KINGDOM: 1

kINGdOM: 1

Rise

David Browning-Paine

ISBN 978-1-7390905-0-0

Dedication

For my children: Samuel, Rebekah, Finley & Casey:
My inspiration, and my drive.
You truly are the *Brightest Beings in All the Sky.*

For Leah, you helped me to *Rise*, and for you I will *Shine*.

For those departed, and still yet to come; forever my heart travels with you.

When the earth was new,
Before man was made, when the dark
was still great, a small thing was done. With
eyes that could see true and by the hands of those
that knew, a seed of kindness was given. It grew despite
the dark and so, in turn gave to hope. To men, for they alone,
amongst all those that had come, would seek, this gift was given.
A gift of substance and meaning and given as it was, a new light
too, was tendered. In time men would open the door, rise above
their place and draw back the veil. But not yet, for men first
need learn how to be, how to see, and how to be kind.
Then, once wise they would shed their burdens,
Rise up high and shine, at last, truly the
brightest beings in all the sky

Unburdened we Rise, Enlightened we Shine

Prologue

Makikangas, Finland, September 1977

"I have already said no. Why are we still talking about this?"

No one answered. No one wanted to be the focus of his annoyance, despite the group's, earlier, lengthy debate. Eventually, and mainly because it had been his idea, Baros spoke up.

"Well ok, I'll say it; I think you're being unreasonable," a pause, a deep breath. "Also, you say on one hand that we're a partnership, all of us, and then, when it suits you, like now, you say that it all belongs to you? That it's all yours?" More silence, then: "It doesn't make any...."

"But it does belong to me. It's my technology. I own it. I discovered it. I said no."

Another pause.

"But Kurt Norkamp, he...."

"Fuck Kurt Norkamp," Harket flashed. "He was here. He used my tools; he used my fucking lab. You all did," he looked around the room, and then back at the man before him. "That means, like it or not; it *belongs* to me."

"But it's not really *your* 'lab' is it? It's our...."

The lights dimmed and the equipment hummed. Contrary to the temperature outside, and the snow piled against the door it was warm in the room. With the equipment running the fans were struggling to keep things comfortable. Baros waited for a moment after the sound stopped before coming back in and joining the group. With him there were fifteen.

Harket looked from one to the other. His eyes, despite his anger, were ice blue, and calm.

"Tell me then Baros, please, if not mine, then who's lab is it?"

Baros didn't answer. Even standing with his cohort, he feared Harket's anger. He'd seen it before, many had, it was something people talked about.

Harket was a young man, a few years older than the main group yes, but still young. But that didn't stop his anger from having power. Perhaps it was his name, who he was, perhaps it was something else.

"I didn't mean it like that. That's not what I meant."

Harket cocked his head. "Really? Right. So what did you mean then? Because that *is* what you just said?"

Baros hesitated.

"I just meant that.... it's just that...."

Baros looked at his colleagues for support, but none met his eyes. He drew a breath and looked back at Harket. He was wishing he hadn't started this. It had seemed so straightforward when they discussed it earlier.

"No," Harket said flatly, waving his hand and cutting him off. "No. I pulled you all together. It was me; it was my idea. I started this. I sponsored you and I funded all of it. And you were happy to agree with me and go along with it while I squeezed the academy for the cash to pay for it, for all your shit." He sneered and waved his hand again. "But now, when I say *no* to you, when I say *stop,* you say, 'it's not my lab' and, 'it's not my tech'. Now, when I say *no,* you decide that *you* own it yourselves. That it's *yours* to control?"

Again, Baros looked at his colleagues. He could see the split clearly. Khaled, Fielding, Hersch and Kekulé plus one or two others were standing closer to Harket. And that spoke nothing of the larger group that were not here tonight. The rest stood closer to him.

It was probably unconscious, likely a coincidence, but if subtle, it still seemed obvious.

For this had been coming, it had been building. They all knew it. A season had changed, the sun had set, and something had shifted, amongst them, as a group, and with their relationship with the man that sponsored them. Baros suspected Harket's reaction was less to do with the proposal, than it was the conflict that was rising. And if not, then he suspected there was something else, something less honest at play.

"We don't want to *own* it, not like that. Lens is showing promise. I've explained it. We have returned 38 over 82 and our heat barrier is less than 18 percent. That's amazing. It's all better than predicted. Its viable, it is, we just want access to it, to use it, to share it...."

"But it's not yours."

Baros rubbed his face. He wanted to say 'it's not *yours* either' but didn't. He feared Harket as much as anyone, perhaps more. He had seen things the others hadn't, quiet things, dark and frightening things. And he had been, in the past, closer to Harket's father so had heard things others hadn't.

That said, it didn't stop him from standing and voicing his objection now. Regardless of the target it made him.

"We are asking to use it for this control, to test it against the model. We're not asking for much. You have seen the metrics, I know you have, so you know the criteria. You've never objected in the past; I really don't see why you would now? It doesn't make any sense Tore."

Harket smiled.

"Oh it's *Tore* now is it? First names now? Ha," he scoffed. "You are smart Baros, really, you are, I've said it before, perhaps the smartest of all of us. But you are *not* as smart as you think. There are things that even *you* do not know. I wonder how much you believe the things you hear from my father, from others, out there? I wonder what you think of the things that are said about me? Do you..."

Baros shook his head.

"No, I don't think of it, any of it. I'm not interested in that at all. All we want...."

"*All you want.... Oh all you want?*" Harket mocked.

This annoyed Baros. Yes, he had heard, yes, he was aware, of course he was. But then, so was everyone else. They had been for some time. Much longer than this request had been contested. Truth told, the rumours Harket referred to were no less than confirmation of the things they'd worked out for themselves. And *seen.* None of it was difficult to come by, not really. Not if you looked and listened.

But no, *this* had nothing to do with *that.* In fact, Baros really didn't care about *that.* It didn't affect him or the projects he worked on. So he ignored it and refused to engage when others gossiped. Which of course they did.

What he *did* care about; was the integrity of the work, the controls, the process, and of course, when and if they came, the results. He was here because of his own intellect, on the strength of his ability. Apart from the obvious, it had very little to do with Harket, junior *or* senior.

And Harket, the one before him now, be he the man they talked about or not, was squashing the life from something that he and his closest had worked on for more than a year. Kurt Norkamp *did* 'discover' it. That was true, he was the one. But that didn't matter. Nor did it matter who paid the lease on the building they used, or who had 'acquired' their instrumentation. The *only* thing that mattered; was the science. It was really very simple.

"Stop it." Baros said flatly.

This made his colleagues lift their heads. Baros suspected most were wishing they'd chosen their lectures over this awkward confrontation. Harket's face coloured and his eyes flickered with anger. But Baros didn't care, he'd gone too far to go back.

"Pardon?"

"Stop this idiocy. We all know," he gestured to the room, "*everyone* knows how you squeezed the academy for funds and resource. We know it because you were proud of it and told us. But you did it because you wanted to, because that was your agenda all along." He knew he was on dangerous ground. "And we all know how you've worked to pull this group together, how you moved, how you pursued us. But again, this was always and *only* to satisfy something apart from us. We are grateful, of course we are, all of us, I am grateful," he touched his own chest, "but again, it was something else, something *you* needed to do, and nothing to do with *us,* as people." There was some nervous nodding amongst the group, which Harket did not miss. Baros went on: "Tore, *we* are here on merit and because we choose to be *and* because we're smart. That is why we were chosen for the Foundation, remember? It's why your father selected us. It's also why you picked us for this, for Skogselv."

Harket stood up and made as if to speak. Baros cut him off before he could:

"But that aside, all we are talking about here, now, is the work, the *science*, the controls. I am not interested in the argument you have with your father, none of us are. Nor are we interested in your anger or the gossip that surrounds us all here. We are *only* interested in using VX3C6H6 within the partition matrix of the scope, for project Lens. It's just this, just the science we are interested in," he gestured to his colleagues. “Beyond that, honestly, you can do what you like. It’s really none of our concern. But with this,” even if running short of options, he was wary of issuing an ultimatum, “but with this, I feel *we* should insist.”

There was quiet.

The fluorescent lights buzzed, and the air conditioning hummed. Beyond that the only sound was that of the students fidgeting. Baros glanced at Vanessa and Alexia. They both nodded subtly and held his eye. Again he wished Proctor had been here.

And then Harket began to chuckle.

“*Skogselv....*” he said ironically. “Fucking Skogselv.”

He pushed himself away from the table and moved out into the room. He began to laugh properly, quietly at first, then louder.

He looked at Baros, and then the rest gathered, and then at the room in general. He walked away and around the central table laden with burners, flasks and testing equipment. He continued to laugh, fully, loudly. Moving slowly around the room, touching surfaces, laughing all the while he came back, eventually, to where he’d started. His face was red and his eyes wet with humour but his laughter now, at length, was gone.

He approached and stopped before Baros, taking a moment to steady himself.

Finally.

“You know,” he smiled, “I knew it would be you, I did, I just knew.” He glanced at the others, and pointedly at Alexia and Vanessa. “I think I knew from the start, from the very beginning,” he gestured to the others gathered. “Even those who stand next to me, *closest* to me, would not speak this way Baros Scaraides. None would. None would have the courage to speak their mind so honestly, to say what they think, what they *really* think."

He poked Baros gently in the centre of his chest, a smile still on his face, if no longer in his eyes.

"But *you*," he poked him again, harder this time, "you have courage, you have the strength of mind to do it." He shook his head and stepped back, and then to the whole room; "*this* is why I chose this man," Harket gestured to Baros, "*this* is why we are here, now, in this moment. Because *this* man had vision and is not afraid. Because this man has courage and *sees* the way forward." Now he touched his own chest, his face soft, "despite my idiocy."

He smiled, but his eyes remained cold. Then softly.

"That, or you are just very stupid Baros Scaraides?"

The room remained quiet and waited.

Baros returned his gaze but said nothing. Eventually Harket went on.

"Very well, my friend, very well, you have persuaded me. For the sake of our little *Forest River*, you may have the VX3," he glanced from Baros to Vanessa and Alexia standing with the group, and then back to Baros. "But that is it Baros, just for Lens, just for this one," he held up his finger. "And all protocols must be strictly maintained, at *all* times. There can be no exposure, no mistakes. Much is at stake here, much, much more than these....," he gestured, waving vaguely at the table, ".... experiments."

Baros smiled but said nothing. If he was offended, he made no show. He no longer trusted Harket to keep his word normally, much less if provoked.

Harket held his eye for a moment longer, watching his reaction, before smiling and patting him on the shoulder.

"I am excited for project Lens my friend, really," he turned to look at the rest of the group, and then back at Baros, the warmth of moments ago now fully gone. "I just hope that you do not fail...."

3 years later - 2400 kilometres away

Baros picked it up.

"And with the J5 still unstable, neither the polymer nor plasma charges will fire. We won't be able to control acceleration and we'll be back to where we started. It's a 'particle thing' Vanessa," an inside joke.

They all smiled, briefly. Then Vanessa:

"No, I don't mean *that*, I mean, I understand what you're suggesting, of course I do. I just don't understand why we're still pushing *this* model. Am I missing something?"

She gestured to the control.

Baros now.

"What? Apart from the obvious? Look, we still need to understand the variables. And we need a workable alternative to the latest...."

She shook her head, exasperated.

"No. Jesus. I mean why are we still doing this, when it *already* works...." she looked from one to the other.

"You read my notes, right?"

Silence. She pressed:

"Tell me you read them? Please. Alexia put them in your boxes? You would have seen them coming in?"

Both men looked confused, then sheepish. Proctor responded first.

"Shit....no, I didn't see them?" Then he looked pained. "Shit, sorry V, I'm not saying they weren't there or anything, I'm sure they were. It's just.... look, fuck, all this back and forth is killing me, both of us actually. I came in late yesterday, and I didn't see them, honestly. There was an issue with the flight, and then traffic and stuff..... look, I'm sorry.....really...."

Baros shrugged his shoulders and clarified.

"I didn't see them either." He had no excuse, so made none.

Vanessa allowed herself a huff, which was more of a sigh.

"Guys, seriously, I described it all in there, in *detail*. Took me ages to write up," she might as well have not bothered. "Christ." Another four hours she'd not get back.

"Sorry," Proctor repeated.

Baros shrugged again.

"I'll be glad when we're settled here."

Which meant *fully* here, in Lágymányos, and not split between the *Academy*, and here. It wasn't just the inconvenience, flights, travel, etc, it was more the trauma of it.

Not that they were markedly better off. They were warmer of course, with better access to normal, modern things, and there were no rats. But there were also no windows so they had no idea what kind of day it might be outside. It was quite disorientating, if each were honest.

Vanessa nodded, acutely aware.

"Yes, right, of course," and then: "Look, the point is, the scope *works*. J4 was oblique, of course but adequate, and stable."

Now Baros looked confused.

"It worked?"

"Yes, we ran it for over five hours on Wednesday, Alexia on the front end, me in here. As agreed,"

She looked from one to the other.

"Guys....?"

Baros coughed self-consciously.

"*Agreed*?" Proctor asked.

Baros scratched his head and looked sideways at his colleague.

"Err yes, actually, now I think of it, that might have been me." said Baros. Proctor scowled at him, before turning back to Vanessa.

"Ok, ok, so let me get this straight," he looked past her at the equipment. "You ran up J4, and it sustained?"

Vanessa nodded.

"Yep. For five hours. We had to *remove* the rod in the end and turn it off manually. It wasn't running down on its own. There was no degradation. Zero."

It was quiet for a moment. Then:

"Five hours. Shit. That's big," it was Baros. "This is exactly what we've been working towards."

"Yes, 5 hours, it was amazing. Completely stable, no frequency flex and all dial-in, dial-out's worked too."

"Fucking yeah," Proctor beamed. "And to think, three years ago..."

"But guys listen, it more than sustained, it actually *received*."

Now both men looked up, confused. Baros, slightly alarmed, came to life.

"Well, that's clearly not possible, we all know that."

Proctor backed him up.

"Right. No one else has anything even close to J2 yet, let alone J4. It took us two years to get from J1 to 2 and the Chinese haven't even got a viable carrier yet."

Baros again:

"And the guys at Cambridge are miles behind that. Mike Faraday told me last week that they haven't even finished the first extrusion."

Vanessa held up her hands.

"Look, I'm just saying that J4 sustained. We have the print outs here," she turned and picked up the sheets from the bench which she offered to the two before her. She reached over and pointed at a series of figures for both men to read. "See here? And here...." She stood back and waited a moment. "And then," she absently looked at her watch, "at about 10:21pm we received."

Baros frowned, looking up from the data in his hand.

"I still can't believe it sustained," he was just beginning to smile. They had worked so hard for this, risked far more than they ever had to lose. He looked at Proctor who was still reading the printout. Vanessa pressed.

"Did you hear me? I said it *received*."

Now Proctor lowered the page and frowned at her, his mind buzzing with the news she had just delivered.

"Surely just RRS, or static bursts?"

Vanessa shook her head.

"No. I mean that's what we thought, at first, and attempted to verify. I spent four hours trying to verify that, actually. But no, on interrogation it's not that, this has got a PCIS."

An uncomfortable silence, and then Baros.

"Sorry, remind me.... PCSS?"

Vanessa rolled her eyes.

"PCIS; Persistent Complex Identifiable Structure."

Another uncomfortable silence.

"Complex Structure?" Proctor asked eventually. "What kind of complex structure?"

Vanessa showed a little frustration.

"Guys, it's *in the notes....*" she huffed again, and then; "Ok. First, it's persistent, there are no variances, measured both medially and laterally. Second, it's structured, uniform, and it's in two distinct parts. There are some elements, the first parts, that look like numbers, or a code, possibly coordinates, I haven't got much further than that. And then others, the latter parts that look like a UCDNS."

They were all quiet for a moment, a long moment. Then Proctor.

"Ok, just so I'm 100% clear," the paper was quivering slightly in his hand. "Are you saying that our experimental scope, the one we've worked on, fought tooth and nail for, for *years,* battled for, and eventually cobbled together with whatever we had to hand, in line with his drunken 'hunch'" he pointed his thumb at Baros, "not only actually fucking works but has received *legible* comms from.....from.....where?"

"From outside our zone." Vanessa said, definitively.

More silence.

"*Zone?* Outside our *zone?* Please, what the fuck does that mean?" Proctor asked, a touch of panic in his voice. "Dont fuck about."

"It means, extraterrestrial," Baros was looking at Vanessa. "That is what you're saying isn't it? We received comms, *real* comms on Lens, on our new scope from an *extraterrestrial* source?"

She nodded slowly.

The two men looked at each other, then back to her.

Proctor held up the paper. He had not seen *this* as part of his morning. He took a breath.

"A code, and some Uniform, Circular, Descending, Number Sequences, from *outside* our zone. From a potentially extraterrestrial source."

".... using a scope with a sustaining J4 Strio core we made in the garage." Baros looked at Vanessa, then at Proctor, then at the ceiling chuckling nervously.

"There's nothing 'potential' about it guys," she answered. "I verified it. It couldn't have come from anywhere else."

"Christ."

1: Fake News

Kassiopi, Greece. September 2018

Probably preaching to the choir here but do you know what happens if you don't wear proper, closed-in shoes for a while?

Your feet spread.

That's right, they spread. Think about it, nothing to contain them, nothing to hold them in.

They spread.

Like a chicken.

And then you have big wide chicken feet.

Which could be advantageous, in certain circumstances I'm sure, like, if you're an actual, live chicken.

But if not, then it's a pain. Especially when you're in a rush, and you're trying to squeeze your fat feet into a brand-new pair of sneakers, after a full six months in budget flip-flops.

But it's a necessary evil isn't it.

Is it?

Well obviously, that depends on what you consider 'necessary ', and evil, of course, but in this case let's say: yes.

Because you've got your first, tentative, speculative, exploratory meeting with a broadsheet, *'journalist'*, who wants to talk to you about serialising your car crash of a life, sorry that should have read 'adventures', in one of the big Sunday broadsheets.

I mean, that's big right?

That definitely warrants shoes doesn't it. Closed in, no toenails visible kind of shoes.

Yeah, right, so here I am, feet quietly screaming at me, deep in the back of *Tom's Place*, my go-to expat breakfast, come restaurant, come coffeeshop, come cocktail bar (only on a Friday and only after 8 pm), place.

Whatever, you can call it what you like, Tom's not fussy, he's only in it for the money.

Anyway, it's sunny, obviously, why else would I be here? And the tourists are just beginning to stir with the obligatory scooters buzzing up and down the main drag and the smell of bacon, exhaust fumes and dog shit wafting back and forth through the open sides of the diner.

I felt good. Today would be a good day. My skin was a bit tight from yesterday's sun and I had drinks to look forward to later with Stelios, my dive buddy. We were catching up after a busy few weeks and needed to plan our next trip. I was hoping for a visit to the Hole of Ha in Liapades, something the tourists talked about. Somewhere I'd never been.

But then Stelios was Turkish wasn't he, so the truth was; literally anything could happen.

So anyway, here I am, I've got my shoes on, what's left of my hair is brushed in a nice side parting, and I've cleaned my teeth. Oh, and I've had a good think about what to talk about. You know, how I should tell the story, how smart I need to sound, how aloof and after-the-fact wise and cynical I need to come across.

Yeah, so I'll be completely honest with you, that's not going to age very well.

You'll see.

Anyway, Helen's late. Helen Gouda that is, from the Telegraph or Times or something. I confess I wasn't really listening. But that's rude, I should've been shouldn't I. Notwithstanding *my* part in this, *she* bless her had flown all the way over here from London just to meet with me, factor 50 and draft publishing contract in hand, with desperately high expectations that she'd encounter an intelligent, worldly, sophisticated man.

Oh, dear god. I do hope she booked a couple of excursions to make the trip worthwhile.

"You want a toastie?" Tom interrupted my thoughts. He was hovering, nosey bastard.

"Thanks Tom but no, I'm waiting on someone, we'll order together. Another coffee tho please..."

"A laaadyyy?"

Jesus.

"Actually Tom, yes a lady, another journalist, from London. She's coming to ask me about the local area, you know, like a review of hospitality and stuff, on *this* side of the island. She wants to know how welcoming local businesses are and whether there are any issues with money grabbing, nosy old bastards."

Tom stared at me.

I stared at him.

And a taxi squeaked up outside.

We both looked over as she tumbled out of the ten-year-old Merc, sun hat, local map (she'd come up from Corfu Town), and shades in hand. Plus, a massive, colourful, string beach bag over her left shoulder. I watched her, clumsy, flustered and pink. Exactly as I imagined - we'd exchanged a few *telling* emails.

I instantly felt better about the latte on my shirt (and shorts).

A few moments later Helen came in, her composure returning now her feet were on the ground, and she scanned the room for me. I'd rehearsed this bit, been through it a few times in my head, you know, the; pretending I hadn't noticed her bit. The; pretending I was buried in an intelligent looking Greek newspaper, never mind the fact that I still couldn't read Greek. But of course, Tom, bless his cotton socks, happily ruined that for me with a loud.

"Hey Mr Matthew, is this your laaadyyy??"

Bastard.

Now it was a heady time, the late nineties, early noughties, reflected in the music and pop culture of the day,

I guess. There was still a little bit of anxiety perhaps, a legacy of Thatcher, the last decade, and the still quite recent cold war. But it was mainly full of promise, full of expectations, politically, socially, both locally and globally, I think.

Blair was still in, and the Tories were in disarray, happy days. But I was still young then, (see above) naïve, angry, stupid. I also had bad teeth and dressed like a moron which was pretty standard for where I came from. And I was sheltered, like, really sheltered. Not that I knew it, no one does when they're nineteen do they. I thought I was across it all, you know, life, love, and all the complex relationships, interactions, and choices etc. But I wasn't, nowhere fucking near it.

I know that now. Actually, I've known it for some time.

But that's not what she'd come to talk to me about. I mean it might have been what was motivating me, what had always been and was still then buzzing around in my head like a frantic wasp caught between my Nan's front window and her crusty net curtains. But no, Helen, at least as far as she was aware, had come to discuss something else.

So, we fast forward past the awkward pleasantries and the ordering of refreshments and the obligatory chat about the airport and the weather back home etc. And then we're talking about family, hers, mine, and Tom's, who seems, all of a sudden, incapable of taking even the most basic of hints. And by hint, I mean; 'Piss off Tom', and 'Haven't you got customers?' and 'Please leave us alone,' more than once. In Greek, AND English.

Yes, I could speak it but not read it. Shameful.

Anyway, we got past that, and were getting a little closer to the reason for our meeting when she repeated *the* question. It's the question that, it has to be said, is almost entirely, alone, the thing that made my mind up about her. It was simple really, and at the same time savage and cutting and told me three important things about Helen Gouda.

First, she was smart, like really, really smart. Second, she'd done her homework, and by that, I mean she'd read the notes I'd sent her and followed the breadcrumbs, at least as far as she could anyway. And lastly, most importantly; She understood the loss, the gain, the change, the pain, in relation to *me* anyway. As much as I'd described it. And she had, in some small way, lived it with me, at least as far as she'd been able to. And that took my breath away to be honest, it really did, it took my words away too, for a moment. It also made me feel more than a little uncomfortable, which was weird in the moment, bearing in mind the aforementioned anticipation.

Tom left the table like he'd been stung in the anal gland, bless him. He knew. He knew what she *didn't* know. He also suddenly noticed that, yes, he did actually have customers. I know, right?

And Helen, for her part, went all pink, again. Bless her.

Awkward right?

Yeah, it was, for a little while. We sipped our coffees and waited for the moment to pass, the warm breeze drifting through and the smell of toasted cheese sandwiches replacing the scooter exhaust and making my belly rumble.

Anyway, for the most part it did pass, thankfully, and we got back to talking.

She told me about herself. I mean, she'd given me the bio stuff when she'd first made contact, and it was all very nice; upbringing, education, work history and achievements, personal interests, pets etc, all the usual. But now she told me about her, you know, the stuff you tend not to write down, the stuff you wouldn't tell someone unless you were comfortable, and confident in the longevity of the relationship.

She was a talented musician and loved to sing. She also gave a shit load of time to a couple of charities for the visually impaired, can't remember the details, but I was impressed. And she was single, albeit intent on being a mother at some point. Which was nice, even if I did think she may have left it a tad late.

She asked about me, I assumed so I could tell her corresponding things. So I talked about my feet, Stelios and our drinks later, and the ants I'd found crawling across the kitchen floor that morning, that I guessed were chasing the juice from the watermelon I spilled en-route to the waste bin yesterday evening. Like, that happed to everyone right, it's just here, in the heat the little fuckers are everywhere.

Anyway, the rest, the stuff about *me,* was gonna be in the book, right? I didn't know what else to say, my life, here, as far as she was concerned, and now at least, really wasn't that interesting. Deliberately so. You'll see if you keep reading.

I was kinda grateful when we finally turned to the matter at hand.

She wanted to know what the set up would be, what the initial premise would be. She wanted to know where I would start, how I would frame the first few moments. Would I tell it in first person or not, what would be the first few hooks upon which the story would hang, etc. I found it interesting, really, because I'd never thought about it as a story. I mean, I'd created the whole thing, I'd 'lived' it, hadn't I, I'd been there, done that, as it were.

Sort of.

The point is I had notes, of course I did, lots of them, I could never have remembered it all, but this was the first time I'd told it to anyone, like a story. And rather stupidly I'd never really given much thought to how engaged a reader or listener might be with the narrative. Which again was weird based upon the circumstances.

But that's ok, because she had, obviously, like, that was her job.

Anyway, we chatted comfortably for a bit about the details, introductions, chapters length, descriptive narrative, dialogue etc. She was very encouraging and seemed more than happy for me to tell it *as me*, which I loved. Not sure anyone else would but hey.

We had cheese toasties, another coffee each, and made good progress. I'd seen the draft contract earlier and said I would review but couldn't see any reason not to sign. We agreed the terms of production, you know, how much content I would be expected to provide, who'd do the editorial and the deadlines I'd be working to, how many interviews I would be expected to sit through etc. She also explained what PR and marketing I might be asked to do, what it would look like and how we would fund it.

It was fun, light, and friendly. We had a giggle, and for me it was a nice escape from my normal. A normal, just to be clear that was entirely self-inflicted, so no, before you ask, I'm not seeking sympathy.

And then *again*, as before, it opened up in front of me. The vista of what my life would look like for the next year or so, working with her. And I liked it, I really did. I mean, there was a fair amount of guilt rolling around in my belly, of course, but I liked the idea of it all. Plus, I liked her, if that's relevant. She had integrity, and a certain innocence about her. I don't mean she was naive or anything because contrary to the initial impression she gave, she was sharp as a fucking razor. No, I just mean that she didn't appear to have much of a concept of the sort of dishonesty I'd been witness to back in the day.

Not sure what she'd be like *after* all this but whatever.

Also, not sure how she felt about me then, but she *definitely* liked the sandwich.

Anyway, the question? Back to this. Because I know it's killing you. Or at the very least I'm hoping you are mildly curious. I mean, because if not then there's a good chance we're wasting each other's time.

Which would be awkward wouldn't it.

So, what was it? What was the question she asked that changed it all for me, that shook me? Because I had others you know, other hacks, authors, journos who wanted to 'talk'. Over the years there had been a few. I mean, aside from several other unrelated, and much earlier forays into this territory I'd undertaken, which I'll come back to much later, *this* particular thing had been out there in the public for a bit now.

I'd had a number of calls, and a couple of visits too. One from Mike Elohesra at the Sun, who, let's be frank, was a dick and more interested in the Sambuca than me. And then from Sophie, a magazine editor from the Netherlands. She was cute, *very* friendly, if you know what I mean, and I was flattered, even if her magazine had very limited circulation. I'd have asked her to stay for a while, but she was only really interested in me signing and the kudos attached to it.

Plus, Tom didn't like her. He said she had a lazy eye.

Which was a shame because he hadn't seen her piercings.

I'd also been approached by a couple of book guys who wanted a novel length manuscript from me. They both offered tons of cash, and a decent royalty's package, which was tempting, and would have been fine, (even if I didn't need it) except they weren't offering to help, and both had deadlines I knew I couldn't work with. I just wasn't built for doing shit like this quickly. Plus, it all felt too big, you know, too much of a commitment, in the circumstances.

So, it had to be pretty significant to make me chuck *all* that away without further thought didn't it. It had to be pretty heavy to stop me in my tracks like that.

Yeah, it did.

And it was.

And it was simple too, easy really, and truly insightful, if in equal measure truly harrowing, truly sad, and as I said, left me feeling weird.

And it was this:

.....

HA! No. No way, I'm not going to tell you now. Like, obviously!? I mean there'd be no point reading the book if I told you now, would there?

Too much of a spoiler, obviously.

But it was deep, right?

Yeah, it was. *Too* deep, possibly. And definitely, under the circumstances contextually fucked up as well. And for the meaning of *that* you'll need to read all the way to the end. Because whilst my story, my 'adventures' are filled with accounts of me lurching from one complete fucking mess to the next, for the most part with good humour and unfailing optimism, that's not true for all of it, how could it be? No, there's pain too, plenty of it, confusion, fear and loss.

Some real dark stuff.

Plus, lots of moving parts, people, places, ideas and interests.

Oh, and a good measure of luck, good and bad, to round it all off.

All of which, as I'm sure you've deduced by now, led me *back* to here, to sitting at the back of *Toms Place*, in this beautiful little town on the northeast coast of Corfu, sipping latte and listening to a very smart lady tell me how much she connected with me, how much she identified with me.

All the while feeling a little nauseous and uncomfortable about the bullshit I was feeding her, despite the faultless cheese toastie and coffee that Tom told everyone was the 'best on the island'.

Which, I'm sure you'll agree now sounds farcical and improbable - no not the nausea, or the coffee, but the 'talking to a very smart lady' bit. Yes, good, of course. And, honestly, like you, I would laugh if it wasn't true.

But it is.

And that's the thing, isn't it? About truth.

It's as often uncomfortable, as it is reassuring.

Not because the truth is an absolute, because it isn't, and there's more on that later. But because it exposes shit and forces you and those around you to reckon with something. And whilst it's not always clear what you're reckoning with of course, most of the time, it's your *choices.*

Now I'm not talking here about the virtues of truth or honesty, not really. I'm saying that if I'm *honest,* I've made choices in my life, like everyone has, where I've told myself I had no option. Where I've told myself that I 'did the right thing,' that 'it's what anyone would do' or that 'I had no choice'.

But that's bollocks, at least it is for me and all the people I know. And that little statement is far more significant that it might seem.

You see, you choose to go to work, to school, to pay your mortgage. And you choose to be law abiding, etc.

And I know what you're thinking, I can hear it, Jesus, I've said it myself, I've *shouted* it out loud.

'I have no choice'.

'I didn't choose that'.

'The choice was made for me'.

But that's bollocks, you know it. It's nonsense. You choose everything. You choose all of it. Always. Every time.

You look at the facts, assess the risks and consequences, and make a choice.

Ok, so what? So, I'm right, why are we talking about this? What's this got to do with the other stuff?

Good question, here's the answer.

Because reasoning with the choices we make, acknowledging them both *as* choices, and as one's made far more consciously than we lead ourselves to believe, brings us closer to the truth about ourselves? Closer, in fact, than pretty much anything else. And that's because the truth about us, if we're 'honest' can only really be *measured* by the choices we make. It can only really be measured by *when* we make them, and by *why* we make them.

And that's how this ties in.

Because all of this, is, and was a choice. All the stuff I was doing now, had done in the past, and was lining myself up for, in the future - was choice.

Now, you'll read some stuff that might make you think otherwise, great example: the meeting I was currently having. But don't be fooled, and don't lose sight of what I've just said. We all choose, all day, every day, everything.

And that is why we are free and why, in my opinion, there is such a gulf between the best and worst of who we are.

But enough of that, now back to the lovely Helen.

We finished up. Helen wiped her face delicately with the napkin, I wiped mine on the back of my arm, standard. She gathered her papers and slid them into a clear plastic wallet which she then put in her string bag. She'd mentioned a couple of excursions she had booked for tomorrow and the day after, and then was heading home. I wished her well, we stood, shook hands, and I walked her to the door. I then watched as she went down the steps to the taxi Tom had called. It had been a good meeting, one, I'm sure she was going to think went well, and formed the foundation of a solid working relationship. One, I felt went well because I hadn't made a complete dick of myself.

But I did feel guilty. More guilty than I should have, because, like I say, I'd been here before, or close to it at least. Plus, I'd actually pursued this. Maybe it was the fact I liked her, maybe the face-to-face part of it. Maybe it was the question she asked me, and the strange feeling it stirred up inside. And you'll see this as you go on, I'm not one to chat on about 'feelings and shit'. But this was strange. It was like something had shifted, like something significant had, or *was* going to happen.

Perhaps it was the weather, perhaps it was just going to rain later, the late summer storms here could be pretty spectacular. I looked up but the sky was faultless blue, no clouds in sight, which there normally would be by now, if a storm was due. I looked out at the sea, visible between the buildings opposite. It was calm, and the air was light and warm. I wondered why her being here, her questions had so unsettled me. I wondered if I was just tired.

I watched the taxi until it was out of sight, then went back in and settled with Tom. He took the euros, obviously, he had to, but still grumbled that it wasn't worth the drachma. He, like a lot of the older folk, missed the old currency, and had zero loyalty for the new. He'd have taken dollars over euros, given the choice.

Anyway, Helen was gone, my course was set, and I had work to do, something to distract me, something in front of me, at least for a time. It felt good, sort of. It felt, regardless of its validity, like I had something worthwhile to focus on, something that might lift me from the pit I'd been wallowing in, if only for a short while.

So, on that basis, you know the improbable truth bit I mentioned earlier, plus the lie I spent time creating to make the truth what it was, *plus*, if you want to find out *how* I got here, *back* here to Toms place, read on. And, if you want to know what my *choices* were, you know, if you want to find out how a young lad, a lad with zero aspirations, zero expectations, and less than zero prospects, became something so much more, read on.

And then if you want to find out just how much that cost, and how much the world changed to make it so, read the rest.

Or just wait for the audio book. It's up to you.

2: Sand

London 1999

"Listen to me son, this is important. Right, in order to survive here, in *this* place, in this shit hole, you're going to have to grow some balls. You're gonna have to be a man, someone of *substance,* you know this right, look around you, you've seen it."
I looked around, he went on.

"But to succeed, to really succeed, which is an entirely different proposition;" a bit of judicial finger wagging; "You'll need to be a man of intelligence. You'll need knowledge, and insight, and to be ruthless in everything you do," a pause: "Well, nearly everything."

A big smile before he went on.

“And furthermore,” he winked, “you like that word son? ‘Furthermore’? It's a big word for a little lad,” he ruffled my hair. “And *furthermore*, if you want to be a man of power, then of course, apart from the obvious, you’ll also need to be a man who knows how to use that power, how to *wield* it. Do you know what wield means?”

I honestly think I was eight or nine right now, I didn't have a clue. He went on before I could answer.

“And apart from looking after your mum and your little brother you'll need to be independent of thought, resourceful and have a complete absence of morals," now gesticulating.

"Do you know what morals are, son? No?” I shook my head. “Never mind. Just remember that these are the qualities that make all great men. These and *more* are the qualities that make men Kings!”

A wink, another theatrical pause and then:

"Are you gonna be a King son?"

I nodded, of course I was. He smiled and looked at me funny.

“You know what? I think that just maybe you are,” he looked away, at nothing in particular, a bit of a sad expression on his face, and then back at me as he carried on: “But of course, remember, it's all abstract as you well know, hot air if not...”

“Sounds like bollocks to me...,”

Ha, not really. That's not what I said, I wouldn’t have, not for another few years anyway. No, instead it went more like:

“Ok Dad, thanks.” or something similar, something a nine-year-old might say.

And then a bit later when he was two or three Tennents Super-Strength deep and up to his armpits in cabbage and rice:

"Spot me a tenner for some fags Dad?" remember I was eight or nine.

A clip round the ear is what I got for that, regardless of his inebriation and the sauteed veg he scattered across the carpet. A bit of good old-fashioned corporal, I think they used to call it.

But seriously, it was a good talk, that one, the; 'what makes men Kings' talk, and far more significant than I thought in the moment. It's one I've never forgotten; one I've referred back to again and again. That and the 'everything has six sides' one that I never really understood at the time, even if I liked the sound of it and later found it somehow relevant to everything that was important to me. But it's what he thought, the power stuff, the 'man' stuff, based upon the fact he considered himself an actual, real-life gangster. Now we're not talking about the trousers drooping halfway down round your baggy arse type of hood rat gangster. Nor the 'alright bruv', tab in hand type either. No, he was old school. Stanley knife carrying, tattooed hands, crew neck shirt and dm's. And here I'm not referring to the 'Direct Message' of today's promiscuous cohort. No, the term dm, in those days anyway referred to a Doctor Martin shoe, or a boot to be more precise.

And with that complex, that belief, comes a system, at least it does if you come from where he did. It's a system of living that provides no space for authority. There's no space for subservience. It's a code. It's driven in, resilience, resistance, like a rusty tent peg hammered from above. Stroke after stroke of the mallet. Blank, savage impacts, one after the other, of the weight of deprivation he suffered, the poverty and inequality in which he, and all his friends lived.

Deep I know, bear with me.

So, is it a choice then? This attitude, this look? A social cliche perhaps? No, it's far from that. The tattoos, the shirt, the boots, all of it: are armour. Essential and inseparable from the boy inside. Has to be. And so, it goes on, breeding, growing, deepening. Until the boy, once all buck teeth, skinny legs and no confidence becomes a hard, scarred, muscled young man. Angry at everything, powerful in his anger and political frustration. Weaponised by his music and clothing and contemporaries and intelligent beyond all societal expectations.

A mouthful, right? Yeah, but is this unique? No, of course not. We all do it, you, me, all of us, you know we do. We all build walls around us with bricks and mortar made of image and projection, language and culture and belonging. Normally current, normally contemporary.

This was my Dad, me too whilst I'm about it, and all of my mates.

Or at least during and up to the end of my time in the *Gardens* that's what I thought. I'd seen the photos when I was round at my Nans. I'd seen his school reports, met old friends, heard the stories etc. We'd even walked the estates and sat at tables in the pubs and working men's clubs where he'd sat as a youth. Love that word, don't you; 'youth'. It has power it's like a two-way mirror. I knew it, or rather sensed it when I was called it. I know it now but for different reasons.

But he had been there, really, he had grown through that youth and into the man I knew, in the way I believed. And yes, he had built his walls with bricks I understood and mortar I had handled myself. But life isn't linear is it. You know that. It's not like a train that runs point to point along a track devoid of intersections. I like that word, intersections. I'll come back to it.

No, life is not so simple as to provide a clean, pure narrative. It's not so one dimensional as to allow a man, or woman, or whatever you choose to identify yourself as, the luxury of a smooth and uninterrupted journey from point A to point B. A journey that allows his or her walls to stand, a journey that allows him or her to remain unchallenged.

And so I found out.

But 'found out' is slightly misleading, apologies. It engenders a perception. It conveys an appreciation of things I still have no real appreciation of. And I don't, I really don't. It's nearly two decades since I began this journey, two decades since the fabric of my life was torn. Since the walls I had begun to build, using tools he'd given me, using the materials he'd shown me, crumbled. But that isn't the word either, again, as you'll find out. It's not nearly the word. No, because 'crumbled' imagines a gentle erosion of said status. Crumbled suggests a gradual weathering of the quo. And here, in this, it's entirely inappropriate.

But again, you'll see.

It was a sunny day. Still warm in early September. An Indian summer I've heard it called. Nevertheless, it lifted spirits after a shit summer, mine, Mums, Danny's. And as such I was looking forward. Not to anything in particular you understand, just forward. In a way I didn't, couldn't really when the nights started drawing in a bit closer to Christmas.

And to clarify, for your benefit, this wasn't because of some undisclosed trauma, some hook upon which I'm gonna hang my yet to be revealed angst, if indeed my angst itself hasn't already been made plain for all to see.

No, instead I looked forward because I like the sun. Simple, yes? Disappointing maybe but honest. Not that it removes the leverage an upbringing like mine and a cultural and political ethnicity fed to me throughout my formative years has upon my persona. Indeed, it would be accurate if not fair to say the home, the prospects, and I use that word deliberately, *prospects*, and the day to day were grey. Not the RAL 9035 I've spotted Wetherspoons using on the walls of their gents toilets, which it has to be said I've wasted far too much of my life looking for.

No, instead it's the grey of fatigue. The grey of disengagement, of disenfranchisement - if such words exist in any real sense. It was bleak and it was obvious, even if I couldn't see it from where I was - inside it.

And maybe I couldn't but a part of me felt it. It felt it and sought the light, instinctively, looked forward when bathed in the unseasonal and unexpected warmth and soft yellow of a late summer morning.

Whimsical and poetic, lovely. Bollocks.

Anyway, I was up early and to work, or at least en-route early. I'd woken Danny and kissed mum and was on the bus for around 7. It was packed, rightly so. And voices rose in competition. It seemed like the sun had cheered all, imbued all with a newfound optimism. Or perhaps it was always this way. Perhaps I just hadn't seen it before in my blinkered ignorance, my channelled misery.

But that's not unusual, is it? Ignorance.

Ignorance that by its simplicity and isolation breads misery.

I mean a fish doesn't know it's in water, does it?

Bear with me.

It just is where it is, with no comprehension of anything else, of any other state of being.

Well, that, in my unwelcome opinion at least, is blinkered ignorance.

I was that fish, I know that now and in fact consider that the first step.

'The first step of what, fish don't have legs?' I over-confidently and optimistically hear you ask. And here I pause, a little self-indulgently, more than a little theatrically before I answer with:

'Wrong question.' obviously ignoring the legs thing because it doesn't suit my narrative.

'Wrong question?' I hear you shrill.

Yes, and there it is, a line from a movie. Can't remember which one for sure, but possibly Jerry Maguire, that sweet little fantasy that we all know carried Tom Cruise from heartthrob into middle aged douche.

Fantastic line though, regardless.

So anyway, wrong question.

Right.

As if not only is the narrative of the outcome steered by the subject but so is the scene, the scenario and the setting. It's like the confidence of the subject alone, the conviction of their 'self' carries enough weight to negate the possibility of deviation from a predetermined outcome. Fascinating.

Irrelevant of course, but fascinating.

But it is the wrong question, sorry.

Why?

Well because obviously there exists a right question. Which you can only see when you know what it is. Still with me?

Ok so what's the right question?

Aha, that's easy:

You see it relates to the fish and to its comprehension of its place. You see, if it can somehow, unlikely as it seems, conceive *of* itself and then *of* the water then it follows that it might eventually conceive of more.

Right?

So, it follows then, that if you are self-aware enough to perceive *of* your place, you'll perceive the existence of other *places* won't you. You'll conceive of other planes of being, of textures and colours and patterns of life you wouldn't otherwise see. And as you do so your awareness deepens and you see more, and as you do so you also see less.

Less? You ask, probably fed up with all the bollocks by now. Stay with me, please, it gets better.

Yes, less.

I liken it to laying on the beach face down. Not face actually in the sand but an inch or so above, like, just high enough so that if your eyes are better than mine you can focus on and see the actual grains of sand directly in front of you. Well, this is it, for most of us. We see the sand, struggle for most of our lives to focus on it, to identify it, to count it and account *for* it. And we do actually, probably better than we'd allow ourselves credit for. But it's a proper life's work isn't it, and it leaves little room for much else. And I say that because I've seen it, I've lived it. Been buried *by* it.

But here's the thing, here's the questions, the fish, the sea, the 'planes of existence' etc.

If you can stop for one moment. Just stop and look at the sand, not *at* the grains themselves, not *at* your income, your kids school reports, the crime rates, the latest box set, how the back lawn needs mowing, whether your brother-in-law is actually mental or not. If you can look and *see* that it is just sand, all of it, it's just *stuff,* then you'll be able to rise won't you. You'll be able to rise up onto your knees. And as you do, like I said earlier, if you'll permit a degree of condescension in my tone, you see more, so much more than what's right in front of your face.

Providing your swimming trunks are buried in your butt cheeks, which we all know can be a distraction.

But if you're still following me, which I very much doubt, you'll appreciate that whilst you can see more you can also now see less. The grains of sand you studied so closely before, counted and named as your own now become part of something bigger, something vast and confused and chaotic. But is it chaotic, really? Isn't it the case that everything you were previously so focused on, previously so concerned about just ticks along nicely without you anyway?

Perhaps, perhaps not.

Perhaps it is chaotic because it has no pattern, it has no uniformity, at least not within the context of anything you've known before. But that doesn't mean it's not there, does it?

Maybe the pattern can *only* be seen from a distance. Maybe there is an order and method and synchronicity to it all, which can *only* be seen from afar. Very far.

So, the right question?

Back to this.

The question you should have asked when you calamitously asked me a little while ago: 'What was it the first step towards?' is simple. The right question is as follows:

'What is the *next* step?'

Easy right.

Yes. It's the right question because of all I've said above. It's right because if you're still asking "what is it the first step towards?" then frankly you're still laying on your belly like an overweight, elephant seal, staring at the sand. And you'll excuse my tone, but this is important.

So, is the answer even a thing? Is there an answer? Like a real one? An answer that saves you and me from looking stupid? That saves us from floundering like freshly pressed farts? No, sorry. I know that's disappointing but, really, there's no answer that flips that coin, we are stupid, own it, take agency with it. And I'm not just saying that to offend your twenty first century woke sensibilities. I'm not even saying it for the *sharp intake of breath* that your right wing bigoted, offenceophiles that saturate mainstream media chase daily. I'm saying because it's true, I'm saying it because it's kinder than the alternative.

So, the answer? Yes, right, before we descend any further into this self-indulgently monologue of smugness. It's easy really. The answer to 'What is the next step?' is:

Rise.

Now back to the beginning

3: Transcript

"Danniel."

Just the hum of the lights:

"Danny."

Nothing.

"Really? Nothing? That's how you want to play this?"

Nothing, more humming.

"Danny this is really easy mate, you can either sit there like a child sulking, or you can man up, and tell me what happened."

Nothing. Silence.

Some huffing and puffing and little chair scraping.

"Danny, we're trying to help you."

Nothing.

"Danny!"

Another chair scrape, and a sniff.

"Christ Danny, I've got too much on to be pissing about like this."

A bit more silence, and then;

"Ok look, I've been patient. You're wasting my time. I've let you have some space, you've had your moment. Now you need to talk."

Again, nothing:

"Danny."

Nothing.

"Danny!"

Silence.

"Jesus Christ. Ok fuck it. You've had your chance, I'm too busy for this. You can talk to the judge. I've tried to help you. We've been here too many times for this now mate. You can face the consequences now. It's on you. You can face up to the consequences, and you know plenty about..." blah, blah, blah.

Apparently, the opening 'few' lines.

Not that I could ever know for sure, of course, or could consider the transcript to be completely accurate. Because we know we can't trust the feds, right?

Maybe.

But ok, I concede, if not this then it probably wasn't far off.

Based on what I saw, and what I knew of him.

Either way Danny, my brother, or Zip and he was known, hadn't answered. And this was hard reading for me because I knew he'd have wanted to, I knew he'd have been super defensive, irrespective of whether he has reason to be or not. He was just built that way. Maybe it was the casual bullying, the regular, statutory doses of spiteful, demeaning violence I'd visited upon him during our years as kids.

As was my right, as the elder brother.

Maybe it was instinct, you know, the whole do or die thing we couldn't help growing up with, *where* we grew up.

Maybe it was just his intellect.

Either way it was tough to read, really tough to listen to as he said nothing.

"I honestly don't think you understand how serious this is Danny, we've been here far too many times. This is the end of the line mate."

And again, nothing, silence. Which in actual fact, if I'm honest is far from nothing. He should've reacted, he should have laughed, or spat or stabbed the fucker with the pen that I so wished was laying on the tabletop between them. But nothing.

Initially I'd doubted that he was even in the room. Until I'd seen the CCTV, which in itself was something, under normal circumstances I wouldn't have been able to do. But he was. And that on its own was shocking, his appearance, his walk.

I'll tell you about Danny now, if I may. And by doing so perhaps tell you a little bit about me and Dad.

There was all the normal stuff, stuff you'd expect. Anger, of course, smart mouth, obviously. He had a few really shit tattoos, loved the footy, drove us mad with his fucking video games. Plus, the girls loved him. No seriously, they loved him. His floppy hair, his sideburns, his manner. He was funny, irreverent, kind and a bit brutal too. A good mix. He was a good, bad boy. Hated school, fought all the big lads, which turned out to be pretty much everyone cause our Danny himself was not a fag paper over 5'6". And generally tore up the place, as was to be expected, as was the plan, if indeed a plan had been written for him.

But he wasn't a disappointment. Not at all, far from it. He was loved, I loved him. Of course, I was fucking horrible to him at times, as was my right, as was expected, as was necessary. But that didn't mean I didn't love him. And he knew I'd have killed for him, without hesitation. I'd have set fire to the world if I thought it would save him.

Because his bones were my bones, his flesh, the skin, the muscle, the tender places of his mind and body were mine, the same as mine, made of the same thing.

He was me, and I was him.

So, I loved him, and in that love was hope, unspoken of course, cause that's just the way it was. It was mine, Mums and Dads. It was hope that his smart mouth might be more, that his wit, his street smarts, his dealing and fighting and efforts to create a space for himself, might become more.

He would've reacted, he would've done or said something. No doubt in my mind.

Unless.

Unless what?

Honestly, I don't know, I can't picture it, I can't see it through the fog of my concern for him. Different of course if it had been someone else. Easy if it had been you, if you'll forgive me. But Danny? I don't know. It blinds me. I don't think my mind, for all my arrogant self-aggrandisement and smug socio-political clichés can see past my own fat arse. Or in this case my fat, wounded heart.

But I've considered this, long. I really have, you'll find out just how long if you keep reading. And I've searched too, not just myself but the world in which I thought I lived. That's what this is all about to be fair. And it's led me places, this search, that I never thought I'd visit, places I confess I had no comprehension even existed. And in this search, this quest, as it became, I transcended the usual, the accepted version of life, this system of class, of political choice and quasi democratic recourse, of legal and social justice. I mean, I'm not so sure I knew it as I was doing it, but I've definitely seen behind the curtain. I've definitely risen above and dove deep and wriggled through and between and come at length, eventually upon the truth. Well, *a* truth at least. And you'll see the relevance of *that* statement a bit later if you have the patience.

Bollocks, I know. And self-indulgent, obviously.

Seriously though, I did come upon something. Something true, something real, something entirely unexpected and fundamentally unwelcome. But this something wasn't what I'd been looking for was it. It wasn't the *sand* of why Danny looked the way he did in the grainy images. It wasn't the sand of why he didn't react the way he should've, behaved the way the man I knew him to be, would have behaved. It wasn't even the sand of why he was in that cell, that interview room, red knuckles, cut face, dead eyes.

They let him out at around 4am, which is bullshit, wankers. He said he'd been fighting, I didn't believe it, there was something off with the whole thing. I took him home and made him a 3-egg omelette while he showered. Then we both went to bed.

Next day I collared him early, before he could slip out. I had work later so time to talk now.

"You're fucking mental fella," I was peeved. Not that I had any right to be really. He'd made me plenty of late-night omelettes if you get my meaning.

"One more of these and you're gone bro, one more, seriously," I held my finger up to illustrate what ONE might look like. Just in case he wasn't sure. I was helpful like that.

"Fuck off dickhead. I'm not a retard."

I shook my head, all superior like, a thing you only get to do if you're older and smarter, of which, let's be fair I was only really making about 50%.

"Mums gonna do her nut fella, she's gonna do her absolute fucking nut."

Danny rolled his eyes, something he did a lot, we all did. Shrugs, eye rolls, all that kinda stuff. But here's the thing right, even though he did it a lot, this time it was different. It was different because he genuinely looked like he did give a shit, like he *was* bothered. He knew the old dear would be mental, that she'd lose her shit. That was a given. He knew too that this could easily be it for him, that this could do him, for real, he could go down. But there was something there, something on his skin, something in his face that told me that this wasn't why he was bothered.

It made me a bit nervous to be truthful, in the moment. I hesitated, very unlike me, just a bit, just long enough to let the thought grow some balls. And in that time the door went, the old dear came home and my god all hell broke loose. Sure, she went bent, all over him, shouting, screeching, proper fucking horrible really. Even if it was all out of love it was still hard to watch. Eventually I stepped in, and like some kind of biblical Saint took his shit and made it my own.

Little fella sat behind me all quiet and subdued. I knew he was grateful even if he'd never admit to it. I ushered the mad woman out of his room and made her a cup of tea. She had a crumpet too.

At length, and seriously, I mean at length she calmed down and stopped spitting fire. I gave her some paracetamol and a hug and told her about Chelsea and her new baby and Frank's dog Benny who took a shit on Tammy's front doormat. It cheered her up, the spiteful old cow.

But that's not fair really. She wasn't spiteful, not at all. She was tired, worn down by mine and Danny's shenanigans and general enthusiasm for the game. She was worn by the grey backdrop in which we scurried like panicked rats. And really fucking broken by the old man's death. She wasn't spiteful really. I mean if she saw an elderly man tipped out of his wheelchair whilst crossing a busy road she'd laugh like a horse whilst she ran to help. But who wouldn't? Not because of spite though, but because she could see the farce, she could appreciate the timing, the creativity, the energy that went into these things.

In fact, she was kind. Actually, all sorts of kind. Flawed of course, like the rest of us and desperately lonely but kind. And she loved us, me and Danny. And Chelsea and Frank, Benny and Tammy, Big Nige. And all the other neighbours, freeloaders and scum that floated in and out of the estate with the high tide.

Strangely enough she also loved the old man, even though he'd left her under a bit of a cloud and now would never come back. I mean 'strange' but of course it's not strange really is it, not in the moment. Again, like the fish, it's all I knew. My parents separated, and my Mum still loved my Dad. It was normal wasn't it, it was standard.

Perhaps not for all, I'd learn later.

Anyway, Danny came out of his room, proper sheepish, sad looking too.

I felt for the little fella.

"Sorry mum," he said.

The old dear looked at him, marmite all round her chops.

"Come here you little bastard," she replied putting her fag down for a second.

And there you have it, my story complete, if only for the omission of the whole fucking point. But seriously, it's a chapter done isn't it. You've met me, me Mum and Danny. And I've told you a little about Dad.

And now, I guess we can move onto the main event.

I was working late, I hated it, much preferred early starts, early finishes. Brian, my *manager*, as he liked to refer to himself, twat, at Bar Shit made me stay on for another 45 minutes to finish the bottle-up. I'd get paid of course so that was good, but I'd miss Mousas kebabs, which was bad.

I'd known Mousas son Ahmed at school. Real dickhead if I'm honest and flash too. Thought he was something else. Truth was he smelled of onions and everyone knew his dad was on the Sex Offenders Register.

Later though, found out he was cool, Ahmed, not his Dad. Just a kid doing his thing, like we all were, nothing to see here. But seriously, he told me what life was really like above a kebab shop, not nearly so glamorous as you might think. And the money he flashed, he earned it all, every penny. His dad made him graft evenings and weekends and drove him like a proper bitch. His life was brutal, like mine, different colour, different smells perhaps but just as shit.

Anyway, we connected post-school, as youths, that word again.

And we were close. I stopped smelling the onions and started respecting his graft, even if I did despise his old man and construct that forced this hand to mouth upon us. This was just the beginning you see. My eyes weren't properly open yet, but I *had* started to see what I could see and I understood the injustice, the disparity.

You see, something they don't think of, the politicians, the policymakers, the town planners and the marketing exec's, is that all us kids, the kids that live in the shit, in estates, that dwell within the grey, amongst the garbage and the rodents, that know instinctively, before we even try, the doors will be closed to us, we *see*. We *see* because our fucking school buses drive through your world, our heads are full of your colours and diversity and bullshit opportunity. Even if we know it to be just that, bullshit.

And that's the beginning, the foundation of the primal, base aspect of our rage. It's why my Dad was a skinhead. You know it if you think about it.

But back to Ahmed.

We were tight because a man needs his friends, doesn't he? Of course, Danny followed me everywhere, younger brother, standard. And as I've said, I was horrible to him, at times. But the three of us, plus Danny's mate Flyn and Ahmed's cousin Tariq made it work and held back the tide.

In our own little way.

Anyway, it was the evening after Danny's early morning omelette, the last in a long line of late-night zygote based savoury snacks to be honest. Perhaps it wasn't obvious earlier but that's why mum went so nuts. She was sick of buying eggs.

But seriously, I wanted to get back early, kebab in hand to make sure Danny was ok, to make sure he was behaving himself. But obviously Brian saw that off, said it was a 'necessary evil'. Prick

I got back and it was gone two and I was Hank. The estate was quiet, even Frank's ugly dog kept his tongue as I walked past his place four doors from mine. I stopped briefly to survey my kingdom before I went in, the deep canyons of grime between the high rise and tenements. It was quiet but not silent. Dogs were barking, somewhere. And cats were screeching like maniacal wizards. Standard.

I looked across at the lights in the building opposite and wondered what life was like in there. Did they bottle-up for Brian at 1am for £8.26 an hour and in the process give away a piece of their soul? Did they make omelettes for delinquent siblings and sedate irrational matriarchs with marmite and paracetamol cocktails on the regular? Did they fuck. Too busy shooting up and pissing in their beds.

But I also thought they probably didn't question their place, or their purpose, or the corrosive vomit they ingested daily as they spent their time and giros watching Jeremy Kyle and Jerry Springer crucify the ignorant. Notice I didn't say 'innocent'.

I guess it was just me then.

My eyes were drawn away from the mattresses and broken bikes stacked high on the opposing balconies and down to the street below.

The streetlights cast a sick yellow glow I was told was healthier for the average man's eyes. To me it just looked like the road had bad kidneys. Kids were in bed, the subways empty and only the taggers were still out, blazing up and down the sides of government buildings, transport depots and railway sidings.

I never got it, personally. I never got what the buzz was from painting *Cock* or *Fudge,* messy and illegible in massive bold italics. I mean, I got the likes of Banksy and his contemporaries but believe me when I say these rats were far from that. To me they were just junkies, their drug: the acetone and cellulose in their cute and colourful shakers.

They were dickheads too, let's not forget that.

Anyway, I noticed the car. It hadn't been there earlier, I think. It was black, or blackish yellow in the sodium vapour haze, and new looking too. All of it not entirely unusual, even the new part. See, the corner boys had a good time around here, so it wasn't unusual to see a bit of splash, a bit of mint.

What was unusual though, and what, quite frankly sent chills up my spine was the fella leaning against the car with his arms folded across his chest, staring at me.

I know right. Drama.

I mean, I was tired and stressed and hungry, so I wasn't really sure what I was seeing for a moment. But I stayed and stared back, and he didn't move. Now during the day he'd have been far too far away to hear me call right, but at night. I'm sure if I'd tried, he'd have picked it up a robust 'Oi, fuck off!'. But I didn't call, did I, I just watched, like an idiot. Eventually, despite myself my empty belly won over, and I gave up on the thrilling exchange. I moved away from the handrail and on into the flat.

It was quiet, as well it should be and I shouldn't have been alarmed, but I was. A man doesn't grow to become one in these parts without a sense of self, without a sense of change. It's like the air feels different, you know, like the weight of impending doom can be felt before it arrives. I liken it to the air that's pushed along in front of the tube on the Central Line. You can't see the train, and maybe, if your deep into your Gods Kitchen Trance Anthems with your headphones on you can't hear it either but you sure as fuck know it's coming.

I felt it, there, in the living room. I'd shut the front door quietly and all the lights were off and from the little I could see everything seemed to be in its place. But it wasn't, was it?

Now, I've thought about this a lot, I've had time. Was Brian involved, no I don't think so. Was the guy by the car? Yes, pretty sure. And now, many moons removed: was it the faint sting of an aftershave neither Danny or myself would've worn?

Yes, probably. And I say that because we were smelly little rats and barely washed let alone bothered with any new man grooming nonsense. That would change in due course, of course but that's an aside. Oh and by the way, that wasn't because Mum didn't try. Jesus, I remember the spit washes by the school gates and the strip washes in the kitchen sink like they're burned into the back of my head.

But that's another aside.

Back then I knew it was wrong, my senses knew it, it stood out. I'd been jumped on too many corners, bundled into too many garages for an old-fashioned regulation kicking for me not to have had the instincts for it. Mum was working. Danny would be asleep, but something was off. I moved into the kitchen and then back out and down the hall. I stood like a lemon outside his room for ages, wondering what I thought I'd find. Also, slightly nervous he might be having a Tommy. If you don't know, don't ask.

Eventually I cracked the door and poked my head round. His room was semi dark too, like the rest of the flat. Only unlike the flat, I could see, even in the dark, that shit definitely wasn't where it was supposed to be.

I pushed the door wide open and flicked the light on.

Aside from the fact that it was a full-on hodgepodge of dirty socks and half eaten bananas it had also been turned upside down. Like properly. Mum would do at least a half dozen crumpets when she saw this. But although all of that fizzed through my foggy noggin the thing that stood out, that rose like a turd from the deep was the fact that he wasn't there.

The hairs on my arms stood on end instantly and I felt sick as I wondered where the fuck he might be. I was also hungry, as I may have mentioned and so I thought about the omelette. But that just led me to thinking about the police station and in turn to wondering what the fuck he was doing there anyway.

Fighting he'd said, but he'd been sheepish, proper unlike him. I don't mean sheepish like when the nutter attacked in the morning. I mean, that's to be expected, right?

No, I mean he was sheepish with me. Highly irregular.

But what else was irregular? I thought about it for a moment. Last night, yes. Now, his room trashed beyond anything I'd seen before and that fucker outside. 2am and he's casually leaning, arms folded, against a car I'd not seen before staring me out. Trying to intimidate the man.

I spun around and darted out of the flat. I ran to the balcony where I'd been standing before just in time to see doors being slammed and the vehicle speeding off. I stared at it. I blinked and rubbed my face and held my breath. I genuinely couldn't believe my eyes, honestly. It took me out. It was like a punch in the balls.

Danny, my brother, was *in* there. He was *in* the back seat, I could see him, the back and side of his head, his shell suit jacket. I could see him; he was in the fucking car.

Fuck. Fuck. FUCK.

Yeah, well that's what happened, that's what I told the police, here's a bit more of it;

"Did you get a look at the number plate?"

"No."

"Did you recognise the motor?"

"No, it was dark. Jesus."

"Did you recognise the individual staring at you?"

"No of course I fucking didn't. Do you think I'd be here now if I did? Me and Ahmed and Tariq and Flyn, if he was back from juvenile detention, would be out there dealing social justice if I knew him wouldn't we?"

Pricks.

That's what I thought and said then. But I was scared, and I was panicking and ignorant and looking at sand. The nutter went more nuts, as you can imagine. It took more crumpets than the One-Stop could supply me with to calm her down. The doctor sorted her in the end whilst I cleaned up the bananas.

I put his room back together and stared at the walls for a couple of days. Brian called wetting himself because he had no staff. I told him I'd stab him in the eye if he called again so I guess that was me done bottling.

Mum slept a lot and the liaison officer: 'Fat Julie' came and went, her handbag and her arse both bigger than our sofa. She smelled funny too, which I think led me, much later, to thinking about what I could smell when I first walked in that night.

I called Brian to apologise, Julie made me. But he was having none of it. Said Chloe had stepped in, that he might even make her up to assistant manager. This pissed me off. Not because I thought I should be but because Chloe was a devious bitch, her dad always dropped her off in his X5 and she smoked more weed than anyone doing £8.26 an hour could ever afford.

Another door shut before I could even try the handle.

The police were shit. Julie said they were doing all they could, course she did. DI Butt, or Detective Inspector Marcus Cherry Butt as I'd later find out was beyond fucking her and fucking useless. Is that the same thing? Anyway, I mean, maybe we'd have gotten along under different circumstances. He was older than me, obviously but I could see we'd had similar experiences. He wasn't uncomfortable in the estate, in our flat, like Julie was.

But that didn't mean he knew what he was doing. I may have told him this too. If I remember correctly.

So, after the interviews, the forensics, the normal missing persons investigation shit, plus a few days of waiting, of dreaming about how I would key Chloe's Dad's X5 and set fire to Brian's girlfriend's horse I decided to get out. Julie said it was a bad idea, she said I looked angry, like I might do something stupid.

She wasn't fucking wrong.

Stupid is what stupid does, as my Mama used to say...

Another line from a movie, one I do know but I'll let you ponder.

I made my way to the Grub. I'd called Ahmed and he was meeting me. The Grub was the old West Ham Labour on St Andrews Rd. It was dirty and smelled of stale beer and shit but did little pies from a glass hot cupboard behind the bar. Maggie and George, the stewards, had been there for yonks and had always let us in. Maggie said she'd rather have us boys in there eating her pies than outside cutting up gang members. Of course, she was right. Apart from the MSG in the pastry it was a perfect plan and kept us wannabe hoodlums out of more trouble than we ever knew.

Ahmed was waiting in a booth at the back.

"What the actual fuck!?"

He stood up when he saw me and grabbed me in a fat hug.

We sat for an hour drinking shandy whilst I relayed what had occurred. He asked me a couple of questions but nothing significant.

Eventually:

"So, what was he doing in the cell? Who'd he been fighting?"

"I dunno. That's what I'm out to find out. The little fucker told me nothing."

Ahmed shook his head.

"I can't believe it. Look, I mean, he's not one to hesitate with his hands and that, but seriously, if he was actually fighting, I mean like a proper battle surely we'd know all about it, right?"

"That's what I thought."

I sipped my drink.

Ahemed went on.

"I mean, I know he had beef with that Polish twat a couple of weeks back but...."

"Nah, it wasn't that, can't have been, we'd have heard about it. Besides, that was all over that bird, the skinny one, the one Marcin was shagging, you know, the one that threw all his shit out the window over Penton."

Ahmed nodded and smirked.

"Fucking Marcin...."

"Fucking dirty bitch. Case said she was shagging his dad too."

Ahmed laughed and then we sat quietly for a moment.

Eventually.

"Have you spoke to Tariq?"

“Nah man. His old dear got cancer a couple of weeks ago. Only found out on Saturday so I've left him be. Something to do with her panchus or whatever."

“Pancreas.”

“Yeah, that's it, panchus.”

"Shit "

"Yeah."

I sipped my drink.

Ahmed picked his nose a bit.

"So, what about your Dad, and his brothers?"

"What about them?"

"You know, can you ask them?"

"What about? About Danny and his fighting? Or him being a dick, or him being kidnapped?"

"I dunno. Yeah that, all of it I suppose."

Ahmed sucked his lips and sat back shaking his head again.

"Man, you don't go into that without a plan bother. You know the score. It's a whole different world."

"Yeah, but this is Danny dude. Our little brother."

I felt the first stirrings of indignation.

"I know that fella, but it don't work that way does it. It don’t matter. You go in with a plan or you don't go in at all."

"Fuck’s sake, " I sat back. He was right. Ahmed's uncles were not to be fucked with. Turns out, and by the way I'm glad I didn't know this as a kid, that Ahmed's Dad kebab shop was actually a washing machine. The shit that went through there beggars belief. I mean Mousas himself was legit, sort of, and the family flat above the shop was too, so by association Ahmed. But behind it all was this whole fucking mess of drugs and sex trafficking and money laundering and god knows what else.

They were nice enough people, don't get me wrong. They had me round loads for birthday celebrations and such like. And if I hadn't known, and let's be honest I didn't *really* know did I, then I'd have thought his uncle Faridabad was a doctor and his uncle Sam an accountant. They looked that way, not at all like they'd cut your testicles off for spilling an ounce of crack.

But anyway, I digress. Ahmed was right, nice as they were, they would consider access to them, to their network, which would be what I was asking for, to be at a premium. If I went to either of them half cocked, without a trade, I'd be balls out, spinning on the kebab rack by teatime.

"Look," Ahmed took a breath and looked round in case he was being listened to. Which of course he wasn't. Ridiculous.

"Look," he repeated. "I'll talk to Mousas, to me old man. I'll try and see if he can have a little word or something."

He winked.

I looked up from the table as Ahmed went on.

"But you know fella, you gotta stay low. I mean like *really* fucking low. Don't come round, don't show your face. If they want to, they might have a look into it for old time, but seriously if they don't then just walk away, fucking leave it brother. Ok? Promise me?"

I nodded. I knew. I wouldn't push.

4: Arabs and Paddies

Maggie came wobbling over to the table.

"You alright boys?" I nodded; Ahmed remained silent. She was a lovely but nosey old cow. Ahmed had been caught out before.

"How's your mum Squidge?"

I saw Ahmed smirk. They stopped calling me that ten years ago, bitch. But she was only being nice. Plus, her and mum had done the whole school run together with her boy Justin when we were just rugrats so she kinda knew me that way. I shrugged my shoulders:

"She's ok I suppose. Bit mental over Danny."

Maggie grinned, as she gathered our empties. What teeth she had were yellow and filthy and her hair looked like she'd combed it with a sausage roll. I'm sure it had its own community of badgers.

"Oh Danny, Danny, Danny. He is a boy that one, ain't he?"

I looked up at her, but she was moving away, chewing her gums, and shuffling her gammy leg. George said she'd been a looker once, which I found hard to believe. But then he'd been all over, seen the world as he liked to say. True, he was a weathered old fart but clever too, could've been a taxi driver. He was alright in my book, my favourite of the two of them if I'm honest. Maggie scared me a little.

I watched her creep back over to the bar like a lame northern tree bear, possibly in search of honey. She was muttering and I considered myself to have got off lightly. She obviously didn't know that Danny was gone otherwise I'd have had the whole fucking Spanish. She got to the bar huffing and puffing and put the glasses down. George came over to her just as Ahmed piped up:

"So, what you gonna do then?"

I looked at him.

"The fucks that supposed to mean??"

"I mean what you gonna do? You gonna stay here, or go home? You wanna get something to eat?"

Shit, I was wound.

I took a breath.

"Sorry fella," I sat back and rubbed my eyes. Jesus, this shandy had made my mouth dry, and my eyes were itching from lack of sleep.

"I dunno. Fuck."

"Squidge?" Now George was at the table. Heavens.

Now, to be fair the light could've been better, although it was only just past lunch time it was pretty gloomy back there. But regardless, I could see the concern on his face.

"Fuck George I haven't been Squidge for ten years," I was irritated, even if I did have a spot for him.

"Bollocks to that. What's this I hear about Zip?"

God's sake, we were adults, we had names.

I threw my hands up.

"George, I dunno what to tell you."

Ahmed could see I was getting stressed. He coughed:

"George, now is not a good time fella."

Jesus were we now in a seventies teatime sitcom weren't we? Not a good time? Next, we'd cut to an ad break for Vagisil or hair removal cream.

I breathed out to calm myself.

"He's gone, George and to be honest I don't know much more than that. He got pulled for fighting the other night then the next night, when I got home, he was took. His room was fucked, there was shit all over the place and he was took. I saw them take him; I saw their car."

Ahmed was looking at me like he wanted me to calm down.

"What?!" I could feel the blood in my ears.

George placed his hand on my shoulder, and I could feel the strength in his bony old fingers.

"Calm down son," he said gently, soppy old sod.

And I'd have shrugged him off with a bit of mouth and a swagger if I'd had the chance but instead he said something else, something that surprised me, something that changed it all and opened the first little crack in my wall:

"He wasn't fighting Squidge. Zip wasn't fighting."

I went still, Ahmed went still, and George's bony old fingers dug a little deeper. I turned in my seat and focused on him properly, conscious for the first time that I had all sorts of pie and shit all over my jacket.

I wasn't really aware of it at the time but in the gap that I filled with turning to George and brushing flaky pastry onto the floor Ahmed left.

Now, I need to address this because he wasn't a small man. By any means. In fact, well I may as well confess now: that I had, once or twice, to my shame referred to him as a fat cunt. Only in jest you understand. We were mates and he was more than a little bit chubby. But free food, right?

So, you can see, even though it didn't occur to me in the moment, I was distracted, him leaving so quickly, so unexpectedly and so unobtrusively was not something I would have predicted. Or anticipated.

Great word that: unobtrusively. Would the opposite of that be obtrusively?

Probably.

But anyway, back to George, George's fingers and the MSG all over my Gazelle Classics.

"What did you just say George?"

"I said he wasn't fighting."

There aren't many moments in life like *that* moment. It's entirely possible that I've added weight to it over the years, that I've imbued it with intrigue and significance that simply didn't manifest at the time. It's possible that it's nothing more than a construct of my overdeveloped imagination, my overreaching analysis of every little crack and sniff I ever came across.

You know like that cheesecake you had round your Nans when you were six, a cheesecake you've never been able to find or better. Or like the night you had with your mates after your last day at school ever, never to be matched, never to be replicated. Even if it was a bit shit by today's standards. Even if it wasn't nearly so special in the moment or as your memory might suggest.

So, I looked at the cheesecake and frowned:

"Why would you say that, George?" still not fully conscious that Ahmed had gone, still lightyears away from working out why.

George looked over his shoulder and then back at me. His face was lined and wrinkled, and his eyes looked tired. He shook his head:

"He wasn't fighting Squidge, he got jumped. I saw it." Another glance over at the bar before coming back to me. "It was me what ran out there."

I struggled with the idea of this old dinosaur running anywhere if I'm completely honest. Nevertheless, something was clearly amiss.

"George..."

"A couple of fellas, neither of which I recognize although I could tell who they were." George tapped the side of his head and smirked. He loosened his grip on my shoulder and began creaking his way round to sit where Ahmed had been. It took a while.

That's when I noticed the fat cunt was gone. Sorry.

I frowned.

"What are you talking about, Sausage?" He hated that as much as I did Squidge. Banned it, in fact after Euro 96.

"I saw it son," he ignored the familiarity. "I seen them sort before. Did I ever tell you I served in Aden? I was there in 60 and again from 63 to 65." He picked at the table whilst he thought about it, his eyes a bit watery and his skin all thin and fragile looking.

He *had* told me. Multiple times.

"I was nothing, you know, back then, just a signalman, like you. But I saw them others," leaning forward. "Not the soldiers, I'm not talking about soldiers cause that's what we were, we all did the same thing really" he looked round, like Ahmed had before. "No, I mean the killers, I'm talking about the killers, cause we, I mean the likes of you and me," he pointed: "never got anywhere near it."

Staring off into space now whilst he conjured up images of the day. Faultless blue sky, hot sand, loads of Arabs, shit food, strong coffee.

"I fucking hated it out there mind, you never knew where you were," he rubbed his eyes. "Made some good mates though, mates I've still got now." But his face dropped a little even as he said this as he remembered most of them were dead by now. I sat still and waited for him to carry on, I had nowhere important to be for a couple of hours and had calmed down a little since earlier. Plus, irrespective of the moment I did have time for his stories.

"They're dead now," stating the obvious. "But I knew some for many, many years Squidge. Served in Ireland with the same company you know, late seventies, just before I got out. Things were bad over there then."

Now this intrigued me cause my mum was born in the mid-sixties and she and Maggie used to do the school run together. Something didn't add up....

"How fucking old are you, George?"

George looked at me, but he was somewhere else.

"Nasty fuckers them paddies," he said leaning forward. "They killed Mike Frindle and Jimmy Scott. It was all over the news. Semtex in their ABSV. Blew the fucker up. I was close, I saw it. Got one of Scottie's teeth stuck in my ear, it was in there for the whole of May Bank Holiday."

This is why he was my favourite. What adventures.

"It was all over the news," he repeated.

I nodded. I wanted him to keep going so had to be careful how I responded.

"Knew his missus too, Eileen, nice girl. Bit too tall for my liking but nice anyway. I gave her the tooth when it came out, it seemed like the right thing to do." He went quiet for a bit, but I didn't mind. Mum would be asleep and Julie, if she was still there, would be working her way through our fridge. I needed another drink and a piss, but I didn't want to disturb the old fella.

Eventually he came back to me.

"But that's why I know them, those fellas," he poked the table. "That's why I know their type," he lowered his voice. "We didn't do 'em, you know, the paddies what blew up Mike and Scotty. They got done of course but it wasn't us. These fellas come over, from London I think," he paused whilst he thought about it. "No, it wasn't London it was somewhere else, some kind of farm or out in the sticks somewhere. Rhymes with Merryfield, or Merrywold, or something like that...."

He paused but his mouth kept moving as he searched his memory for the place. Eventually.

“I looked it up when I got home, a sleepy little place. Just a village out in the middle of nowhere. With a base and an airfield. Lovely little green as well.”

He was drifting.

“Anyway, these five fellas came over, all serious and quiet. Tried talking to em of course, don't you say I didn't,” I hadn’t said a word: “but they weren't interested. Senco thought one of em was a poofta but I dunno."

He shook his head and looked down at the table.

I gave him a moment.

“Fucking Senco....”

Drifting....

"What happened George?"

He looked up at me, but I wasn't sure he saw me. Maggie would be over shortly and then I'd lose him for good.

"George, what happened? And what do you know about them fellas that jumped Danny?"

I could hear voices at the bar, probably punters arguing with the old bat over the change she'd given them. You had to keep your eye on her.

"George?"

He came back to me finally, but he didn't look happy.

"What Squidge?" As if we'd not been sat here for the last ten minutes sharing war stories and talking about Arabs. Ok, a bit of licence there but you know, you get my drift. Anyway:

"Fuck’s sake Sausage at least finish your story," not so chill now all of a sudden, was I? He looked at me then over at the bar with a frown.

"Maggie's not been...," he seemed a little lost suddenly. "Old cow’s been moaning about her leg again. It's all the bloody time now. Doctor wants it off. Says her sugar's all wrong and she's gonna go blind."

I didn't know what that had to do with her leg.

"Shit fella."

He sighed heavily.

"She was a looker, you know, once. I had to watch her; all the lads wanted a piece of her. She used to dance as well you know."

He was proper waffling now. Christ.

"Not being funny George but I'm not fucking interested. What happened to Danny?"

He snapped back, the dreamy look on his face melting away. His eyes focused on me, and he frowned.

"He was in here. He was talking about his mate, the bloke he met. I don't know anything about him mind, he just said he met some bloke who knew stuff about him, who upset him."

This was better.

But what the fuck!? What bloke? Who was he talking about? Danny wasn't easily upset. Whoever this bloke was he needed a slap.

"What are you talking about George? First, you're talking about soldiers and next Danny's met a bloke who knows him?" I was shaking my head and starting to get agitated again. I needed to calm down, I needed a piss.

"When did he meet this bloke? What stuff did he say to Danny?"

I knew before I asked that it was a waste of time. George might see people come and go, him and the old Scab might hear a bit of gossip here and there but the chances of them knowing anything important was zero.

But George thought he did know something.

"You know I like Zip don't you. We've always had a soft spot for you boys, always looked out for you."

I nodded, my eyes starting to glaze over. God, I needed a smoke, and a piss.

"Do you know why though, Squidge?" I sensed another moment. Not a unique moment maybe. In fact, more like a continuation of the previous one, with all twaddle in the middle removed.

"Go on," my eyes refocused. Could this be an answer to the whole school run / Justin / the old Scab being fucking ancient conundrum that poked me in the bum hole a few moments ago?

He sat forward and breathed on me. Smelt like a full English breakfast with day-old cat shit on the side. I blinked as he began:

"See, there's a lot of things you dont know Squidge, proper bad stuff, proper dark."

I shook my head, but he went on before I could jump in:

"For starters Justin ain't our son. He's, our grandson. Our boy Terry got into some bother and here we are."

Here we are? Here we are? Fuck me he was paraphrasing like he was on speed. I shook my head.

"Jesus George thanks, I didn't know that mate. But seriously, there must be more to it than that?" Not sure if it was in anyway helpful right now, but it was definitely a bombshell. "Like, what about the decades in between then and now? Justin's *older* than me."

George moved his mouth around like he was still chewing the cat shit.

"Like where's your boy now? Where's Terry? What's that got to do with my mum? What's that got to do with me and Danny?"

I was wasting my time with this one. And he was 'A One' wasn't he. Oh, my days.

I couldn't hold it any longer, I had to piss.

"Sorry George, I gotta piss, but please can I have another shandy. And whilst I'm gone have a little think out using your words to tell me what the fuck you've been banging on about."

I slid out of the booth and made my way to the loo at the back. It was proper filthy in there, always had been. It stank, there was chewing gum in the urinal from 1976 and piss stains up the wall you could've peeled off. I finished up and went back out.

George was gone and there was no shandy, so I thought I'd cut my losses and see what Fat Julie had left in the fridge for mum to eat. I wasn't getting anywhere here, and I could catch up with George tomorrow. Actually, bollocks to that, I'd get a kebab instead. Ahmed slunk off nice and quickly earlier so at the very least he owed me a can of pop.

I put my jacket on and walked to the bar to pay for my drinks. Maggie said not to bother but then took a fiver for the pie anyway, which in actual fact was more than I owed for both. I didn't argue, I'd had plenty off them both over the years, plus she clearly needed the cash for toothpaste and shampoo. If she was careful she might have enough left for a comb and some mouthwash for George.

Outside I turned right and started towards Mousas, my mouth already watering at the thought of his fatty goat.

Should probably get the nutter one whilst I was there. Fuck Fat Julie though, she'd clearly had quite enough.

I put my hands in my pockets and picked up the pace.

I woke at about four, kebab and salad all over. Mum was asleep and the windows were open, so I was freezing. I stood up and put my coat back on before walking the flat to make sure the front door was shut and locked - it wouldn't have been the first time. She'd eaten a bit of her food and we'd had a row although now she was snoring like a fucking steam train. She said Julie thought I was selfish, that I should have been here, looking after her. Which was code for saying that *she* thought I was selfish etc, etc. Stupid cow. Like I didn't spend my whole fucking life looking after her.

I did feel a bit bad though, I mean it's not like my expedition had been fruitful. All I'd discovered was that Maggie may well have been an exotic dancer, and that George was fucking useless when it came to remembering anything of value.

Plus, I'd left Mum alone with a woman that was more interested in our fridge than our missing family member.

Just getting comfy back on the sofa, having also shut the windows, when I noticed the piece of paper in my coat pocket. I pulled it out thinking it was a receipt, it definitely wasn't gonna be a fiver was it, Maggie saw to that. Holding it up I squinted to make out what was written on it, handwriting for sure.

Now, again, a little 'authentic moment' as they might call it. So far removed from the moment, with so much dirty stinking water under a bridge that can only be described as 'rickety', it seems like I may have known there was some significance to the writing on the paper. Like a window of enlightenment opened before me and I saw a willowy old man with a stick and a very long beard showing me the way.

I fear the truth may be closer to me not actually giving a fuck, I mean at that precise moment. And that, I think, is the truth. Not a truth that plays well on screen when they turn me into a miniseries, starring Damien Lewis as me, Sigourney Weaver as the nutter and Jack Nicholson as the old Sausage. In that version I'd sit up, shake myself down and have a full-on white man's epiphany. And that's not racist by the way, it's just the way they'd film it.

Anyway, that's not what happened.

I fell asleep, Babestation on mute and the paper gripped loosely in greasy, fag-stained fingers. More Ewan McGregor in Trainspotting than Lewis in Friends and Crocodiles. Which was great by the way, Steven Poliakoff, genius.

I slept awkwardly, and on the sofa all night. And before you start stressing about posture and sleep apnoea, firstly it wasn't a regular thing, maybe once a week at most. And secondly, shut up, none of that shit existed in the nineties.

Anyway, I did sleep, a bit, and I dreamt. And they were weird. I dreamt I was floating, like a bird or a discarded carrier bag, high above a field. Initially I thought it was Blackheath, or Clapham Common, but then I looked about and there were no high-rise buildings anywhere to be seen. In fact, all I *could* see was more field, more grass in every direction, and in the far distance, too far to see clearly, some hills or mountains or something. It both felt very old, and like I'd been there before.

I rose higher still and then hovered, fluttering in the air like a flag. I was watching the grass as it began to snow. Lightly at first then heavier, large fluffy flakes, driven by the wind until all the grass was covered. I thought it would melt and the grass would be revealed again but I watched, and the snow continued to fall, hour after hour, day after day. And the days sped up, as did the weeks, months and seasons. And then the years. They were flying past, I was hanging above, and the snow was falling all the time. And now the land, that once was grass was covered in thick ice, many metres thick. So thick in the end that the land lost its features and became flat and eventually even the hills in the distance disappeared. And then I felt a vibration and heard a voice.

And then I woke.

Fat Julie had her own key, probably a good thing. She woke me up with a cup of tea, with plenty of sugar, and then bustled around picking up my crap from the night before. It was gone nine and Mum was in the shower. The TV had turned itself off and I had a raging head. Think it must have been the draught from the open windows. Now, my superior decision-making ability showed itself and came to the fore. Because as Julie was busy cleaning up goat, lettuce and pitta together with the ripped and torn wrappings from my delightful takeaway she would, it's entirely probable also have picked up the piece of paper with the writing on, that had I found in my pocket the night before.

At this point she may have read the writing and binned it, or eaten it, who knows, it would've depended on how hungry she was. Either way though I would have lost it. If she read it, and I didn't know this sipping my tea that morning, and by the way despite the size of the handbag and her arse Julie made a decent cup of tea, far from outstanding you understand, like it needed *work*, but it was passable.

In my opinion.

Anyway, as I say, if she'd actually read it I'm pretty sure she would have passed it up the line. A few questions would no doubt have been asked which may have led places, sure, but ultimately, knowing the competency of Detective Inspector Marcus Cherry Butt I'd hazard that we'd have got nowhere off the back of it.

And if she'd binned it then there's every possibility that I'd have lost it forever. And then we'd be properly fucked wouldn't we. Because, and believe me when I say I'm not trying to leverage any emotive response from you now, I'm smug enough to know I don't need to, we'd have nothing to talk about. I'd have no story. You'd be lost, without purpose in life, bereft of the very foundation of your existence.

No of course not but you wouldn't be sitting there thinking 'who the fuck does he think he is?' and 'did I remember to turn off my hair straighteners?' and 'have I got clean pants to wear tomorrow?'.

But seriously, if she'd picked it up, we'd be having a very different time, the two of us. You'd be playing rounders in the back garden with your kids instead of sitting, feet up on the sofa desperately trying to understand what I'm banging on about. And I would probably be floating somewhere in the North Sea, a turd, shit out by some fat bird who fancied a kebab from Mousas on her way back from the Academy.

Because you see, I wouldn't have let it lay would I. You know that, at least you should do by now, Danny would've known that, the Sausage knew it. I'd hazard that Ahmed knew it too, even if the fat cunt did try to stitch me. He may have slipped out that afternoon, he may even have avoided me when I dropped into his dad's at tea time. But I caught up with him eventually, oh yeah, I can assure you I properly caught up with him, but that's for later.

Anyway, let's just go back to the Sausage, to the note he left in my pocket, to the note that I only still had because it was stuck to my dirty, sticky fingers rather than on the floor or in Julie's sweaty handbag. And the note itself, the writing? Did it tell me about Danny, about the men that took him, about the man he had met that 'knew' stuff?

No.

None of the above, disappointingly.

But it did tell me something else, something arguably as significant, something that, in hindsight, changed EVERYTHING. And what was that I hear you ask? What could it have told you that was so earth shattering? What could a few lines of scratchy old handwriting have told you that could have had such an impact?

Easy.

It was my Dad's address.

So, I should probably take this opportunity to apologise for the language. It's obvious and it's 'in your face', I understand that. And it's not easy for some to read, including me, weirdly. However, it reflects who I was during the times I write about.

You see, when I was still at home, when Danny was still there, shortly before, shortly after etc I swore a lot. I mean it's not like I don't swear now but then it was part of my DNA, it was in my breakfast cereal, the water from the tap. It was in the wallpaper at home, the carpets. It was in every breath and thought and it was perfectly normal. Like breathing. My teachers swore at me, my mum did. Every fucker swore; excuse me.

It was everywhere.

Sorry not sorry.

I mean, maybe you can cope with that, and that's good, really it is. But maybe you're struggling and find it gratuitous. If so, then I apologise.

But I can't promise to stop. In fact, if I'm honest, and at the risk of losing a few of you, it's gonna get a little worse before it gets better. It's just a reflection you see, nothing personal.

So, you best buckle up.

Anyway, onwards.

I went back to the Grub to see George, but he wasn't there. I don't mean straight away. I left it for a couple of days. Playing it cool, you know? No? Me neither.

Truth is Mum was a mess and Julie had taken time off because her cat died, or her Grandmother, can't remember which. But tragic, obviously.

Tammy popped in, pissed about her doormat obviously but it was a welcome distraction for the Nutter. Also, Chelsea called, was gonna come round with the new baby but changed her mind when she found out I'd be there. Oh yeah, Chelsea was an ex-girlfriend, this is awkward, probably should've mentioned that sooner. Baby wasn't mine though. We'd stopped all that nonsense long before, kind of. Anyway, that's another one of them stories for another time. The list is growing, we'll move on.

Mum's sister: Bean popped in too, all the way up from Bournemouth. Not sure where the name 'Bean' came from now I think about it. In fact, it's a bit weird if I'm honest. She was older than mum by a couple of years and a proper liability. But it was company for the old dear so, you know, there's that.

So, as I was saying I went back to see George but he wasn't there. The old Scab said he'd had a fall and wasn't well. I'll be completely honest, I'm certain she said he'd 'fallen down a well' which of course he hadn't. Anyway, after a moment or two of panic I found out the truth and that he was down St Thomas's, in good hands. I heard a bit later that he'd had a bleed on the noggin and was actually in a bad way.

I was fucking angry to be fair. I should've gone straight back, kebab still on my face if necessary. But I didn't.

I've thought about this a lot. About why I held off, why I didn't push a little harder. I think it's because I didn't want to lift the lid on that thing, that fucked up scenario where my Dad was alive when he should be dead. Or he was still dead, but I'd find out something about him that I really didn't want to know.

I also think that it's like when you buy a lottery ticket, until you actually check it and find out you're no luckier than the millions of other chavs desperate for some bling and bit of 'fuck you' for all the wankers that stepped on your neck throughout life, anything is still possible. I mean until you know you *haven't* won, in theory, you *have*. Or at least you haven't not won which, I'll admit is definitely not the same thing but it's close enough for now.

I was also tired, sad and a little bit lost.

I was sad that Danny was gone, sad that I didn't know what I should be doing about it, and sad that Chloe had taken my fucking job. And I was lost because of course the person I'd naturally have turned to, you know, to help me find a lost brother would've been, you've guessed it, my little lost fucking brother Danny.

Bean left me a fiver, bless her, like Auntie's do, which mum used for fags, perfect. She also left me her number and said I should call; said I'd be welcome round hers anytime. I was there when she left and she kissed me goodbye, all teary eyed. I suggested she buy herself a new razor for her moustache and that cheered her up.

I tried to go and see the Sausage but couldn't get in as I wasn't family. The old Scab said he was getting worse not better which didn't improve my mood. But was that important? In the grand scheme of things? No. The Sausage was dying, that was a pretty big deal, my feelings about it were irrelevant.

I did go and see Maggie, you've probably gathered. I couldn't imagine the Grub without her and her pies. I know she wasn't dying but to be honest I couldn't see how she'd keep up with all them rascals without her other half. I mean, people were kind enough to her, but she was a fucking mess, and her leg was proper bad. I reckoned the Association would be in touch soon.

Didn't see Ahmed though, he stayed clear, that hurt if I'm honest. Without Danny he was my 'go to'. And it both confused and hurt that he wasn't around.

Anyway, you'll be getting bored of my meanderings, so I'll crack on:

I'd much rather have tracked down the stranger that George said had 'befriended' my little brother. I mean it did occur to me that it could have been the same person as whose address I had scribbled down on that greasy piece of paper. But if I genuinely had thought them to be a stranger then, like the lottery ticket, anything would've been possible. And tackling an 'anything's possible' situation would've been infinitely more preferable than this.

Instead and as it was I just had a sick feeling the whole time. Like nausea, like I wasn't going to *be* sick, I just felt sick. I didn't have to 'track' anyone, or hunt anyone, I had an address. There was no challenge, I just had to man up and get there.

'Get there?' I hear you ask.

Yeah, get there.

You see the address George scribbled on that piece of paper was for a property on the Isle of Wight.

The Isle of fucking What!?

No 'Wight' not 'what'

Wight?

Yes, Wight.

Great. Right.

No 'Wight'

Ok whatever, so that's bollocks for a start. How was I supposed to get to the Isle of Wight? We had no car; I had no car. I had no cash either, thanks to Chloe, Mum and Maggie - the three bastard robbing musketeers. But I did have friends, didn't I, and a few 'favours' I could call in. First there was Stevie, Chelsea's brother who owed me £40 for some gear. It had been going on a while, so I didn't feel bad calling it in.

Next was Jason Donovan, I know, don't say it. Ridiculous. Anyway, this fella owned me for a couple of blades I sorted for him for a special 'school project' he was doing, it was a policy of mine not to ask questions. This plus I promised to put a word in for him with Skinny Mitch the local 'product manager'. Which was complete bollocks if truth be told, Skinny Mitch and I were not currently on speaking terms after I shot his mums cat in the arse with an air rifle I'd found in someone's shed over on the Western. It was almost brand new. The air rifle, not the cat.

Anyway, with these and a few other bits and bobs, like £15 from Mum's elderly friend Miss Milly for cleaning out her dust bin and mowing her front garden, I scraped together a couple of hundred quid. Quite frankly, it was more cash than I'd had in a while, what with eggs, crumpets, and kebabs, in recent times, weighing heavily on my personal finances.

Not that I minded though, I had no aspirations for retirement.

It was funny though, wasn't it, how I'd considered myself totally skint before, even though without too much effort, in this situation I had been able to pull together a reasonable sum. I wondered why I hadn't done it before, you know, when mum was shaking cause she'd run out of fags and coffee, or when Chelsea rang me begging for help with formula for her kid, not, and I'm at pains to point this out, that it was actually any of my concern.

I did help though, just so you know, I bunged her £20, it was all I had.

I think it just felt different this time, like it didn't matter if I used up all my favours, if I left all the cupboards bare as it were. It was weirdly liberating. It felt like, and I'm reluctant to say this, like I wasn't coming back. Which, of course, was stupid. The Nutter was there, wasn't she, and she needed me. Bean, for all her promises, would be on the pipe by now and all but useless to anyone but her plumber Dave who made regular and planned visits for more emergencies that the war commission had to deal with. And her kids were brats, they were all too far up their own backsides to notice cousins, aunties, and the extended family.

So, I would be going back, of course I would, Mum needed me, I had lads running bits for me and they'd need paying. I wanted to see the Sausage too if I could. I'd also look in on Maggie if circumstances permitted.

But I got it together and that's the point. I bought a ticket and packed a bag. I bought a shit ton of crumpets, fags and even a bunch of nice forecourt flowers for the Nutter before I left a note and departed. I mean if I'd had a phone and left a number for them to call, Julie would for sure, the Nutter would too. Fuck I'd be surprised if Franks dog Benny didn't call. They'd all be moaning at me, all be saying how I should leave it to the police, that I was being selfish and irresponsible blah blah blah. Except Benny, of course, he'd just breathe heavily and drool.

But drool or not, I had to go, I just had to.

I'm hoping you're beginning to see why.

5: Red Funnel Chunder

So why the Isle of Wight? I'd find out, obviously, in due course. But while I sat on the Southern Railways service bound for Southampton I pondered on the significance. I knew about the scooter rally and the music festival on the island, we all did. I knew they had nice beaches too, a mate at school had been there once as a kid. In fact, he tried to claim he'd actually been abroad, back when anyone from school who went abroad for a holiday was treated like fucking rockstar. He got rumbled though, when Iris the dinner lady told us the truth. She was a spiteful old witch and knew his parents. Think she used to walk their dog. Obviously, I was as happy as everyone else to chop the little twat down to size but I gotta say I did feel a bit for him and his little sister. Who coincidentally I had reason to think fancied me for a year or two in middle school.

Totally unrelated.

Anyway, I knew there to be one or two cultural reasons why a man like my Dad might be drawn to the Isle of Wight although I suspected that outside the times when the scooter rally and such like were actually ongoing the place would be pretty much like any other. Perhaps it was a mixture then, of the glamour and occasion plus the rural and quiet pace. Unless of course he knew something I didn't, which was entirely possible, or knew someone who lived there. I mean Bean only lived along the coast a bit, so it was possible, wasn't it?

Maybe, possibly.

All just assumptions as I watched the countryside speed past.

Gotta say I felt uncomfortable on the train. If you exclude school trips to the obligatory safari park and Museum of Natural Shit, it was the first time outside the big smoke on my own. So apart from my destination I didn't recognise any place names. The accents were funny too. Some were proper rough like southeast of the river whilst others, dead posh like that bird Hermione Granger off of 'Harry Potter and The Ginger Knob Head'. Remember that one?

Me neither.

I imagined some of the kids on the train excitedly receiving their letters inviting them to Hogwarts, whilst simultaneously grooming their ponies and stirring their marmalade.

They obviously lived very different lives to me.

The journey was quick, much quicker than I had imagined it would be, and I started to wonder what I'd spent my fourteen quid on. I made my way to the Red Funnel ferry terminal like a startled virgin before fumbling my way onto the ugliest boat I'd ever seen. I felt less bad about the kid who got knocked about for claiming to have gone abroad now. If he'd thought this boat was anything other than a shit little ferry then he deserved all the dead arms he got. Twat.

Anyway, across the Solent we went, eventually. I was sick twice in the 25 minutes it took to get there although, thankfully, I did it at the front of the boat so that the rest of the foot passengers got a chance to share my experience. But if I'd expected gratitude, I fear I would have been disappointed.

Happily, though, I didn't give a fuck.

I was disappointed however, when we finally docked, with the Isle of Wight. Proper disillusioned. I don't know what I expected to be fair, but it definitely underwhelmed me. I mean, perhaps I was too used to the buzz and noise of the smoke. And being on the train and then the ferry, with all the seagulls and the briny sea air and chatter of kids I didn't have a chance to consider my change in circumstances.

Now however, when the ferry had finished its turnaround and was fifty or sixty metres back out to sea the quiet settled on me like a depressingly wet dog blanket. It smelled too, not like wet dog, more like fresh shit, and fish, and wet grass. In fact, it smelled a bit like the canal that ran parallel to the private garages at the back of the estate.

I'll come back to that canal later.

But I'm dithering aren't I. I mean we haven't come all this way just to talk about how it smelled have we?

No, that's right, we haven't.

But maybe that's the point. Maybe the point is that we, you, and I, aren't really ready to face what's in front of us. You, because what's in front of you is the same as what's behind you. It's the same wake up alarm, the same commute, the same faux excitement for a weekend filled with exactly the same shit as the last weekend. And I'm not criticising, really, I'm not. That's not me, I'm not one to poke at things more vulnerable than me.

Of course, now you've spat out your tea, but that's because you haven't been listening. I said I don't poke, it's true. I observe, comment and, on occasion, voice a considered 'opinion'. But I'm not turned on by making others who have less than me, who are less *able* than me feel bad. I don't take pleasure, ok so maybe a little bit of satisfaction on occasion, but no actual *pleasure* from exposing those more vulnerable than me.

And make no mistake you're one of them.

'Me? You say?' More tea on the floor, and this time all down your nice Aran cardigan too.

Ponce.

Yes, you.

'Outrageous', you shrill like an overwrought Edwardian Governess. Ponies and marmalade.

But I'm serious, and not at all poking fun at you. You see, it's not a case of you being vulnerable, it's more a case that you've selectively evolved to suit your environment. I wanna call you the Sabre Tooth Tiger but that engenders images of ferocity and dominance - which is definitely not what I'm aiming at. Instead, I'm going to call you the Aye-aye.

That's right you're a Long-fingered Lemur native only to a very specific environment. Madagascar, I think you'll find. Look it up if you have questions, my mate Dave was there.

The point is, that if your environment changes, you're fucked, literally. Your specially evolved digits are fucking useless if the food you eat, the ONLY food you eat, ceases to be available.

Truth is, you sit there in bed, or the conservatory, or possibly under a very expensive beach umbrella reading this trite and you consider yourself immune to the pitfalls and poisons of the sort of life *I've* lived. But actually, you're living hand to mouth too aren't you. Your holiday has taken you a year to save up for unless you've bought it on tick. Your car is on finance, probably without GAP insurance because 'it'll never happen to me,' and your conservatory is on the mortgage. That's providing you've been lucky enough to get a mortgage in the first place. Which if you did you only managed because Mummy leant you the ten percent in the first place.

Boomers, bastards.

More likely you're facing a decade of rental payments whilst forcing yourself to shop at Aldi. Yay. All the while trying desperately to raise a deposit, which in itself is a target that keeps moving. An almost impossible task with student loan repayments and both Tesco and the big energy companies declaring record profits.

Unless of course you're Chloe in which case you're busy shagging your boss for tips and pay rises whilst callously sponging off your Daddy, your only plans in life being the Peugeot Roadster you're trying to convince the aforementioned to buy you from Westover.

Oh and of course, your next score.

What I'm trying to say is that you think *I'm* vulnerable, close to the edge, living hand to mouth, but in truth it's you, not me. You see, I own fuck all, so I've got fuck all to lose and therefore fuck all to gain. I'm not obsessed with possession, or status, or income. I'm not climbing anything, I'm not on my way anywhere. So, I'm already both above it and below it, aren't I?

You on the other hand will never rise above it, you'll never climb off that wheel. You'll always be teetering on the edge of a total cluster fuck. Think about it. One driving ban, one error of judgement at work, one tiny little fuck up and it'll all come tumbling down. And you have no safety net.

You go to a garden party, a friend's surprise 40th. You have a few sausages off the barbeque, two cans of cider, a game of Swingball and then, later, a glass of bubbles thrust into your hand to toast the birthday girl.

You drive home, because - 'you've only had a couple' and 'you'll be alright'. On the way, your missus drops her phone between the seats. You glance down, you don't see the kid running out, and you hit her.

The kid dies, don't worry, this is all bollocks so don't get all wound up. But yeah, the kid dies, you get breathalysed, and convicted of drunk driving, causing death by.... etc etc. You lose your job, cause you can't drive. The neighbours stop talking to you, you don't get invited to anymore parties, and your kids struggle to look at you.

And now you can't afford the mortgage, and your marriage is on the rocks, because 'she dropped her phone' and 'you never wanted to go to the stupid fucking party anyway'..

'What?' 'What about the £12k we've got squirrelled away in the Nationwide Building Society?'

Hahaha. What about it?

Your mortgage / rent is at least grand a month, your food shopping, utilities, and council tax is another grand minimum. And don't forget your car payments, phones, and your Netflix account. You're literally four to five fragile little months away from either tasering and kidnapping your bank manager or kipping, kids and all, around the back of Bensons for Beds.

Make no mistake.

Other out of town furniture retail outlets are available.

But me?

Well, I'm free. I have nothing and therefore I have nothing to lose. I have no ambition, no vision. I have no aspirations, no burning desire to achieve anything. I have no skills and therefore no tidemark of disappointment to wash up against. I have little academic knowledge so no ladder of *further* education to climb. And I'm not about to compare myself to anyone either.

Read that again if you need to.

Of course, I grew up with kids like me, but I also grew up with kids who had shit. Their parents had shit. But it was never about opportunity or education or ownership where I came from. It was about survival. For their parents it had been about survival too, even if they did have money. It was about getting up and living the day, living the moment. And if you made it through and you had a couple of quid then happy days.

That's why mum always had fags isn't it, and why if she wanted a crumpet or some pills, I fucking made sure she had em. Because the cash, it wasn't really mine in the first place, was it? It just happened, at that moment, to be in my pocket.

Anyway, back to my original point. You're not ready to talk about it because 'ready' infers control. And you definitely ain't in control. See above.

And I don't want to talk about it because it's hard to write about walking across an island looking for a terrace house with a low stone wall and old-fashioned wooden sash windows in an interesting and engaging way. I mean the paint was flaking off the windows and the front 'lawn', if you want to call it that, was overgrown but other than that I'm drawing a blank.

So, cutting rapidly and slightly clumsily to the chase; here we are.

Sweaty palms, sore feet from the walk and proper desperate for a shit (they won't have Damien Lewis saying that now will they) I stood in front of the crap wooden door and wondered what the fuck I was doing.

What was I hoping to find? Who was I hoping to find? I don't know, I really don't. I was confused about how I got there. One minute I was peering round Danny's bedroom door to find him gone and the next I'm thousands of miles away, well ok seventy-five if I stretched out my arms and stood on one leg, standing outside someone's front door.

Wtf?

What did I know about my Dad then? I've given this some thought to be fair, I had by then too. He died when I was thirteen and Danny was eleven. Babies really, shocking.

He worked away a lot, he was a decorator, always had been. Fucking hated painting though, so mum said. He'd been in Scotland, St Andrews if I remember correctly and then Newcastle upon Tyne in the weeks before.

We got a call on the Saturday morning after his two-week stint away. Should've been home late on the Friday but we assumed, well mum did, Danny and I were too busy shoplifting fags and Red Bull from the One-Stop to notice that he'd got held up. It happened a lot, it was no big deal.

Phone call was his boss Dean Peters, who was nice enough but to be honest, and I did notice this even at that tender age, looked like he'd never lifted a paint brush in his life. Only met him a couple of times but he was always dressed wrong for a mush that runs twenty-five brush hands. Had a funny accent and big special watch too, I remember that well.

Anyway, Dean called. There'd been an accident, Dad had been crushed by some piece of machinery and wasn't coming home. We couldn't even go and see him. *We* were crushed, fucked, devastated. Mum fell apart, honestly, she just totally fell apart. There was a funeral, obviously and Bean was there with her pristine kids and big shoes. Uncle Knobhead was too, back then he and Bean were still on speaking terms, not my name incidentally, that's what everyone called him.

Anyway, it was all over pretty quick, and I don't remember many of the details. Not just the funeral, I mean all of it. The visits by concerned relatives and neighbours. The flowers, the cards, the casseroles. The kind smiles and sad expressions people put on when talking to us. It was done within a month and then we were back in the mix. Danny was fighting at school, the Nutter was doing extra shifts and smoking like she was on fire, and I was back to doing deals and intimidating people.

Standard.

The pain didn't go though. That never went. I felt cheated, like I'd been promised something but then it had been taken away. That lasted for a long time, not sure it ever went.

But what about him? Dad. I mean, what did I know or remember about him? Well, I'll start with the physicals. Cause that's the easiest bit. I remember his skin was quite tanned, pretty sure he had some Spanish or Italian in him somewhere along the line, poor fella. And he had tattoos; S.K.I.N.S across his knuckles on one hand and that funny honeycomb, hexagon thing on the back of the other. He had a few others too, and scars which he tried to keep hidden. Difficult when you've got two curious little rascals darting about the place. The scars he said were from his time in Vietnam but even then, I knew that was just banter, he was too young for that shit. His hands weren't big, but they were strong, and the skin on his palms was hard. He had one of them big watches too, like Dean, although he nearly always took it off when he was at home. I figured Dean must have bought it for him.

He had a kind face, smiled a lot. I can still picture it now. Blue eyes that seemed to see everything, and short hair, like shaved a bit at the sides and back. Although not as short as when he'd been my age, Nan showed me. It didn't occur to me as a kid but in the time since he'd gone and because I'd eaten so many pies and seen so many builders and painters in the Grub, I realised that he didn't really look like a decorator either, not like any of the red nosed sarcastic piss heads I knew anyway.

Yeah, so he wore the white overalls and carried his Brush Mate and extension pole with him when he left on a Monday, but he never came home with paint on him, never, not on his hands, no splashes on his face. He could talk shop of course and hold his own in the pub when it came down to football and all the other bollocks. I remember him having good banter, and I think a bit of a dark sense of humour too, at times.

I remember him carrying me on his shoulders, I loved that. I thought I could touch the sky, fuck that was nice. And he was good with Danny too, when he came along. Funny how that's in my mind, how he was with my little brother. Good to mum too, she loved him, like I say she was proper broken when he passed, even if things were a bit shit between them just before the end.

It wasn't right was it. All those good memories pissed up against a wall. I mean there's families out there that struggle for just *one* good memory, and they're having to put up with one another long term. And then there's us, bags and bags of sunshine actually, more than I can properly describe. Cause even though I've gone to lengths to tell you how shit life was on the estate, I'm only really talking about the time since Dad went.

That's when the colour went. That's when the clouds came in and we all thought bollocks to it, all of us. Cause what was the point? There was no point.

I lifted my fist and banged on the door. Of course, nothing happened. What did I expect? Dad to come bounding out, shirtless, with his 2" fine bristle gloss brush in hand? 'Hi Squidge (yes it was his fault and perhaps why I fucking hated it so much) come on in, I've got some cutting in you can help me with, and oh, by the way did you see the Bashir interview with Princess Dianna?'

Yeah, right. Bollocks.

I dunno, fantasies I suppose but I did kinda, naively hope he might be there. And I did concoct a frankly bizarre scenario. It involved him ruffling my hair like I was eight and us reliving the 'qualities that make men kings' conversation. Brought a little tear to my eyes if I'm honest.

But anyway, none of that happens in real life does it. None of that nice shit can ever happen to real people can it. No because then we'd have no interest in the bullshit rom com with Hugh Grant playing a floppy, mop haired loser desperately chasing a spiteful self-obsessed sociopath called Linda. And there's always a dog, isn't there? I mean I know Benny and he's ok in small doses, dribbles a lot mind, but these posh dickheads in the movies always find time to have a dog, normally a big one. They never fucking walk it or take it to the vets to have its sex organs removed but they still seem to make out like it's part of their soppy story.

Bollocks to that. If I had a dog I'd call it Stabber and I'd train it to bite anyone driving a Range Rover or riding a horse.

Anyway, no, good things don't happen like that, not in real life. Instead, it rains, or you can't get tickets, or you're skint, or there's no one home.

So, I stood for a full five minutes which is a long time. I mean if you've ever done it, you know, knocked on someone's door and waited for them to answer, I'll bet Hilary Clinton's entire budget for the legal defence of her sex pest husband you've never stood for more than thirty seconds. It's ridiculous.

I knocked a couple of times but nothing. I wandered round the side and peered, stalker-like through the front window but nothing. Eventually I put a note through the letterbox. Surprised? Yes, me too, but like a yet to be molested Boy Scout I had come prepared.

Then I walked away.

I had Dad's smelly old sleeping bag, some bin liners, thick socks, and some snacks. Also had an umbrella so I'd be fine in a doorway for a few nights. I had considered this possibility. You know, I wasn't a complete wanker and was happy to try again tomorrow, to keep trying until I spoke to someone, anyone in fact. I'd try the neighbours if necessary. I didn't take lightly to leaving the smoke and chasing halfway round the world after a wispy thread of hope like this. Ok a tad dramatic perhaps but I'd be fucked if I was going home with nothing.

I walked into town; it was Ventnor on the south east coast of the island if anyone's interested. Sounded like a fizzy drink to me, not a sleepy little town filled with the nearly dead.

Didn't have to go far, the address I'd been to was just on the outskirts, in the village of Wroxall. I mean it was a proper walk but doable in a couple of hours and I wasn't fussed about wasting four quid on a taxi. There were plenty of shop doorways in Ventnor, and I know I'm making assumptions here but, there didn't seem to be a lot of competition for decent spots. Nor was there an overt presence of official looking individuals who may seek to move me on at the very moment I got comfortable.

I spent the next few hours wandering around trying not to look dishonest or homeless, which, to be fair I was precisely both. I walked along the beach and had a sit down on the bandstand overlooking the sea and even had a paddle. It was lovely, to be fair, all sandy and clean. Eventually I found a lovely Honda motorcycle dealership next to St Catherines with a large overhanging roof section at the front which I suspected would suit my purposes. I'm gonna call it a porch from now on, if that's ok?

Anyway, another hour of wandering, lurking, and avoiding the very posh looking Royal Hotel before I returned and settled down. It was dark and quiet and to be fair, a lot nicer than it would've been back home if I'd felt the need to be outside. I was starting to see the charm of the place. It was deathly quiet, apart from the faint sound of the sea, and there were literally no smack heads, no blacked out M5's cruising around looking for opportunities to murder people and very little dog shit. It was really quite tidy too.

Yeah, I kinda liked it.

Until about 3am.

'Why until about 3am?' I hear you ask.

Forgive my optimism, but my life literally depends on you still being there...

Because at 3am I was taken, yes taken.
'Really?'
Yes. Really.
And then things got proper sideways.

6: 120 degrees. If you'll forgive me...

This is where the narrative starts to change. Written by the same person, me, obviously. But it's changed because I was changed.

You see, I did try to write the first part as me, now, with words I use now, language I use *now*. But it was rubbish, inauthentic. I know that sounds glib and woke but it's true. Now, me, right now, I have no idea what those streets, those estates, those defence mechanisms look like. I am a million miles from that. So, writing it as me, now, just didn't work.

The only way I could take you there, authentically, was to go back there myself, to be me, actually *in* it. Not 'innit' obviously, but in it. Immersed in, mobilised by and as fully *me*.

So that's why the cheeky chappy. That's why the tone and sarcasm, the swearing, which I addressed earlier. It's why I reference my political anger, my suspicion, my distrust. It's why, and this still lives within him, that cheeky chappy, why I tell you I love my mum. Why I loved her then, why I love her now.

Because she's still in it, in that shit, in the grey. She's still there, sort of.

Anyway, more on Mum later. Now I'm gonna tell you about Terry.

7: Surf and Turf

Right. I don't know where I went initially. I was picked up roughly, hood over my head, hands over my face, really strong arms around my legs and upper body. And then I was dumped into what I can only assume was the boot of a car. Probably an M5, if anything like poetic justice exists.

I was driven for probably 10 minutes and then dragged out, again held tightly, and kept quiet. To be honest though, I didn't need any persuading to keep quiet, I was shitting myself. I may have, genuinely, shit myself.

I was carried for a bit before being put down again, a little gentler than before if I am honest. Then I was sat up, my hands pulled round the back and cable tied to a pipe and my feet cable tied together. And then it went quiet, for a good hour before someone came back into the room, I was in. And I know I was in a room because the air was still, and I could smell oil and petrol and sawdust.

The light was switched back on and the hood was pulled and when my eyes finally adjusted, I looked up into the face of...

No, I didn't know them, no fucking idea. Excuse me.

But seriously, I had no idea.

"Do you know who I am?"

I shook my head, my banter curiously absent.

"No."

The bloke, big and fit looking stared at me. He had cold eyes, like he could see me, but he couldn't see me. Like the way I might look at a chicken breast as I was chopping it up for mum's favourite *El Paso* chicken fajitas. Other pre-packaged Mexican food options are available.

Oh, and buy the way when I say big, I mean he really was big, like massive.

"What's your name?"

I swallowed. Such a cliche.

Didn't answer though, I was so disoriented.

The big guy continued to stare at me like he was trying to melt me. He asked again.

"What is your name?"

I stared back, he had a funny accent, maybe that was normal here.

He was late thirties, mid-forties tops and fit, like super fit. Clean shaven and looked like he looked after himself. Like one of those city boys who pulled down 250K a year and jogged everywhere. Groomed and healthy and so relaxed with their fortune. Wankers. But no, this fella, although he clearly looked after himself, he didn't look like a trader, or a banker. He didn't look like he jogged for fun either.

I looked at his hands, big and strong but clean. And his clothes, they weren't the sort of clothes the Turks in the blacked out M5's back home wore. He wasn't dressed to impress, or to intimidate. He was dressed for travelling, for movement. And he had a big watch on, just like Dads, just like Dean Peters.

Fuck.

"Last time laaitie. What is your name"?

I hesitated, just for a few seconds more. I was scared, I had no idea what he wanted, I was terrified. It was all fucked up. It was all too much. What was I going to do?

He sighed and started to move. I knew, before it happened, what that meant. There'd be pain, agony more likely. There'd be decisions too, you know like the one the gangsters force their captive to make in the movies. 'Tell us what we want to know, or we'll kill Benny the dog'. What a dilemma, what a thing. I mean if they said Chloe then I'd have kept schtum but the dog??!

Seriously though the big fella, his resignation, his cool terrified me. I blurted out:

"Squidge! Fuck, my name is Squidge."

And the room was quiet. Like, it was quiet before but now it was really quiet. Dramatically quiet. He stopped and turned back to look at me. He stared at me for a full minute before eventually moving back to stand in front. Finally, he opened his mouth.

"Where did you hear that name?"

I didn't like the way he moved. Like a cat staring at a laser pointer, moving quietly, carefully into position. It made me shiver; it made me sick. But then he asked me that question and I gotta be honest I wanted to laugh. I mean I hated that name. Not when my Dad had called me it. When he'd called me and Danny, Squidge and Zip, his two little fart busters, we'd loved it, beamed with pride in fact. Mum hated it, well, she made out like she did, but I know she'd have given anything to have that sort of nonsense back under her roof later on.

I hated it now because it just reminded me that he was gone. And people that I didn't like used it. Drug dealers used it, the police, Mousas, Maggie, ok maybe that's a bit unfair but still, it was my *Dad's* name, for me, just for me. It shouldn't be used by others. But it was, and after so many years it was the only name a good deal of people had for me.

Under certain circumstances, and for good reason, I might include myself in that.

Case. In. Point.

So how to answer.

I drew a blank. I mean, it was my name, what could I say?

"I don't understand," I stuttered like a nervous schoolgirl. And I think that was probably the first time in my life those words, in that order, had ever come out of my mouth. It just wasn't good form, you know, to admit you didn't understand, not from where I come from anyway. Oh, and yes, I'm talking about the 'I don't understand' bit, not the 'nervous schoolgirl' bit.

Although, to be fair, the same could be said of both.

Anyway, the big guy with dead eyes looked at me and raised his eyebrows which in turn raised the tension in the room in ways I can't adequately put into words.

"I mean, it's my name. It's just my *name*."

He stared without speaking.

"I've always been Squidge, I mean it's not my real name of course but it's what everyone calls me," verbal fucking diarrhoea now.

I was scared, really, I was, I was crapping myself. But even in that state the oddness of his questions struck me; 'Where did you hear that name?' Not; 'Thats a shit name', or; 'What the fuck does that mean?' What's your real name?' or even; 'That's a bit odd, what is it short for? What does it stand for?'

I know that's a lot of options but seriously, who does actually call their child Squidge? For real?

Nobody right?

But no, none of the above. Instead:

'Where did you *hear* that name?'

Like, mental. Very specific and mental. I mean if I'm not mistaken, and I very rarely am, it seems like he knows that name, like that name has something about it, right? It also means, and I'm taking leaps here, that it seems like he knows of me but doesn't actually know me. You know? What!?

Right so all of this is whizzing through my head as I'm sat sweating and cable tied to an inch and a quarter BSP incoming mains cold water pipe. I jest, of course, it was actually a 22mm copper gas pipe.

Which in itself was a mistake because, first: it should have been 28mm, and second: the copper is far more fragile than the BSP, so not really an ideal hostage anchor point. If you're a purist.

But really? Honestly?

Yeah, fuck.

He knew *of* me but not actually me. So why was I here? Why did his goons put a bag over my head and chuck me in the back of their BMW? How did he know *of* me? How could he have heard that name? Had he followed me? Did he know Danny? Did he *have* Danny?

My brain was starting to wake up, the anxiety and terror slipping away. This wanker had Danny, he knew where he was. What the actual fuck?

"Where's Danny?" I asked, my voice low and strained, I was getting stressed, very quickly.

The big fella said nothing, but his eyes told me he was thinking about the question.

"Where's my brother? Where's my fucking brother," I can't properly describe the rage building inside, but it was like it was something new was growing there. Sure, take me back a couple of weeks, and if I'd been quick enough, I'd have had no hesitation in jumping over that balcony back at home. Three floors up wouldn't have entered my head. It was Danny, and I was the fucking *Batman*. Bollocks to gravity.

But here, as I struggled against the cable ties, a thick red mist was rapidly descending.

"You wanker. Where's my brother? Where's Danny?!" I was growling at him, all thin and wiry and not the least bit physically intimidating, certainly not to this big cunt.

Nevertheless, he shifted backwards slightly.

"Who's Danny?" He shook his head. "What are you on?"

I exploded, I did. All the days and weeks of anxiety built up inside. My panic at not knowing where my little brother was, the sheer brazen neck of these fuckers that took him. The state the Nutter was in back home, bouncing off the walls, working herself to death. My grief and turmoil over my Dad, and soon probably the Sausage. FUUUUCK!

It was like a volcano.

I went berserk, really, mental. I snapped them cable ties like they were fuck all, which I gotta be honest surprised me far more than the big fella. With startling, hulk-like strength and speed I jumped at the bloke, feet still tied together but fists, elbows and nut buzzing, I knocked him flying. He went back, tripped over a nice Draper socket set and bumped his head on a woodworking vice on the bench behind.

It wasn't a top of the range socket set but not the basic one either. It was the sort you'd get for your eighteenth Birthday from your Nan with the hope being that you still had it when your kids were buying their own first motors, you know so you could use it together. Unless of course you sold it for a line of smack and some top of the range Adidas Predators.

Anyway, the poor fella was sparko before my first blow even caught him. Didn't save him though, and I'm not proud. Turns out I can be a proper nasty cunt when pushed. And I was pushed, like really pushed, hopefully you'll forgive me that.

Anyway, I beat the shit out of a man that couldn't hit me back, broke him up, blood everywhere. There was some growling, a bit of spit and a fair amount of language my Nan would've been shocked at. Bit ashamed of that to be truthful.

But it seems that irrespective of all that I did it quietly enough because no fucker came. Seriously I rained down all sorts on that guy and no one came to see what was going on. When I was done, my initial rage spent, I stood up and surveyed the room. I found something to cut the ties off my legs before I checked he was still alive. Then pinched a few bits: cash from his wallet and a single ID card, a gun, yes an actual fucking GUN that was tucked in the back of his trousers, so cliche. Also, I'll try and use that word a bit more going forward if you don't mind, love it, 'trousers'. Oh, plus I nicked his watch, fuck it, why not.

Then I put him in the recovery position, I'm not a complete wanker, and crept out the room.

The corridor was dark and quiet, I guessed the property to be empty and so moved quickly to find a door. I perversely wondered how many bedrooms it had and whether it might be warmer than the porch at Honda garage. Idiot. But I did consider exploring upstairs, seriously, I mean maybe Danny was up there, maybe there *was* someone else in the house who couldn't have come to see what the racket was, even if they wanted to.

I stopped, the front door was there in front of me, just at the end of the hall. I cursed. The big fucker could wake any second, despite the beasting I gave him, and the other guys, and I was sure there were at least two, could return at any moment. It was stupid, possibly suicide but fuck it, there was no way I could leave without knowing for sure.

So, I dashed back, against my aforementioned better judgement, stomach doing its bollocks and my nerves shot to pieces. I raced upstairs like a mad kangaroo three steps at a time, my theory being that I was screwed anyway so best get it over with quickly. Going room to room, kicking doors it was obvious no one was there, even if it looked like someone had been at some point. Had they kept Danny here? I didn't suppose I'd ever find out for sure, but either way it was safe to say he wasn't there now. I was gutted, and relieved beyond words, all at the same time.

Not relieved beyond sick though, no, I puked a bit at the top of the stairs just to mark my territory. You're welcome.

And then I ran back downstairs and shitting myself that the sasquatch would come barrelling out the garage behind me any moment. I proceeded at speed down the hall and finally eased my way out of the front door.

Now outside I moved across the front yard, keeping hidden in the shadows as I went, listening all the time for the sound of voices or an approaching car. It was deathly quiet, eerily so, or maybe that's just me and my default understanding of 'city quiet' over 'everywhere else in the world quiet'.

But no car came, no voices called out and I got away. Which was good until I realised I really had nowhere to go. I mean these fellas had a base of sorts, they had resources, transport etc. I had a tatty rucksack, smelly sleeping bag, a bin liner, and no ticket for the ferry. These fellas might have been proper shady hoods, but they were also legit, at least when compared to yours truly.

Shit.

Plus, I was cold.

The adrenalin was wearing off, my hands hurt, and I was proper hank too. I wondered if there was anywhere open at this time of night, a 24h garage, a late-night chippy or kebab shop. I thought about it then discounted it.

First of all, it was Ventnor, on the Isle of fucking Wight. Second, I was sort of on the run wasn't I? I mean, when these guys did get back to the place they had me they were gonna be pissed. No doubt they'd come looking for me, I know I would.

So takeaway outlets with big plate glass windows and bright lights weren't the best place to hide were they. Nor was it smart to be out casually strolling along the only A road on the island in the middle of the night. I mean knowing where I was, considering what had just happened it was....

FUUUUCK!

The car was on me before I knew it was coming. I think it was the tall hedges and general twists and turns, or it could've been the fact the car was a limited-edition stealth model, Vorsprung Death. But anyway, they saw me, I know they did, straight away. I jumped in the bush next to me quicker than a fart, literally. I mean it was instinct, nothing more. Luckily though, that I didn't actually fart, I mean in those circumstances I'm really not sure how well that would've turned out.

But back to the bush, apparently, they call it a hedge as mentioned above, which is nice. Anyway, I jumped in and fought my way through, cuts, scrapes, and blackberry juice all over me.

As soon as I was through though, I ran like Ahmed's uncles were chasing me. My hair full of leaves and shit and my skin itching with both anticipation and citric acid. Straight across the field I went, arms and legs pumping like a fully loaded Ben Johnson and sleepy pissed off cows and rabbits scattering before me. I had no idea where I was going, it was fully pitch black, unlike anything I was used to.

Back home dark meant that yellow haze I spoke of earlier. It never got proper, fully dark on the estates. Here though, Jesus I couldn't see my hand. I'd have been cautious under normal circumstances walking along the high street. And yet here I was, mad as a sack of tripping squirrels barrelling across this field without a care.

And I could hear them behind me, tyres scraping, doors slamming and voices shouting; 'Excuse me gov, can we bother you for a little chat?' or something along those lines. But I gotta confess, and not deliberately trying to be rude, I wasn't hanging around to indulge. There were torches too and I may have heard a dog, or tiger can't remember for sure. It didn't help me though, last thing I wanted was their torches showing me which way to go. I mean in hindsight it might have served a purpose but at the time. You know...

Another small hedge, a little bit of barbed wire and then I was off again, faster than if I'd been bitten on the arse by a rabid nun.

Anyway, you'll laugh, but the funny thing about running like a shoplifter on probation across a field on the south coast of an island in the English Channel in the pitch-black dead of night is - you never know where the grassy bit ends, and the sky bit begins.

I know, very provocative. Not really me is it right? I'm more of a fuck it, twat and bollocks kind of guy. But still the principle applies however you phrase it. And that's what it is you see, a principle. A principle of gravitational pull. The sort of gravity, if there is indeed more than one, that pulls you down when you are up. You know, like when you run, full tilt off the edge of a fucking cliff.

I mean I knew it was coming, like the tube train I mentioned earlier, that impending sense of doom, of occasion. Not so much the smell of sweaty builders on their way home from a gruelling 6-hour shift that you get on the Central line, but you get my drift.

Other tube lines are available.

But seriously, I was fucked wasn't I. I mean I couldn't see it, taste it or hear it. I couldn't stop either, I couldn't slow down. I just ran, kept running, and ran straight off the cliff. Boom.

The drop was sixty or seventy feet, ridiculously vague I know. But I don't know do I. I was out, gone, unconscious. Not from the impact or some dramatic, and kudos attracting life changing injury, that I could dine out on for the foreseeable, even if that was just chips, cheese and coleslaw. No. Not me. I just fainted, like the big brave boy I am.

I woke up later though, much later, you'll be glad to hear.

And things just, kept, getting weirder.

8: Lakes and Mountains

The boat was shit. Not shit like the ferry to Cows. No *that* was shit because it was bare painted metal, huge fucking rivets everywhere, like millions of them, rust and dirty water. Plus, it stank of fish and diesel and vibrated worse than a twenty-year-old washing machine. Oh, and it had a bit of sick down the side too. Dirty bastards.

This boat was shit because it was small, like tiny, and chopped about all over the place. Not that I should've cared really, I was in and out. The pain was remarkable, truly remarkable. I'd seen loads of movies with people getting carved up, seen a couple of kids run over for real outside my middle school by an alcoholic divorcee in a Range Rover too, see fucking Range Rovers! Plus. Plus, I'd seen Mike the Bike stabbed in the foot. Which was weird because why would you stab someone in the foot? Never properly got to the bottom of that one.

Anyway, I'd seen pain before, kinda knew what it was all about, thought I did anyway. But nothing prepared me for this.

I mean nothing. I was beside myself. It was like an out of body experience, I can't think of any other way to describe it. I think the sleeping was just my head going 'you know what, fuck this, I'm done'.

Which was fair, to be fair.

But when I wasn't away with the fairies, I was banging about left right and centre. It was dark, I was piss wet through and covered in my own blood. At least that was until we got to Jersey. I know right, how do I know there's even a place called Jersey? Because I listen right, I'm not always in my head you know.

Anyway, when we got to Jersey we transferred back on land and they patched me up or something. And when I say 'patched me up' I mean cut me open, moved my bones around a bit and then stitched me back together. I had no idea who they were, no idea. Could've been Gary Glitter and Michael Barrymore for all I knew. Didn't know, didn't care.

But they stitched me up, drugged me up, slapped a couple of casts on and popped me in a helicopter. Like you do. Lovely.

Or it would've been had I not been tripping on the best 'over the counter' you could ever wish to come by. I mean I'd have loved it, seriously, being airlifted at any other time of my life. Like, if that had happened to me back on the estate I'd have been set for life. Forever after known as Airlift, or Chopper or by some kudos garnering derivative.

You know how it is, I could've used that for literally years. Indeed, after said *years* I wouldn't even have to explain it anymore, it would just be, like there, and no one would question it, and the kids would talk about me in hushed tones.

I'd be a fucking legend.

But no, it was wasted cause the reality is I didn't have a scooby. Seriously, I kinda remembered the sound and was aware of the vibration. And I remember it all being very urgent, or secret or something. But not much more, the drugs they gave me took not just the pain but also any sense of time and the world around me. They were fantastic.

We landed, eventually, much later than I assumed we would. I mean how far away were the major hospitals in London anyway? And then I slept, and slept, and slept.

Waking up with the sun in your face. Waking up warm and comfortable, no aches or pains, no banging head, no anxiety of what the day might bring. It was a background thing wasn't it, the anxiety, the physical pain or discomfort. Sometimes it was at the front, obvious, and the first thing you noticed. Sometimes not so much, sometimes barely noticeable. For me it was always present though. At least since Dad had gone.

I'm sure that's not unique, is it?

Anyway, I couldn't remember not waking up both hungry and worried about what I might be able to eat that day. That was until I started earning for myself and I could sort myself out with food and stuff.

But it didn't stop the anxiety, the pain. I mean, I was only young but my bed was shit, things weren't good at home and I was always in some scrape or another (and if I wasn't then Danny definitely was) so there weren't too many times I woke up feeling a hundred percent. Guess I was luckier that some though, at least I did have my own bed and mum wasn't putting fags out on my legs for fun.

I woke up with the sun on my face. I was comfortable, like really comfortable. My head, my back and legs, all perfectly snug and happy where they were. Why would I want to open my eyes? I knew the reality wouldn't be as good as what my body was describing to me.

I could hear voices, birds and the breeze. And I sensed that the warm sun wasn't the 'through the window' type of sun. Not the type that warms even on one of those Baltic mornings where the ice and snow never gets to melt. Had plenty of them in the flat. Where the ice on the inside of the front door stays till after lunch. On those days we'd sit, me and Danny in front of the big front window from about 10am and let the sun warm us up. Such extravagant indulgence.

This didn't feel like that though. This felt like real sun, like I was actually *in* the sun.

Sounds weird but I'd never had a tan. Seriously, never. You'll not be surprised to learn that I'd never been abroad and done the whole pool-beach thing. I'd never sat with a book lazily laying across my chest, sunnies on, early drinks and aftersun followed by souvlaki and a carafe of Rose at the local taverna to look forward to. I didn't have holiday memories, holiday snaps, holiday aspirations. Mum took us to Bexhill once. And obviously we'd been to see Bean in Bournemouth once or twice but if I'm honest it was all a bit stressful and shit. It was a faff, a hassle. Too many rude idiots from town for the weekend, all doing the same thing, and the locals all la-di-da and rude cause we were spoiling the ambiance.

I was little, but I could tell. Beans kids fucking hated us, thought we were scummy. Took us out one evening and left us down the seafront whilst they got a taxi home. Said they 'lost us' but bollocks to that, they did it on purpose. The nutter was livid, fell out with her sister big time and we never went back. I didn't know if holidays in Spain or Greece would be different than that but hoped so. If not for me then for the millions of die-hards who packed up and flew off every year.

I opened my eyes.

I *was* outside, in the sun, properly.

I laid for another moment to get my bearings before lifting my head to look around. First thing I saw were the kids. There were three of four little kids running around chasing each other on a big lawn. First instinct was that I was on the Common, or maybe the Heath, as per my dream. But that went soon enough. I looked past the kids to the cars parked on the drive. I mean, I call it drive but it was nothing like any drive I'd ever seen. And the cars, Jesus, they must all be gangsters, whoever I was staying with, they must all be gangsters.

Then I looked at the building. A hotel, clearly. And then it all started to click. The big lawn, the driveway and cars, the building. I glanced the other way and saw the water, a pond, actually no, a lake, a fucking huge lake. I squinted and realised that there were buildings on the opposite side, but they were tiny. Fucking huge lake.

I turned my head back to the hotel to see someone making their way over to me. From here he looked like a PE teacher, tracksuit, smart hair, purposeful mince. He was smiling too, like he knew me or fancied me. Bollocks, what was this? Where the fuck was I?

"You're awake then?" as he got closer. Funny accent.

I didn't say anything, I just watched him come.

"Micha," he held his hand out for me to shake as he came alongside. I looked at him and then his hand. And then I looked down at myself and wondered what I was doing lying down, my brain was still half asleep. Self-consciously, I tried to sit up but struggled, like, *really* struggled. I didn't seem to have any strength in my arms, and everything felt so strange.

Anyway 'Micha' was there, wasn't he.

He grabbed me, across the shoulders and helped me up before rearranging the pillows and cushions so I was comfortable. Then he stepped back and tried again;

"I'm Micha," hand out as before. This time I took it and replied quietly.

"Squidge," unsure whether he thought I'd insulted him or told him my name he nodded, still smiling, and then stepped back.

"You're probably wondering what you're doing here," and then without waiting for me to agree or disagree, went on; "You had a bit of a fall, I'm told. You've been here for a little while; you've been asleep for a little while."

I was confused. Where the fuck was here? What the fuck was going on?

One minute I was on a ferry to the Isle of Wight, the next I was here. Actually, was that 'lake' the Solent? Were the buildings opposite just the buildings on the south coast, Southampton or Christchurch or France or something?

I looked back at Micha.

"Where am I?"

His smile slipped a little. I mean he was still smiling but there was something else there too. Ignoring the question, he looked instead at my legs and began fussing. He pulled the blanket off and examined the bandages, both legs were wrapped. Next he touched my feet, rotated my ankles and flicked each of my toes in turn.

"Can you feel that?" looking back up at me.

I nodded, embarrassed. I'd never been in hospital, rarely been to the doctors. And mum wasn't a hugger, so it was a bit weird being touched by another person, especially a mincy little man.

"Where am I?" I asked again. "What happened to me?"

Micha finished his checks before re-covering me with the blanket.

"Are you warm enough?" still ignoring the questions.

I nodded.

"Good. Someone will be over to see you soon. I'm glad you've woken, it's nice to finally meet you."

And with that he was gone, hair, tracksuit and tight little walk fading as he went back across the lawn. I watched him go, wondering what I was supposed to do now. I didn't know where I was, probably on the Isle of Wight but apart from that, no clue. I didn't know what was wrong with me, why I'd been 'asleep' and for how long. I didn't have any of my shit and I didn't know anyone. Shit I could have been in Lake Geneva for all I knew. Even if I didn't know where Lake Geneva actually was.

I laid back against the pillows, damn they were soft, and closed my eyes. I could hear the children playing and even the occasional hum of a boat or something out on the water. The birds were there, in the background, not giving a shit. But it was nice, warm, soft and pleasant, even if I did have a growing sense that I shouldn't be there.

And then I thought about Danny. And then I remembered what actually happened, the rage, the beating, kicking, spitting. I remembered the feeling of strength, of overwhelming, all-consuming rage. Then the running, the panicking, the sprinting and fear and the end, the void. I remembered the fall, the drop. My lungs filled with air, my stomach lurching up into my chest as I fell and fell and fell.

And then the black and cold and sleep.

I opened my eyes again; the sun had moved and there were different noises. I looked over, some of the cars had gone as had the kids that were buzzing about earlier. Instead, there were guys in white setting up what looked like a barbecue on the lawn close to a gazebo thing.

And it was a nice lawn, I gotta say. Perfectly flat and even, no divots or holes, no nappies or McDonalds wrappers or dog shit. Big too, plenty big enough, just on this side of the buildings for a game of 5-a-side. Someone clearly looked after it.

Anyway sorry, so yes; I did like a barbecue, I've gotta be honest. Not that I'd get to have any of that, I couldn't move even if I wanted to. They hadn't started cooking yet but I knew when they did the smell could kill me, assuming of course that they weren't already intending on basting me up and using *me* as the main course.

You never did know these country folk.

Not so many birds this time of day, not that I had a scooby what time of day that might be. I mean, the sun was lower in the sky and there seemed to be less noise coming from the water but other than that I had no way of knowing.

I was hungry, I mean it hit me all of a sudden. It wasn't the smell or anything, because they hadn't actually started cooking, it was more just the thought of it. And, like, I'd been hungry before, obviously, but something had been switched off, I don't know how else to describe it. Well, I can tell you it was properly switched on now. I got a cramp, seriously, a big angry, bollock squeezing, cramp. Couldn't remember the last time I had one of those, possibly when the obligatory school chunk; fat Charlie Arsewhistle stole both my Dairylea Dunker *and* the Pepperami I'd literally, just 5 minutes before, lifted from the new Chinese girl back in year four.

Bitch.

And I know some of you are going to say that's karma, justice even, and that's fine, you can make that judgement if you like. With no context. Without taking the time to find out my circumstances. Without thinking about just how desperate I may have been, to have been driven to such lengths.

I say piss off, I was hungry, and she wasn't looking. So, finders keepers. Plus, both he and she, at the time, looked like they needed the carbs far less than me.

Anyway, just as I'm wondering whether I need to crawl across the lawn to get *myself* some ribs and coleslaw, or crawl across the lawn to save myself from *being* the coleslaw, I saw another visitor making their way over to me. This time it was a woman, or girl, or something. Apologies but I've never been sure where the line is between the two. She was young and attractive though; I do know that.

"Hey," all bright, breezy, and informal. Ponytail, blue eyes, great teeth. She held out her hand and unlike Micha, I took it straight away. And possibly held onto it a bit too long as well.

"Hi," I responded, weirdly shy. Fuck, what was that? I'm not shy, no matter how well they look after themselves I'm never shy. But shit, I was now.

"I'm Freya, I'm on your team."

I nodded. Didn't have a scooby what she was talking about. I had a team?

"Ok."

"You hungry?" she smiled. Strangely enough my cramps had disappeared. "You look hungry."

Rude. But I nodded all the same.

She was busy fussing with my legs, like Micha earlier, checking bandages, poking, flicking. Didn't feel as uncomfortable as when Micha did it though.

"Got any pain?"

I shook my head; I didn't think so. Not sure I'd know if I did.

"Good. Cool, cool," she smoothed the blanket back down before standing back up. "I gotta say, I've been looking forward to actually meeting you. You're a bit of a celebrity here you know."

A celebrity? WTF? What was she going on about?

"I'll take you over when they've cooked something. Think they're doing the usual burgers and sausages plus a bit of the fancier type of stuff too. Probably won't be ready for half an hour or so. In the meantime, I'm going to pop back in and get something to put over your shoulders, it's probably going to get a little nippy later on."

"Ok," was all I had. Really? Jesus.

She was really pretty, young too so I guess in the girl category but still, she was lovely. And whilst none of that was helping, it has to be said it wasn't the only reason I was tongue tied. The facts that I didn't know where I was, I didn't know who these people were or what the fuck was wrong with me, were, shall we say, 'playing a part'.

But soon enough she was back and wrapping me up in a thick black cardigan. It wasn't mine; I mean how could it be? Seriously though, I'd never owned a cardigan, not one. Danny would've kicked me in the balls and called me a ponce, and rightly so. But under these circumstances, with the lovely Freya brushing herself against me I guess I could make an exception, Zip would understand.

She stepped back.

"Better?"

I nodded but wanted to say more.

"Can I ask?"

"Yeah, what up?" She'd been about to turn and head over to see how long the food was going to be but stopped and focused on me. It was a little disconcerting to be honest. Not just because she was attractive but also because there was something about her, something familiar, something I felt was known to me.

"Where am I?" I asked, suddenly apprehensive about the answer. "Who are you?"

She didn't answer straight away but instead looked away, back over to the house. Eventually back to me with a strange and slightly sad look on her face.

"I don't think I'm the right person to talk to you about that, sorry." She clearly wanted to though. I looked over at the house myself and saw someone standing on the big back steps watching us. For a second, I thought it was the massive fella that zip tied me to the water pipe. Yeah, that's right the same fella I beat the juice out of before making good my escape off an actual cliff.

Good plan.

But no, wasn't him, just some other big fella, at least he looked big from here. He turned and went back through the doors and disappeared.

Freya did an awkward little cough to clear her throat.

"I'm sure it'll all be explained to you very soon. Thing is, you've been very sleepy up until this morning, so it's been a bit tricky." She was definitely feeling uncomfortable.

"Let's get you something to eat first, not too much mind, not for your first meal. And then we'll see if Terry's free...."

So, Terry?

Yes Terry.

What the actual fuck?

I didn't know Terry of course, not this one anyway. I mean I knew *Terry's*, shit loads of em, they were everywhere, like Dave's or squirrels. There was Terry the Knee who'd had a dodgy knee forever, something to do with kneeling down on a fifty pence piece, bollocks if you ask me, it was more likely to be a pound coin. The there was Terry Plumb the electrician, I know, don't say it, Terry Pratt who was a total dickhead, Terry Minor, an ex 'friend' of my Nan, who I kept well away from as he was only just now out on licence following a spell at her Majesty's pleasure for 'firearm offences'. Proper nutcase. Tell's you a bit about my Nan, that does.

Plus, there was Tezza, Tel, Turtle T, and Paul, whose real name was Neil, but got called Terry cause his dad was Terry (actually it was Paul too, fucking wierdo's, don't ask). So, I knew a few.

But not this one. I'd heard his name, as you'll recall a few days ago, I think? And I say 'I think' because firstly I didn't know if this was the same guy the Sausage was referring to and called his son, and secondly, because I had no idea how long ago that conversation was. Was it a 'few days' ago, or was it longer? No idea.

But anyway, sorry, no, I didn't know him. In fact, I hadn't known *of* him either till the Sausage fessed up reference Justin's dad. Still not sure why he told me, might be about to find out now I thought on it.

And as I thought on it I also wondered how the old fart was. I hoped he was clinging on; I'd have a story to tell him now wouldn't I? Maybe not as random as the stories he told but still, a good couple of pints worth I'd say.

Anyway, Terry. Yes, he'd said his son, Justin's Dad was called Terry. I mean, could it be the same guy? It's conceivable, however unlikely. Why would it be though? I mean the Sausage had given me the address and seemed to know something. But what? And what were the connections?

And if it were his Terry, then what? Who gave a shit? Was it important?

All these questions running around in my head made me feel like inspector Morse, when he's trying to piece together all the clues and loose ends that Lewis was too thick to understand all the while trying desperately to avoid falling into a vat of whisky.

Of course, I'd have much preferred to have likened myself to Ludlum's Jason Bourne over Endeavour Morse. But I've got far too much to say for myself and I'm not nearly so well groomed.

As Bourne that is, not Morse, he was a scruffy bastard.

Anyway, Terry. Who the fuck are you?

You'll be glad to know I didn't have to wait too long for my answer. Freya came back over to tell me the food was more or less ready. Said they'd plate something up for me but on reflection, I'd need to go inside to eat it. I wasn't in a position or disagree so just nodded. And with that she released the brakes on the clever chair bed thingy I was strewn across like a dead dog and began pushing me over to the house.

I have nothing against dogs by the way, I hope you understand.

Inside the ceilings were high and it felt old and expensive. Not old like the sewerage works in Beckton. It was posh, lots of fancy plaster and paintings, you know the sort of thing. It also felt odd and out of place for the south of England. I mean, it was a while since I'd last been to visit Liz in Bucks Palace so you might not call me an authority, but I gotta say, I wasn't feeling typical English architecture. I probably don't need to labour the gaps in my knowledge here, but you know, it was a feeling.

Freya took me through to a big, ornate dining room and pushed me up against a massive table. It was dark and shiny and like the lawn outside, big enough to play 5-a-side football on (soccer for the uneducated). It was so big I expected to be joined by others, some possibly in a Sunday league kit of some sorts. But no, I sat alone for a few minutes before she returned with a plate full of juicy meat, crispy potatoes and weird looking salad. Obviously, I left the salad and dived into the ribs and stuff hoping that the napkin she gave me would be big enough to wipe the shit off my face when I was finished.

It wasn't, see below.

So, I guess I wasn't the most civilised of people back then, not now either to be fair. But I still prided myself on being reasonably well presented. You know, I didn't *want* to be a scruffy looking rat, it wasn't a *choice* of mine, it was just circumstances. My old man, he'd taken pride in how he looked. I remember it well, the boots, the pale jeans turned up at the bottom so you could see his laces, the beanie and the green bomber.

I thought it was normal as a kid and only later realised he dressed that way to say something. I talked about this earlier. I think it was something that needed to be said when he was going up. You know, like a social statement, a statement that was like a flag planted in the ground for everyone to see. It made him part of something, something I personally couldn't clearly identify as even still existing when *I* was growing up. I think it may have been gone before he'd finished growing himself to be truthful. But still, it gave him an identity and gave him status that spoke for him, in front of him. And true, it would have been this status that shielded him from the worst of the shit he would've had to deal with as a kid, but I think it also limited him.

I saw this with my own eyes, with kids I knew.

You see, parents with strong loyalties to any group always draw their kids in. They can't help it. It could be religion, it normally is. Or it could be an obsession with the big man - talking about Elvis here, obviously. It could be with footy teams, a strong, secular social group, or perhaps strong political views that lead to things like veganism and dreadlocks and recycling,

Yeah, I know, that won't age at all.

But all of the above, although not intended to, end up capturing kids. It ends up shaping them, often as not, at the same time as tying them up and holding them back. They shape a narrow view. They provide a false reality. They made kids stand out, not blend in. And, seriously, you've gotta be a fucking idiot to think that your kid 'standing out' is gonna be anything but catastrophic for them. Really.

I mean, unless they're a child prodigy of course, you know, like they can play the flute with their belly button and a twiglet whilst swimming with Piranhas, or they end up competing at Wimbledon before they're potty trained.

Other than that, make no mistake, it's Munchausen by Proxy.

So no, I didn't wear dm's or a crew neck Paul Smith shirt. Neither did I have s.k.i.n.s tattooed across my knuckles before I was in long trousers. But I still took pride in how I looked, I'd still prefer to look like I belonged to something rather than nothing at all, even if it wasn't obvious at that moment in my dressing gown and borrowed cardigan.

I finished my protein and felt sick. I'd probably not eaten a great deal to be fair but it was my first meal for...for how long? God's sake, I had no idea.

No idea at all.

I was about to find out though.

9: Mid-range

I was wiping my face with the very small napkin when he walked in.

He was big, bigger than me but not as big as the big guy I'd beaten up the other day. On this basis I thought I could probably take him. If my legs worked. If I had a big bat.

Anyway, he moved round the table and sat down opposite me, then moved a bit because opposite me was like twenty odd feet away. He pulled his chair until he was close enough for me to gob on, and then sat down.

"I'm Terry," he said. I didn't gob on him by the way.

I looked at him, trying to gauge what I might gain by being a smartass.

He was fit looking, like the big fella before. Bollocks, let's give him a name. Let's call him Bob, it's easy to type and easy to remember. Plus, you know he could actually be a Bob or a Robert. Maybe, at a push a Robin? No? Ok let's stick with Bob.

So, he was big but not as big as Bob. He looked fit too, like Bob. Actually, I'm gonna amend that to Bob the Giant, because he was fucking huge and it's funny.

And yes, you've guessed it, he had a big fancy watch. WTAF? Maybe they all got them when they took the job at 'I'm a Dickhead Ltd'. But no, my Dad had one so that couldn't be true. Anyway, he was, albeit different looking facially, with dark hair, a spit of Bob. Like I say, fit looking, smart but casual, with cold, steady eyes. This fella smiled though, so that was nice.

He repeated himself, which made up my mind reference being clever.

"I'm Terry."

"Hi Terry. I'm Squidge."

He smiled again.

"We know that mate," he looked over at Freya who was standing quietly, close to the door.

"Listen Squidge, we clearly need to discuss a few things but I'm feeling like you may not be ready for all that yet. So, in the meantime I'm just going to tell you where you are, how you got here and why you're in that chair."

I nodded, now glancing myself nervously over at Freya.

"First things first, welcome. This is a special place. Special to me, special to a great many people in fact. Maybe, one day it will be special to you too."

A creepy fucking hospital on the Isle of pissing Wight? Was he drunk?

"You are currently in the care of your team; Micha, Freya and Anders, who I think you've yet to meet," Freya was nodding in the background. "These guys are based here in

Bellano permanently along with the tech and support staff whilst most of the rest of us use this as kind of a base from which we operate remotely."

Excuse me??

"It's fair to say actually that you're kinda lucky to find me here right now. I'd normally be out in the field; a good deal of my workload is actually in central and eastern Europe and I'm busy developing contracts in Asia Minor. So, a lot of the time I'm pretty much incommunicado,"

Excuse me??

"So, as I say, this is Bellano, or Le Grande Casa to be precise, The Big House. We've been here..."

"Excuse me?" I was shaking my head, now a little bit sweaty. "But, *where* the fuck are we? Did you just say Bernardo?" I looked from him to Freya and then back again. "Where the fuck is Benardo? Am I still on the Isle of Wight?"

Terry looked at me. He had an honest face. And he was honestly pissed at my swearing.

"No Squidge. You're not on the Isle of Wight." He looked over at Freya.

"He only woke this afternoon, sir. We've not had a chance to debrief him yet."

I glanced at her to see her looking nervous. Fuck this areshole it wasn't her fault.

Terry looked back at me.

"Squidge you're in Bellano, northern Italy, close to the Swiss border. On the banks of Lake Como."

He stood now, pushing his chair back under the table nervously. No, sorry, he wasn't nervous, he was agitated. I shook my head again.

"What am I doing in Italy? Where the fuck is Lake Combo?"

"Como, Lake Como," Freya corrected me gently.

Terry pressed on.

"Ok. So, you were on the Isle of Wight, as you know. You ran away from some *guys*. You ran off a cliff and we picked you up."

I would've nodded if I was any clearer. I mean, yes, I knew I was on the Isle of Wight and stuff happened but...

"We didn't know you were going to be there. We were in the area as part of an exercise. How can I say this?" he paused, and I really hoped he knew the answer because I sure as shit didn't. "We had eyes on a foreign asset, who we believed to be watching us, or at least trying to track us. It's complicated."

He had started pacing. I tried to follow him but honestly all I could think about was that I'd always wanted to go to Italy.

There'd been a school trip to Florence in year ten. Obviously, we were lightyears away from being able to afford for me to go. And then there were the Italian exchange students that came over in August. Of course, none of them were ever placed in the estate, that would've been death by acute deprivation, but we still saw them. We were always friendly of course, I mean it wouldn't do to chase, intimidate, and try to set fire to teenagers visiting from a friendly European neighbour. Definitely wouldn't be good form to push the little ones with glasses on into the canal when we caught them in a compromising situation.

Anyway, Terry was still going on.

".... the house and from there it all went a bit out of shape. I'll be honest with you though, I thought we'd lost you. Frankly, if it wasn't for my team leader, Gretto and your speed off that cliff it would've been a very different story, I'm sure."

He stopped pacing.

I looked at him again and then back at Freya. Who was Frank?

"I don't suppose you picked up any of my stuff?"

Terry smiled but shook his head.

"Sorry, the only things we recovered were what you had with you at the time," he looked over at Freya. "I think it was just the gun and socket set?" Freya nodded.

"Did you have anything else with you, back on shore?"

"Well, yes, back in Ventnor, but..." I frowned, "Sorry but what did you say you recovered?"

"A handgun, a Glock 19, I think. It's a bit battered but still serviceable. No serial number on it though, been filed off unsurprisingly. I assume it's not yours?"

"No, not the gun, the other thing?"

I'd forgotten about the gun.

"Err, the socket set?" he started pacing again. "Yeah, it's a Draper, I think. Nice one too. I mean it's not top of the range or anything, but you'd certainly be glad to get it for your eighteenth birthday or whatever. Actually, we were wondering what the significance of it was?"

Jesus I really was a fucking weirdo.

"Significance?"

"Yes. Why did you have it with you? Was there a data file hidden somewhere inside? Was there an engraving? Was it personally significant to you in some way? Did you use it as a weapon?"

A brief pause.

"Er, no, I just nicked it. I think."

I had nothing else. Really. I couldn't remember it; I mean I remember the socket set itself but I defo didn't remember taking it. Like, why the fuck, when fleeing for my actual life from men with the means and motive to do me in *properly*, did I choose to hang onto a bloody socket set? And a mid-range one at that?

The deeper this rabbit hole went the weirder it was getting.

"You nicked it? Do you mean you stole it?"

I nodded.

"Yeah, I guess."

"Right," Terry glanced up at Freya, an eye roll milliseconds away. "Listen, I'm sure you're going to have a lot more questions. Freya here, and Micha plus my number two, Waterman can fill in a few more of the gaps. I'm going to be unavailable for the next ninety-six but will make some time for you on the bounce."

He was talking like a soldier now, all digits and acronyms. He stopped and came to stand in front of me.

"Squidge, it's good to see you, really, better still to see that you're ok and on the road to recovery."

He held out his hand which I took. Big, strong hand. Big watch.

"You're in good hands here, I promise. And safe. And when I get back, I'll explain what we do here and why you're with us."

I nodded again. So many questions, so many confusing, conflicting thoughts.

"How's Bob?" I blurted out before he could go. Honestly it was bothering me. Which is odd considering all the other things that should've been bothering me. I mean it was necessary so I can't apologise but it really wasn't me to beat the living daylights out of someone who couldn't fight back.

"Bob?"

"Yeah, the guy, the big guy at the house. I mean, I'm calling him Bob. At least for now. He could easily be a Stuart or Nigel, but I think Bob is easier to remember..."

Terry frowned.

"That was you?"

"Yeah," I looked down. "I kinda just lost it a bit."

"A bit?"

I looked up at him, ashamed but not afraid.

"Yeah. It was everything, you know Danny, the way they fucking just took him. And then me. My Dad. Sausage."

Terry sniffed and looked up at the ceiling. He was obviously thinking about what to say. Eventually.

"Listen, don't lose any sleep over it. We had eyes on them for a bit, afterwards. There was an ambulance and a bit of activity. But he walked out, after a while."

I let out a breath.

"That was really you?"

"Yeah. I mean he tripped and everything but yeah, things got a little fucked up."

Terry raised his eyebrows.

"I'll say."

Freya came over and coughed to interrupt.

"You're looking tired Squidge,"

Terry looked from me to her and nodded his agreement.

"Yeah, yeah, of course," he said, stepping back and turning to leave the room. "But listen, we'll tidy everything up in a couple of days. Get some zeds and get cracking on your rehab and then we'll look at the next steps."

I nodded again, not really sure what zeds and rehab meant.

Freya nodded goodbye to him and then he was gone. She turned back to me clapping and then rubbing her hands together.

Jesus, was she planning on eating me?

"Right superstar, let's get you back to your room and washed up, you're probably exhausted. It's a lot to take in. And tomorrow's going to be a full day, lots to do so we need you fresh."

And with that she released my brakes and wheeled me off, like a dead dog on a stretcher, through and out of the dining room and into a maze of corridors to God knows where.

The next couple of days were bloody awful. I found out I couldn't walk anymore, at least for the moment anyway. I found out why too. Apparently when I jumped, or rather ran off the cliff edge I was going quick enough for me to more or less clear the rocks and shit at the bottom. And I say more or less because I mean not quite.

Like, I made it out as far as the water but because I fell so far, I went in deep, deeper than, let's say 'would have been ideal'. I hit some rocks, broke some legs, so what. At least I wasn't dead. There's always a silver lining if you look hard enough.

Freya said it's because I blacked out. My body was all flexible and stuff, so I didn't do more damage. I'm happy with this, it certainly sounds better than saying I was saved because I fainted like a limp wristed drama student.

Anyway, I was rescued by these guys, who just happened to be in the area, and brought here via all sorts of very exclusive transportation methods. Most, if not all, contravening the international border agreements through which they passed, I surmised. I was told that I was pretty banged up, so time was 'of the essence'. I'm not sure asking any further questions about that bit was going to help me so I left it there.

Freya agreed, as she massaged my right leg, the worst of the two, from my calf all the way up to my groin.

FML I was glad Micha wasn't doing this.

"Just accept you're here, you're safe and you're well on the road to getting back on your feet."

There were three fucking brutal looking scars on the right leg, one just above the knee and two below. Just the one long one on my left leg thankfully. And then on both a series of small round scars that looked like bullet holes.

"How long was I out?"

"You've been here for just over two weeks. Your legs were bad Squidge, we had to pull them out straight, and then insert metal plates and stuff."

All of which if I'm honest scared the shit outta me even if I had already suspected it had been more than a couple days. It was like a bucket of cold water. What about Danny? What about the Nutter? Jesus. And the Sausage? Fuck's sake, I'd only intended to be away for a few days.

"Your Mum's ok you know. She's had a visit and knows where you are. We haven't told her everything, but she knows enough."

You haven't fucking told *me* everything either have you? I thought.

"She alright for money?" Was what I actually said. I was thinking about all the usuals, fags, coffee, crumpets. Plus, she was shit with change and was always forgetting to pay for her parking at work. I could imagine the bills piling up.

"She's fine. She's fine, it's all in hand."

It's all in hand? What the fuck does that mean?

To reassure me she rubbed my inner thigh. I closed my eyes and concentrated on not getting a boner and soon enough she moved away, and I thought of another question.

"And she's being watched too," Freya continued before I had a chance to ask it.

"What?" I opened my eyes.

"Your Mum, she is being watched. I mean that doesn't sound great does it, put that way. I should've said we're keeping an eye on her, you know to make sure she's ok."

I nodded, not at all sure how I felt about that.

"Right."

"Yeah, I mean with you not there, bless her, she is a little vulnerable, isn't she?"

I'll say.

But what did that look like? Sorry but I couldn't go swashbuckling around central Europe not knowing if she was ok, *really* ok. I needed to get back. What the fuck was I doing anyway? I needed to sort my shit out, well my dopey fucking legs at the very least and then make tracks home. She'd be doing one, even if Fat Julie was still there. She'd be going proper mental, no matter what these guys had told her. And how did they get close to her anyway with the police lurking, and I mean, I genuinely hoped they were lurking, didn't I. Or did I? I was so confused. Jesus this was so fucked up.

Freya saw my face and stopped rubbing for a moment.

"Hey, listen she's ok. She really is, I promise." She looked over her shoulder briefly, then back to me; "Look, I'll try and get some current intel. I'll try, if I can, and arrange a quick call too if you think that'll help?"

I nodded, relieved she was picking up on this.

"Yeah, it would. Thank you."

She nodded and smiled.

"We're on your side Squidge, I promise. It's all good, it's all gonna work out, I promise."

I tried to return her smile, but I think I just growled at her a bit. She didn't notice and went back to teasing me, sorry I mean rubbing my legs. Which was nice, no matter how shitty I was feeling.

I had proper physio as well with Micha. He wasn't nearly so camp as my first impression led me to think. Not that it mattered either way to be fair. If he got me on my feet, then I couldn't care less whether he was Julian Clary or Chuck Norris. Nice guy actually. Not so military as some of the others, and I'm including the lovely Freya in that. I mean she wasn't all Sergeant Major or anything but there was something about her that made it obvious. You know, she was professional, obviously, but there was more. She was very ordered and spoke in a certain way that demonstrated a disciplined mind. Plus, she was toned, really well presented and always on point - with everything.

If she was military, then I suspected Micha to be a civilian. He was funny, friendly, and camp as mentioned before. But also, less formal and happy to tell me stories about other people in the building. I learnt all about the comings and goings of the casual staff. The affairs and the bullying, the money that was owed to this person and that and the marriages that were in trouble. I got the names of all the important people, the shift pattern, and a good idea what the security guys did day to day.

I mean I wasn't fucking interested in most of it to be honest, but he seemed happy nattering away, so I let him talk, plus, it was all information wasn't it. Asked him the odd question as well, you know, tactfully. Good plan too because he told me stuff, I'm sure Freya would've held back on. Like what this place was, you know, the 'organisation'. Turns out it was a private security firm called AMOS. I know right. Pretty sure there was an Uncle Amos on Emmerdale once upon a time. Great name. Great sideburns too if my memory serves me right.

Anyway, they had places all over the shop, proper international. And they worked with governments to keep important people safe. People of all nations and political persuasion, apparently. Pretty sure that's security speak for 'terrorists' but whatever. Well, that's the front at least, that's what he told me, what I suspected he was told himself too.

And that was ok, for the moment at least, I mean it was a fucking site more than I knew before he started work on me.

At some point I also met Anders. He *was* ex-military. A big blonde Swedish lump. Hair all up his arms and bushy ginger eyebrows that should really have had their own postal address. When I say he was big I mean bigger than Micha but not as big as Terry, and defo not as big as Bob the giant. I concluded I could probably take him too. If he wasn't looking. And he was asleep.

Anders was the bender. I mean he's the guy who bent me up and forced me to move. Like, Freya looked after my skin and muscles, Micha was nice to me, checked my wounds and encouraged me to walk with the frame they gave me. Like a little old lady.

And Anders picked me up and bent me. I had arms and legs going everywhere and a good deal of discomfort to boot. Actually, it was fucking agony. Like, really. I'd have stabbed him if he hadn't been so jolly. I'm not joking. He was like a happy, mediaeval torturer/motivator. His bushy fucking eyebrows moving on their own, completely disconnected from his face and his big gammon hands gripping and twisting my back and shoulders and pelvis. God it was awful.

This went on for a bit. Freya massaging me, Micha gossiping and Anders trying to kill me. It was good though, I gotta say, despite the pain. Within a week, even though I was pissed at Terry for not coming back within the '96' and filling me in on the specifics, *and* doing my nut with worry over Mum, I was feeling amazing, and walking too. Freya gave me a couple of sticks and some exercises to do, you know like walk across the lawn to sit on the bench under the citrus tree by the water. Then walk back. Horrendous.

But seriously it was nice to be able to do it. To have a bit of freedom. To breathe a bit of the clean air without someone chatting at me.

I watched the kids playing. Turns out they were staff kids, there was a creche here. And they were looked after by Micha's missus, I know, don't say it. There were seven, eight if you count the baby, Janea, and they all seemed to get along. I watched the comings and goings too, like the bread guy, the florist and some maintenance men that cut the grass and did a bit to the house like window cleaning and mending stuff. There was a mailman too, well actually a woman and she was as fit as fuck. I mean it would've been a tough one to call between her and the lovely Freya.

She wasn't the slightest bit interested in me though. Standard.

Then there were the security guards who were all definitely ex-military. They kept mainly out of sight but were always visible at the gate. They did rounds too, and when I'd watched for long enough, I could work out their shift pattern and patrol routes. People came in, through the gates and parked in the driveway. Men in suits and very shiny cars, women too although not as many. I didn't pay much attention to these, they all looked like businessmen or politicians, none of which I would have recognized even if I had been taking notes. I wasn't well known for my insight into the world of international current affairs if you get my drift.

But anyway, back to me.

Not sure what she was giving me but six days after I first properly came round, I was walking without the sticks. She said she'd never seen anything like it, that there was something special about me. None of which meant anything to be honest, I'd always healed quicky, I guess I just had good genes. I was eating better too, better than I ever had at home. I mean, I'm not a fussy eater but I know what I like, you know. It's like I'd never say no to stuff, especially when times were tough, and they really were on occasion. But looking at some of the shit the Nutter put in front of me made me want to vom, and I'm not the only one. Since I started earning and could choose, I'd become a little more discerning, even selective perhaps. However, that all went out the window here cause the food always looked so good. Basically, no matter what it was, I got stuck in, and it showed.

Apart from salad. Don't give me salad.

I also started reading. Crazy I know, I never saw myself as a reader. I mean Danny read on occasion but not me, I didn't have the patience, even, or perhaps *especially* at school. But here, when Freya, Micha and Anders were done rubbing, annoying and brutalising me there wasn't much else to do. I knew all the kids outside by name, and the staff. I knew the menu and the rotation of guards, even got to chatting with them when they were not being watched by the officers. And I call them officers because I don't know what else to call them right. Were they Agents? Caretakers? Death Eaters?

I mean they didn't wear a uniform, at least not in the traditional sense. They wore the same or similar clothes as each other, dark, plain, hardwearing, as did Terry, but it wasn't really a uniform. So, they weren't officers like you might be thinking. But they were something and there was an order to them, like, there definitely was a bossman - Terry, and then his minions in ascending or descending order.

But anyway, I knew them, most of them, quite well. I also knew the local guys that came and went as I mentioned earlier. Not the mailwoman though, she avoided me, she thought I was a pervert. But apart from that, once I got my head around the day-to-day stuff I was bored. Obviously.

Back home I'd have been out running, no not the kind of running that bankers and surveyors do. I mean I would have had shit going on, like usual, loads of shit. I might have had a job too if Chloe hadn't decided to suck Brian's dick. But if not then I'd have been busy, super busy whatever I was up to. But here, I was climbing the fucking walls man. Freya bought me a couple of books the same day she bought me my new clothes. They weren't the same clothes as the Wizards wore but they were decent. Comfy too.

Got shoes as well, which was nice. It meant if I wanted to go a bit further afield I could, I was sick of wearing slippers and felt like a wet sack striding about the grounds in my tartan dressing gown.

So yeah, I read, a lot, actually. I got through a couple of novels first and one short story about a spaceman that turns out was actually Santa Clause. I know, mental. And then I moved onto something a bit more challenging. Seeing I was interested / bored Freya gave me some political stuff to get started on. I said I would as soon as I'd spoken to Mum. She nodded and then mugged me off with something about waiting for the right moment.

I let it go and got on with her books which, to be truthful, I fully anticipated to be complete dog shit. How wrong was I. Fucking insane, honestly. I mean they were fiction, at first, and so just made up, but as I moved from them onto the nonfiction my eyes were opened wide. The shit that went on, honestly. I'm not sure how much I retained, you know from a factually correct point of view, because my memory's not all that, right, but it definitely widened my view. And it gave me the taste for it. I confess I learnt a bit, you know, about history or whatever, and the intricacies of diplomacy and democracy. And even if I couldn't tell you the next day what I'd read the night before, it definitely formed the basis for hunger for knowledge that developed later.

So, this continued on for nearly five weeks before anything changed. By then I was jogging around the garden three times a day and spending an hour each morning doing weights and shit in the gym in the basement. With the food, the exercise, massages and physio I was looking and feeling better than ever. Definitely better than when I bedded down for the night in the porch of the Honda garage in Ventnor.

Scan, the house barber sorted my hair and I gotta say I cut a dapper figure when I looked in the mirror. Which, it had to be said, was a relatively new activity for me and not just because we didn't have one in the flat, bar the one Mum used to pull out her moustache hairs. No, if I'm honest I'd never been too fond of what I saw in the mirror when I did look, so I tended not to. But now, I'd go as far as to say that I'd started to take on a similar, toned, capable look as some of the guys around me, the officers that is, not Micha. Bless his chubby little pork pie belly.

Freya was impressed. She said so. Said my legs had not only healed well but that they had filled out and were stronger than before. We weighed me and it turns out I'd put a fair bit on and was now up to thirteen stone, fat git. Which was fucking amazing for an underfed, addled, nervous estate rat like me.

Next day we started training in self-defence, which I thought would be hilarious until she kicked my ass. It was fine, it was in front of everyone, and they all cheered when she laid me out flat on the grass. But no, seriously, I was embarrassed, I mean that's obvious right. Think it may have been the point too. She knocked the wind out of my lungs which hadn't happened since year 10 when Neil Wheelhouse tripped me up in the middle of a proper physical game of British Bulldog. But bollocks, I got back up and we carried on, and again the next day, and the next. We'd been at this for about a week and a half when Terry returned.

And fuck me, it all went off then didn't it.

A car and two black 4x4 Merc's came lurching into the drive, dust and shit everywhere. Security then came out of the building pushing all of the day visitors out in front of them and into their respective vehicles. They in turn fucked off with corresponding clouds of dust and shit and great deal of muttering. Security then shut and locked the front gates, the first time I'd seen that happen during the day since I'd been here.

Next Terry, at least I assumed it was Terry plus a couple of others were helped from the car and moved into the house. I was a nosy bastard, no, really, I was, but in my new clothes and with the knowledge I'd gained in recent weeks I decided, on balance, on this occasion at least, to leave it. I'd catch up with one of 'my team' in a bit and get the latest. It looked like some calamitous shit had gone down and I guessed my mug wouldn't be essential viewing. Plus, I had another couple of circuits to complete before I was finished for the day and was now well off the pace. And I say circuits, but it was more of a square, or a squared off circle or hexagon or something. Fuck it, you know what I mean.

Had breakfast with the staff the next morning, eggs, bacon, sausage and those little bread rolls you can't get back home. Standard. I hadn't been in the big dining room since the last time Terry was here. As I was finishing, I got chatting to Mick the chef. No not an Irishman, actually a black fella from Nigeria whose name nobody could pronounce. So, they called him Mick because the last chef had been called Mick. Jesus and Mary. Anyway, Mick was an excellent chef, really. He and his team catered for the whole estate, all the different people, staff, visitors working and visiting at all hours. Honestly, not a job I'd relish.

Anyway, whilst as a chef he couldn't be faulted, he did have a few foibles, if you know what I mean. Interesting word that, 'foibles', might put that in the same word bag as 'trousers'. Definitely under-used.

Anyway, it was nothing serious. Nothing that would compromise anyone or put anyone in harm's way. Just personal stuff, you know, and a weakness shall we say, for Italian girls.

So, on that note, Mick had this girlfriend, a local girl, per his MO. Apparently, she lived up the road in a place called Noceno, which when I say was 'up the road' I mean exactly that, up. It was a fucking hike, like seriously. Everywhere was from here. Her name was Claudia, and she was young, and lovely, which is of no consequence whatsoever. But she *was* from 'outside' the compound and as such was privy to, and the subject of a bit of local gossip.

Normally she came and went, bringing 'ingredients' and stuff, sometimes staying for quite a while. Today though, she wasn't allowed in, obviously. But she had told Mick a few days before that there was some weird shit going on in the surrounding area. Like guys checking into local hotels without obvious holiday plans, blacked out vans doing the rounds and other stuff that wouldn't normally be going on, stuff that made Mick worry.

He was ex-military, South African, I think. Anyway, he had scars and shit all up his forearms and a couple on his face and it occurred to me he could probably do a good deal more with his filleting knife than chop root veg for casseroles. Side note: his casseroles were fucking lovely, like really. Bean made us a casserole once, she called it 'Sausage Surprise' like some nervous, frustrated, hypochondriac, which, to be fair, is exactly what she was. Anyway the 'surprise' bit was that she didn't put any sausages in it. Not even the Linda Macartney substitute soya bollocks. So basically, it was minestrone soup, with big ass carrots and onions.

Anyway, Mick had gone to Waterman, Terry's no.2, Waterman had sent a couple of guys out to snoop around and that was that. Only it wasn't.

Right now, see, I'm getting the same butterflies I had just before I knocked on the door in Wroxall. The same as when I opened Danny's door and saw his bananas. So, Mick tells Waterman, he sends minions out and then a couple of days later the 4x4's, the dust, the gates and then Terry. Shit, I had a bad feeling, as I'm sure you can appreciate. Didn't stop me eating though or slow my routine. I mean, I never had a routine before. Not that I didn't know how to get up and do shit when I had too. But it was always shit that I *had* to do, like school, or community service. Or when not at Her Majesty's beck and call I was doing my own shit. Still had to do it though, if I wanted to eat, if I wanted the Nutter to be relatively sane, if I wanted to keep Skinny Mitch and his line manager Mad Rufus off my case.

But here, I could've sat on my arse all day, at least *today* I could. No Freya to push me, no Anders chasing me around the gym so he could snap something that, I quite frankly would've been happy not being snapped.

No Micha either, telling me the latest in the Micheala, Jacques and Pauli love triangle saga. Was Pauli going to tell his wife about Micheala? Was Micheala pregnant and if so was the baby Jacques or Pauli's? Did either Micheala or Pauli know that Jacques was actually a lad called Steven Graham from Tonbridge Wells who took night school lessons in Italian at the Tonbridge Wells Girls Grammar School. Apparently, he only came out here for a summer season but 'got stuck'.

His words not mine.

Oh, and by the way; who calls their child Steven Graham, two first names? Seriously, just make your fucking mind up will you.

Anyway, without all that distraction I could please myself and do fuck all if I wanted. But I didn't. With great pride I surprised myself by doing all and more of the shit I would normally do, if there were other people pushing me.

My plans to pop in and catch Terry went out the window as I circled the garden for the fifth time (third session of the day). I was buzzing, my lungs felt great, the air by the lake was amazing. My legs felt strong, and all the massaging had ensured the scars hadn't hardened up. I even felt like my eyes were better, I mean the tiny little houses across the lake I could barely make out a few weeks ago now stood out clearly. All reds and yellows.

Jesus I was hungry though, fucking hank to be honest, but other than that I could've kept going. I turned away from the water and jumped out of my skin. Terry was right behind me; the big fucker had managed to creep up on me which was a bit unsettling.

"Hello Squidge," he said calmly, even if his eyes were saying something else.

I looked him up and down and a dozen questions popped into my brain. Not the questions I'd had when he left the last time telling me he'd be back in '96'. No, those questions were already locked, at least the ones I hadn't had answered by 'my team' and all manner of other people here, in his absence.

Instead, the questions that sprang to mind were:

"What the fuck happened to you?" and "What's wrong with your face?" both of which actually came out, unfiltered. Now, I have been told that my lack of filter is 'charming', under the right circumstances. Yes, that's right, the '*right*' circumstances. Really not sure these fitted into that collective.

He didn't answer straight away. Instead, he turned and looked out to the water. Eventually, back to me:

"Do you like it here?"

I nodded.

"It's ok."

He smiled; he knew.

"I apologise for not being here."

To be fair I didn't need an apology, I was having the time of my life. I shook my head.

"It's ok fella," not at all sure I could call him fella.

He smiled again and took a breath.

"I've been overseas, and I got caught up in something."

I shrugged, I'd assumed as much, not that it was any of my business.

"How have things been here? You're looking well."

I nodded.

"Yeah, you know. Food's good, my legs are getting there," Didn't really know what to say if I'm honest. He didn't seem bothered.

"Look, obviously we need to talk. I need to tell you some stuff. I should have told you before I went but, you know, we had a mission critical timeframe with no wriggle room," I really didn't know, not a fucking clue. "And anyway, I made the wrong call before I went and should have made time for you."

He paused and took a breath.

"Of course, I'm here now so it's not all completely screwed but, you know, it might have been."

I looked past him and saw the security guys hovering close to the house. Pretty sure Freya was back there too. I started to get that uneasy feeling again, like I was looking through a very small crack into a room full of all sorts of scary shit. I shrugged again; the gesture was very 'me' but strangely becoming more unfamiliar by the day.

But I got the feeling I wasn't the only one on edge.

"Well, I ain't going anywhere, so you know, whenever."

He nodded and looked across the water again, then up into the sky like he could hear something. Wasn't making me feel better.

"Ok," he said. "Let's do this."

10: Gorilla Face

Through the main back doors, the big dining room off to the left, the corridor leading to the accommodation across and to the right and the stairs to the kitchens and staff dining rooms, gym and workshops also to the right but not as far as the corridor. Complicated, I know, but not my design, so sorry not sorry.

I followed Terry across the lobby, past the dining room and then to the left. We went into a corridor, kind of opposite the accommodation one, and carried on for a bit before we came to a lift door. I gotta be honest I had no idea there was a lift and to be frank it really didn't look like it belonged either.

Doors opened and we went in, it was nice, there was a mirror. Terry pressed a button, scanned a pass and the doors closed. We then went down which, I must say, surprised me. I mean, I knew there was a basement, as previously mentioned but I was pretty sure I'd been round it and I was equally sure I hadn't seen a lift. Anyway, the lift went down a few floors and then stopped and the doors opened majestically. Actually, they just opened slowly, not really the same thing is it.

Security guys immediately outside the doors stopped us and checked Terry's pass and then gave me all sorts of evils while Terry explained who I was. They let us pass after a few moments and we went on down another corridor before passing through a scanner of some kind. Next through a fuck off heavy door and into a big room with screens and computers and shit.

There were nerds with headsets sitting at the computers and a buzz of chat all around the room. On the wall at the front was a huge TV with a mess of different images and text constantly moving and updating. I'm sure the nerds knew what they were looking at but if I'm honest it just made me dizzy.

Terry spoke to a couple of his stormtroopers and let me take it in for a bit before leading me off to a smaller *meeting* room on the right-hand side, with a load of people already sitting down. I didn't know anyone in the room and felt uncomfortable straight away. I wished Freya was there, or Micha, I'd have even settled for Anders providing he didn't chase me round the table. Actually, I didn't care, anyone I knew would've made me feel more at ease.

Terry told me to sit while he got me a diet coke *and a glass* which I gotta say threw me a little. It was such a normal thing to have in front of me, apart from the glass, in such a weird and totally not-normal moment.

"Right, we're all here?" Terry asked one of the guys opposite.

"More or less, we're just waiting for Paul, he's on a call with Istanbul. Shouldn't be a minute."

Terry nodded, not bothered. Good, I wasn't bothered either, Paul sounded like a douche.

"Ok that's fine we can get started without him. First..."

The door opened and Paul came in.

"Sorry I'm late, got held up on a call."

Terry nodded.

"Everything ok?"

Paul scrambled round the table to take his seat. Which incidentally was opposite mine which is totally irrelevant. Nice chairs though.

"Yeah. Targus is struggling with point on option B, but we've made contact and dropped the links so it's only a matter of time."

Paul sounded like he knew something I didn't. Seriously though, was he talking the same language as me? Terry's face didn't show anything although his voice was cold.

"Don't leave anything to chance. This needs to be carefully handled, there's a lot riding on it. Make sure you've got eyes on. And ensure our asset if fully briefed on the trap door."

"Yes, of course, it's in hand. The trap door is in place and the asset has the protocols" Paul responded while looking down at his notes whilst Terry went on to address everyone without acknowledging Paul's reply.

"Ok, we're all here, that's good." he looked at me before he went on. "I owe you all an apology, particularly you Squidge, I should've done this weeks ago, but circumstances got away from me." he smiled at me, but I wasn't sure why.

"So, let's start with some introductions; firstly I'm Terry Carter, I take lead here in Bellano and manage the Strategic Resource Placement or SRP. I also manage the wider team in southern Europe. We cover offices in London, Paris, Barcelona, Lisbon, Geneva, Berlin, Rome, Athens, Vienna and Sofia. We have working cells in all other major cities within states where we don't have a permanent residence." He gestured to the guy sitting to his right.

I was still struggling with Lisbon.

"Hi Squidge, I'm Carlson Verge. I am OPD for the footprint and manage day to day operations of our teams and all shared resources. The acronym OPD, it's just Operations Director." he smiled at me. I liked him. "Um, Terry, have you actually told Squidge who we are? What do we do here?"

Terry shook his head.

"No, but then I'm not sure how much I *need* to tell him," now looking at me. "Squidge has an inquisitive mind, and, er, let's say *hasn't held back* in making friends in the time he's been here."

Carlson nodded but then looked at me.

"What *do* you know then young man? About us? What do you think we do here?"

Fuck, I didn't have a clue. He'd put me properly on the spot.

I mean I'd seen the uniforms, the guns that the security guys carried and obviously they'd rescued and brought me here so there's that but, honestly. I knew Terry had been out and about causing some kind of trouble and Freya had mentioned the politicians and businessmen that they helped. Other than that, though I was floundering.

"Um," I sat up in my chair and cleared my throat. "So, um. Right. So, you're a security firm, a private security firm right. You're all ex-military, well most of you are, both your operations and support staff." I was probably doing better than I thought I would. "Your clients include politicians and private businesses across all border's alliances. You have resources everywhere and are well organised. I mean, your security guys are well organised, I've watched them."

I stopped there; I wasn't sure where else to go. I mean, I knew they had a great gym and had bread delivered every day at 6am but not a great deal more.

Carlson nodded.

"Oh, and you're called Amos."

This drew a little smile.

"Ok. Terry, I think it might be worth a quick rundown of Amos and its business model."

Terry looked a little uncomfortable albeit he nodded his agreement.

"Yes. Ok. So, Squidge, Amos or Allied Multinational Operational Security is a private security company founded in the Netherlands a little over 20 years ago. As you correctly stated we are staffed by a high percentage of ex-military personnel from all nations. We operate across the globe and have access to an enormous pool of resources. We work for governments and large corporations and endeavour to look after their interests as aligned with any contracts we have with them."

"Ok."

"With this in mind we provide close protection services for individuals and projects, resource management and security services in places where local circumstances dictate its necessity and other ‘services’ shall we say as and where required.”

I mean, he could have lifted a red flag at the moment he said those words and it wouldn't have drawn my attention as much as his gay little phrase ‘shall we say’. What the fuck did that mean? What was I involved in? Was I being naive?

Terry went on.

“We move people, money, and items of national importance. We secure agreements, we keep secure things that people want secure. I mean, I'm not trying to simplify it more than necessary, but it really is just that.” he took a breath, clearly wishing to move on and back to his introductions.

I nodded, happy with whatever. I mean, I think I knew enough for the moment.

"Does that make sense, Squidge?" Carlsberg again. Probably the best security professional in the room.

Just a little joke there. Sorry.

"Um, yeah, I suppose."

“Good. Right, thank you,” Terry picked it up and gestured to the guy next to Carlson. He in turn started talking straight away. And then the one next to him, all the way around the table. More acronyms, more clever, mind boggling shit about who they were and how many hundreds of footprints, resources and people they managed. I wasn't interested, seriously, I hoped it wasn't obvious but really, I couldn't give a shit. These guys, who were they to me? Why did it matter? What they fuck was I doing here, a kid from the estate who only a couple of weeks ago was bottling up for Brian the

Bollock and desperately trying to keep my mum from losing her shit by filling her up with marmite pissing crumpets.

And I'd been here for weeks now, hadn't I? I mean I was recovering and recuperating obviously, but still, beyond that, I'd just been waiting, hadn't I? But waiting for what? For Terry? I hadn't had a smoke for weeks and felt an almost irresistible need for a kebab, or Fray Bentos pie. And a shandy. What I had no desire for was more of this shit. Or more waiting arou....

I jumped as Paul the douche spoke directly to me.

“So Squidge we really wanted to get your take on this. How quickly do you think Saffren is going to move against Couco? We're trying to understand how deeply his roots go, how closely his ties with the Manento family extend and what effect the cross-border merger will have on his decision.”

I think a little bit of poo came out. Seriously. What the actual fuck?

"Sorry?"

"Oh, I apologise, I'm, I'm not sure how...." he glanced at Terry.

"No, no. I'm sorry? Why are you asking me? Who the fuck, excuse my *French*, is Magneto?"

A few weeks of bottled frustration showed itself. I looked from Paul to Terry to Carlson feeling like now I'd popped the cork, I wasn't going to be able to put the genie back in the bottle. Like a big gas bubble rising from deep in my belly it just came up, and I couldn't stop it:

"Am I seriously expected to be able to answer that? Is my opinion even the slightest bit relevant? I mean, who the fuck do you think I am?"

"Squidge...." Terry started but just the use of that name set me off.

I looked at him, and realised, beyond the name, I had absolutely no idea who he was. Nor, whilst I was about it, why he or his men just happened to be there, you know, loitering as you do in the English Channel, conveniently close to white cliffs of Ventnor ready and waiting to pick me up when I plopped out like Saturday morning turd.

"No. Fuck off. Fuck off for fuck sake, all of you, no," I paused, and then; "What's going on here? Seriously? Why were you there? In Ventnor? You know why *I* was there, right? Terry? You know my brother's been kidnapped, don't you? You know I couldn't give the slightest shit about your OPS and your SRPs or whatever, right? You know I'm *only* here because I can't fly, and because I fell down a bullshit fucking rabbit hole, that *you* made?"

I looked around the room. It wasn't all men, there was a stern looking woman at the end farthest from the door who looked like she wanted to inject me or check me for head lice. Scary old witch. She looked every bit the headmistress of Crunchem Hall.

Ok so maybe it wasn't all men, but they did all look miffed. I pressed my 'advantage'.

"My brother's been kidnapped, right? I saw it happen, Jesus fucking Christ. I'm only here because the police are wankers, and completely incompetent, and I was duped by a Sausage into pursuing some reckless and stupid fairytale I thought might help bring him back."

I took a breath, the red mist just starting to form at the corners of my vision and my ears were beginning to buzz. I knew it sounded weird, like I was reading the synopsis of a Guy Ritchie movie but bollocks, it was true. I was also aware that I was red in the face and spitting all over their nice table. I'd have wiped it off if I'd had long sleeves.

I glanced at the faces round the room again, but I couldn't give a shit. Give me some dough or take me home, I'd had enough.

"I didn't ask to be dragged over here. This is on you. If those blokes hadn't been watching you, they wouldn't have grabbed me, and I'd never have jumped off that cliff. It *your* fucking shit I'm dealing with here and I've got nothing to show for it." I was waving my arms about like a fucking lunatic.

"Listen, I can see that you're unhappy..."

"Really? What gave that away? Fuck sake you're sitting here talking bollocks about bollocks, quizzing me on shit I know nothing about. All the while I *should* be out there looking for the cunts that took my brother. I'm grateful for the massages and breakfasts and all that, oh and for including me in this pointless and completely irrelevant fucking board meeting but enough is enough."

"Squidge..."

"No, stop it. Stop calling me that. Jesus. Who do you think you are? You don't know me. You know fuck all about me, about where I've come from, about where that name comes from."

"Apologies...."

"Jesus Christ, what the fuck is wrong with you? I'm done. I don't need your apologies. Just give me some money and open the gates. And if you can't do that then bring that nice helicopter round the back and take me home. Seriously, I'm fucking done."

And with that I stood up, I was a bit cross.

The room was quiet, I mean, if not for the air conditioning, you could've heard a mouse fart. But it felt good to purge, to get a little of my frustration out. I knew I'd been rude, ungrateful even, but I really didn't care. It didn't matter, did it? If I wasn't out there either looking *after* the Nutter or searching *for* my little brother, then nothing mattered. That's why I'd left the flat. That's the reason I was here.

I looked at the faces in front of me, I had not the slightest ounce of fear. If Danny had been in the next room I'd have carved a route through these fuckers with my fingernails.

Terry was looking at Carlson and thought I could see a trace of a smile on his face. Eventually he nodded and stood.

"Thank you everyone," he said quietly to the room. Then to me: "Matthew, come with me please."

Terry left the room before I could argue so after standing awkwardly for a moment, belly fizzing, hands itching, I picked up my diet coke *and glass,* which I only noticed then was cracked, cheap fuckers, and followed him. I was certain he would be taking me back upstairs so I could pack. That was cool, I wouldn't be missing anything here for sure.

Instead, he went the other way and into a smaller room off a corridor on the opposite side of the situation room, left hand side. I followed him in, sheep like before I knew what I was doing.

"Sit down," he gestured to the seat in the corner. Oh, shit and bollocks this is where I find out I can't leave or if I do it'll be conditional to me sacrificing a lung, or a leg.

I sat, again without arguing and waited while he paced a bit before sitting down himself. He was clearly in pain, possibly a broken rib, either that or he needed a massive poo. I'm going for the latter.

"What can I call you?" again, quietly.

"I don't give a shit, you can call me anything, I'm cured."

Terry smiled.

"Ok, well if it's all the same I'm going to stick with Squidge."

Prick.

I nodded and shrugged at the same time, which you've just tried doing yourself, and discovered it's not as easy as it sounds is it? Amiright?

Anyway.

"Suit yourself."

"I know you don't value apologies but here's one anyway; There's an awful lot of very clever, very manipulative, 'interested' parties out there. I'll get to that in some detail in a minute but the whole thing before today, in fact including today, has been about establishing who you are. Locking in your identity. It's been about establishing that you really are who you claim to be, who we hoped you were."

I must've been frowning like a lowland gorilla. Sigourney Weaver would've wet herself. Terry, bless him, just ploughed on.

"And that's important because of what comes next. Suffice to say you've proven yourself, that is to say I, and *we* are confident that your identity is confirmed."

Jesus Christ, more bollocks.

I nodded, still frowning, both confused as to how I could possibly be someone *else*, and kind of understanding the principle too. Even if I hadn't a clue why it would be necessary.

"Ok."

"Right, so here we are." He paused as he planned what to say. "Your Dad was never a decorator; you know that right? I mean I'm sure he could paint if the need arose, he could probably hang paper too but that wasn't him."

I nodded again.

"Right?"

"I knew your Dad since we were kids, and yes, you're right I am Terry, George and Maggie's son. I'm sure they've told you 'I got into a spot of bother'? Anyway, me and your Dad, we grew up together, school, youth club, everything. We were skinheads, both of us, well into that scene. Jesus, we had some good scraps with the punks, Jason Kybert, Barry Steel and the Boyson twins. Big battles with all our gang and theirs down on the old Merrell-Sydenham sidings. Bricks, bottles, even knives, your Dad was proper handy, a dirty little scraper, very quick hands."

I remembered the tattoos on his hands then, and the boots. I didn't smile but I kinda wanted to. Terry went on.

"In fact, he hung onto some of his clobber, I saw him wearing it years later." Slightly wistful.

He paused whilst he pictured himself as a kid. Eventually.

"Anyway, we both applied for the same apprenticeships, we did it together, the careers officer said it was a good idea, even though your Dad was much smarter than me. I mean, had we pursued that properly he'd have gone on to do really well, I have no doubt."

I would have smiled if I believed a word of it. Was he really talking about my old man?

"But that's not what happened. Instead, my spot of bother happened. It's a bit shit but the short story is I got a girl pregnant, the wrong girl if you know what I mean. Anyway, she had brothers, and her old fella had a crew, and they were going to do nasty things to me so I had to disappear. I mean, the baby was given up in the end, that's how Mum, Maggie as you know her, got Justin."

"So, Justin *is* your son?" I said recalling him from school. He was a biggish lad, chubby, soft, but otherwise forgettable. As mentioned, Maggie and the Nutter used to do the school run together. Justin used to come over for tea now and then, when we were little, I remembered playing Connect Four with him. Lost touch in recent years though, like you do. I think he went to college or Uni somewhere up north. I also remember him never mentioning anyone other than George as his father.

"Yeah," he looked sheepish: "Ashamed to say I wasn't around much when he was growing up."

I'll say. I'd literally never seen his mug before, not once.

Terry pressed on:

"Anyway, your Dad, he did me a solid and came with me, you know when I went. We joined up together and didn't look back. We weren't the only ones, you know, you'd be surprised how many youngsters join up to escape some kind of trouble. In some cases, I've heard the judicial system offers it as a form of quid pro quo settlement of a 'social debt.' In my case it was more about saving my skin, plus it kept the Grub safe for Mum, Dad and Justin, sort of."

Which made me think of Justin again, and now specifically George and Maggie. I mean, as much as I wanted to ask questions about my Dad, and me, and all this bollocks, I couldn't help thinking about this fella, sitting pretty here, while the rest of *his* family struggled like fuck back in London. Did he know what Justin was doing now? Did he know his Dad was on deaths door, that his Mum needed her leg off and had forgotten how to brush her hair?

"When did you last see Justin?" I asked before I could stop myself.

He frowned.

"Too long ago, for sure. But we're not here to talk about that...."

I shook my head.

"True, but I didn't bring it up."

Now he grimaced. I think I'd got through a bit. He took a breath and looked at me steadily:

"No, you're right. You didn't bring it up, I did. But I don't want to talk about it."

"What about Maggie, and George? You know George is in St Thomas's, right? He been rough...."

Terry looked like he wanted to stand up and pace. He also looked pissed that I was getting into stuff he wasn't prepared for:

"Squidge, sorry, listen I don't want to talk about this, really, not now. And you're quite right, with them there, and me all the way over here, it's far from an ideal situation. But trust me when I say it's not as simple as you might think. I am involved, and I do care...."

"Right," I nodded.

There was a pause, whilst he decided if he could carry on from where he left off. Eventually I pushed it back:

"So, my old man was in the army then?"

Terry looked relieved and took the bait straight away.

"Yeah, well sort of, for a time at least. I've already told you he was smart, but I don't think you appreciate how smart. I certainly didn't. He aced every test, every single one, the physical and aptitudinal. I mean he learnt languages and code and command strategy really, really quickly. Complex stuff. It's funny how he excelled then but not whilst at school. I mean, I assumed it was the self-motivation thing, you know as opposed to being told he *had* to be there by parents or whatever...."

I think I got that to be fair.

"Well anyway he got noticed, obviously, and was quickly pulled out of the squad and fast tracked. He was into MI within a couple of years of joining."

"MI?"

"Military Intelligence."

Terry smiled as he saw my face.

"I know, this is all a bit of a shock, a lot to take in, I'm sure. But I owe it to you, we all do."

Gorilla faced again but he ignored it and went on.

"He took me with him of course, not straight away, I had to work hard to get in, but he sponsored me and pushed me. When I got there, he was already heading up two sections, had a team of over forty under him, super clever Squidge, super clever. And fucking hard too, took no shit, pushed his own agenda and delivered. They loved him, absolutely loved him.

He trained us up, me, Carlson, a few others, some you've met, some you haven't. Thing is, when we were at school, I was the loud one, I was the leader, if you know what I mean. He was quiet, you know, he didn't stand out, not really."

I knew a few like that.

"But now, as an adult, with all this confidence and all these resources he was the man, he was the one people followed, he was the one *I* followed."

I could see that too. I'd have followed my Dad anywhere.

Terry went on:

"A couple more years and he appointed Dean Peters to his position whilst he went on secondment to...."

I stopped him.

"Wait. Did you just say *Dean Peters*?"

Terry nodded.

"Yeah, Dean. He was there early on too. Him and your Dad did a couple of tours together whilst I was still at Rheindahlen...."

I held up my hand again. Fuck this, I wasn't having this.

"Dean Peters? *Dean* Peters??"

Terry nodded:

"Yeah. Why?"

This was making me angry;

"Fuck you. Dean Peter is or *was* his boss. He used to decorate for Dean fucking Peters. The only tour they did together was of Blackpool Pleasure Beach."

Terry sat back:

"Sorry, look, I know this is all hard to hear, I get it, I do. And whilst I understand you don't want to hear it, it's all the truth, and it's really important that you know the facts...."

"Know the facts?!?" I was going a bit red again; "He fucking *died* working for Dean Peters you cunt. How's that for a fucking FACT?"

Terry put his hands up defensively, but I ignored it:

"What's fucking wrong with you? What the fuck are you trying to do?"

Terry remained silent. For sure, he didn't like being called a cunt. Sure too, that he was running out of ways to make me see things his way.

Eventually he took a breath, and spread his hands:

"Squidge, Matthew, I'm not trying to wind you up, I'm really not, honestly. I'm sorry this is hard, I am, I *really* am" he rubbed his chin, and looked up at the ceiling whilst he composed his thoughts.

I gazed at his neck, the fizz in my belly fully back, and wondered if I should punch him in the Adams apple. Finally, he looked back down at me:

"Look, I can either tell you, or not tell you, I don't mind. Honestly, it's your call. It's no skin off my nose either way...."

I stared at him as he pushed on, balls fucking of steel:

"I just want you to know who we are, I want you to know why you're here. You can decide what happens after that."

I was simmering, like a pot of new potatoes that had been on the gas hob for 45 minutes, just ready to blow my lid off and vent my shit all over. But I also had enough about me to know that, beyond the bollocks he was spouting now, I had no other reason to hate on Terry. I looked away, frustrated that I'd got so wound over it all, and awkward about how to move things on.

"Can I go on?"

Fuck me he was relentless. But I nodded anyway, kinda grateful that I didn't have to do the work myself:

"If you must," I said, like a 12-year-old girl.

Terry nodded, and rubbed his hands together, nervously.

"Right, so where was I?" he looked up, and then it clicked: "So your Dad was seconded to weapons development, well weapons deployment research really but that's a bit of a mouthful. Anyway, he got fully involved, as was his way, and helped deliver a few projects for those guys and even assisted in the development of a new propulsion system using a mineral extraction technology known to the Americans but new to us. It involved a substance called Striochatheneamylist which can be extracted from certain rare rock deposits. It's an incredibly complicated process involving lots of steps and lots of expensive and complicated equipment. Your Dad, as much as he assisted with the development of the tech that used this 'Strio' substance, whose properties I'll get into in a moment, was perhaps the only person who had visibility of the whole process, you know from setting up with the raw materials to all the technical, science stuff. He was a project guy at heart you see. He retained the data and could see the steps required. Given an end goal he could visualise the steps, the resources, critical path, stakeholders, risks, deliverables etc. He had that kind of mind. Of course, now I say it, it sounds like he was superhuman. He wasn't, he was just a man, a very, very smart and capable man surrounded by almost limitless resources and lots and lots of other very smart, driven, committed people. The perfect storm I suppose."

"Fella, I hate to interrupt your story, but this is bullshit. Clearly."

I'd calmed down, not completely, but mostly, and had sat quietly and let him talk but I'd had enough now. Apart from the made-up life, the manipulation of sad and very real facts about who my Dad was and who he worked for, the whole thing was getting into the realms of science fiction now. And I really wasn't interested.

"This is bollocks. I'm sorry. You wound me up, and I shouldn't have got angry, but I did. But this," I gestured to him, and the room, and everything; "It's got nothing to do with me, it's a distraction and it's bollocks. You know why I'm here. I've made no secrets about it. The man you're describing, that's someone else's Dad there. You want me to be wowed by this but I'm not. Don't get me wrong it's a fantastic story, very entertaining but as far as I'm concerned, it's complete and utter bollocks. My old man was a decorator, a fucking brush hand. He left on a Monday morning, was gone for two weeks at a time, did commercial and light industrial decorations for a firm in Derby. They had twenty brush hands and seven or eight vans." I was shaking my head: "Jesus he was clever, but he wasn't the man you're describing."

"So, who am I describing then?" Terry answered quickly. Prick.

"James fucking Bond, I don't know! I mean Jesus it's great you thought so much of him but honestly, I don't know where you're getting this from. He weren't in the army, my Mum would've told me."

"Would she?"

Wanker.

"Yes Terry son of Maggie and George, if that's really who you are." I was getting annoyed again. "Oh, and if you're trying to piss me off again you're heading in the right direction."

"Ok, ok. I get it, you're annoyed, and you think you're wasting time, you think *I'm* wasting your time."

"Oh, you get it?"

"Yes, I do, I really do. But listen to me. Would she have told you? Yes, you're probably right. But did she know?" Now he shook his head. "No Squidge, she didn't."

I scowled. Truthfully, it never crossed my mind to use that word before in conversation let alone write it down, but in this case it fits. If I could I'd have growled at him, cursed him, shouted all sorts of cunt at him. But I didn't, I just slid forward slightly, the fizzing in my ears that had been there earlier returning in a rush. It grew loud and the edges of my vision begun to tint red again.

"I've gotta warn you now fella that I'm pretty close to losing my shit. Don't talk about my Mum."

Terry held up his hands, again, like he was a fucking lollipop lady.

"Calm down, listen..."

"If you tell me to *listen* one more time, I'm gonna bite your fucking face off."

If only Bob had taken note the way Terry did following that mildly alarming statement. I mean it was alarming for me, totally out of character, notwithstanding the aforementioned Bob. But then I'm not suggesting it was particularly alarming to old Tez, you know, to have some skinny kid, high on diet coke and organic Swiss sausages threatening to eat him.

"Ok ok. I'm sorry. You're right let's get you out of here. Let's get you on your way home. Come on." And with that he was up and out the room, would've been a top doorman this one, diffused the fuck out of me.

I sat for a bit pondering what I actually would've done with his nose once I'd bitten it off. I mean, it's not like I *hadn't* had breakfast and I'm sure it wouldn't have gone unnoticed let's face it (no pun intended). So no, on reflection he probably made the best move, for the both of us. I stood up, legs a bit shaky and followed him out.

Back in the lift he stood quietly, as did I. It felt awkward now, like I'd gone too far, like the friend I might have had was gone. I hated that, you know the feeling that you've overreached, overreacted to something. And you've made a fool of yourself. That's caused me a ton of trouble over the years, seeing or hearing something, and instantly pinging off like some demented jack-in-the-box only to discover I'd got it wrong. And then having to crawl back, to apologise.

Wasn't easy on the estate, in the school I went to. Hadn't been easy at home either. Mum was cool, but she was hard too, when pushed. And we know Danny was as happy to swing as he was to talk. So yeah, it was a shitty feeling.

I glanced sideways at Terry. Thought about saying sorry but chickened out.

The lift stopped and the doors opened, and I followed him out. We walked back up the corridor and into the central lobby where he stopped.

"I'm sorry you feel the way to do, son, really I am."

I didn't know what to say now I'd calmed down a bit and was out of that fucking basement, so Terry filled the gap.

"I made a promise, you know. To your Dad, to look out for you, to keep eyes on you. I'm gutted to say I failed Danny. And I'm sad to say I've not exactly excelled with you either."

He paused waiting for my explosion. It didn't come. Instead, I felt my eyes prickle at the mention of my little brother. And the promise he claimed to have made, whatever that was. Terry pressed on.

"I'm going to let you go, we're gonna take you home, all the way and make sure you and your Mum are ok. But that's not it. That's not the end."

I was relieved to hear those words. As nice as the lake was, the grounds, the food and, yes, the company, I couldn't shake the feeling that I was somehow a prisoner here, or that I didn't belong here, that I should be somewhere else. Maybe it was just my piss poor view of the world and the fact that until I went to the Isle of Wight I'd never even been on a proper bloody train. I think I was missing home. Maybe that was all of it, I was just missing home? I half smiled, and frowned, at the same time.

"What does that mean?"

He shrugged.

"It means, I'm going to keep eyes on you. I'm not going to let any harm come to you."

"But why? What am I to you?"

He looked at me straight.

"I've been trying to tell you that for the last couple of hours."

Ok that was fair. Now I shrugged. Shit loads of shrugging going on. It was a shrug fest.

"Right, yes, I'm sorry I got all bent down there. I just..." I didn't really know how to put it into words, how to say it. I mean, until I was home, I wasn't going to fully believe I wasn't being held captive here, but on the flip side I didn't really have a great deal to complain about did I.

Why had I gotten so pissed? Up until an hour ago I hadn't really known I was stressed. Maybe it was Paul. Maybe it was the fact that Terry hadn't come back with answers when he said he would, or that Freya never arranged the call with Mum she promised to.

Maybe it was just the sheer fucking randomness of my situation.

Terry sensed half a painful apology brewing and did me a solid.

"It's fine, really. Don't sweat it."

Now I felt weird. I took a deep breath.

"Can we walk outside a bit?"

Terry nodded, and then gestured over his shoulder at the stairs:

"Sure. Unless you wanted to go pack first?"

Prick.

I shook my head.

"It'll wait five."

Terry followed me out onto the lawn, and we walked over towards the wall that bordered the lake edge, not too far from where I found myself when I first opened my eyes all those weeks ago. The sun was low in the sky but there were a few boats still out there and one guy on a parasail thing.

Ponce.

I turned to Terry:

"What I don't understand is; if you was keeping eyes on me, looking out for me, Mum and Danny then why were we in that scummy fucking shit hole? Why were we hand to mouth, scraping by? Mum's been doing 12-hour shifts for yonks, since Dad died for fucks sake. I've been doing deals just to survive, and Danny...." I paused. "How is that looking out for us?" I wasn't angry anymore, but I didn't hold back either, bollocks.

Terry turned to look out onto the water before eventually turning back to me.

And here's where I learnt about the sand.

"If you spend a long time looking closely at something, you cease to see it, you cease to see what's around it," he looked back at me as I thought about that: "Don't look too closely at the grains, they'll only mislead you."

I shook my head:

"But..."

"It was the safest place Matthew, for all of you. You were hidden in plain sight, somewhere they, where *he* wouldn't think to look, somewhere where you would all have some semblance of freedom."

And so, with each answer comes a corresponding question.

"Hidden?" That *was* my question, but shouldn't it have been 'sand? What the fuck you talking about fool?' Possibly, but the thing is, I think I already knew what it was, what he meant by sand. I asked again:

“Hidden? From who? Who is *he?* I don’t understand, why would you say we needed to *hide*?”

He smiled kindly.

"It's a hard thing, I'm sure, to find out that what you thought was your reality is actually a fabrication. A very elaborate and well-constructed fabrication.”

I was shaking my head like a wet dog. WFT?

“Sorry but you’re not making any sense. What are you *talking* about? Why would we need to hide? Who were we hiding from? And....”

"Squidge, I’m sorry, I know you don’t want to hear it, but your life, it's not what it seems. You’re not who you think you are, and your old man, he wasn't a decorator. He was a soldier, an engineer and a spy."

11: Bonnie & Clyde

I had my bag packed and five grand in my pocket - all in untraceable notes. I loved it, I felt like an international bank robber. I mean, I could probably legitimately call myself an international Cadbury's Creme Egg robber after seeing off that old lady behind the counter in Smiths, Waterloo before I got my train to Southampton. Didn't really have the same ring to it though, did it?

It was the day after the night before. I hadn't blown up on Terry, even though I felt like it. I dunno, I think it was easier to hear bollocks, or uncomfortable truths, or a clever mixture of the two when standing, hands in pockets, on the edge of a beautiful Italian lake than it was whilst sitting in a grey, airless basement.

Diet Coke or no Diet Coke.

Regardless,

Freya came to say goodbye, all teary and daft. She gave me a book about some old bald guy, obviously. And then she checked my scars one last time before she kissed me on the mouth. It took me by surprise, I can't lie. I mean she was gorgeous, really lovely, so I can't imagine what possessed her. Anyway, our moment was interrupted by Micha bouncing through the door, complete with a cake and a tea towel. Yes a tea towel and a fucking cake, of all the things I wanted to take on a helicopter. I said thanks, graciously of course before tactfully suggesting he give the cake to Mick and Claudia, or throw it in the lake, whichever was easiest. I'd keep the tea towel for Mum, she'd love it.

I gave him a hug and together the two of them walked me out to the back lawn. It was all very sepia; you know the kind of warm orange that good memories go when you look at them from a distance. A few of the staff and their kids were there, plus the bread guy even though we'd never actually spoken. Terry too, and when he saw me he pulled me to one side.

"This isn't the end you know. I'm gonna help you find Danny. We're working on it now; we have been since the beginning. And as I said, we're going to keep an eye on you."

I kinda knew that already even if I didn't say so. I nodded.

"Yeah well don't get too close, you know, I've got business to take care of and I don't want you upsetting Mum."

I didn't really know what I was saying. I just wanted to go, to get back to something I knew. I could start again then, once my feet were back on the ground. Plus, I had a bit of cash in hand now so I might be a tad more productive. And I guessed, if Terry was gonna insist on being somewhere there in the background then I could always reach out if the need arose.

The helicopter came in a bit early, flying up from the southern end of the lake and fuck me was it noisy. I mean obviously we've all seen Arnie hopping on and off of them on screen, but I was proper surprised by the scale of it.

Everyone took a step back and Terry told me to keep me head down as I went over to it. I climbed in and belted up and the driver, or pilot as I've since been informed, told me to put my headphones on so we could talk. Great, from almost slightly cool to fucking space cadet in one swift movement.

Anyway, in a moment we were taking off and my stomach was in my mouth, how were we even in the air? This crazy fucking machine lurching up and the ground getting smaller by the second. I looked out of the window as we banked left and circled back over the big house and then it all went to shit.

So, you've all seen Scarface, right? At the end where the Columbians come in over the walls and shoot the shit outta Al Pacino's big house before shooting the shit outta actual Tony Montana himself? 'Say hallo to my leetle friend!' and all that? Well, it was a bit like that, or at least I assume it would've been had I been on the ground to see it. I mean apart from all the coke, you know, the frankly industrial quantities of class A powder that Tony was casually throwing about. Yeah, other than that it was pretty much the same.

But I wasn't there, was I, I was escaping again, by the skin of my teeth, again. Sounds like I'm being flippant doesn't it. I don't mean to be, really, it was fucking awful to see, to experience, so I've no desire to make light of it. And even though we were moving away I could see the gates come down, the flashes of gunfire, the swarm of black suited fuckers pouring in, some even coming from the water. I actually saw Terry fall, pretty sure Freya too but I couldn't be certain and then we were clear and moving away.

I was screaming at the pilot to go back but he was having none of it. Bullets were pinging off the fuselage, (another one for the word bag). One even came through the floor of the cockpit and passed straight up and back out through the windscreen. Fuck knows how it didn't hit the rotors. But it didn't last long, soon we were too far away to make it worthwhile shooting at us.

I tried to look back, to see what was happening but the windows were angled wrong and all I saw was water and the green of the lake shore rushing by. I was sweating, my heart was hammering, and I felt sick.

Again, I begged the pilot to go back, or just to turn so I could *see* back, but he just shook his head. He wouldn't even look at me. It was infuriating, I was raging, and screaming and shouting at him but it made no difference.

I kinda understood though, on some level, despite my panic and fear. I knew if we went back, we'd die. But that didn't make it less excruciating, you know, to just be flying away like we were. I wanted to *be* there, to help, to, I dunno, be *accountable* for something. Anything would be better than being the flaky fucking chav I was, making the most of a set of very fortunate circumstances.

I hated it, and raged, and hammered against the window and door for a moment but we kept flying and moving away.

And then I discovered that the pilot, Alex, had actually shit himself. Properly. And it stank. I'm not gonna say it was a useful distraction, but it was a distraction. I wasn't completely surprised, as I say, it was terrifying, see above.

But I was glad it wasn't me because it was actually quite embarrassing.

Anyway, I offered to take over the controls while he went into the back for a strip wash. Ok so no, I didn't have a driver's licence right, but that doesn't mean I didn't know the basics, and this looked pretty simple. Anyway, he declined, which I initially thought was rude. I mean, it was always good enough for me and Danny growing up. In fact, I've got fond memories of Mum wiping us down in the kitchen sink with a crusty flannel. Certainly, better than risking death at the hands of the 'push on the tap' shower attachment thingy.

But whatever, Alex explained that I wouldn't be able to control the *bird* and bless him, he then explained, at length, with shit in his pants, why I'd struggle. You know the technical aspects of that belief, the 'collective pitch control', the 'anti-torque pedals' etc. I mean I couldn't help admiring the fella, his commitment to my education in the face of such trouser squelch.

Turns out however, and this is a little painful to say, that in fact he hadn't 'had a little accident'. No, he'd been shot. At least one of the rounds just before the one that I mentioned earlier as having passed straight through had actually hit him and ruptured his bowel. It had hit the bottom of the fuselage below the cockpit, passed up though and into the pilot's chair before splintering and cutting through his backside and into his soft bits.

Truly harrowing.

The brown stains and dribbles were his poo mixed with a frightening quantity of blood. And I think until you've seen for yourself, what a person bleeding out looks like you'd never be able to picture it. There was so much blood, so, so much.

I don't get queasy easily, I really don't. I mean with the obvious exception of a little English Channel, Red Funnel chunder I'm normally pretty good. I've seen dead cats and all sorts. Saw the top of a dead fella's head once where the crime scene guys hadn't properly covered him with their hazard blanket. They'd pulled him out of a skip behind Woolworths.

But this was different. I don't know if it was the smell, the blood lapping at my feet or the fact I knew, well we both knew, that he was dying. Like, what could *I* do? No seriously what the fuck *could* I do? His life was leaking out the arse of his trousers and there was absolutely no way to stop it...

All this whilst we were racing along the lake three hundred feet up, looking desperately for somewhere to put down. Jesus I was conflicted. On one hand I wanted him to land as soon as he could so I could get him some help and on the other, I was double crapping myself at the thought of the Columbians coming after us.

Fuck sake.

But he hung on, Alex did, my absolute fucking hero. He could have checked out, any time. And if he had, I wouldn't have held it against him, I mean I would've died of course, either by burning to a crisp in a white-hot ball of aviation fuel fed fire or by drowning whilst trapped in the shit and blood filled cockpit of a bullet riddled helicopter.

Sure, I'd have been disappointed, but I wouldn't have held it against him.

He didn't though, Tupac bless his soul. He hung on, growing paler and getting weaker by the second. Eventually, approx. twelve clicks north and on the opposite side of the lake we saw it, a small flat area of grass. Turned out actually to be someone's rather large back garden. It had a jetty with a small but expensive looking cruiser moored, and a few trees which were far enough up the garden to leave room for the bird. I watched Alex closely, listened to him too, on the headphones as he struggled to breathe, to stay alert and in possession of his faculties. It made my eyes water, I don't mind telling you.

He made his approach without the usual reserve and with none of the normal checks and we dropped quickly, quite roughly to the ground, bounced around a little and then settled. I helped him switch off all the dangerous shit before jumping down, running round to unbuckle him and lift him down. I was panicking, I was crying, and I just wanted to do something to help him. But it was a mistake, a wasted effort. The seat, the belt and everything, was all that was holding him together. I just made it worse moving him. He was dead before I had him laid flat on the lawn. His last words to me, as his insides fell out, were something about being sorry about Danny, and then ‘home’, or ‘gnome’, or ‘foam’, or something.

I couldn't believe it. I was covered in blood and shit and shaking like a fucking jelly. My hands, I could barely get them to do anything. I looked round to see two old people making their way purposefully towards me, thankfully quite a way off still. They looked pissed. I wasn't surprised, I mean the grass looked lovely and now it was covered with dead helicopters and even deader pilots. I couldn't focus, I didn't know what to do next, I had no context into which I could put this experience. I looked down at Alex, his face was all relaxed with his jaw kinda sunken. He'd been a handsome guy before, obviously, he was a pilot right. Now however he was just a dead guy. My hero for sure, forever, but still, just a dead guy.

I heard voices, old and thin, like the angry pensioners you get at the post office when you're there trying to top up your gas meter key with a hooky fiver and they want to spend four hours posting a fucking letter. I glanced up, conscious that I was on their property, that I had no passport, and that I didn't speak a word of Spanish or Italian or Klingon or whatever they were going to be screaming at me. Bollocks. BOLLOCKS!

What do I do?

What do i do??

The radio.

Fuck, yes, the radio!

I stood up, the rotors had fully stopped spinning, so I didn't need to duck. I leaned into the cab and pressed a few buttons. Eventually I got some service so tried to call Terry, or Carlson or *anyone* back at the big house. No response so I tried again. No response, I didn't even know if I was doing it right.

FUUUCCCKK!

I jumped back down and looked at Alex again. He must have something on him of use. I had a fumble, checked his pockets, rolled him a little and checked his back etc. It was sticky and gross back there, but I got his wallet and a couple of other bits.

The old man, the first of two, arrived. Screeching and shouting at me. Fuck him, I ignored him whilst I climbed back into the bird. I had a good, proper rummage about and turned up a walkie talkie, a gun (yes, another gun), some magazines, no not Top Gear or Bella but bullets, or rounds or whatever the fuck you call them. Also found a big arse knife, a compass thingy and a small first aid kit.

The second pensioner arrived and joined the first. It wasn't a man, just a hairy old lady, I've heard it's not unusual for these parts. She had a stick and seemed to be threatening me with it through the windscreen of the helicopter. I ignored her too whilst I finished stripping the cab of anything I thought I could use. I grabbed a bag and stuffed it all inside before jumping back down, on the opposite side to Alex and the two elderly muppets. I needed to move, the Columbians would've followed the flight with binoculars and seen us in trouble. If they had any sense, they would then have had someone follow us over land to see where we eventually put down. I would have. They might even have an aircraft of their own. I needed to get away from the helicopter, away from Alex, even if it did pain me to leave him lying there. And I needed to do it quickly.

FUUUUCCCKKK!

I jogged up the garden towards the house the sound of Bonnie and Clyde fading behind me. Thankfully they'd left the back door open so I dived in and scouted for car keys, like I say, I couldn't really drive but needs must.

I knew they'd be following me, or at least one of them would so unless I wanted to be hitting Nana on the head with the Yellow Pages I needed to be quick. I checked all the usual places, hooks, drawers, small glass bowls filled with cables, business cards, buttons and pens but nothing. Bollocks, bollocks, bollocks.

I was about to give up when I saw them on a dresser next to a row of coat hoots. Strangely these were closer to the back door than the front and the hooks were filled with waterproofs and wet weather gear. I grabbed the keys and moved on through the house to a door I assumed led to the integral garage, It opened straight away but there was no car. There never had been one either, couldn't have been. The whole space, a double, double garage, you know double length, double width, was taken up by a 1:16 scale model of Ancient Troy - early period. I mean obviously that's a complete guess, and well after the event so it could easily be Corinth or Ephesus. At the time I confess all I thought was; 'WFT?' Followed by: 'Where's the fucking motor?'

Back through the house, the sound of old people approaching just reaching me now. Through the kitchen, another glance at the coat hooks and I noticed the wellies this time too. Back out of the back door and round to the front to see if the car was parked on the drive. It wasn't. And as before, it never had been. Because there was no drive. Fuck.

What was going on?

Where was the car?

Where did they park it?

How did they get about?

I looked at the keys and it dawned.

Back around to the rear, and a jog down the garden passing the second old crusty as they were coming the other way. I passed the helicopter on the opposite side to Alex again, sorry but I couldn't face him, before carrying on down to the edge of the water and the wooden jetty.

Yes, there it was. The car, or the closest thing to it, the boat.

I ran down the jetty, jumped on board and got it started. It fired up straight away, a healthy rumble and gurgle, which was a huge fucking relief I can tell you. I then untied it and went back to have a play with the shiny levers and buttons. It was a lot simpler than I thought and I had it out on the water before the fastest of the grey wizards had even got as far as the end of the grass. They were wailing and waving at me, and I could see they were red in the face and I'm pretty sure it wasn't gout. I mean, to be fair it must have been a pretty shit Saturday for them. There was no footy on the TV for starters, then some wanker drives and parks a dirty great helicopter on their nice garden, without asking. He then dies, and shits on the lawn and his skinny deaf mate then runs up and down a couple of times before stealing their nice (new) boat.

And to top it off he also pinched the freshly made garlic bread baguette that was left cooling ready for lunch.

Bastard.

12: My Cousin Vinny

I drove the boat out into the centre of the lake before continuing north. Well, it turned out to be more northeast, but I didn't know that at the time. I needed to find somewhere to park up so I could think about what to do next.

Actually, it turns out to be 'moor' rather than park, but I didn't know that either, did I.

I had some cash, at the time it actually seemed like a lot of cash, a few semi useful bits and bobs and a gun. Great, I mean what the fuck was I going to do with a gun? I mean, I'd struggled with a 60-mile train journey and one night on the Isle of Wight. How was I going to cross half of Europe, and get myself back onto the estate with no passport, five grand in dubious Sterling, a hunting knife, compass and St Johns Ambulance first aid kit for five?

All whilst being pursued by Carlos the Jackal and his crew of ruthless assassins?

Ridiculous.

I kept going for a bit whilst I scanned the maps Gandalf had kindly left in the cab. I noticed straight away that there was a lot more water to the south of me than to the north, plus all the bits that weren't water, you know, the green bits, looked a lot more like mountains to the north than they did to the south. Was that good or bad? I didn't know. Perhaps I could hide better in the mountains, perhaps I'd just freeze to death, or get eaten by a snow leopard or a yeti. Perhaps I didn't need to hide. I mean who's to say they were even bothered about me, beyond that of me being a potential witness. Did they, and I'm referring to the Columbians, even know I was in the chopper? Maybe they were just shooting at it because that was their SOP?

Fuck. I didn't know, couldn't know.

And here's a thought, did the Columbians make it into the basement? Not the basement with the gym where Anders tried to tie my arms and legs into a clove hitch, and the canteen and kitchen. I mean the other basement, the special one with all the nerds. It seemed pretty secure to me. It was at least three floors down, and there were lots of doors and shit to get through. I guess it was feasible that Carlson and Paul, ok possibly not Paul because he was a douche, were safe and well down there drinking diet coke and inventing acronyms. I hoped, as the thought occurred, that perhaps a few of the others would have made it down there too.

Bollocks, I headed up the *Mera* River, a dirty little waterway that joined the lake at the very extreme north-east. I drifted upstream for another hour before parking up against a small wooden jetty at the top of another, much smaller lake that I'll be honest took me a bit by surprise.

I was exhausted and desperate for a poo so after I tied up the boat I went below. Full of the best intentions I ended up falling asleep on the bog, for at least 40 minutes. Eventually, legs numb and arse aching I sorted myself out before crawling into the, surprisingly and pleasantly, prepared bed and died. Not literally, obviously, otherwise how would I be doing this. Idiot.

Anyway, I slept, not as well as Alex or course, God rest his soul, but still, pretty good.

I dreamt I was back in the helicopter, only this time Alex collapsed before he could land, slumping sideways in his seat with blood dribbling from his nose. Instead of panicking and crashing straight into the lake I took control of the machine with my mind. I flew it, or carried it, hands glowing, Magneto style and then landed it, like before on the end of Chas & Dave's lawn. Then, before I could go round and check on Alex I became a bee, buzzing and floating around, dipping in and out of the flowers in the beds up and down the sides of the garden. Eventually I headed back to the hive where I took a massive shit in the honeycomb. All the other bees were pissed and started buzzing and stressing and then I was myself and the honeycomb was just a huge expanse of hexagonal shapes below me, which slowly turned from golden yellow through to green and then white. And then finally I was there hovering like a helicopter, high above a vast landscape of frozen snow and ice.

I could still hear the humming and buzzing.

When I woke it was still dark and I was disoriented. I expected to be cold, you know, after my dream, but instead I was hot and sticky and, I mean, obviously they weren't, but for a moment, in the dark, I thought my hands were still glowing.

Anyway, following a rummage, for which I was developing a bit of a knack, I scoffed some biscotti, the garlic bread I stole from Chas and Dave, and some weird looking buns filled with kumquat flavoured custard. I'll be honest, they tasted like foot sweat, but I was proper hank, and I knew I'd need the energy. The water tasted a bit metallic, but there was plenty of it, so I was grateful. And as I still had some of Alex's insides on me, I had a quick strip wash before laying back down for another couple of hours.

No dreams this time, which was good.

When I woke again, while I waited for the sun to come up and the smallest kettle in the world to boil, I had another quick rummage. I happily bolstered my collection of utterly useless shite before making a cup of Lipton's 'tea', I know, don't start, and restarting the boat. I then, hesitantly, began my journey south.

Having given considerable thought to this, I knew I was taking a risk. And when I say considerable, I mean at least the seven or eight minutes it took me to poo the night before, *before* I fell asleep.

The Columbians, they could have people out on boats looking for me. They could have me as a target. But equally, they may not have any interest in me at all. I mean why would they? What was I to them? I was just some random skinny kid from an estate in London who got tangled up with something I had no business being involved in. Clearly the people at AMOS had fingers in pies that had nothing to do with me.

And whilst I said all of that to myself, over and over again, there was this other little voice telling me that I *was* significant, that I *was* 'someone'. But I told that little voice to fuck off because I couldn't get my head around it, could I. I couldn't seriously look at that because it would mean that some, if not all, the shit Terry had been talking about the day before was true. And that would mean my Dad was someone completely, fundamentally, different from the man I thought he was. It would mean he'd lied to Mum, and to us. And it would also mean that Danny had probably been taken, not by some low rent drug dealing knob heads, which I was starting to believe, following my international adventures, I could, at a push, knock the fuck out, but instead by someone with a whole lot more to gain.

It was a head fuck, it really was. So, I decided, after consideration to err heavily on the side of 'no fucking way' and head on downstream to see if I could pass Bellano unnoticed before slipping into the crowds in either Como or Lecco. I had dark hair, could say 'marguerita' and 'cao' quite convincingly and I had a compass. How hard could it be?

The helicopter circled the compound. I watched the gunmen come over the fence and vehicles smash through the gates. I saw the black boats pull up on the water's edge and more guys come in that way.

Then I saw the orange flashes as they started shooting, and watched as people were cut down. I watched them all fall; Terry, Mum, Maggie, Mick...

The helicopter moved, swinging and lurching to the right, dropping initially before rising again and moving away. I heard Alex grunt and knew he'd been hit. I offered to take the controls which he accepted before he painfully stood and tried to move past me into the back.

But as he did his insides spilled out. They fell on the floor between his legs like a wet towel, heavy and slick. I looked at his face, but he was smiling. I looked down to see more, and more came out. It was pouring from him, a cascade of red and blue and brown.

It spread out across the floor, rising up to lap at my feet. And still more fell from until he grew pale and fragile crumpled down, his body just an empty paper shell. And then the helicopter was falling.

I tried to control it, but it was no use. It plunged down, faster and faster, gathering speed until it smashed violently into the surface of the lake. It pushed on in, water forcing its way into the cabin, gushing through broken glass and gaps in the fuselage.

The water mixed with Alex's blood and turned red. And as it rose higher and higher, I reached for the door, desperate to escape, struggling to breath, but as I looked through, I could see someone holding it shut from the outside.

And then I felt the heat. It started in my belly and grew. It was like a fire, hot and sharp and soon my whole body burned. I looked at my hands, they were glowing again. My hands and arms, and soon my whole body glowed, yellow at first and then increasing in intensity until I shone bright white, like the brightest star.

And then the heat and the light overcame me, and I exploded and the water and the shit and everything around me vapourised and I was alone and floating in the air, high above the land, high above the lake.

I sat up, the hard wall behind me cool on my back. My face and hair were wet with sweat, and I'd been sick. The memory of the dream was mixed with the horrific reality, and I couldn't clear it from my mind.

I was shaking, and I knew I'd been crying.

All I could think about was Alex, and how he'd saved my life, but I'd been unable to help him.

I sat and watched the dim reflected light of the moon through the small window creep across the wall. Eventually I lay back down and drifted off, my mind filled with questions I couldn't answer...

Now unless you've ever woken up in an Italian police cell you're gonna struggle to fully appreciate how shit it was. I'm pretty sure they didn't have, at least not back then anyway, an Independent Police Complaints Commission. And I say that because it looked like anyone who had the nerve to complain about the accommodation would've found themselves thoroughly disappointed with the response they got.

Not as disappointed as me though, it's gotta be said.

It was dirty, like proper dirty. I honestly thought I'd gone back in time and was gonna find myself standing before a mediaeval court of the common pleas. I thought the guy that was here before me probably had leprosy and the one before him had simply faded away to dust.

The rats were bigger than the ones Maggie kept as pets in The Grub cellar and the bugs, I mean I use that word loosely because they didn't look like any kind of bugs I'd previously encountered, crawled up and down the walls like they were competing for a place on the Italian gymnastics' agility squad. Better quads than me, every single one of them.

But I'm making light of it aren't I. I'm painting it with a brush I made from a few fragmented memories of my own, an actual revisit many years later when compiling my 'Memoir' and scenes from Schaffner's 1973 Papillon. It was fucking horrific of course but nowhere as harrowing as a French colonialist prison at the turn of the century.

Truth is though my memory does get a little patchy when trying to recall the more traumatic episodes of my adventures. I mean, not all of them. I remember Alex getting shot in the shitter very clearly. I remember him dying, like it was this morning. There's lots more I remember in vivid high definition too, some of which I'll get to later, some I'll spare you from.

Now though, I'll get back to the nineteen-year-old English kid with no ID, no passport, an unregistered firearm, a suspicious quantity of cash and some mouldy tuna sandwiches found cruising down the middle of Lake Como in a recently stolen and very expensive motor yacht - also conspicuously close to the still smouldering ruins of a large privately owned estate destroyed during a very recent terrorist attack.

Yeah, I know.

I was so preoccupied by the Columbians that I didn't give a second thought to the idea of the Mafia, sorry I mean Carabinieri.

Anyway, here I was, my shit confiscated, my boat sanitized and returned to its owners and my anxiety levels so high I'd 'worried myself sober' if that's even a thing.

The guy with the keys was trying to convince me that I was to be hung, drawn and quartered at dawn by the sheer force of his greasy, leering face and the jangle of massive keyring. I was so beyond simple stressing, that I actually *wanted* to wind him up, to get him going. I wanted to see his eyes when I told him my mum had NEVER eaten a pizza and that Diego Maradona was a cheating cunt. But it was pointless, he just laughed at my hand gestures and carried on mocking me with his dubious clichés and very large chin.

Eventually a senior officer came to fetch me. Lurch unlocked the cell, and I followed the other guy first to the lav so I could have a luxury toilet break and freshen up and then down the hall to an interview room.

I assumed I'd be quizzed on my identity first, then on my movements and activities over the last few days. And I wasn't disappointed. At least I think I wasn't disappointed as they made absolutely no fucking effort whatsoever to allow for the language barrier. I mean none, none at all. The officer questioning me just kept repeating himself over and over again. I shrugged, over and over again, in every which way I could. So much so I began inventing new ways to shrug so he wouldn't get bored.

Lurch took me back to the cell after about four hours. I'd had nothing to eat or drink, so was a bit grumpy when he prodded me in the back of the neck with his truncheon. It was then I learned that he understood more English than I knew Italian.

There was no hope of us being friends after that. Nor of me meeting his mother and little sister.

Next day I was summoned again. Lurch led me there but kept a sensible distance this time. It was early and the sun was still low enough to be shining through the windows and straight into my eyes when I was seated. I therefore didn't immediately see the suit lounging smugly opposite me.

The officer was there again, this time plus an interpreter. I was grateful, well I would have been had his skills been a match for the chest hair that poked out the top of his shirt like an agoraphobic ferret. He introduced himself and told me I was under arrest for theft, loitering and some other bullshit to do with taking a shit in Laurel and Hardy's boat. Also, for wandering about the countryside with no ID and for my suspected involvement in the landing of a helicopter on the back lawn of the town Scout Leader / paedophile. With a smelly dead guy.

I shrugged again, my plan being to begin rotating through the 468 specific and individual shrugs I had settled upon overnight as being a true representation of the core values of the much-maligned gesture. I didn't get a chance, the suit coughed and butted in.

Rude.

"Sir, I may introduction myself to you."

I raised my eyebrows momentarily transported into an episode of Only Fools and Horses. I shrugged.

He tried again.

"I was Carlo, I am in your lawyer. You are a mine."

Jesus, he was a bit forward.

"Ok."

Carlo smiled and rubbed his hands together before looking sideways at the officer. The officer in turn looked at the interpreter who relayed the brief exchange.

The officer looked pissed and went off chattering like a monkey on speed. The interpreter bravely told me what he could be arsed to of the officer's tantrum, before standing dramatically and holding out his hand for me to shake.

"I hate Scout leader; I wish you shit on his face. Death to him."

I shook his hand, not really sure what the fuck was going on and then he left. It occurred to me later, and I have sympathy for this, I really do, that the interpreter may have, at one time in the past, maybe as a child, been invited to the Scout leader's bungalow after the meeting to see his 'scale model'. I looked from the officer to the lawyer and then back again. It was obvious that neither of them knew what was going on either.

"Can I go then?" I asked sarcastically, speculatively, without the faintest hope of it actually happening.

"You go may yes. But remain in me," Carlo was so impressed with himself I didn't have the heart to laugh at his efforts. And to be fair, they were a million times better than anything I could do. They were also clearly, relatively effective. I nodded and stood, more than a little surprised, and completely ready to be laughed at before being marched back to my cell. But that didn't happen, so I held out my hands for Lurch to remove the cuffs. Which of course he refused to do until after Carlo and the officer had finished arguing at the front desk over paper and permits and places of residence. At least that's what it sounded like to me although it could just as easily be an argument over whether pineapple should ever be seriously considered as a mainstream and acceptable pizza topping.

Which, seeing as you brought it up, I have to say; yes, it should. I mean tomato's a fruit right, so why are we discriminating?

Anyway, they eventually agreed on something and Carlo signed some forms and told Lurch to let me go. Which he did, reluctantly. I rubbed my wrists and thanked him politely, without mentioning any of his family members. And then we left.

A couple of minutes later I was out in the sunshine following Carlo across the street to his car, slightly dazed and more than a little concerned that a large part of the prisoner release process had been missed. I breathed in the air, once again reminded how clean and fresh it tasted compared to back home and the armpit-like smell of the Bellano police cells.

I looked out onto the lake for a moment before I got to the car, the last of the mist was burning off and water was coming to life with boats and ferries and all the usual water sports and stuff I was used to. I was envious, happy to be out of course but envious of the freedom these fuckers seemed to enjoy without the anxiety of being shot at. Carlo snapped me back to the moment.

He told me to get in the back seat while he put his briefcase in the boot and took his jacket off. The street was quiet but before he'd finished farting around another vehicle, a fancy metallic brown Mercedes pulled up and a couple of purposeful looking guys, one suited and one less so climbed out. I watched from the front seat as the smart one strode urgently into the police station and continued watching when he came back out and made his way directly over the zebra crossing to us.

Oh shit, what now?

I heard him talking to the lawyer for a spell before he came and opened my door.

"Out you get old chum," he said, "We're from the consulate, you need to come with us."

Now I'm a trusting soul by nature, I'll give anyone the benefit of the doubt but when a thousand miles from home without a passport or any means of looking after myself, my natural instincts to take people at their word, are somewhat suppressed. I shook my head.

"Who the fuck are you?" I mean, I'd asked the same question on the Isle of Wight, and again in Bellano and on neither occasion was I able to make sense of the answer. Nor was I able to take advantage of the information I was given.

I remained seated.

"My name's Colin Askwith, I'm from the British Consulate in Milan. It's taken me an age to get here, so now, be a good chap and jump out."

I eyed him suspiciously, wondering what the differences were in my chances of survival with him or the lawyer. Was he with the Columbians? Was he with AMOS? Was he with the British Consulate? Was he the son of a wealthy ageing novelist who spent his early inheritance and spare time chasing about the country abducting skinny, malnourished, discombobulated chavs in shell suits?

Fuck knew.

And did it even matter anymore? I mean my anxiety was past caring, it was on a break. I wasn't Jason Bourne, I wasn't going to fight my way out of anything. I had no survival skills beyond making deals and scaring school children so really, what fucking choice did I have?

"Can I see some ID?" I asked sheepishly, apologetically.

I felt angry, I was sick of this shit. I just wanted to see my mum and fall asleep on the sofa covered in coleslaw. I think he could tell, in fact I think I saw a little bit of genuine compassion on his face. He reached into his jacket and showed me his ID badge, all official looking and completely useless to me. What was I even looking for?

"Ok," I said and climbed out stiffly. He helped me, which I wasn't expecting.

"Come on old chap, we actually don't have a great deal of time," now I was out of the vehicle and in the sunshine, I could see a nervous sweat in his brow. Plus, he was looking over his shoulder and scanning the street in both directions. His colleague was now standing close to the lawyer, very close. They were talking quietly so I couldn't hear but I knew the lawyer was being told to stay still and keep quiet, that much was obvious. I'm really not sure how that made me feel. I mean, was I being kidnapped (again) or was I being saved (again).

Besides I felt a bit for My Cousin Vinny, he seemed nice.

Fuck sake.

I allowed myself to be led to the car where Askwith seated me in the back. There were snacks so I was briefly distracted. Moments later the other guy climbed in the driver's seat, and we set off. I looked out the back window to see the lawyer throwing his jacket on the ground. I had no idea what this would mean for him, although I suspected it would be more than the face value of surrendering his client / prisoner to a British diplomat.

Anyway, before I knew it we'd wound our way through the tangle of narrow town streets, pushed on up the hill and were barrelling south along the SS36. It was nice to be on the move, and when we weren't in tunnels the scenery was fantastic, mountains, twisty turny roads, big trucks threatening to smash you off into oblivion on every sharp bend. I wished at the time that I had some chat, some sparklingly clever banter I could amuse you with. Truth is though, I was exhausted. If it wasn't for the fact I could easily have been hurtling towards my untimely and untidy death I could've slept.

I didn't sleep though, it was too early in the day, instead I ate the potato chips and chocolate wafers without even checking whether they were there for me. Bollocks, it wasn't my fault, the Gestapo hadn't fed me for the best part of three days. If necessary, I'd apologise with good grace to Askwith and his butler for my misstep later. In the meantime, I was content to enjoy the sensation of a semi full belly and my hands not shaking.

We stopped for a bit after about 45 minutes on the road and Askwith went and made some phone calls. I tried to talk to the driver, but he wasn't interested, or maybe he was pissed that I'd eaten his snacks. Either way I didn't care.

When we got going again, I did nod off, sorry to say, although it didn't seem to bother the chaps up front. Eventually I woke up and saw the sun was low in the sky. The countryside was beautiful, a bit flatter now we were further south, and much greener than I imagined it might be. We passed loads of typical and very picturesque villas and houses, initially quite well spaced out. The closer we got to Milan however the denser the buildings became, to the point where there was very little green to see. My full belly of earlier was no longer enough to keep me chill.

"You have awoken" Askwith in the front.

"Yeah," I replied, nodding, a bit groggy still. "Where are we going?"

Askwith smiled to himself, Jeeves remained quiet.

"Truth be told I'm a little surprised it's taken you so long to ask."

A bit more semi suburban stuff went by.

"I was tired. And hungry."

Another smile, or smirk I couldn't decide. I wasn't as immediately drawn to this posh twat as I had been the suspiciously straight Micha. Come to think of it, the poor fella was likely gone now so I best not besmirch his name with my slanderous imaginings.

Anyway, this guy seemed a little too smug to be real. I really wasn't sure.

"So where are we going then?" I paused, "Oh and I'm sorry if I ate someone's lunch."

I caught Jeeves looking in the mirror, all I could see were his eyes though, so I had no idea if he was smiling or grimacing. No idea whether he could understand me either to be fair. Askwith turned in his seat.

"Relax old bean. I've told you, I'm from the Consulate, Karol here is my staff driver. We were notified of your predicament via the local branch of the Italian State Tourist Board. Seems word of your misadventures reached the ears of a prominent expat who felt it prudent to notify us of your presence."

"Lucky me."

"Indeed, lucky you."

"But you didn't drive all the way there for some kid caught on a misdemeanour did you."

It wasn't a question. Askwith turned back to face front and he and Jeeves exchanged looks.

"A little more than a misdemeanour wouldn't you say?"

"Maybe," shrugging again and brushing the crumbs off my absolutely filthy clothes. "But you haven't really answered my question have you."

He turned again.

"Why so suspicious? Why would you not view the intervention by your government a welcome distraction?"

He had a point and his comically raised left eyebrow knew it. I stared at him for a moment. I wasn't trying to intimidate him, what would be the point. I was just trying to see what was behind the chat, the smooth caramel of his exterior. I'd been through too many scrapes in the last few weeks not to be wary.

I shook my head.

"It would be welcome," I tried, "If it was genuine."

The eyebrow hovered, quivering slightly like a pigeon caught by the crosswind of a passing Tesco delivery truck. Askwith stared at me and then smiled again.

"You really are jumpy aren't you." he spun back round and spoke to Jeeves in Italian before he re-addressed me.

"We'll be there soon. Panic not. We're taking you to a safe house first for a debrief and a wash. Then, when we've got your documents in order, you'll be on the first plane back to your council estate."

The smug, posh dickhead.

Weird wasn't it, how quickly I felt the red mist descending nowadays. I mean back when me and big Bob were getting acquainted it took an age plus a whole shed load of button pressing. Now though, a bit of banter layered with a significant degree of deceit and dishonesty was enough to get me going. But I looked at myself, I mean I really looked. I was still hungry; I hadn't eaten properly in days. I hadn't slept either and I had no 'stuff' to help me survive out there on my own.

I was gutted. I genuinely thought if I'd made it as far as Lecco, I could have gone all the way. Instead, I'd been picked up by the trainee Agente fresh from college patrolling the lake *off duty* in his girlfriend's mom's boat. And now, here I was sitting in the back of someone's car who I was beginning to feel might cut my throat at any minute. If I'd had a plan, if I'd had someone or somewhere to go I would have given in to the rage. But I didn't. I just sat and wished for more chocolate wafers.

13: Sausage, Eggs and Aromatic Annulenes

The big roads were behind us now and it was all multiple lanes of traffic, lights, signals and noise. The car turned and turned again, in and out and through the various quarters of the city. It did occur to me that I was kinda lucky to be experiencing Italy, even if it was from such a strange perspective.

Finally, we turned into a courtyard and stopped. I clocked the gates being shut behind us just before Askwith came and opened my door.

"Out you hop matey, there's a hot meal, a shower and some clean clothes for you through here," and he marched off, far less anxious than he had been when I first met him.

I followed but kept my eyes open.

Through an open door, right down a passage, left, up a flight of stairs, left, left, right and then to a room four along from the corner. Askwith opened it and ushered me in.

"Clean bed, clean clothes. Shower is at the end of the corridor and food is downstairs, simply follow your nose."

He turned to leave but then came back.

"Oh, and best not chit chat too much with the other 'guests', there's a whole range of reasons why you're all here. And not everyone is going to be going home as soon as you, I'm afraid."

And then he was gone.

I stood for a moment and breathed in the quiet and the space I had to myself. It was glorious. He was right though, I was jumpy. I think it went back to the old dilemma: If he was genuine, Askwith, and he really was from the consulate, and I really was going home then all was good. Terry had been bullshitting me or was delusional and I was just an unlucky dickhead.

If he was lying however then it was possible, as completely mental as it sounded, that the shit Terry had told me was true.

I was jumpy, angry and confrontational because I was desperate for the former even though my rapidly evolving instincts were pointing at the latter.

I was also fucking cream crackered.

I slept well, but still wasn't ready to get up when Jeeves knocked on my door at 8:00am. I sat up as he came in and placed a few bits on the table. It was the usual stuff for a man being repatriated following a spell in a foreign jail having stolen a boat and garlic bread baguette.

He didn't say much and shut the door when he left. I'd had a shower the night before but had another one anyway, I wasn't sure when I'd get the chance again. I mean, if I was taken home, it would be back to baths or those push-on bath tap attachment showers, and we all know what they're like don't we. And if they took me into a dark alley and strangled me then I at least wanted to have a clean arse for the coroner.

Having dressed, I headed downstairs with all the bits Jeeves had left me in the bag. Askwith was waiting in the dining room, a big, old-fashioned cafeteria-style place with booths, tables and benches. There was a counter with hot food waiting and a grim looking lady with a ladle. Askwith was sat reading the paper, legs crossed like he was Prince Phillip. He looked like he'd slept well and had made time to oil his moustache.

"Morning old chap," he greeted me brightly, lowering the paper for my benefit.

Wanker.

"Morning."

"I trust you're well rested?"

"Yeah, I slept, thank you."

"You most definitely welcome old chap." Askwith then stood and nodded across the room to Jeeves who was lurking. "Now have yourself some breakfast, the eggs royale are sublime. And then Jeeves will bring you across for your debrief and to validate your documents."

He smiled down at me whilst folding his paper.

"You really have nothing to worry about. You're going home old chap, your adventures are over."

I nodded, the thought of sausages, bacon and beans filling my head. But it's funny isn't it how one thought can so fluidly lead to another. I'm not sure it did before, you know when I was just running bits back home. I mean, everyone knew I was smart, I knew it. But it was street smart wasn't it, not really people smart. I wasn't worldly wise, to coin a phrase. I couldn't read people that weren't *my* people. I couldn't plan or anticipate scenarios beyond those within which I lived. Clearly.

But now my mind was bigger. Sorry but it's the only way I can think to describe it. I could see more, I could think faster, handle multiple thoughts and likely outcomes at once. I mean I wasn't Stephen Hawking or anything and I wouldn't have been able to vocalise any of that back then, but it's true.

I know that because the thought of breakfast, and in particular sausages, lead me to thinking about home, and about him, Sausage. I momentarily wondered how he was but moved on quickly, because that wasn't why he came to mind. No, it was something he'd said to me, one of his stories.

It was the one where Scottie's tooth got wedged in his ear over the May Bank Holiday. It wasn't Scotty, or the tooth I thought of though, it was the guys, the quiet, serious team of operatives that were brought in to 'deal with' the paddies that blew the squaddies up. I had listened to Sausage as he told me that story. I'd listened because he was also describing the type of men he'd seen Zip fighting with the night he got pulled.

Quiet men.

Confident men.

Cold, purposeful men.

I looked up at Askwith and saw him. I think he saw me see him too, I think he saw it in my eyes, that realisation, that dawning of the truth. Maybe I should've, right then jumped up, whacked him with the sugar bowl that was on the table in front of me and ran for a window. I could have. I could've punched him, used the skills Freya had taught me to take him down. Maybe it would've worked, maybe I would've got to the door. I thought about it, I really did. The whole scene played out in my head as I maintained pleasant eye contact.

I didn't do any of it though did I? Of course not. I knew there were high walls, metal gates, men with guns and probably dogs. Plus, I didn't know Milan, where would I go? I knew it would be pointless, that I would be laughed at, that they'd catch me half in - half out of the window like a ferret in a letterbox. So, I sat and waited and hoped the moment would pass. And it did.

Askwith sighed.

"Anyway, I'll see you in a little while over in the lounge," and then he turned, nodded at Jeeves and was gone.

The sausages were probably nice, I don't know, I couldn't taste them. Maybe the thought that they might be my last should have enhanced their flavour, but it didn't. Was that because I was a miserable git, or because I was still considering jumping out of the window? I don't know.

I sized up Jeeves as I chewed my breakfast. He wasn't any taller than me, but he was stocky, you know, thick neck, thick hands. He didn't want to look directly at me, so I had free rein. He was wearing dark clothes, not the same as the AMOS guys but along those lines. I couldn't see a watch, but he seemed alert and capable.

Serious even.

Bollocks.

I finished my food and took my plate over to the counter before crossing the room to let Jeeves know I was ready. He looked at me as I approached. I'd expected to see hostility in his eyes, some kind of threat even. But it wasn't there. He didn't smile but it was on that side of the spectrum rather than the other. I wouldn't say he looked friendly; I mean that would be going way too far, but he didn't look like he was limbering up to choke me out either.

"You ready?"

I nodded, not sure what I was agreeing I was ready for.

"Follow me."

We left the canteen and headed back down some corridors before crossing the courtyard where we'd come in the night before. Back inside via a door opposite and some more corridors, left, left, right, blah blah blah. Eventually we entered a room with some desks, filing cabinets and old-fashioned Post-Office type paraphernalia. There was a narrow little nerd with glasses perched on the end of his nose furiously stamping what I can only assume was outgoing mail.

He stopped when he saw us.

Now this was interesting.

And strangely reassuring.

Karol spoke for me.

"This is Squidge," he turned to me with an enquiry on his face. I leaned forward and pointed to the form laid out ready on the tabletop between us and Penfold with my full name on it.

"That's me."

Karol looked down and nodded. He then looked across at the postmaster.

"Ok?"

Penfold nodded but said nothing.

"Good," Karol said to me. "I wait outside. Come when you are finished and we go across," he pointed at a space in the corner of the room I assumed to be representative of somewhere else back across the compound. Which made me giggle a bit if I'm honest, a nervous, childish laugh.

I mean we all do it don't we. When you're telling someone, you've got the dentist a week next Thursday at 11, you look at your watch like it's somehow got a week next Thursday on it. And then when you tell your careers advisor in Clapham that your friend's sister's boyfriend has family in Goa, you point vaguely in the direction you think Goa might be. Like they can see it from there, like maybe if they stood on a chair and squinted they'd actually be able to see the palm trees.

Ridiculous.

Karol seemed to think so too. Or maybe he thought I was ridiculous, not sure. Anyway he turned and left me with Penfold and together we spent a thrilling 40 minutes filling in forms and writing my name. He made me stand against the wall whilst he took a small Polaroid which he then laminated onto the inside page of my temporary, 'diplomatic' passport.

Not sure about that word, 'diplomatic'. I mean in this context. That's what Penfold called it but its real meaning took me somewhere else. You see it has its origins in official and significant text and documents, however its meaning and use has evolved to represent a set of negotiating principles or behaviour aimed at not upsetting people. So, it's kinda rich to apply it to anything associated with me, my documentation, my travel plans and my most recent activities.

I'll just leave that there for you, it's not important, but it did make me chuckle.

Eventually Penfold was done. He handed me the relevant bits before shaking my hand and wishing me well. He was kind of pasty, but I liked him, he was probably just iron deficient. Plus, he had not asked anything of me beyond that demanded by his role. Which was pleasantly refreshing.

He led me to the door and opened it to reveal Karol on the other side just finishing a cheese and cucumber sandwich. This surprised me because I didn't have him down as a cucumber man. Penfold nodded at us both and then shut the door, pretty sure he would've had some of Karol's sandwich if I wasn't there, plus if I wasn't mistaken, he looked quite keen to get back to his pile of outgoing mail.

Karol finished chewing, at length.

"You have everything?"

"Yeah, I think so," I gestured to the bag in my hand.

"Good. Come," and he was off again, brushing crumbs from his clothes as he went.

Back the way we came, back out into the courtyard and this time to a vehicle that was sat waiting. It wasn't the same one we'd arrived in but at least it was a car and not a windowless van.

"We go Consulate now," Karol gestured to the front passenger seat.

I climbed in and put the bag between my legs. He jumped in next to me and started the engine. We made our way through the gate and guards and then we were out on the street. It was still rush-hour, with loads of busy Italians preoccupied with the commute. The roads were full of traffic, but it seemed to be moving, at least better than the cliches would suggest. And there were tons of pedestrians too, all walking to and fro. It was ridiculous but even after my night's sleep, the shower, the food, and the time spent with Penfold getting my paperwork in order, I was still plotting an escape strategy. I was pleased it was busy out, it would make abducting me harder. This plus I'd yet to have a shit so was significantly heavier than I might have been.

Karol wove in and out, heading all the time towards the centre of the city. The buildings got bigger and the roads narrower until after about 25 minutes we pulled into a barriered entrance. He showed the guard some ID and told him something that sounded important before the guard lifted the barrier and we moved on inside. It was only then, once we were actually inside the compound that I realised where we were, the actual British fucking Consulate. And I say this but even then, I was making assumptions. I mean, there may have been a Morris Minor parked in the corner and a gent with a bowler hat and umbrella taking afternoon tea at a small white table in the middle of the courtyard, but I was still nervous. It wasn't until I saw the signs and the flag and whatnot that I knew I was safe.

And the relief that came over me was intense, like proper debilitating. I was glad Karol kept the vehicle moving for another few moments because I'm not sure I would have been able to walk. I felt like crying, seriously. I embarrassed to say that because I'd probably had a fucking holiday compared to whatever Danny was going through, compared to what Alex went through, bless his soul, but it was true, I felt like crying.

When the car stopped, I climbed out and Karol led me into the building via a grand old entrance off the rear of the courtyard. It looked like it had been there a lot longer than the British Government had wanted it for a consulate. We signed in just inside the door and then did the whole corridor, left, right, left, corridor, left, right, right thing. We gradually moved through the complex from the 'back of house', or 'shit' areas into the posh and well looked after bits. Karol knew where he was going, so I just followed and basked in the feeling of being at home, away, like a thousand miles away but still, kind of at home, in a legal sense.

We met with Askwith in a plush lounge, just like he said we would, all big windows looking out onto a grand square, big curtains and bookshelves filled with dusty, unread pornography. The furniture looked like it cost more than Mad Rufus' entire stash and the carpets had clearly been handmade by albino pygmies in the farthest reaches of Papua New Guinea, back before that kind of thing was frowned upon. There was even the stuffed head of a big ass deer on the wall and I was surprised not to see Askwith smoking an arm sized cigar, foot up on back of his kneeling man servant with a 12 gauge shotgun casually draped across his right shoulder.

14: The Whisky Drinker

He was actually sitting in a modest, Swedish designed office chair sorting through his morning at the desk. He looked up and smiled.

"Ah, welcome chaps," he seemed happy, then shouted: "GLORIA.... GLORIA, CAN I GET COFFEE FOR THREE PLEASE? OH, AND SOME OF THOSE DELIGHTFUL CHOCOLATE WAFER BISCUITS TOO?"

Gloria was either a long way away or dead. Either way if she didn't hear him someone else would and I was confident we'd all soon have beverages. I also noted the request for chocolate wafers and felt an *underwhelming* wave of remorse at having noshed them all the day before.

"Sit, please," he pushed his papers to one side and gestured to the seats in the centre of the room. He then came round and sat opposite me, with a disinterested looking Karol to his right.

"Good breakfast?" he enquired.

I nodded, feeling a measure of remorse at my earlier hostility, albeit I knew I was so crap at being threatening he wouldn't have noticed.

"Splendid."

Really? Who the fuck said 'Splendid' anymore?

"Ok, so here is your itinerary," he handed me a typewritten sheet. It was strange, of course I'd never been repatriated before, but I was sure the holidaymakers who dropped their documents whilst parasailing overactive volcanoes were not given an itinerary laying out their journey step by step from the Consulate to the front door of their 3 bed semi. I scanned it and the hairs on my neck stood on end.

"Why so much detail?" I enquired before I could stop myself.

Askwith looked at me, his pigeon eyebrow quivering as it soared majestically above his face. He said nothing for a moment and then glanced sideways at Karol. He in turn stood and went to shut the door just as Gloria came stumbling through with a tray.

"Sorry Mr Askwith, the kettle was on strike."

Gloria staggered around the room avoiding furniture as best she could before dropping the tray from waste height onto the coffee table between us. She was 146 years old if she was a day, and so wrinkled she made the average elephant scrotum look like polished plate glass.

Askwith thanked her and Karol guided her firmly out of the room before shutting the door.

"Almost entirely without merit, seriously, no redeeming features at all. However, she's been here since Mussolini himself was in short trousers so unfortunately we're stuck with her."

"Not for much longer I'd hazard," again, before I could stop myself.

Askwith smiled.

Karol came back and cleaned up the coffee that had splashed across the furniture whilst Askwith pressed on.

“Right. Now at the risk of telling you things that may, unintentionally place you at peril I should perhaps divulge one or two pieces of critical intelligence. In the interests of engendering peace of mind.”

The wafers, at least the ones not swimming in coffee, looked amazing.

“As no doubt you keep telling yourself ‘You are just a kid from an estate’ blah, blah, blah. No?”

I didn't answer but I also wasn’t sure if I fancied a wafer anymore.

“But unless you really are debilitatingly thick, which I have to confess has been a serious concern of mine at times, you will have begun to pick up on the basic fact that there is more to your story.”

Askwith crossed his legs and picked up his coffee. He sipped it noisily.

“Maybe.” I offered weakly. Fuck sake, here we go again.

“You, due to circumstances far beyond your current comprehension *and* control, are of interest to one or two, shall we say, ‘committed parties’.”

He seemed to like that phrase. I didn’t.

“Why?” I didn't fancy the coffee now either. “Why can’t you just send me home?”

"Oh, I can, I can. And indeed, I will," he placed the cup down and fidgeted a bit. Karol remained impassive. Askwith went on;

"But before I do I feel duty bound to arm you with one or two little gems of pertinence."

Karol frowned, perhaps 'pertinence' was too far even for him.

Askwith stood and paced a little before eventually settling on the corner of his desk.

"Your father..."

I rolled my eyes and felt the tension immediately return to my shoulders. Fuck sake.

Askwith saw but pushed on regardless.

"Your father was a colleague of mine, of sorts, a very dear and deeply missed colleague. As you may or may not already be aware he worked for British Intelligence on a number of very, how shall we say, 'dark' projects. That's not to say of course that he only moved in the shadows. No, by all means he was a valuable diplomatic asset and well respected, despite the tattoos on his hands." Askwith smiled as he saw that one land.

But it did land, didn't it. It was like stepping into a warm room after having been outside in the snow.

"He was a dear friend." Askwith repeated.

I looked up at him, glad to hear a little gravel in his voice. He went on;

"Thing is old chap, when you are so well respected, and he really was, you attract a degree of unwanted, perhaps unwarranted attention. And not just from those who would traditionally be described as hostile. You see there are those within the company, within other similar companies too, with special skills and access to 'things', like him, like me, who serve, and do so, loyally for life. Then, of course there are those with similar skills that serve only for a time before they fade heroically into the wallpaper, perhaps with a small dog on their lap and a glass of quality single malt on an occasional table next to them."

He stood and started pacing.

"But then, and this really is the crux, and would perhaps explain your presence here with me and my good chum, there are those who serve only for a time before the call of enterprise provides too great a temptation. These fellows, as human as they unavoidably are, represent, unfortunately, our greatest concern. You see enterprise, and the world of corporations and finance and distant, let's face it; oblivious shareholders have no place meddling in the affairs of state."

"And yet they do," Karol said quietly in the gap.

I looked at him and saw something on his face. Was it anger? Was it sorrow? Was it a little milk froth from the frankly lovely cappuccino we'd all just had? Gloria. Who knew!

Anyway, I looked back at Askwith having noted Karol's thing.

"And yet they do." Askwith himself looked at Karol and I could see an exchange of something. They'd clearly been together for some time, perhaps they'd shared more than coffee and long drives into the countryside.

"So, it transpires over time that interested parties evolve into political and financially motivated 'cells'. These 'cells' as we refer to them, are regrettably nearly always threaded through with those that once served. Less of the whisky drinker, and more of the action man type, if you get my meaning."

I think I did. Fit, capable, big watches?

"And with knowledge gained during a period working under the umbrella of their respective state sponsored intelligence agencies they represent a unique and worrisome threat."

"But aren't there rules? Like, this must be...." I felt a bit of an idiot, I didn't really have the words. "Was my Dad one of these action men?" I was remembering his watch.

Askwith shook his head.

"No, he most definitely was not. And yes, there are rules, a great many in fact, complex and well-constructed pieces of legislation. However, for rules to be effective there has to be a potential for policing them, if not all, then at least some of the time."

"Was he a whisky drinker then?"

Karol shifted in his seat.

Askwith looked pained.

"I would like to think he may have been, had he been given the chance."

I nodded. The warm room feeling lingering.

"So, rules. You see, policing the masses is easy, relatively, within your own demise. You set the rules, you enforce the rules. You have peace and accord. However policing organisations that straddle borders and who claim no real sovereignty is a tad trickier. Plus, it somewhat goes without saying that some of these 'interested parties' are in themselves agents of the state. It's like they operate with the soul public interest of financial gain, albeit cloaked heavily behind power plays of intricacy and skill. But ultimately, somewhere along the line there are nation sponsored agendas being scurrilously pursued."

I wasn't confused, not really. I knew what he was saying. I just couldn't understand why I was in the fucking room.

"So how to police another sovereign state, who claims to be a friend via all the usual and well-established means but who is also working furiously behind closed doors to frankly pull down your trousers and spank your bare bottom?"

"Tricky."

The eyebrow again.

"Indeed. Tricky." Askwith settled again on the corner of the desk. I noticed then, having grown accustomed to his tone and voice, his physical presence. He was smart, of course, and perhaps a little old fashioned. I'd seen that straight away, when he snatched me from My Cousin Vinny. He was also slim and deceptively younger than his pompous vocab and manner might indicate. His moustache was defo Captain Peacock even though I suspected he saw himself as Magnum PI, but actually, under the brown corduroy jacket he was quite fit looking. His hands too, they didn't look like they played the piano much.

"Look, as much as I can see you enjoying this discourse, your plane," and now he looked at his watch, a big, fancy watch, "will be wheels up in a little over three hours. I will therefore cut to the chase."

I nodded, once again unsettled.

"Your dear father, *my friend,* was a valuable asset. He was 'significant' and therefore of 'significant' interest to said parties, all of them as it turns out."

"Who are these 'parties'?" not really wanting to know the answer.

"Good question, and one I'll answer quickly, time is slipping. First," pulled down the index finger of his left hand with the index finger of his right, "and most importantly, is his own government. Of which I was and still am, a loyal servant. It's rather complicated dear fellow but suffice to say your father was looking to distance himself from some of the less pleasant aspects of his duties. His employers, which I am most definitely not, I was always just a colleague and a friend, were less than inclined to permit this."

He pulled down his middle finger.

"Two. An international privately owned security concern operating under the moniker of AMOS, or Associated something, something, I don't know, it bores me. Again, suffice to say they wanted to 'employ' your father beyond his service, in the pursuit of various, less than socially responsible activities."

He paused as he considered his next sentence.

"And three?" I looked at him, and then at Karol.

Askwith checked his watch again and then cleared his throat.

"Yes, and three. Ok." he straightened his jacket and then pulled down the third finger of his right hand. "Three. Is another privately owned and suspiciously well-funded outfit. They go by the name of Six and whilst maintaining many of the aforementioned qualities and characteristics remain our greatest concern. At present."

"Who are they?"

Karol shifted in his seat again.

Askwith smiled.

"People with whom we sincerely hope you do not have occasion to spend time."

I shook my head.

"But why would I? Why would any of these fuckers want me?" And then it all crashed in on me. Danny, Terry's men 'watching' my mum. Big Dean, the Sausage, Alex and the helicopter. Bob the giant.

"Have they got Danny?" I stood anxiously. Karol rose to his feet slowly, warily.

"Now calm down old chap." Askwith, hands out placating me. "There's lots more I can tell you, but we must be prudent."

"Prudent? What the fuck does that mean?" I'd forgotten about the wafers now.

"It means you are needed at home, as I believe you have yourself come to realise. And as I say, your plane will be wheels up in too short a time."

I was breathing heavily. I was anxious, angry even. Not with Askwith, not with even Gloria. But fuck. What was going on?

"Where is Danny?"

Askwith studied me for a moment.

"We are your friends Matthew, really we are."

I was a little taken aback that he used my real name but pressed on.

"Who has my little brother?" my voice was lower, calmer. But I felt a rage building.

"For the moment at least, we believe Six has him. At first, we thought AMOS but after Bellano we're not so sure."

I shook my head. This was mental, proper mental.

"For the *moment?* What does that mean? What are you doing about it? Who the fuck are you anyway?"

"We are taking you home, that's what we are doing. We're keeping you safe and taking you home."

I thought about that for a moment. It actually made sense, sort of. But it also felt like a hand job when what I paid for was a blow job.

"But that means nothing. Terry was doing that."

"Terry?"

Oh shit.

"Yeah, Terry Carter, Maggie and George's son."

Askwith shook his head.

"Sorry old chap but there is no Terry. Maggie and George Carter did have a son, yes, he was friends with your father, they joined up together, very close I believe. Sadly, however our Terry Carter met with a rather messy end whilst deployed with the UN in the Balkans in 1991. Terrible business really. I don't think they ever really got over it."

What. The. Fuck.

Karol coughed.

"Yes. Of course. Listen, Matthew, you really need to make tracks. You asked me why your itinerary was so detailed, and I have told you. Undoubtedly you are going to have more questions, that is only proper. However, sadly, your presence here, at this time is less than ideal whereas your presence at home, with your mother, is, at present, essential. Can we leave it at that for the time being? Put a pin in it?"

My god I could feel my guts churning. The rage was still there but now it was mixed with fear. Really, I was scared. I'd never admitted that to myself before. I knew what was happening, the details were vague, cloudy and fucking weird but I knew what I was facing, even if I didn't know why.

"Ok." I didn't have anything else. Well, that's not strictly true, I had plenty. But we didn't have time and I was aware my stress would only grow the longer we talked about it.

Askwith held out his hand, he clearly wanted to impress upon me his good intentions. Personally, I wouldn't have completely believed Jesus at that point, but I was backed into a corner of necessity.

"I have no doubt that you are finding it increasingly difficult, daily I'm sure, to trust what you are told. This is demonstrably evident, but it is not without cause, so you have some sympathy."

Demonstra what??

"But I would ask Matthew, that you try, and find a space to think, to work your way through your thoughts and, in a quieter moment, perhaps the memories you have of your father, and of your childhood. Perhaps there you will find something to anchor you, something to steady your ship?"

It was a curious way of putting it, but it made sense. It was a nice thing to say.

I nodded and shook his hand. It was strong and his grip was warm. I think I too wanted to part with having left a good impression. At least better than the one I left the two hairy old Italians whose boat I soiled.

"Take care Matthew."

Karol was already moving across the room, with my bag in his hand. Cheeky bastard.

"Thank you," I said before turning and leaving the room quickly. I didn't look back, that would've been wet.

Behind me I heard:

"GLORIA WOULD YOU BE SO GOOD AS TO POP THROUGH AND CLEAN UP THIS GOD-AWFUL MESS PLEASE!?"

15: Guns and Roses

Back down the corridor and into the shit area again. Left, right etc, etc and then boom we were out into the daylight of the courtyard. Karol made straight for the car whilst I lingered a moment to take in my last of Milan. Mum would be so proud; I mean, I couldn't fucking tell her anything of course, but she would have been if she knew. I'd been to Italy, who'd of thought.

I was feeling good as well. My legs, my lungs, even my hair was looking good, I'd noticed in the mirror that morning. And the clothes I was wearing felt good, comfy you know, and decent quality. My body had filled out and my skin was a healthy shade of skin colour, rather than the grey death of northeast London.

So, I was feeling good, and I was looking forward to seeing mum, of course I was. But behind that I couldn't help feeling a bit depressed at returning to the estate, the kebabs, the numbness that came over me when I was on the bus or doing my deals, or just looking out the window. Lake Como at dusk was a far cry from dirty carpets, Babestation on mute and goat meat pittas.

But mum needed me didn't she, so I had to go. Plus, Askwith said my presence there was 'essential'. Maybe this was to do with Danny. Maybe me being there would focus attention, maybe the police had made progress, maybe I could make progress. Something I clearly wasn't doing now.

"You come Squadge?"

I smiled, fucking dickhead. But I went anyway and climbed in next to him.

"It's Matthew by the way."

He nodded and handed me a business card.

"This Giles, friend of Cubby," he pointed to the number. "He will help if need, a very good friend." I assumed the Cubby he referred to was Wooster back there. Karol wasn't finished. He turned the card over in my hand.

"And this Stanislas, my wife brother, brother. He very good man, lots of good connection, many cars. He help too if need."

Christ.

"Right. Shit. Thanks." I was grateful, don't get me wrong. I mean I was happy to be 'connected'. It's just, I wasn't sure how useful these dodgy sounding fuckers were likely to be. Giles sounded like he could help me buy a county if I had the funds, and the other fella Staisbob or whatever was defo a Russian gangster. 100% he wore a leather jacket and shiny slip-ons.

At that point I'd rather have had Karol himself.

He took the card back off me and wrote another number on the back.

"This me," he said, handing it back. I nodded, a little choked to be fair.

"Thank you."

"Call international, I answer," patting me on the shoulder.

A few moments later we were back out on the street, ducking and diving and weaving in and out. I guessed this was just the way, although it did occur to me that this way of driving might have been necessary, based upon my very 'detailed' itinerary.

The traffic was lighter now everyone was at work, so we made good progress through the city to the SS36.

I saw signs for the airport, it looked to be about 40k to the northwest of the centre so I settled in for the drive. Karol stopped after about twenty minutes for fuel and snacks and then we were off again. I glanced at the sheet and noted his compliance with the itinerary. It settled me, I was finally getting on a plane. I had some onion rings and nodded off.

When I woke, we were pulling into another barriered entrance with a guard post booth in the centre. Karol leaned out and spoke to the guard who looked like Mr Bean and handed over some documents. Looking through the chain link fence I could see military and civilian aircraft along with all the usual gubbins, fuel trucks, baggage wotsits etc. There was a bit of movement but generally it was quiet. Not what I'd expected at all.

Pretty soon, having had a good old butchers at me Mr Bean let us through. I didn't mind really; I was flattered and I wasn't gonna judge. Karol drove on through and began winding his way across the vast plot to our spot. Now I was going to use the word rendezvous there, but it sounded a bit poncy, so I dropped back off to my default. Might save it for later though. If that's ok.

Anyway, it was another couple of minutes before we pulled up in front of huge fucking hanger, like massive. I mean, it was just like in those movies where rockstars or politicians use private jets to sneak here and there at the speed of light. I'd fully assumed they'd put me on a commercial flight, you know holidaymakers, kids, writers doing a bit of research for their second novel, a much harder sell than the first and a lot harder to get down, so I've been told.

But no, it was U2 and Guns and Roses for me. Fuck, this was amazing. Would there be champagne and little packets of nuts on board? My own personal TV, deep pile carpets and a freakishly long legged, blonde hostess desperate for me to notice her and offer her some 9-mile-high overtime?

Karol switched the engine off and turned to me.

"You wait. I check."

I nodded, thinking about the nuts and what, if any, magazines they might have on board...

"Ok." It wasn't worth the effort to correct his English.

He got out and walked over before disappearing through the single door on the side of the slightly battered green metal wall.

Then it occurred to me.

Never mind the nuts, what was I actually going to tell Mum? I couldn't tell her about the Isle of Wight, she'd be really fucking hurt. She knew I'd gone off looking for Danny, but she didn't know about the wooden door in Wroxall, she'd be pissed at that. It's not like I could tell her about Bellano either could I. I mean, what would I say? How could I explain the stuff that happened, the stuff I was told. About Dad, and the army and shit. And then there was the police station, Alex, Freya, if that was actually her name. Fuck I couldn't tell her anything, not even about Captain Peacock.

And how long had I been gone? I counted on my fingers, 4, 5, 6, 7. Shit, it was getting on for eight weeks, or was it nine. Never mind Danny disappearing, fuck, I had disappeared. For eight, no nine weeks. She'd he loopy by now poor cow, seriously, she'd be in bits.

Suddenly I was anxious again. Anxious to see her, to give her a hug. I'd need to have a fucking good sort out when I got back to the flat, I knew that. No doubt the flat would be full of stray cats and fag butts and stacks of unopened parking fines. I wanted to show her my scars, bollocks no I couldn't do that. But I wanted to see her. I needed to tell her it was going to be alright.

Shit.

Fuck, where's that lump gone?

I looked out of the window but there was no sign. In fact, there was no one, and crucially no bird either. I mean, was that what they called planes as well or did that only refer to helicopters? Whatever, he was taking his sweet time. He was probably having a sneaky sandwich, bastard.

I waited another couple of minutes and then thought, fuck it, I'm going in. I got out, put my bag across my shoulders and made sure the car was locked. Karol had left the keys in the ignition, so I took them too. And then I made my way over to the door he'd gone through.

It was a grey day but there was no wind, so I listened at the door before I opened it. I'm not really sure why, now I say it. I mean after the business card and phone numbers and the trip to the actual fucking airport with Mr Bean and the promise of a private jet, I'm not sure what I didn't trust about it all. But there was something.

Maybe it was just that instinct thing again, the same one that saw me reach adulthood alive with all my fingers and toes. I mean it wasn't unusual on the estate to see lads hobbling about if you know what I mean. And lots of reasons for it too, some due to interactions with a certain kebab dispensing family business, some because they just couldn't keep them to themselves. Mad Rufus was well known for it, it was like a calling card. But both Danny and I had all our digits and I guess that counted for something.

But I couldn't hear anything so just thought fuck it and went on in, I mean, what's the worst that could happen?

I tried to open my eyes, but they were stuck shut. So much so I honestly thought I was dead. And then I heard noises and realised my hands could move. I probably wasn't dead then. I brought them up to my face and felt something sticky.

Bollocks this can't be good.

The sounds were a little way off so sitting up slowly I gently wiped and scratched at whatever was on me until I was able to see.

It wasn't properly dark, but it was gloomy, you know, like I was in someone's garage with the door half down. Not that I'd ever had occasion to be in that kind of scenario.

No sir, not me.

Anyway, I scanned around and shit my pants. Not literally, and not like Alex either bless him. No, I looked and saw and realised that I definitely wasn't a rockstar. Bono didn't wake to find himself laying in a pool of someone else's blood. Blood that has only recently poured, probably, from the massive hole in the back of his new friend's head. I mean, I say that, but I've heard the Joshua Tree tour got a bit tasty at times...

Anyway, Karol lay three of four feet from me. He was properly dead, there was no mistaking it. And I'd been laying literally face down in a lake, not the slightest bit of an exaggeration here, a LAKE of his blood. I was red from head to toe, my new clothes fucked, my chances of hoping on the 10:55am BA3242 bound for Gatwick fucked with them. My bag was gone, as were the car keys. As were any hopes I may still have had of seeing my poor old Mum today.

I sat up properly and looked at Jeeves. He looked like such a sad, discarded piece of litter it made my heart ache. And I know that sounds wet as fuck, but I can't lie. Him and Alex, they'd been good to me. Alex was obviously slightly higher on that list on the basis he actually saved, or at the very least prolonged my life whereas Karol here, God rest his soul gave me his phone number. But still, they were both heroes. And they didn't deserve to die protecting me. Especially not Karol here, he was ugly, no offence intended, and possibly, on balance and based upon today's information, one of the good guys. Not that Alex wasn't good, it's just he was really handsome and possibly, again based upon today's information, working for the bad guys. Or one of the groups that fell into the 'bad guys' category.

God it was complicated.

And yet it wasn't, was it.

Karol was dead and I was fucked. That's actually pretty simple.

The sounds grew louder and then some lights came on. I blinked while my eyes adjusted. I must've been a fucking sight, covered in blood, like something out of a Hammer Horror. But it wasn't funny was it, because these fuckers, whoever they were had killed Jeeves and scuppered any plans I may have had for returning home and paying Mums parking fines.

Who were they?

Was it AMOS again? Was it Six? Was it the fuckers that took Arnie's daughter in Commando? I think they were bin men, weren't they? I looked up but couldn't really see anyone. But then one of them spoke.

"Hello Squidge," and it was a voice I thought I knew. It had an accent I recognized, and it was low and kind of gruff.

Whilst I held my hand up to shield my eyes there was a jangle of keys and the squeaking of a metal door and then a figure stepped in a bit closer, into the light.

"Hello Squidge," again.

Oh fuck.

Bob the giant.

Was I dreaming? Not sure.

Was I tripping? Most likely.

Fuck it was hot. I was sweating, I knew that, regardless of my state of consciousness. And I stank as well, like really. Worse than poor Alex had when his insides fell out. I had been asleep, I knew that. I'd dreamt of mid-range socket sets and of flying off a cliff strapped to one of those stupid microlight wotsits made of Micha's floral shirt and a massive garlic bread baguette. Skinny Mitch's mums' cat was there too, just staring at me, all hostile and cat-like.

And I'd seen Mum, and Danny and we'd all stood in the kitchen at the flat and talked about our days.

We did that you know, on the regular. It was one of the things I was a bit proud of. One of the things I really missed. Pretty sure none of my smackhead mates did anything like that.

I saw mum as she was now too, or at least I thought it was mum. But then I realised it wasn't, it couldn't be. She was too smart, too clean and *together*. She wasn't sitting in the flat, quietly going out of her mind, smoking and chewing her gums. Instead, she was smartly dressed, hair brushed, and travelling. I couldn't make out where she was going but it felt strange, not just seeing her like that, but also because it was so real, so clear, so immediate.

I came too, groggy and with a dry mouth.

I sat up. Again, it wasn't dark, there was light coming in through small round windows along the wall in front of me. I stared at them for a few minutes trying to understand why they were there, in that way, all in a row. And then I realised I couldn't hear anything.

Shit.

They must've hit me so hard I'd gone deaf. I've heard of that happening, you know, when people have a shock or some kind of trauma and they go grey overnight or lose their hearing or start speaking fluent Welsh. I wondered for a moment why they'd hit me. And then I wondered whether being deaf was worse than being blind, or worse than being Welsh. I was very confused. But it was bollocks wasn't it because when I reached up, I realised I actually had earplugs in and headphones on over the top. I wasn't deaf at all.

I looked at the windows again and then turned my head and saw a matching set on my side of the building and then I worked out why I had earmuffs on. It was to stop the sound of the aircraft preventing me from sleeping.

THE AIRCRAFT?!?

I tried to stand but smacked my head and back on all sorts of metal and shit behind me.

Fuck. Shit. Bollocks.

I looked around and saw pallets of stuff covered with green netting, all strapped into place with heavy duty webbing. And bare bench seats along the edges with shit loads of equipment hanging and strapped in above. Also, three or four rucksacks hanging opposite me which I guessed were parachutes but only after the event. Definitely a military plane, or at the very least a commercial cargo carrier. Now I felt rather than heard the rumble of the engines at the same time as I saw Karol's body laying untidily in the corner next to the chemical toilet. He was wrapped of course so no leakage, but I realised, or rather hoped he was the source of the smell rather than me.

Which made me feel bad.

I sat back down.

What the fuck was going on?

Where was I?

I wasn't on my way to Crawley; I was pretty sure of that. I mean, how would they explain the dead guy sausage over there by the shitter to UK Customs. Plus, it felt like a long time since I'd woken with Big Bob in my face. I tried to look out of the window but the chains they had me on were not long enough. Fuck it.

I sat down and started counting rivets.

It was a bit later, sorry, I don't know how else to write that, was it hours, days, I'm not sure. I'd got up to 2343 rivets. Some of those were 'assumed rivets', due to there being objects in the way but being based upon what was before and after, I was pretty confident. Let's call it; predictive rivet reasoning.

Anyway, a lot of rivets later the plane began to descend, I felt it and the engine vibrations changed and pretty soon the whole sensation was different as we prepared to land. It was a good landing, I think. Certainly, smoother than in the helicopter but I didn't really have a lot else to compare it to.

At length the plane came to a stop and the engines were turned off. I took my earmuffs off and removed the plugs and let me tell you what an absolute pleasure that was. I hadn't known it at the time, but I was pretty sure my head was about to explode. The relief was wonderful and put me, despite all that was apparently stacked against me, in a great mood. I mean I could've murdered a bowl of Frosties or a cheese and pickle sandwich but other than that I was on top of the world.

A few minutes later there were boots and voices and whining and grinding as doors opened and men came and went. Someone popped in and collected Karol with a sack truck, you know, like the draymen use to deliver crates of Budweiser, which I've gotta say I found particularly distasteful. No, more than distasteful, actually I found it really upsetting. He looked like a roll of fucking carpet draped across the bottom. My mood darkened quite a bit then.

But then Bob appeared, and I cheered right up.

Why? You ask. Surely that should have had the opposite effect? No?

Well, no, and here I confess a degree of smugness, which as you'll know is most unlike me. He had a few, how shall I say, 'marks' on his face. And when I say 'marks' I mean scars, gross lumps and a frankly disturbingly weird looking nose. Oh, and one or two gaps in his teeth for good measure. I mean, my smugness was measured closely against a sliding scale. You know, like did my beating enrage him so much, that he killed Karol just because, you know, he's a cunt? Cause if that was so then fuck me I felt like shit. But on the other hand, if Karol was always gonna go, God rest his soul and my beating could be seen as a bit of proactive, before the fact, in your pocket kind of, retribution, then great, happy days even!

But I wasn't sure. I really wasn't.

But I also didn't think it mattered. They had me. I was alone, no one to turn to, no idea what I was involved in really, and at the same time in possession of all the information I needed to scare the living shit out of me. They could do whatever they wanted now couldn't they. There weren't any cliffs to jump off, there weren't any boats to steal, or wafers to eat. At least I assumed there wasn't, come to think about it, where the fuck was I?

I looked at Bob and he smiled.

"Welcome to South Africa, Squidge. Welcome to Johannesburg."

Oh bollocks.

16: Roy Keene

I was helped into the back of a van by a man/woman called Gerth. Massive, hairy and with frankly biblical BO. But I was glad of the help because I was far from agile, I felt like an old man. Looking out the windows I saw a few others climbing into various vehicles and then we were off, a lovely little convoy of murdering ex-military psychos and a bewildered south London chav.

As crap as I felt I couldn't help looking out of the rear windows as we made our way from the airport, which seemed to be on the outskirts of a large built-up area, out into the sticks. It wasn't particularly hilly at first although I caught glimpses of hills or mountains in the distance. I tried taking to the driver, a black guy who I quickly named Mick, just because. But he either wasn't interested or couldn't understand me.

I persevered for a bit, telling him about my Mum and then that time I stole a lad's bike from outside John Menzies on the High Street but returned it when I realised it was actually a girls bike and I couldn't have sold it for any more than a fiver.

I felt shit, pinching a kid's bike, which he'd probably borrowed off his little sister just to then throw it in the canal. That's why I took it back.

Anyway, he never came back for it, I think it's still there now, even if John Menzies isn't. In hindsight I should've just let Mike the Bike have it for the twenty B&H he offered me.

Oh well you live and learn.

But Mick here wasn't interested. Not at all. Just rude.

Hey, no big loss though, he had a number 16 Roy Keane Man United shirt on so probably wouldn't have had anything sensible to say.

Eventually I gave up, sat back and tried to enjoy a road trip through the South African countryside, or bush as they call it in Australia. I know that from watching Neighbours. And I'm aware that Australia and South Africa are in different counties. Just thought you'd be impressed. Shit, whatever.

And on that, I mean, if I survived what stories I could tell right? The Isle of Wight, Lake Como, helicopters, boat's, jets and now South Africa. Fantastic. The grandchildren would love it. Yes, apart from all the killing that is. Yes, fantastic stories apart from my kidnapped brother, lies, conspiracies, international intrigue and all the dead people.

But still, South Africa, right?

Yay.

But it was beautiful, I mean once we got out of town, and it opened up. The hills, the fields, the colour, was amazing. And the sky, it was huge, like fucking huge, unlike anything else I can describe. And the air tasted so different, at least what I could taste coming in the open window at the back. It tasted of burnt earth, flowers and trees and maybe a little bit of poo. No, actually quite a lot of poo. But that was ok, it wasn't entirely unpleasant.

And it was sunny too, in October. At least I think it was October. I mean it was when I'd left on my little train. So that didn't make sense. Right so I found Danny's half eaten bananas on September 14th or possibly the 15th. It doesn't matter, the thing is; that was a couple of weeks before I jumped off the cliff both physically and metaphorically (another one for the word bag). I then spent a few weeks 'asleep' as the lovely Freya put it.

Bless the lovely Freya.

And then another five, no six weeks in Bellano waiting for, arguing with and 'escaping' from Terry, or whatever the fuck his name was - Arther, Gavin, Miguel, whatever. Another few days then with Lurch, My Cousin Vinny and finally Wooster. And all that before these lovely chaps thought to shoot my driver in the face and then include me on their summer vacation to THE OTHER SIDE OF THE FUCKING WORLD.

So basically, it was about November or maybe early December. And it was sunny so that was fucked up. Not that I was complaining, I mean let's be honest I didn't have a scooby what to expect so I'd just have to get on with it wouldn't I? Might actually get a tan though. I mean if I was to be buried in a shallow grave in just my underpants at least I'd look a bit better than I would've this time last year. Good enough for the worms anyway.

We drove for about three hours with a short piss break halfway. Mick didn't get out of the van when we stopped, pretty sure he was part camel, but I was busting. I was busting again when we arrived at the house and hungry too. But that's ok cause they took me through and locked me in a back room with no food or water for another three hours the very moment we got there.

Finally, someone brought a tray of food and some water. I've no idea what the food was, I think I blocked it out in favour of avoiding starvation. It was gone in seconds, as was the water and then I felt sick. But I wasn't sick, I sat myself in the corner and tried to focus on forgetting where I was, the massive hole that was in the back of Karol's head and the way they had casually picked him up and took him off the plane.

It got dark quickly, and I fell asleep, but it was shit. I dreamt of Alex and Karol and Bob the giant. He was chasing them down a corridor towards a kitchen. The corridor walls were made of crumpets, the floor pastry and the kitchen, when we got there was an authentic historical replica of ancient Troy, albeit with a modern kitchen worktop and appliances. When he caught them, he picked them up with a giant pair of tongs and dropped them into a food mixer. Then he switched it on and mashed them up to a paste which he used to make a sandwich. As hard as I tried, I couldn't look away, my hands were cable tied behind my back to a water pipe and my head was held rigid by Anders obscenely hairy arms. I woke as he was bringing the sandwich over to me to eat, his face all mushed up and distorted.

And then it was morning.

More food was brought in, thankfully not human meat paste sandwiches, plus a nice glass of fresh orange juice and then I was left for another couple of hours.

A few things occurred to me after I'd eaten and was sat waiting for fuck knows what. Firstly, that I'd actually been kidnapped, that's right ME. All that talk about Danny and then here I was. I mean, not a lot of people can say that, can they, that they've been kidnapped, or that they knew someone who had. Ok, so I knew two, me and Danny, but on average, if you're really honest I bet you don't personally know anyone.

I mean you might know a kid from school whose parents were splitting up and whose Dad grabbed him and pissed off to hide with family in Turkey, until Interpol found him and dragged him home. Or that one time there were all those police including the local swat team camped outside the chip shop next to St Mary's primary school because Big Gary the scaffolder had his ex-missus locked in the guest bedroom and was threatening to cut out her silicone implants. He never did by the way. Got tasered, jailed for 26 weeks and is now a born-again Christian living in Stoke Newington, apparently.

But anyway, other than that there can't be many people who actually know someone who's been properly kidnapped, like actually abducted and taken overseas and held against their will.

And I say 'against their will' here because it's generally accepted that most kidnappees would be rightly pissed off at having their liberties so significantly restricted. But I gotta be honest, I don't think that applied to me, not for any more than about twenty percent of my 'incarceration' anyway. If you exclude the little bit in Ventnor and again the couple of days in the cells in Bellano before My Cousin Vinny sprung me, it really hadn't been too bad.

The second thing that occurred to me was that someone would be looking for Karol. And not just him, probably me too. I assumed Askwith would be, at the very least, but hoped others would be too. I mean, I assumed he would have informed someone in the UK that I was on my way? Like customs or something. And I assumed therefore that someone would be now asking all the questions.

Like; 'where is he?' and 'what?' and 'no?' and stuff.

I mean, I had no idea if that was the case, but hoped, if it was, that someone had the good fucking sense to let my Mum know, you know, that I was ok. Or rather that I *was* ok, just before I wasn't. That I wasn't dead, or at least that at some point I hadn't been dead, even if I might be now.

Fuck, I hadn't thought that through properly.

Anyway, whatever, people would be looking, for me and for my mate Karol. And if *his* family were anything like my imagination said they were, they wouldn't take this shit, his disappearance, or whatever, lightly, nor, when they found out the truth, his death.

No idea what any of that meant for me. It didn't matter really. I just hoped it would mean that Bob the cunt finally got what was coming to him.

Like I say, they left me alone for a couple of hours. Then I heard vehicles outside, doors slamming and voices. At first, they were quiet, and I couldn't make out what was being said but after a few minutes' voices got raised and shit went down.

Whoever had recently arrived was either dishing out a ton of shit or was getting some. Next, I heard footsteps and a bit of clattering and banging before my door was opened and a couple of heavies and a young girl came in.

The heavies were standard, I'd seen quite a few by now so apart from their size and body odour I was past stressing. The girl however was something else. I mean, apart from the obvious, like, she had boobs and stuff, I wasn't really prepared for her. She was covered in crap and had cuts and bruises all down one side of her face. And she'd been crying, her eyes were all puffy and red.

I kept quiet, I really didn't fancy a beating and I dare say if they were happy to do that to her, it wouldn't bother these goons to knock the absolute shit outta me. It would be a light workout, nothing more.

I waited, really not sure what I was supposed to do.

The girl looked at me and then turned to the goons.

"Will you two wankers fuck off."

Now I've seen a bit, I mean there's not much that surprises me when it comes to human interaction, with the obvious exception of violent, messy death. Which I gotta say, between you and me, I'm still struggling with. But the rest, you know the 'normal' stuff, I'm pretty much all over. You could even say I'm a little jaded. Perhaps, if you really wanted to stretch things you could describe me as cynical. That said, every now and again something surprises me.

And this was one of those times.

This 'girl' telling these big ugly, and clearly very physically capable hardmen to fuck off, was one of them. That and the fact that they did exactly as she told them. They left, and left the door open behind them. I really didn't know what to make of it.

She turned to me and smiled and then noticed I was looking at the open door.

"You wanna have a go?" she said, gesturing.

I mean, yes. I wanted to have a go. But something in the way she asked, plus the way she casually dismissed the goons that had accompanied her made me hesitate. I shrugged my shoulders.

"Oh, you shrug? That's good, I like a guy that shrugs." she moved further into the room, keeping eye contact with me all the time. "Are you retarded? Is that why you shrug? Or do you have an attitude? Because a guy with a good shrug plus a bullshit attitude are exactly what I'm looking for."

She moved to the window and pulled the curtain to one side.

I just stared at her, desperately resisting the temptation to pout, shrug, roll my eyes or tell her to piss off. She was hot. Like, beneath all the blood and scabs and shit in her hair she was fit. Almost as fit as Freya, possible more so, if she cleaned up ok.

"I get it, you don't know what to say do you. You're intimidated. I'm not what you expected," she glanced over her shoulder at me. "But what *were* you expecting? Because you must've been expecting something, right?"

Again, I had nothing, all the ways I would normally deal with a girl with a big mouth, she'd already called out. I was fucked.

"Nothing to say? You wanna shrug again, is that it?" Now she came close, like *really* close and stood with her face inches from mine. I could smell her, her eyes were brown and her skin almost entirely unlined, apart from the puff, and there were little beads of sweat on her forehead and cheeks. Her teeth were white and her mouth full and soft.

"You wanna fuck me?" Her voice was low, and quiet.

My legs felt like jelly, and my head was banging. I was completely disorientated. I was still hungry and tired and recovering from a pretty shit time. I mean, of course I wanted to fuck her, but then, I'm sure she was used to that. And actually, in reality, no, I don't think, at that very moment, I did. Not right then, not with her being so 'in my face'. Who did she think she was? I had standards, right?

I shrugged.

Shit and bollocks.

She shook her head.

"Another shrug. Fantastic. Fucking pussy."

She turned to leave, and I just stood and watched. My body ached and my mind was fizzing and blinking like an old fluorescent tube light fitting. Shrugs and eyerolls had served me well enough on the estate, had saved my neck in fact on more than one occasion. The theory being that if you didn't actually commit either way you always had somewhere to go.

I was getting the impression here, however that conviction was preferable to fence sitting. And I did love a fence.

She reached the door, and I knew she'd close it on the way out.

Bollocks.

No, I don't wanna fuck you," I don't know why I said it, it clearly wasn't true, how could it be. I guess I just didn't want to be pigeonholed, to be forced into her box, if you'll excuse the pun.

She turned and smiled lightly, just her mouth though, not her eyes.

"You're a shit liar, Shrug boy."

And then she was gone.

Her smell lingered for a good couple of hours. Plus, I couldn't un-see her face, it was burned into the back of my eyes, like I'd looked too long directly at the sun. But I felt so off balance. She was so out of place, her initial appearance, her banter. I was sure she wasn't any older than me, she didn't look it, and yet she was *so* confident, *so* in control. Who was she? She was fucking gorgeous. Why was she interested in me? *Was* she really interested in me, or was I just a prawn in some massive, intricate game. And doesn't that sound so cliche? Like I'm reading from the well-known Robert Ludlum novel - 'The Underfed Chav who fell off a Cliff.' And then there was Danny, I mean if I was here, maybe he was too? Maybe he was in the next room, maybe he heard me arrive just like I heard her.

And before we go on, yes, I'm aware I said *prawn,* and not pawn.

You're welcome.

Should I call out? Should I call him to let him know I was there? Fuck I didn't know. I was bolloxed wasn't I? No clue where I was, no clue who I was with, why they had me, what they wanted and what the future for me looked like.

The door went again and this time a 'normal' looking guy came in with towels and stuff for washing.

"I'm Franc," he said, still a bit rude, maybe it was a thing here. "Bathrooms down the hall. Lizzy said you stank." He put the towels in my arms and pushed me out the door and down the hall to the bathroom. I went, I didn't have the presence of mind to resist. He could have been walking me towards a bath of lava and I'd have gone.

"Leave your clothes outside the door."

I did, although I didn't know why, I was getting numb to the commands and the aggression. I was fucked.

Not so fucked after a nice shower though, you'll be pleased to hear. You see, I'm not that complicated a guy. I need to eat, obviously, I need to shit, regularly - something you're never going to see on screen in my miniseries, unless Damian wants to use a bit of artistic licence, *and* I need to sleep. Oh, and one more thing, I like to be a bit clean, if at all possible. And I felt amazing after a long hot shower, I really did. There was even a toothbrush which was awesome cause I hadn't cleaned my teeth since the morning Alex shit out his guts all over Laurel and Hardy's back garden.

Look, it's simple really. I get down, like everyone right? But I spring back, especially when it looks like my life depends upon it. Which it has, on more occasions than I like to remember, and not just in the recent weeks either. And I tend not to hang on to shit. Like if Danny snuck into my room before I woke up and had my last fag, the one I'd saved overnight, the one I'd planned on having with my morning brew, literally the only one I had left and *would* have till I got paid in a couple of days, I wouldn't hold on to it. At least not for more than a couple of months. And then I'd let it go, just like that. I'd get over it, I'd move on.

Simple.

So, I came back to the room clean and wrapped in a towel like an Egyptian prostitute, with a bit of a spring in my step. So what if they were dicks, that was their problem. So what if this bitch wanted to intimidate me, fuck her. If they wanted to use me for some bullshit corporate espionage thing, then fuck it, I'd get over it, it wasn't my problem. Whatever they had going on, however it affected me, it wasn't my fault, and it wasn't my problem. As long as I got through it, as long as I kept smiling, they couldn't touch me. And I would get through it, I had to, for Danny and for Mum.

Of course, the small fly in that ointment was the fact that they killed Karol, but whatever.

I got back to the room to find Franc had cleaned it and made the bed. He'd also opened the windows and put some fruit in a bowl on the table. There was also a tray with bread and cheese and all sorts of other grub including pickles and some ham I had no idea about other than it looked wonderful. My mouth started watering instantly, in fact I thought he'd notice so I kept my face turned away.

"New clothes on the bed. Your old clobber was filthy, we burned it. Get dressed and eat something. Leave your towel outside the door."

Proper chatty fucker this one.

I nodded, both surprised and suspicious.

"Ok. thank you."

Franc nodded but didn't smile, pretty sure he couldn't to be honest, maybe an old war injury. He picked up a few bits and then left, shutting the door behind him. I listened to see if he locked it, but he didn't, and that made me feel even more suspicious, like they were trying to fatten me up, and then let me escape only so they could hunt me down. Like, so when they caught me, I'd be fatter and tastier with all the cheese and shit inside me.

Bastards.

But anyway, I went over and finished drying my bits and bobs before getting dressed. I mean, clearly there was a general outfitter that catered to the paramilitary / private security firms, that supplied all their watches, and all their clothes and shit. Because if I'm not mistaken the clothes, they gave me were almost identical to the ones Freya had put on my bed a few weeks ago.

Jesus was that really a few weeks ago? Seemed like yesterday.

Once dressed I had a look at the food. And when I say look, I mean I got stuck in. Proper. I layered cheese on bread, then ham, then pickle, then more cheese. I was up to my fucking elbows in it to be completely honest. So much so that when Franc came back, I had pickle all over my face and cheese in my hair. But fuck me it was good, better even that the casseroles Mick, no not that one, the *other* one, used to dish up back The Big House in Bellano.

Bless Mick.

Made me a bit sad thinking about him then, I mean he was just the chef wasn't he. It was just a job to him, probably nothing more. I sure he didn't ever expect to meet the sticky end that he more than likely did. Poor Mick, or whatever his real name was.

Didn't make me sad enough to put me off my food though, sorry Mick.

Anyway, back to Franc.

"Lizzie wants to see you," he said bluntly. I finished chewing and then wiped myself down before I stood. I know I'd had a shower, but I was conscious that I'd since made a bit of a pig of myself.

"Jesus Franc, can you give it a rest mate, you're giving me a headache."

He stared at me for a moment before turning his back. Miserable cunt.

I put my shoes on slowly, which they hadn't replaced, just cleaned. And then I went to the door and waited for Franc to get over himself. I mean I was grateful for the change of bedding and clothes and food etc, but he didn't have to be rude.

He turned when he saw me.

"A word of warning. Don't fuck with her. She'll cut your fucking balls off."

I wasn't expecting that but actually appreciated it, even from this grumpy twat. And I believed it too. It was all very well being all blasé and thinking fuck it, as long as I got through it, I'd be ok etc, etc, but I kinda wanted to do that with Ant and Dec still in place as well. If you know what I mean.

I nodded.

"Gotcha"

Franc nodded too.

"Follow me."

17: Shirley

A bit of left, right, left, right and then we were in a large lounge type seating area. It was huge, certainly compared to my lounge and even compared to Sally Sissons, the most minted girl at the school's lounge. I mean I only went there once to watch MTV, but she had a fuck off great fish tank dividing the lounge from the kitchen and an equally large TV on the wall with all the normal speakers and DVD players etc. Pretty sure her Dad was an armed robber, or an architect, or whatever.

Anyway, this lounge didn't have any of that. Instead, it had massive sliding glass doors that opened onto a deck that had the biggest barbecue I'd ever seen plus as much seating as there was inside. Barbeques must be a thing here. The room itself had a piano in the corner which was nice and lots of wooden and bone ornaments on various shelves. Oh, and a giant fucking spear on the wall above the fireplace.

Anyway, Franc told me to sit in his normal chatterbox way and then went and got me a drink. When he came back, he kicked my foot.

"Remember, don't be a dick, she'll eat you for breakfast."

I took a breath, then a sip of the water he'd given me and then she was there.

"Fuck off Franc," she said, immediately, instantly charming. Franc departed. Jesus, she was brutal.

She poured herself a drink, definitely not water and then paced casually back and forth a little without speaking. She was looking at me and I was looking at her wondering how close I was to being neutered.

She had changed since before and cleaned up the scratches and marks on her skin. And to be fair she didn't look too bad now, a bit more girly. I mean, before she looked like she'd just come from a fight with a family of crocodiles but now I'd say she'd probably only fought the one, and perhaps only for its last Rolo.

She was all casual and cool looking and, sad to say, even more unsettling.

"You look better," I tried, Franc's warning ringing in my ears.

Straight away I felt like it was the wrong thing to say. But she didn't acknowledge it, instead she stopped her walking and slowly, really slowly came over and sat next to me.

"You smell of cheese," she said.

Fuck sake.

I nodded.

"Yep. I just had some cheese."

She looked at me quietly, scanning my face and then my hands and my body. I felt like I was being examined by either a doctor or by The Predator. I honestly don't think I've ever felt so uncomfortable.

Eventually she smiled and got up and carried on her casual movements around the room. She stopped at the piano.

"Do you like the piano Matthew?"

I wasn't shocked that she knew my real name, I mean bollocks, they wouldn't have gone to all this if they weren't sure who I was, would they.

"Yes. I think so." Trying so hard not to nod to shrug or convey my disinterest with any non-essential body language. She just stared at me a bit more without speaking.

“I love the piano.”

I nodded.

“Ok,” really not sure what she was looking for.

“You are an interesting guy,” she said.

Seriously have you ever tried not to shrug, its fucking impossible. It's like the yes - no game. Because you can't, it becomes the only thing you want to do.

“Why?”

She nodded; I think she understood the effort I was making.

“I'm direct. I want you to be direct, we don't have room for anything else.”

“Ok.”

“Ok?”

Oh, fuck here we go. I mean, this was perfect shrug material here. What the fuck did she want me to say?

"Yes, ok. I will be direct."

She nodded again.

Oh, hang on, now she was nodding, like it was ok for her to nod but not for me to shrug?

"What does that mean?" before I could stop myself.

She smiled.

"What does 'what' mean?"

I huffed, yes, I huffed like a small child.

"There it is."

I took a breath. She was a fucking pain.

"The nod, what did it mean? Listen, I'm sorry, but if you have something to say, please, if you have a question then just say it." I was getting a little pissed. I couldn't help it. I had heard Franc loud and clear but fuck me they'd brought me all the way up here via all sorts of fucked up means and now she wanted to play mind games. Bollocks, the cheese was amazing, but I was done with this bullshit. I knew Franc was in the back there, fist in mouth but the red mist was creeping in.

"Why am I here? Why did you kill Karol? What the fuck is this all about?"

She remained still and watched me. I, for my part, stayed sitting, I was smart enough, even whilst losing my shit a little to know she'd not tolerate any kind of physical shenanigans.

"Did you finish school Matthew?" her voice was quiet, controlled, and her question kinda stopped me in my tracks. I thought about my answer, I guess I was beginning to understand that I would be expected to.

"You killed my driver, you put me, and him, wrapped up like a fucking burrito on a plane and flew us thousands of miles and you want me to believe that you don't already know the answer to that?"

She didn't smile this time, but her eyes registered something.

"You know all you need to know about me."

She moved away from the piano and came closer.

"Do you know where you are?" she asked.

"Fucking South Africa. Johannesburg," it was funny, not adding the 'I think' or the 'um' or the set piece attitude answers was something I knew how to do, even if I was still struggling with the body language bits. And the swearing. I was always going to struggle with the swearing.

"Right. But do you know exactly where you are now?"

"Three hours northwest. There are mountains to the south and the road up to here was a single track for the last 45 minutes so I would think probably around 120k from the airport."

"Ok," she nodded. "Not bad. But you still think you could make it don't you? You still think you could climb out your window and find your way home."

I didn't answer.

"What, no shrug? I thought that was your thing?"

I didn't want to look away from her, I figured it would give her ammunition or something.

"No."

"No? No what? No, you don't think you could walk out of here, or no, shrugging is not your thing?"

Fuck sake.

"No to both."

"Ok."

"Ok?" I was being reckless, but I couldn't stop it, she was doing my nut in.

She smiled and nodded, accepting the dig.

"Matthew you are interesting because you are unusual. Unusual because you are unknown, because we don't 'know' you."

I shook my head, in my opinion quite legitimately.

"So why did you kidnap me?"

She liked that; I could see. It was direct wasn't it.

"Matthew, I'm a nice girl, really, I am. But I grew up with a knife in one hand and a gun in the other. And I've trained in combat and fought right across this continent. I have no problem dealing with things in the most extreme way and I will deal with you and anyone else the same way if we can't move this forward."

Maybe I should have been intimidated. But I wasn't. Dying here, in the sand would be no different than dying in a filthy squat in Beckenham. Dying was dying.

Besides, Mad Rufus would have cut my fingers off for looking at him wrong. Ahmed's Uncles would have cooked and served me to my neighbours in a nice soft flour tortilla wrap if I'd asked the wrong question. I'd sold guns, I'd sold knives. I'd sold drugs and seen people die on them, low life's for sure, but still. I was skinny, pale, a bit sickly looking and not the most well-educated boy but I'd seen enough shit to know I had what it took to survive. This bitch, as fucking scary as she was, didn't frighten me. Fuck it.

"Congratulations."

She tilted her head and looked at me.

"Really?"

"Look, whatever, I don't give a fuck anymore, really, I don't. I'm sorry if that offends you. Franc said not to piss you off, but this is bollocks. Cut my balls off if you want. Thanks for the cheese and that but if all you're gonna do is try and intimidate me then we're done, I'm done."

She shook her head.

"He said you were tough. I think I can see that now."

Who?

"Who said I was tough?" Was she talking about Danny?

She frowned.

"Never mind."

I was exasperated.

"Who are you talking about?"

She paced a bit more before speaking again.

"Shirley. You fucked him up Matthew. It cost me a lot to get him back here and will cost more to put things right. More than I can tell you right now."

I was confused, she'd said 'he' then talked about a woman. I had no idea what she was going on about, who was Shirley? How had I hurt her, or him, or whatever? What the fuck?

"I need you to apologise."

I'm sorry but *what?* Apologise to some woman I'd never met? Who you keep referring to as a man? What was I supposed to have done to her? Offended her? Stepped on her toe? Neglected to hold a door open for her?

"If this is going to work, you need to apologise."

"Sorry but who are you talking about? Who the fuck is Shirley?"

Before she could answer, Bob the Giant came into the room. Fucking great, king knob head was here. I looked past him to see the woman, to see who I had so tragically upset. But there was no one there, no woman. I stood nervously.

"What was going on?"

"Shirley, Matthew has something to say."

I turned to look at Bob, his face all puffy and marked with his nose trying desperately to escape around to his ear. Fuck, did I really do all that?

"Matthew?" she pressed.

I looked from him to her, was *this* Shirley?? No fucking way.

"Um,"

Bob, or Shirley towered above me, his meaty hands hanging loose by his sides, a new big fancy watch on his wrist. I looked at him, and remembered the moments we shared in the garage in Ventnor, the water pipe, the smell of petrol and paint. And then the rage I felt when I thought he had Danny. Jesus, I really went off on him didn't I.

I actually started to feel a bit bad.

"Um, I'm sorry?" I offered weakly.

She shook her head.

"Use his name."

And I so desperately wanted to call him Bob, Bob the Giant, it seemed more fitting than the name his mother gave him. But I didn't, I called him Shirley and as I said it, I really think I meant it.

"I'm sorry Shirley..."

There was a fucking huge bang, and a flash and I flinched and recoiled all at once. Blood sprayed across my face and neck and thick lumps of skin and bone, and other shit splattered all over me, the furniture and the walls and ceiling. Shirley was knocked sideways, violently as his head popped like a watermelon and I fell back, almost by instinct.

I found myself behind the sofa, my hands in fists and my eyes scanning for an escape.

Fucking bitch shot him. She fucking *SHOT* him!

I had bits of him in my mouth and nose, possibly a tooth in my ear. It was hot and it was running down my face and in my eyes, and I could taste his blood, all metallic on my tongue. And I should have been terrified, shouldn't I, I should have been catatonic with fear, shaking and crying. But I wasn't. I was angry. I was fucking furious.

I stood slowly; my face white with rage. To be fair it was pretty pale to start with, and currently covered in blood so she may not have noticed. But I was shaking.

"WHAT THE FUCK!?" I almost shouted.

I stared at her, as she just stood casually, gun down by her side, bits of Shirley on her chest and legs. I couldn't believe how far he'd gone, how far his bits had sprayed and spread. The ceiling was dripping, and the walls were running with him. Incredible.

She looked at me, and then at him.

"Ahh, I'm sorry Matthew, was he your friend?"

I didn't have the words. I wasn't scared of her, really, I wasn't. She was a callous and spiteful, fucking bitch, but I wasn't scared. But I couldn't express my disgust, my horror at what she had just done. To Shirley.

"You're fucking crazy, you're fucking *mental*," I said, quieter than a moment ago, my belly starting to fizz. "What the *fuck* is wrong with you?"

She didn't answer straight away, instead she wiped some of the blood from her neck, it must have been a bit sticky, or itchy, or something.

"He was a bad man, Matthew."

I shook my head, my body still trembling, the heat now spreading to my chest and neck.

"But you just killed him."

She smiled.

"No, I didn't. You did."

I scowled, and frowned, my heart still beating fast within my chest. I was trembling and could feel my skin getting tight and my hands itching.

"Fuck you. Fuck you. You shot him."

"Yes. But let's face it, he was dead the moment he tied you to the water pipe. We all know that don't we?"

"What are you talking about? Why? Who the fuck am I to you? What is this all about?"

She wiped some more blood off before moving across and placing the gun on the piano. Then she turned back to me.

"No one's been straight with you yet, have they? No one has been honest enough to tell you who you are, and what we all want with you, have they?"

I looked at the gun on the piano, blood and bits all over the handgrip, and then I looked back at her. I knew I couldn't reach it, that it was pointless to even try but I thought for a brief moment I might be able to move it with my mind, like I dreamt I did with the helicopter. She saw me look and knew it too. She shook her head.

"No," it was enough.

I could've shrugged then; I was pretty sure I could've got away with a shrug under such circumstances.

I coughed and spat out a little Shirley.

"I don't know what you're talking about." I was still shaking. "You're fucking crazy."

She came back over slowly and held out her hand, blood dripping from her elbow.

"Come out from behind the chair, Shrug boy, there's something I need to show you."

18: Wolweburg

We showered. Separately, although she did offer for me to join her. I mean, who does that? She was a fucking psycho. And then once changed into new clean clothes, thanks Franc, I met her outside by a big but battered 4x4 truck.

"Jump in."

It was all happening very quickly; however, I did as I was told and then we were off.

The track went beyond the house and wound its way up the hill behind. There were shit loads of trees, but I hoped I might get a good view once we got near the top, and hoped too that I might be able to orientate myself a bit. I was still shaking from earlier and my ears were still ringing. Plus, I could still taste the blood in my mouth.

"Still thinking about running?" she noticed me looking out across the hills.

I turned to her. Nutter.

"Would you blame me if I did?"

She didn't answer, instead just concentrated on driving.

I mean, I was angry with her, disgusted by her behaviour. And really uncomfortable with how attractive and brutal she was at the same time, it made me feel weird inside. But it was still nice to be out here with her, with a woman, in the fresh air. And God knew I needed some fresh air.

The track was bumpy as fuck with trees and shrubs close on each side. We bounced around like mad but eventually we neared the top of the hill, and she pulled round into a small clearing. It looked like the track stopped here albeit there were signs that the route extended on further. She got out.

"Come on," she beckoned.

I climbed out and followed her warily as she started walking. Fuck's sake, she was just going to throw me off a cliff. We walked in silence for a couple of minutes before:

"You're wondering whether you could take me, aren't you?" she said over her shoulder. I coughed, bitch. I also noticed the knife on her belt and the gun holstered under her arm. She also had a small pair of binoculars in pouch sitting just above her arse. I kept my eyes on these.

"No," I denied. Although I thought I possibly could. If she was looking the other way. And she didn't have that knife.

She laughed lightly, all girly and whatever.

"You couldn't. Just so you know."

Actually, I think I did know but whatever. Maybe if I'd spent a bit more time wrestling with Freya, I might have had a chance. And then the thought of her and Freya having a wrestle together on the lawn popped into my head. Jesus Christ.

"I wasn't." I insisted.

We stopped after a few minutes for her to re-tie her hair. I couldn't help looking at her neck as she fiddled. She noticed but didn't tease.

"You're unfit Matthew. We need to fix that."

It was unfair. I was a damn site fitter that I was a couple of months ago, all that running around The Big House plus a decent diet had helped there. But she was right, I was puffing like I was trying to blow up a hot air balloon. She on the other hand looked as cool and unbothered as someone who had just shot a man at point blank range. In the head. In her lounge. God, I was sick of washing other people blood out of my hair.

I chose not to respond, and, in a moment, we were walking again.

Ten minutes later we stopped, and she led me slowly though some trees to the edge of a cliff. Well, it wasn't really a cliff, it was more like the edge where the hill went back down the other side, quite steeply. I mean, it was steep, but I was pretty sure if she did push me off, all I'd do was just wander gently down without too much bother. But that wasn't why she'd brought me here, there was something else.

"You see Matthew sometimes you're looking so hard, so *specifically* for your answer that you lose the ability to see."

But I was seeing now, wasn't I. I was seeing something now that took my absolute fucking breath away.

So, the hill dropped away, and the land opened up onto a massive flat expanse. It stretched as far as I could see and was dotted with bush and trees and grass. It wasn't completely flat; in fact it rose and fell gently to suit the rivers that ran across it. But it was flat enough to let me see for at least thirty miles, I guessed.

Out on the plain I could see herds of animals, cows or antelopes or something, and other groups of animals that definitely weren't cows. Plus, there were smaller flocks of what looked like sheep or goats or camels. Listen, I'm a city boy, this is the best I can do, ok.

Anyway, there were also birds and all sorts going on up in the trees both close up and far out where the sky got a bit hazy.

I turned to her but she was as lost in the landscape as I had been.

"What is this place? Why have you brought me here?"

She didn't answer straight away but when she did, I noticed her eyes were a bit wet.

Who's the pussy now then?

"This is our home, Matthew. This is what we are protecting."

I shook my head, glancing briefly back out at the vista before me.

"It's lovely, really it is. It's probably bigger than Richmond Park."

"Thank you," I sensed an edge.

"But you said protecting? What are you protecting it from?"

I was confused, I didn't understand the link.

The Sausage, Danny, Bob, Terry, Cubby, her.

"I don't even know your name," I said a little absently before turning fully back to the view.

"My name is Lizzelle. I was born here; I've lived here my whole life."

Yeah, apart from all the 'fighting right across the continent' bit. Obviously, I didn't say that, I didn't want a kick in the nuts.

"And? Listen, I don't mean to be rude but great, congratulations you live on a big farm or whatever. What's that got to do with me?"

Again, she didn't answer but continued to look out.

"Our land stretches for a hundred and eighty kilometres in that direction," she pointed north, "and ninety in that," she pointed west. "We own it all Matthew, from the base of this hill all the way to the Waldlhe river and beyond into Botswana."

I didn't bother questioning her, she'd clearly get there in her own time.

"And we have done so for more than two hundred years."

"Well done," shit that was terrible, but I didn't really know what else to say. We didn't even own our TV, let alone the flat.

She looked at me, I sensed something brutal coming, it didn't.

"But it's not about our land is it?"

"Isn't it?"

She shook her head.

"No. Come with me."

And then we were off again. Back through the trees, back down the track towards the car. Before we got there though she cut off left and headed east. I had no idea so just followed, trying to fend off the mosquitos and the branches she deliberately let flick in my face. Another ten minutes and we pushed through to another clear spot, again, on the edge of a drop, this time almost vertical.

I hesitated, shit, this was a bit different, and to be honest if she threw me off here, I'd be fucked, for sure.

But anyway, I soon forgot about that when I saw what she had brought me here to see.

Stretching out before me, not as far as before but still, for a good couple of miles was a hole. Like, the biggest, deepest mother fucking hole I had ever seen, or imagined, or had even had nightmares about. It was so fucking huge the vehicles trundling around only halfway down were like ants, tiny, tiny ants. It was crazy.

I got a bit of vertigo, I'm ashamed to say. I thought I was going to be sucked in, the space in front of me was so vast I was struggling to comprehend it.

"What the fuck?!"

She looked at me.

"You ok Pussy?" she reached out to steady me. I let her. She may have been a bitch, but it was still kinda nice.

"Yeah, Jesus, it's just so huge. What the fuck is it?"

She looked back out, like I was.

"It's called Wolweburg, It's a diamond mine."

I stared at it for a few moments. It was nothing like I imagined a diamond mine to look.

"Diamonds are made under super intense pressure deep within the earth's mantle and rise to the surface in massive pipes of molten, igneous rock. Igneous, just means molten Matthew. This stuff hardens and sits for millions of years until we find it, find the diamonds stuck inside it and start digging. We then follow the pipe down, hence the super mega hole."

It was fascinating, genuinely, I'd had no idea.

"My great, great grandfather found it. Story goes; he was out riding one Sunday and stopped to draw water from the spring at the base of the hill. When he got close there was whitey as big as his fist just sitting in the sun. He actually mined it himself on the quiet for a few years. Stopped when his horse died.

"I guess the spring's not there now?"

"Right, yeah, it's a shit business, screws up everything around. But it pays well, made him a rich man."

I nodded; I think I was starting to see a picture.

"And when the pipe ends or we reach the limit of our tech, we stop digging."

"Ok." I was thinking of the dead horse.

She sighed; it sounded a bit sad. I looked across at her and was surprised to see her staring at me.

"Ok? Is that it?"

I opened my mouth and then shut it again. I rephrased.

"Sorry but what do you want me to say?"

She was still looking at me as she reached round behind her back. She was going for the knife, fuck. She was going to stab me. Shit.

I tried to move, to raise my arm to fend her off. I knew this would happen, fuck, I knew it. Franc warned me. I started moving my feet too, to adjust my balance in case she was going to sidestep and throw me off the edge. Fuck, I wished I'd taken more lessons with Freya.

"Here, have a look through these." she said casually.

She was offering me the binoculars and watching me curiously as I did this strange little arm up back shuffle.

"You ok?" she asked, binoculars still held out in front of her.

I straightened up and made out like I was just stretching or something and took the binoculars quickly, kind of snatched them of her really. She let it pass and turned back front, pointing out something on the southwestern edge of the huge pit.

"See the buildings down there, look at the sigs, see if you can make out the writing."

I did as was told, it took a moment to get the hang of the binoculars, or *binos* as we professionals call them in the field. But soon enough the buildings jumped into focus. And once again I was dumbstruck by the scale of the thing in front of me. To think all the earth and rock had been dug out by man. It was amazing, a little disturbing too, but amazing.

Where the fuck did they put it?

Anyway, I fiddled with the focus and stuff and started searching for signs. She waited patiently and in a couple of moments I saw it. I moved away and then went back and read it aloud.

"Ok, it says Coyn, I think, yes Coyn. And then below, I think I can just make out Stuck, no wait. No, it's Sex, no sorry Six. Definitely Six." I lowered the binos and turned to her. "It says Six."

She nodded.

"Genius. Well done," as she took the binos back.

"So that's Six, down there. That's one of their places or they're doing security or something for this Coyn? And who are Coyn?"

"You ask a ton of questions."

Again, a perfect shrug moment. Instead.

"Is that a problem? You've had plenty of opportunities to see me off and you haven't. I don't see that asking a few questions is gonna make a difference."

She turned back to the mine.

"A guy called Peters bought the rights to Wolweburg from my great-grandfather nearly ninety years ago. Coyn bought them off him in the 40s. They started digging straight away and haven't stopped."

"Go on,"

She liked that; it was better than 'ok'.

"At first they used their own guys; you know to keep the drifters and prospectors away. But as the mine got deeper and the infrastructure developed around it the task of security got too big. So, they started using contractors. Small guys at first and bigger, more commercially minded outfits later on."

The 'infrastructure' she was referring to was massive, like a full-size town. I mean, it was all a little way off, there were roads and houses and all the usual stuff you'd expect to see in a town. Plus, all the industrial stuff too.

"And when did they go to Six?" I was thinking back to something Cubby had said about them. And as I did something else occurred.

"So, you're not Six then?"

She turned back to me quickly, a proper heavy frown in her face, the first one I'd seen.

"Are you fucking stupid?"

I took a step back without really meaning to.

"Sorry I just thought..."

"What? What did you just think?"

"I don't know, I just thought you, well I thought there was AMOS, you know, Terry and his guys, British MI and then Six, and I thought that was you."

She stared at me for a few moments, the frown lingering. And then she looked away.

"He got to you, didn't he? Askwith?"

Fuck sake. What was she talking about?

"I don't know what you're thinking but..."

"Yes, you do."

"Look, I'm just a kid from an estate caught up...."

"Yeah, yeah, and I'm fucking Mary Poppins. Fuck you Matthew, stop the bullshit. I know, ok, we all fucking KNOW!"

Jesus she was angry. I didn't really expect that, I didn't see that in her, seriously. Cold, manipulative and ruthless yes maybe but not hot and angry.

I was confused by that plus what she'd said. She 'knew'. What the fuck did that mean? What did she know?

"Lizzelle, can I call you that?" I almost reached out, feeling a bit of a dick all of a sudden, even if I had no clue what I'd done.

"It's Lizzie," without looking at me.

"Ok, Lizzie, sorry but I don't know what you think I am, or what you think I know but I'm really fucked here, I'm really in the dark. I don't know who you are, obviously I know your name, you told me, like five minutes ago after you held me prisoner and then shot a man in front of me. But, like, that's it. I don't know who Six are or Coyn and I really don't know why you blew Bob's face off."

She turned back to me.

"Who the fuck is Bob?"

"Bollocks, I meant Shirley. I just used to call him Bob, you know back before. When I was talking to other people."

She frowned again.

"What other people?"

Jesus, were we really going down this rabbit hole?

"Look, fuck it, it doesn't matter. What matters is who the fuck are you if you're not Six? And why did you kidnap me?"

Now it was her turn to step back.

"Kidnap you? Are you fucking kidding me?? I didn't kidnap you, you fucking moron. I *saved* you."

I shook my head; this was spinning me out.

"*Saved* me? Who did you save me from? I was going home for fuck sake. I was going home to see my mum, to start looking for my little brother properly. I was going home to eat crumpets for fuck sake. I was only where I was because of Bob the cunt, or Sandra or whatever you want to call him. This is your fault."

Ok so now I was getting a little stressed. It was so hard to get any kind of truth, ever. No one ever just told me what I wanted to know.

"Ok, so if you're not Six and you didn't kidnap me then tell me who the fuck you are and why you brought me up here?"

She took a breath, the sort your mother used to take before she told you for the fourteenth time not to put your action man's hand *and arm* up your nose.

"I've told you, my name is Lizzie, this is my land, I've lived here my whole life. Jesus. I don't have another name, I'm not part of a thing, a security thing. I'm not out for that kind of gain. And I killed Shirley because like you say, he *was* a cunt.

He took you back in the UK sure, I'm aware of that and he was working for me at the time. But that was *nothing* to do with me, he was acting alone, because he's a cunt. And then he rescued you in Milan because I told him to, again he was working for me. But he didn't rescue you *from* the driver guy, Karol, or whatever, he was harmless, he was just a driver, he was Cubby's guy. He rescued you from the guys waiting for you back in London, this time *not* Cubby's guys but someone else's. He shouldn't have shot the driver, he had no reason to but like I say, he was a cunt. And I shot him, when I did because he raped and killed a 12-year-old boy yesterday, a boy called Melokuhle from one of the villages just south of my Rangers farm to the east of here. I shot him because he was a bad man Matthew, a man filled with hate and poison and he deserved to die, and I would do it again in a fucking heartbeat."

We stood staring at each other for a few moments. It was a lot.

And she was crying, tiny, dainty little tears rolling down her brown face. I was shocked, really, I was devastated. I could see she was really troubled by it, rightly so, I was. Fuck sake. Fuck and shit and bollocks. Bob, what a sicko, what an absolute, complete and utter cunt.

I stepped a little closer, which she didn't seem to mind. I wanted to touch her, to convey something, I didn't know what, but something. But I didn't. I thought about Karol, I thought about the boy Melokuhle, his parents, his family. Jesus Christ.

I looked at her.

"I'm sorry."

She looked into my eyes and then looked away, then nodded.

"Thank you."

Now I did reach out and put my hand on her shoulder, I couldn't help it, she looked so broken. She tolerated it.

"Did you know the boy?" she shook her head and sniffed. I noticed her hands trembling slightly.

"Not well, but I knew the family. They've lived on this land for generations. They worked for my father. They are family."

I was a bit lost. I'd been solid for Mum when she needed me, and always there for Danny, you know the kind of tough love big brothers dish out. Standard. And I'd been there for Chelsea too, when the fella that knocked her up did the dirty on her, and seriously, she really was in absolute bits for a time. But it wasn't my MO, it wasn't normal for me to be all soft and sensitive. I wasn't sure what to say.

We stood quietly for a bit, her thinking about all the shit she needed to think about, you know, loss, grief, the complexities of managing such a huge tract of land, and me thinking about Shirley's brains running down my face. The dream I had about him putting Karol into a food mixer had a whole different feel to it now. Fucking arsehole.

"I'm not what you think I am. I'm just here, holding back the tide, trying to stop it all going to shit."

I didn't say anything, but I think I kinda knew what she was talking about.

"And I'm caught, Matthew, just like you are. I'm stuck dealing with shit because other people are just out for themselves."

"Are you alone though? Don't you have family?"

She turned and looked out across the mine; my hand fell off her shoulder as she did.

"We sold the rights to the mine but retained the leasehold on the land. We get paid, we get paid big in fact. But it's not always been good for us."

"My family's fucked too."

She looked across at me.

"I know. I'm sorry."

"Why me though?" I tried to move the conversation on. "Why were you sending people halfway across the world to pick up a kid you don't know? I don't understand."

She hesitated before she spoke.

"Matthew, like I said earlier, sometimes you're looking so hard at something, you fail to see it."

I would have rolled my eyes if I thought I could get away with it without being stabbed. Why couldn't people just talk straight? Where was this going? This was like what Terry had said about sand. But it was bollocks. It was saying something, without saying something.

"The stuff Cubby told you, it's not true, not all of it. Ok, some of it is, just enough to make it seem real, but a lot of it is crap. Believe me."

Here we go, version number 3, or was it 4? I stopped her.

"Right, ok, listen, before you go on, I've gotta be honest with you, I'm really gonna struggle here to believe anything you tell me. You understand that right? I mean, if you know half as much about me as you seem to think you do, you'll know I've heard a shit ton of weird and wonderful over the last few weeks."

She nodded.

"I know."

"Right, and everyone has told me not to believe the guy before. So, you'll understand if I don't fall head over heels in love with *your* version. Don't get me wrong," I held up my hands, "I do want to get to the bottom of this fucking rabbit hole, but it's getting a bit fucking thin, if you catch my drift."

She nodded again.

"I get it."

"Ok, so just understand that when you're quoting your lovely poetic phrases and talking in circles about sand and seeing shit and stuff. It don't matter what you think of me, the truth is I *did* grow up on that estate, that's where I'm from. I *am* a skinny fucking rat with no manners and bad skin. And I'm not about fantasising about concepts and psycho bollocks."

"Ok."

"Ok right, good. So if you're gonna tell me stuff do it straight please, do it without any bullshit, without any nonsense."

"Ok."

"Ok, right. Good."

"Good."

"Good."

We stood in silence for a moment and looked at each other before I got shy or something and looked out across the big hole. It occurred to me that I liked her. And that was weird. She spent the last 24 hours fucking terrorising me. I honestly thought she was a serial killer, some kind of twisted, dominatrix nut job. But now, I thought differently. I wasn't sure what she was. Was she just a girl who lived on a farm, who learned how to survive because she had to, who took 'extreme' measures as and when because that's the way it was here? Was she just protecting what she had been entrusted with, protecting the land, the animals, the people?

Or was she a twisted, dominatrix nut job?

I didn't know. I just knew I was starting to like her. Bollocks.

"Matthew, I'm doing this, I sent people to get you because of a promise. Because of two promises actually. You see, this land, not Wolweburg, but the land on the other side, it is mine, yes, but it doesn't really belong to me. It belongs to the people here, to the animals, to everyone."

She actually reached out and took my hand, I nearly shit my pants.

"The land is yours, its mine, it's everyone's. It belongs to every creature that wants it, that makes its home upon it, that raises its young within it. It's not mine, it's not yours, it's everyone's."

Ok, I kinda understood. It was a bit wet, but she was talking about the environment, about green stuff, about conservation and shit. And that in the face of this massive industrial boil before us all sort of tied in. It was a hot trendy topic right now and perfectly understandable from where we were standing. I got it.

"But it's being threatened, it's being spoiled."

I nodded and glanced over my shoulder. She shook her head and frowned again.

"No not by that, dickhead" I looked back at her. "For sure industry, but not this. By the consumption of energy, by the consumption of fossil fuels and natural resources for use in the production of energy. All across the world."

Ah, so she was a fucking eco warrior, like Swampy, that guy who spent a couple of weeks in a tunnel under the A30. Great, no I mean it, I was quite pleased, it was better than the aforementioned alternative. Unless of course she was going to want to move to Wales and live in a Yurt.

"Look I'm not getting into this now, not in detail, I'm not an environmentalist, I'm not a campaigner, I'm just saying, and you should take note. It's complex and there are so many factors, so many contributors and you need to remember what I said earlier; don't look too hard at the details."

I was disappointed and relieved. Maybe she was a serial killer then.

She let go of my hand and took another look out into the void.

"Come on Shrug boy, I'm hungry, and I need to show you something else."

I was a bit confused, but that was almost standard now, I felt confused nearly all the time, so this was kinda normal. She moved away from the edge and started back through the trees. I followed without hesitating; I was hungry too.

Back at the house she led me straight to the kitchen, they were still cleaning the lounge, Shirley was everywhere. I sat whilst she got some bits out of the fridge, more ham and cheese and stuff like I'd had earlier. I was starving, all the walking and shitting my pants had tired me out. We ate in silence, I didn't really know how to make small talk, especially with someone so completely different from me. Like, we had nothing in common did we, zero, zilch.

I was curious though, I wanted to ask how loaded she really was. I mean, this house was massive and had all the mod cons including, but not limited to, a pool, hot tub, big lounge with blood all over it, that barbeque I mentioned earlier and loads of big glass windows. And glass is always a sign of wealth isn't it, think about it - Winnie the Pooh: no money for trousers, also limited windows.

Anyway she clearly didn't need to shop at Aldi or worry about topping up her prepaid electric meter.

We finished eating and she cleared up, again, I didn't really know what to say. Eventually:

"You ready?"

I nodded. "Yeah. Thank you."

"No probs, follow me."

She led me through to the back of the house and then through a door and down some stairs to a basement. Another door at the bottom and then we were in a dark room filled with computers and shit. There were racks with stuff piled high with masses of cables and hundreds of blinking lights. There were also screens with letters, numbers and symbols just constantly scrolling and scrolling. I scanned around quickly and noted the air conditioning and tons of other bits of very complicated looking equipment.

"Take a seat, and don't fucking touch anything," she said as she sat down in a fancy swivel chair.

She started pushing buttons and keys almost immediately and the screen directly in front of her came to life. She then entered some passwords and the screen changed again, and then again. I just sat and watched; I was mesmerised. I'd seen the computers at school, had even attended lessons where they let you use them, but I honestly couldn't be bothered. It was like science fiction to me, all lights and buttons and shit. And most of it was just for writing letters to the Post Office asking where your actual, real letters were. I mean, I remember Bean had had an electric typewriter which Danny tried to use to write ARSE as big as he could once. Got found out and bollocked for touching it. But beyond that I really wasn't interested.

This looked different though, this looked kinda sexy.

"What is all this?" I think I knew. I mean, I'd seen Terry's big room with all the nerds and screens and stuff. I guessed this was something similar.

"This is my den," she smiled at me over her shoulder and I gotta say she was gorgeous when she smiled, took my breath away a bit to be fair. Her teeth were bright white, and her eyes flashed and sparkled. Jesus that sounds wet.

"What is it for?" an obvious question I suppose, but a million times better than my stock 'ok', plus it covered my blushes a bit.

"I hack."

I nodded.

"Do you know what hack means?"

I think we all know the answer to that, I didn't bother replying.

"So, I use it to break into other people's systems, other people's machines. I use it to find shit out, shit that helps me do the stuff I need to do."

Ok the first part of that just passed me by. I couldn't comprehend how she could use this stuff, this equipment to break into people's houses and businesses somewhere else.

It was beyond me, I was a philistine. But the second part, I got that.

"You find shit out. What do you find out?"

"I find money, I find secrets, I find people."

"Ok," which was a legit response to be fair, she was far from finished.

"And I use the information I find to make stuff happen that I want to happen."

"Is that how you found me?"

"Yup." she was typing away like crazy, without even looking down at the keyboard. It was fascinating. I kind of wanted to have a little go myself.

"Cool,"

She paused and looked over her shoulder at me.

"Cool?"

Ok that was fair.

"Sorry."

She nodded.

"I found you by hacking the comms at the British Consulate. I did that because I know Cubby and I know his methods. And I did that having traced you from the UK to Italy. I then hacked the Air Traffic Control at Milan to find your likely flight plan."

Jesus Christ.

"Right. That's impressive."

"I know."

She continued tapping and tapping and the screen kept changing and flicking. I wondered if she might have been better off with two screens, but what did I know?

"But and don't get me wrong, this is very, very cool. But it doesn't answer the question of why does it? Why did you trace me? Why was that important to you? What were these promises you mentioned earlier?"

I waited a moment.

"Thanks for lunch by the way."

I saw her smile even though she didn't turn to look at me.

She tapped a bit more and then a big screen, like twice as big as the one she was looking at blinked into life on the end wall. I must admit I hadn't seen it until it came on. She looked over her shoulder again.

"We're getting to that. Look at the screen."

I nodded and refocused on the big TV in front of me. In the movie, this is where Damien Lewis would put his glasses on and lean forward, chin in hand. I just scooted my chair a little way forward to get a better view. I ended up right next to Lizzy, even though she had her back to me.

The screen flickered again and then an image appeared, there was no sound. It was difficult to tell what it was at first but then I realised it was a street, like a normal street somewhere in a residential area and it was night. There was a lamp post just off centre and the light was sort of yellow or orange. I watched but beyond a small moth flapping around close to the light, nothing happened, and I realised that she had stopped tapping. I glanced sideways and noted that she was watching too.

"Watch the screen," she said almost immediately without turning.

I looked back and wondered why the scene looked familiar.

And then there was movement, out on the far left. I couldn't make it out in detail, but it looked like someone walking past or through, even though I could only see their legs. They moved quickly and then they were gone. Then nothing again but the same moth, now with a friend, for another couple of minutes and then it happened. From the left again, the same direction as the legs had gone came a group of what looked like men. They were all close together, moving strangely, three or four of them. They came diagonally into the picture, awkwardly until they were in the centre of the screen. And then I realised what I was looking at. There were four of them, two big guys on the left and right, one big guy very close behind, almost like they were moving as one. And then one smaller guy, probably not even a fag paper over 5'6" being half dragged, half carried in the middle. I watched as they moved across the screen and I continued watching as the small guy in the middle, the little one looked up, directly at the camera. He looked terrified, he looked in pain and even in the poor light, with the poor resolution of the recording I could see there were marks on his face.

He looked at the camera, like he was looking directly at me.

It was Danny.

19: Bona fide

It was like a bomb going off in my head. That's the only way I can describe it. And it took a while to calm down, with which she was a great help, seriously, unexpectedly so. I mean, she ought to be right, it was her fucking fault I'd lost the plot in the first place wasn't it. But anyway, I did a bit of shouting and stamping and all the usual petulant stuff, like throwing drinks coasters and lightly kicking the brick wall, well away from her computers and stuff, nothing too surprising. And then we went for a little walk, got a bit of fresh air and had a cup of tea. And eventually I was ready to go again. Fucking child.

"Right," we were back in the basement. "As I say I got this tape within a week of it happening and I've been tracking you ever since."

That answered part of the first question.

"And the promises I mentioned, they are to look after my land, this land. To make sure it is cared for, respected and preserved."

That answers part of question 2, or was it 3?

"But why were you even interested in Danny? Why do you have this tape?"

She got up and moved across to a large table in the back area, away from all the screens and shit.

"Come and look at this."

I went over, still slightly lightheaded from my tantrum. There was a map on the table, a huge one. To be fair the table was massive too, almost the size of the snooker tables I remember from the Ambassador Snooker club in Cheam.

"This is Wolweburg," she pointed, obviously. "And this is the surrounding area, and the house, here," she pointed again. "The mine was started in 1921 by this guy Peters, right. And you remember I said that when either the diamonds run out, or we reach the limit of our tech we stop digging?"

I nodded.

"But they're still digging so..."

"Yeah, that right, they're still digging, which is great. Except they ran out of diamonds in 1989."

I frowned.

"But you just said.... but that's like 10 years ago...."

"Right, I said when they run out of diamonds they stop. But they haven't stopped."

"Ok, right, But why? What are they digging for?"

She nearly smiled, but didn't, although I could sense a look of slight satisfaction on her face, like she was beginning to get to her point.

"So, this is where you come in," she took a breath. "What do you know about your Dad?"

Oh, for fuck sake. Not this again.

She saw the look on my face.

"So, you've heard something then?"

I nodded.

"Yeah, something, but to me he was just Dad, he was a decorator. I miss him."

She nodded.

"My Dad was just Dad too. I miss him too," she nodded and touched my arm. "But my Dad was also best mates with yours."

I felt my heart jump within my chest.

"Oh great, here we go, another bullshit 'best mate' story? How many 'best mates' can one guy have?" I said a little sarcastically.

"No, not *another* one. This is not the old *Terry Carter*, *Gabriel Scholari* or Colin Askwith bollocks you've heard before. This is real. I knew your Dad, I sat on his knee, I fell asleep in his arms. He was my Dad's best friend, he was my Uncle, he was family."

She looked a little emotional. I didn't know what to say.

"I don't believe you." I said flatly, wondering briefly who the fuck Gabriel Whatshisface was.

She hesitated for a moment and then:

"He was my Dad's friend Matthew, best man at his wedding," she turned and lifted down a photo album. She placed it gently on top of the map on the table and then glanced at me before opening it. As soon as she turned the cover over there were pictures of him, and then further on dozens of them. Dad in their pool, Dad in a suit, standing next to a big guy who both look familiar and shared a striking resemblance to Lizzy. And the house was there, the big windows at the back, the barbeque, the hill behind. There was even a picture of Dad playing the piano, I could see his watch and another one of him holding a little girl tightly in his arms, long dark hair, smooth brown skin, knobbly knees. It was like a punch in the bollocks, it really was, it took my breath away.

I glanced at Lizzy, and she blushed. Fuck sake she *blushed*. Who'd have thought that was possible a few hours ago.

I said nothing, I had no words, no banter, nothing. Even if I did, I don't think I could've talked without cracking at that point. I flicked through the book, page after page of photos, some faded, some better than others. He was everywhere, so many occasions, so many places. There were even some of me and Danny. I got to the end and stopped. I was breathless. I'd seen more pictures of my Dad in the last five minutes than I had throughout the rest of my entire life.

Eventually, I shook my head:

"The other promise?" I said softly.

She nodded.

"Yeah."

"I can't believe it."

She nodded again.

"Sorry for being a bitch before, I was pissed at Shirley."

"It's ok, really, it's cool," it wasn't completely cool, I still had bits of Shirley's hippocampus up my nose.

"I promised him, your Dad, that I would look out for you, all of you, Danny and your Mum. I've got money, shit more than I could spend in a dozen lifetimes. I've got skills and time, and I don't give a fuck about anything. So, I found you, a couple of years ago. I watched you, I worried about you."

It was all a bit much.

"And when they took Danny, I knew I had to do more."

"But why? Why did they take Danny? Why was my Dad here?"

"And that's the last piece of the puzzle Matthew, the promise I made, and why."

She moved the photo album, gently placing it back on the shelf behind, and then she turned back to the map.

"So, the diamonds ran out in 89 but they carried on digging. But why? Well turns out that below all the igneous rock is another type of rock. It kinda forms the plug that stops the igneous and diamonds pouring back out and down into the mantle. It's really hard but workable, brittle. Well, this rock, this plug, and it's not the only one, there's thousands of them all over the world, contains rare elements and heavy metals, one of which is lithium."

I was suddenly transported somewhere else. To a small blank office, in another basement, on another continent. And I was having a conversation with a big guy who called himself Terry Carter. And he was telling me about lithium, and some other stuff I couldn't quite remember. It made me think about Freya, her face, her bright eyes, her ponytail.

"Matthew, are you listening?"

"Yeah, sorry." I snapped back, a sick feeling growing in my belly.

"So, this Striochatheneamylist, which turns out to be amazing by the way, can be extracted from the lithium using a range of processes, one of which is called..."

"Electrolysis. It's an incredibly complicated process involving lots of steps and lots of expensive and complicated equipment. Dad was the only person who knew it all, he was..." I trailed off. Fuck.

Lizzy just looked at me without saying anything. I was glad, at least for the moment. Eventually she went on.

"Yeah, right. So, he was kind of an awesome guy, as we've said. Anyway thing is this Strio stuff is pretty cool too, and this is where we go back to my first promise. When he found this stuff, he and my Dad were working with weapons propulsion and weapons deployment, military stuff, hard core stuff. But when he, sorry, when *they* realised its potential as a replacement for fossil fuels, or at least an alternative fuel for the generation of power and energy they wanted to do something about it, they wanted to do more than make rockets for dropping bombs on people."

"I don't understand."

"Matthew Strio is amazing. It's an element that could replace uranium-235 and plutonium-239 as the primary fuel source for use in nuclear reactors. It's clean, it's safe and it doesn't degrade. And it doesn't produce dangerous waste. Think about it, with this fuel, we could build cleaner, more efficient power plants, we could provide energy cleanly to everyone. We could remove our dependence on fossil fuels in a single generation."

I was shaking my head, the grains of sand in front of me getting smaller by the second.

"And it's cheap, relative to the radioactive stuff. Plus, the tech is here, we already have it, both for the initial extraction and for its conversion into power."

"Right, I get it, so that fucking amazing. Where's the catch?"

"Oh, there isn't one."

I frowned.

"Really? No catch?"

She tilted her head to one side and looked at me like she would a small child.

"No, dickhead, of course there's a catch. There's always a catch."

I grinned; she was charming.

She went on.

"Strio is fucking awesome, everyone agrees, yeah, its gonna change the world, revolutionise power production, revitalise economies, inject wealth into some of the poorest places on earth. It'll remove our dependence on pollutants, provide clean water, and sanitation. It'll explode the science and space exploration industry and open corridors of research that have previously been unthinkable. It's fucking awesome."

"Right?"

"Right, so, I'm sure in the future it will be replaced by something even better, like properly efficient solar or something that doesn't involve digging bastard great holes in the ground. But for now, it's the thing, right now it's the bomb."

"Great, the bomb."

"Right. Great, fantastic, unless of course you're an oil producer, or an oil producing *nation*, you know, one of those whose economy depends entirely on the production, use and sales of oil. I'm sure you can think of one or two? Other fossil fuels are available, obviously."

"Right, ok, so its fucking awesome but not so awesome for some, thats easy enough. And I sense this is leading to another one of my questions, another one of your promises."

She nodded.

"Correct. You see this kind of thing screws everything up doesn't it. You've got the general population, the *billions and billions* of poor, underprivileged, exploited people wanting something better, cleaner, more efficient, cheaper and sustainable. And then you've got the 1% saying fuck you. I've got the money and I wanna keep the money."

I understood, I'd lived in the grey, I'd lived in and breathed that fucked up set of rules, riding my bus to and fro, watching that shit happen.

"And so they, the 1% do whatever they gotta do to protect themselves. They lie, they cheat, they steal, and they kill. They take over and control the extraction and exploitation of this amazing substance so it cannot be used for good. And here, in this instance, to answer your questions, they send guys to kill the only man in the whole fucking world who knows how to make this shit happen, who knows how to make Strio into a viable fuel and then, when they get scared and think that actually, despite their best efforts he's still out there, still out there and capable of communicating what he knows they go after his sons. First the little one, the one who likes to swing his fists, and then the older one, skinny, a bit pale, with soft eyes, and a soft smile."

It was very quiet, apart from all the humming and buzzing of the computer shit behind us. I stood looking at her, and then the map and then back at her. I didn't know what to react to first. There was a lot in that last statement, like nearly all

I'd been searching for in one go. I felt like I'd taken a massive bite out of a really greasy cheeseburger, too big to chew, too good to spit out.

"Um," I hesitated.

"Sorry." she offered, well aware that she had both unloaded a huge fucking bomb on me as well as complemented me in the sweetest possible way. Well, as sweet as she was ever going to get, I assumed.

Fuck this was awkward.

"Um, it's ok, Thank you." I looked at her shyly. "Um, did you just say that they think he's still alive?"

She nodded.

"Yup. they think your Dad is still alive."

My heart started to flutter a bit in my chest. I took a breath to steady myself.

"And why would they think that? Do *you* think that?"

"I did say some other stuff as well you know."

"Yes I know but, and thank you by the way, for that, but...'

I trailed off but kept eye contact.

She looked at me for a long time, a sad look on her face but also with eyes that seemed alive with hope or rage or something. Finally, she responded, her eyes now sliding away over my left shoulder.

"Oh that's easy really, they think it, because it's true."

I stared at her for a moment, her words whizzing around my brain, burning and smashing into stuff and eventually, slowly, like snow, settling and finding their place. And then equally slowly, like a man in a dream, like a man dipped in honey I turned around to see what my eyes refused to believe. My Dad, my actual fucking, real life, bona fide Dad standing there, right in front of me.

I kid you not, I shit my pants.

"Hello Squidge."

20: Jack in the box

"Hello Squidge, hello son."

I mean, those words, that little phrase, right? I'm sure you can imagine. I'm sure, if you've got this far and are as invested as you'd have to be to have persevered for so long, you'll have at least some basic understanding of how fucking monumental that was.

And it was mental, monu-mental. It was earth shattering. It was genuinely like the earth shifting on its axis, or something equally geophysical. It was like finding out that everything you thought was real and true about your life, was, in fact, not true. Like everything and everyone, every memory, every thought, experience, opinion, ambition, hope, fear and truth was suddenly shown to be false, fake and shit.

Oh wait, sorry, it wasn't *like* that, it *was* that.

But it was also the most gratifying, satisfying and emotionally rewarding moment of my life.

It was like I'd been doing this massive jigsaw puzzle, you know, like the ones of the surface of the moon made up of 29 gazillion, almost identical pieces. And I'd kinda got there or was at least starting to see the picture.

And then he was there, my Dad, back from the dead, in the flesh, looking at me with his own, real, proper eyes, his kind face, a face I knew, a face that was imprinted on my soul. He was there, and he knew me, and he had the missing pieces of my puzzle, the pieces that made it make sense, that made it look like a proper thing, a proper picture.

And then he said my name and grabbed me and hugged me and my god did I fucking cry.

But fuck you if you think that's wet, I don't give a shit. It was the best thing ever, the best thing ever. And yes, I wept like a baby. So did he, so did Lizzie, rightly so.

He held me for a good 5 minutes, it was amazing. I smelled him, exactly as I remember, exactly as I dreamt and fantasised. And I had, really. Losing your Dad at 13 is rough, seriously. Especially if he'd given a fuck about you before he popped. Especially if the memories you were left with were ones you cherished. I mean, yes, I'm sure it's still tough if you didn't get on, if he had been a wanker, or absent. But then it would be a case of going through life being the man you had to be because of his failings. *Despite* his failings. You'd have a resilience already, you'd have a strength inside made up of the pain of his rejection, or cruelty, or apathy.

Sure, you'd spend a ton of time questioning yourself, him, your mum maybe. You'd probably waste a huge section of very precious time and energy thinking that you're a cunt because he wasn't interested. When the truth would be the complete reverse. And that would be sad.

But I didn't have that. Either of those things. At thirteen, I knew we had stuff to finish. He needed to be there, to carry on calling me Squidge for a bit. To carry me in his arms a bit when I needed it, to help me with my woodwork project at school, to tell me about girls. He should've, would've been there to fight my corner, to help me build my walls, to straighten me out when I needed it, to laugh at me when I needed it.

To finish what he started.

Of course, he couldn't do that now could he? I'd already finished what he started, or at least I thought I had at nineteen. Truth is, and this is only a hindsight thing, there was still a lot he could do.

We stopped crying after a while and then my brain woke up to it. And with that came all my questions. I don't know if he was happy or took some satisfaction in the volume of info, I demanded from him or not, but he never stopped smiling the whole time. I mean the questions were initially all about what he was doing there, how he got there, what he knew about Danny etc. But after a while they predictably slid into the whole 'why the fuck did you let us think you were dead for all that time?'

At this point Lizzie disappeared upstairs to get drinks. She reappeared briefly before disappearing again to give us time to work through some of that.

"It wasn't a choice I made. It wasn't like I had option A: Stay around, see my boys grow up, make a go of my marriage. Or option B: disappear and pretend to be dead."

He looked at me and yes, of course, I was listening to him, you know, taking in his words and stuff. But I was also just plain enjoying hearing his voice, again exactly like I remembered it. It was warm and familiar, soft and comfortable in my ear. It's weird trying to describe it, but it just was, just really comfortable in my ears

"I tried to stay in, you know, in the firm, to make the changes from the inside. But it got too difficult. There was a moment when I knew three things reached critical mass, you know like, one on its own would've been manageable. Two, possibly, but three not, not on my own, not on my own and still keeping you safe. Plus, the other options, if you want to call them that, always, no matter how I rearranged the pieces always left you and your Mum at risk."

Two, no three months earlier I'd have had no fucking idea what he was talking about. Seriously, the limit of my experience of 'risk' would've pointed me at a possibility that the council were looking at increasing the rent, or that Mums parking had gone up a fiver a week.

Now though, I knew he was talking about the likelihood of real, physical harm. And the risk of that harm being visited upon us by one or more of a number of clandestine international security organisations.

Mental.

"I was in possession of too much knowledge, too much information. Both about the tech and processes, as well as the political landscape that was driving the controls."

He sipped his drink.

"Plus, I'd been vocal in my reluctance to go further, to *exploit* our asset, to exploit our resources, and to develop the tech needed for what they wanted to do. And the more it was talked about the more vocal I became. I mean I was warned, both by friends and those who turned out later not to be friends."

"I think I might have met a few of those."

He nodded.

"Yes, Lizzie's kept me up to date. I'm sorry."

He reached out and placed his hand on my shoulder.

"I can't tell you how proud I am of you son. You've done so well, you know, dealing with all this, all those guys, all the lies. I'm just so sorry you've had to."

I went a bit red. It was embarrassing, and quite nice. I shrugged, and immediately looked around nervously.

Dad went on.

"So, the scientific community knew, *knows still*, all about Strio. The testing and modelling was carried out by a team in Budapest back in the late eighties and early nineties. It was overseen by the European Commission for Energy Research, or ECER and paid for by both European member states, and others, further afield. Not least of which was the US. All very smart, very public and very well structured. And this was following time we put in back home when it was still test tube stuff, you know like experiments at the academy, burning stuff, setting fire to stuff."

I nodded, I kinda knew, even though my participation in sciencey shit at school wasn't regular or desired, but I remembered the Bunsen Burners and the glass test tubes and stuff from chemistry.

"After a bit of time and money had been thrown at it and despite interference, we managed, amongst other things, to engineer a principle. And by that I mean a standard or method by which the energy generated can be measured, quantified and most importantly, controlled. This principle showed remarkable efficiencies and almost zero emissions and waste. Unheard of."

He sipped his drink again.

"And then it got tasty right because the UK government wanted to keep it quiet so they could use it for weapons, as did three or four private little outfits who we've always suspected to be fronts for bigger players. The petrochemical companies disputed ownership and wanted to squash it, like, completely, to stop it putting them out of business, and they're fucking ruthless son, make no mistake. And then on top of that we had Greenpeace and one or two others wanting to publish the data and spread the word so we could change the world. And why not?"

Exactly, I had no idea. Why not indeed? Fuck the Petrochem boys and their shiny cars and Christmas bonuses. Fuck the weapons guys and their mental desire to shit on everyone. Why not? Why couldn't we change the world?

"And it all came to a head. Some dickhead, or saviour, or whatever, depends on your viewpoint, leaked the Strio tech to the BBC. They did a segment on *Tomorrows World* where Judith Hann showed how batteries of the future would work. Utter nonsense all these years on."

I had no idea what *Tomorrows Worle* was or what Judith Whatsherface would've been doing with batteries. But it sounded cool.

"Anyway, it was a nothing piece, barely received any public attention really. Certainly not interesting enough to get the mainstream going. But it *was* enough to ruffle the feathers of people already invested, you know, materially or intellectually. Because there was never any money in Strio, at least there didn't look to be then anyway. It was more likely to cost economies than line pockets. You know, now that I think about it, that's probably why it was able to remain so low key, because it wasn't of interest to the financial community."

"I assume that's changed, right? I mean, if not, why are people chasing me all over the shop?"

"Similar reasons as me, they want control. Yes, it's changed, now, there's money there, I mean a shit ton of money if you think about it. But that's not why you've been targeted."

I frowned. Hadn't thought about it in terms of me being 'targeted' before. I'd kind of assumed I was just in the wrong place at the wrong time and had a name that seemed to mean something.

"But I haven't been *targeted* really, have I?"

Dad looked up at me, his smile slipping for a bit.

"Yes mate, you have. At least I think Danny was, maybe by accident, and then because of that, because you stuck your head up, and they zeroed in on you."

I shook my head.

"Ok, so if Danny was a target and not me, why? Sorry, that's confusing. Why him and not me? Why not both of us?"

He sat back and rubbed his face before continuing.

"It's complicated Matthew," he hesitated, and looked uncomfortable. "For now, let's just say; it's the way these things work. It's like, you have to have a certain amount of positive in order to respond to the negative. Like I say, it's complex. It's to do with your Locus of control and means there has to be a degree of self-determination left in order to maintain motivation."

I was staring at him. He went on.

"So, I need to go back a bit here, you know, to the fact I was dead. At least, I mean to the fact you all thought I was dead right?"

I nodded.

"So, with that thought, that *absolute*, you were fucked, you had nowhere to go, you had nothing to aim for," he held up his hand apologetically, "And I'm sorry if that's brutal but seriously it's true, I know it is, I saw it."

I should've been hurt by that. I mean, I've thought about it over the years since and *have* been hurt, like seriously. But then, back then, in the moment, with him sitting in front of me sipping his pop, being offended was the last thing I was wanting to do. It did bring a little tear to my eye though, which he saw, which he felt shit for.

He paused for a bit; I think he had a bit of a lump in his throat. Eventually.

"So, *knowing* I was dead, you had no motivation, right? But thinking I was alive would've had you buzzing wouldn't it?"

Fuck, he was right. I mean, I was here now wasn't I, having had nothing more than a greasy note slipped into my coat pocket by a senile old man. And the note had no context, no *anything*, it was just a note, just an address, nothing else. And

I'd gone off like that, selling shit, packing a bag, setting off like some prick Disney character on some great adventure, crossing the continent in search of my owners who abandoned me at a gas station in Illinois.

Wankers.

But he was right. One tiny, insignificant, almost non-existent sliver of hope and BOOM, off I went.

"Without the possibility of something positive, you know, without *hope* all you get is apathy."

"Right so if they'd taken both me and Danny the Nutter, sorry Mum would've lost hope right, she'd have just, what? Not been bothered? Not been able to look for us?"

Pretty sure the 'Nutter' reference would've earned me a clip round the ear any other day, but today he let it slide.

"Yes, maybe. I don't know. But it wasn't about your mum. Again, I go back a bit here, but this is why you're here isn't it, because of all this, because of me. You see, if you thought I was dead, then you'd just *be* as you were, just there, not reaching out, not doing anything to attract attention. You'd be safe."

I nodded, made sense.

"And when I *died* I did it in such a way as to make sure anyone who was still looking for me would give up, that they'd see and know it was over, it was done."

"Right."

"So they all thought I was dead, all of them, it worked, and then something happened."

Right, so immediately I had a feeling, a feeling that I wasn't going to like the next bit. He sat back again and rubbed his face, again.

Before he could go on though I heard footsteps on the wooden stairs and then Lizzie popped her head round.

"You guys getting hungry?"

I mean, yeah, of course. But, like, her timing could've been better. We both looked up and Dad replied.

"Yes, yes we are. Thank you."

"Good cause we've finished mopping Shirley up and the braai is ready to go."

"The what?!"

"Great, thanks. We'll be up to wash up in a mo," Dad looked pleased at the mention of the braai, so I guessed it to be something good.

"Cool, and yeah, give the little fella a scrub won't you, he smelt like shit earlier."

And then the cheeky bitch was gone, footsteps going up the stairs and doors slamming and banging.

Dad smiled.

"You'll get used to it," he patted my shoulder again as he stood. "Come on, let's gets some air, have a beer and then we'll get back into this".

He gestured to the maps and computers and shit, but I knew what he meant. I was glad too, because yeah, I was hungry, and I honestly couldn't contain myself at the thought of having an actual beer with my father, but I was also really keen to finish our chat. I still had so many questions.

We headed upstairs, him first with me following. I was determined not to let him out of my sight, you know, in case he vanished again. Daft I know but I couldn't help it.

Anyway, turns out a braai is like a barbecue. I mean it is, but it isn't. Like, it's meat cooked over wood and coals, outside, socially but it's more than that. It's more social, it's more about the occasion, the fire, the beer, the chat. It's a South African thing, traditional, or something. And the meat's different, there are no burgers or cheap shit, its all-prime cuts and legs of this and legs of that.

Franc was there, so was Shirley but only in the form of a bit of dried blood under Franc's fingernails. Only joking, he'd actually showered so was all clean, still grumpy as fuck though. The two goons that walked Lizzie into my room, what seemed like an age ago, but which was actually only yesterday, were also there plus a couple of the guys I remember seeing at the airport along with Mick and Gerth. Also, a black lady who Lizzie introduced to me simply as Princess. She then handed me a beer and ruffled my hair like she was my great Aunt - Lizzie not Princess, before drifting away to look at the meat sizzling on the coals. I mean seriously, what the fuck?

Dad smiled and moved away himself to talk to Franc leaving me standing awkwardly by the big glass doors. It was then I noticed a few more people sitting at a table a little further from the house. I've never been great in social moments like these, no matter how intimate they may seem. Still not great at it now if I'm honest. I know, I knew then, that I just needed to wander up to people and speak but as simple as that sounds, it's tricky, you know, to overcome that initial anxiety.

That said, the guys sitting apart looked equally uncomfortable, so I threw caution to the wind and went over anyway.

As I got closer, I realised that it was a family, and they weren't dressed like everyone else. I hesitated momentarily and would've turned back, but Lizzie appeared at my shoulder and, linking arms with me, carried me forward.

We arrived at the table and the people stood up, smiling nervously.

"Matthew this is Khayone Gowon and his family; Geraldine his wife, Gumede, Haroon, Jalila, his children. Khayone is the father of Melokuhle, the boy one of my men took, tortured and killed. These are his brothers and sister; this is his mother. I have welcomed them to my home because I am shamed by what my man did."

Boom. Just like that.

Fuck this was awkward.

I nodded, really not sure if this was a good idea or not. I mean, back home you wouldn't invite the family of one of your mates' victims to your barbeque, would you? Like, you'd be asking for it. What with knives and in this case guns and what not floating about there would bound to be trouble. I looked at Khayone and then at his wife. I glanced at his children, and I felt a lump in my throat.

Lizzie unlinked her arms from mine and approached the man. She bowed her head and gently took his hand and placed it on the top of her head, and then she knelt. And if I'm honest I've never been so moved by anything. It was fucking heartbreaking. Worse than when Alex died in my arms.

Khayone, clearly a proud man, was crying, his wife was crying, his kids were sobbing, bless them, Lizzie was crying too.

Without standing she spoke quietly between her sobs:

"I cannot bring your son back Khayone Gowon, father, strong man, defender, but I offer my heart and my sorrow."

Khayone stood still, his hand laying softly on Lizzie's head and his tears rolling. The moment dragged out. Eventually he placed both hands on her shoulders and raised her up before cupping her face.

"You are a good girl Lizzie Bathandwa, your father was our Utata omkhulu. You have avenged our son and shown me your heart. I forgive you."

And then they embraced. I know it sounds glib and a bit trashy, but it was just like that. It was simple and powerful, and I was so moved by it. Maybe I've cut it short, but I can't see any point labouring the emotional bits of it. I'm also not suggesting that a pat on the head and a few tears undid the damage caused by Shirley. I mean, a child had been taken, by one of the very people responsible for his protection. There would be a shift in loyalty for sure, a dramatic and perhaps permanent change in the relationship and trust between the villages and landowners.

Lizzie knew it, I'm sure she did, Khayone knew too. It was sad, more sad than just the immediate and the obvious. And I remember thinking at the time, that this simple moment was more significant that it appeared on the surface.

Eventually they parted, made some small talk before Lizzie led me away. Which was fine by the way, I mean I had wanted to talk to the family up until the moment I found out who they were. And then I'd spent the next few minutes, whilst watching the exchange between parties, trying to work out how to back away without seeming rude.

She took me back over towards the braai. We passed Princess on the way loaded up with drinks and snacks for the Gowon's so I felt a bit better at leaving them, even if I couldn't get the picture of the kids sobbing out of my mind.

Shit we all lost stuff didn't we. Me, I'd lost my Dad, and then later my little brother. And it was easy to get wrapped up in that, to think I was the only one. That's what I meant when I said I spent a lot of time in my own head, you know, just running around that hamster wheel of woe is me.

But fuck it, I wasn't the only one. Everyone lost people, EVERYONE. And some people never got the opportunity to do anything about it. Some people never got to crawl out from under the rock of grief and loss that losing someone could be. They were just trapped there, squashed by its weight, pinned down by its mass. And they just existed with it. No healing, no moving on, no answers and no quest for closure.

Cause that's what this was after all wasn't it. A quest. Sounds crap doesn't it but in reality, that's what this started out as, and what I'd subsequently chosen every moment since, at least in the moments I'd had the freedom of choice.

Fuck, I was a dick. Chasing about after nothing. Nothing more than a little personal and completely selfish peace of mind, when the Nutter was back there in the flat pinned under her own rock of grief, loss and creeping madness she had no means to escape from.

I felt sick.

Lizzie stopped and turned me to face her.

"Are you ok?"

No insults, no banter, just straight.

I looked at her and wondered what we were. I wondered what she was, to me. Was she my friend? Was she my sister (from another Mister)? Or was she, could she, should she be more?

She was beautiful. Like really. And not just her skin, her eyes, her lips and her white teeth. She was fierce, and smart, and brutal, and kind, and soft, and capable. Fuck she was everything I could want in a sister. Like, she'd have my back, she'd have Danny's, Mums too. And she'd be there, loyal, I'd seen that in the basement, the photos, the love she had for Dad, the shared history.

But she also had an amazing body and looked like she could be proper dirty.

I took a breath.

"No, not really."

She didn't say anything straight away. Instead, she looked across at Dad who was still nattering to Franc and one of the goons, Pieter I think his name was. The moment dragged before she turned back to face me.

"You can't stay here you know."

I nodded after a moment.

"I know."

"They'll be coming for him, maybe for you too. If not now, then soon. Too much has happened, too much activity over the last few weeks not to have drawn attention. And even if they don't know, they'll still come, because, hey, you know, why not...."

I nodded again but followed it up.

"How long has he been here? How long have you been safe here?"

She smiled a little sadly.

"Not long, but he's been here many times in the past, it's always been safe. But he wasn't in a good way when he arrived this time, there were people tracking him."

"I'm sorry."

She frowned.

"It's not your fault. If anything, it's mine. I, I mean *we*, left loose ends, loose threads. Plus *'they'* took a gamble and took Danny. It flushed you out and the rest is history."

Now I frowned.

"What loose threads?" I thought back to something Dad had said in the basement just before we came up for air - '*You see, they all thought I was dead, all of them, and then something happened*'.

What happened?

Lizzie turned away again smiling at someone across the deck. A moment later she turned back to me.

"There's another dimension here that you don't know, something that's," she hesitated, glancing over her shoulder before looking back at me. "Matty, there's something else here much bigger than the stuff we've already told you."

A month, no a week, no fuck it, a *day* ago I would've rolled my eyes. Not now. No, now something told me just to listen.

"Go on," I said carefully, remembering Terry saying something quite similar.

Lizzie smiled thinly, noting the intelligence of my response. But she didn't go on, instead we were interrupted by the sound of a helicopter.

21: Flash Bang

We both looked up instinctively but saw nothing, it was dark. Initially no one else reacted but after a moment both Franc and Dad stopped talking and looked round at me and Lizzie. I looked at Dad, a thousand thoughts tumbling through my mind all at once, the most prominent being that I was going to lose him, after only just finding him.

Lizzie gripped my arm.

"Come. NOW," she said with such urgency I snapped to attention and looked back round just in time to be dragged by the same arm she'd grabbed, back through the patio doors and into the lounge area.

I wanted to stop, to force her to stop, to ask her what the fuck was going on. But I didn't. That was the old me, unfamiliar with massive international conspiracies and green as a five pound note me. Instead, I focused on what I saw around me.

The braai was over. Staff, guests, even the Gowon's scattered like frozen peas on the kitchen floor. Pieter threw a bucket of water over the barbecue before running out into the grounds, gun drawn and face all serious and shit. Three or four others went with him, at least two of which I'd never even seen. Someone turned the lights off to the house, like all of them and then massive flood lights *on* in the gardens - the place lit up like the astroturf at Mile End. Luckily Pieter and his buddies were well out of the way by then.

Lizzie pulled me across the room, telling me to keep my head down, hurry up, slow down, keep my eyes open, and look where I was going. All at once. I mean that was fair though, because I did kinda bounce off every fucking piece of furniture in the room enroute to the corridor.

But we weren't the only ones. Franc, Dad and three or four others followed and chased us down the hall towards the basement stairs.

I was shitting myself if I'm honest but even in that state I was concerned that dropping down into the basement would be suicide. It was a dead end with nowhere to hide. Surely it would've been better to head out and jump into one of the battered old 4x4's?

And I would've raised my concern had it not seemed like this had been rehearsed, like this exact scenario hadn't been exhaustively prepared for at some point in the recent past.

Plus, I didn't have time to stop and chat through the pros and cons, we were bursting through the door and clattering downstairs before I could take a breath.

All this time the noise of the helicopter had been increasing. So much so, the rhythmic beating of its rotor was beginning to shake the big patio windows and actually hurt my ears. It was a fucking sight louder than Alex's bird that's for sure.

Anyway, as we went down so the sound was dramatically cut off. Like completely. I tried to glance over my shoulder to see what kind of big ass door I'd missed at the head of the stairs, but Lizzie just shouted at me.

"Get a fucking move on Matthew!"

I did as I was told.

In moments we were all in the basement together. Lizzie let go of me and hustled over to her tech. She began punching in passwords and shit and the closing or deleting systems. Or something like that, she told me after. I watched for a moment before turning to see Franc and Dad swinging shut another big ass door I'd also missed at the bottom of the stairs.

Great, double sealed inside Lizzie's smelly little tech-den, and there was me busily brewing an early evening poo. This could be awkward.

Dad came over, sweaty and nervous looking but far from panicking.

"Sorry. Jesus. We expected *something*, just not this, and not now. Anyway, you, ok?" He grabbed my shoulder, which was nice. He also looked intently into my eyes. I nodded.

"Yeah. Yeah, I think so. You?"

He smiled, actually he grimaced.

"I will be."

Next, he called over to Lizzie.

"How are you doing kiddo? Do we have eyes on yet?"

She shook her head, concentrating.

"In a sec."

I watched this but was also conscious of Franc dragging a helper around and over to where the big map table was, where I'd first laid eyes back on my old fella.

"Let me know as soon as we have an ID and a number. We'll get things set up next door."

Next door? Next fucking door??

I frowned and must've flinched or reacted in some way because Dad turned back to me.

"Don't stress son, we've got this. We've prepared for this, it's all gonna work out".

"Got it!" Lizzie slammed her hand on the tabletop as the images from an array of cameras flickered and flashed into life on the big screen. Everyone turned to see, and Dad, letting go of my shoulder, moved past me to look closely.

Like I said the doors had shut out all the sound from above, so the only noise was the hum of the air conditioners keeping Lizzie's stuff going. So we couldn't hear the helicopter come into land or the subsequent gunfire as Pieter and his team's set about defending the house from the garden.

We saw the flashes though, and the black suited figures as they crept round and into the building, covering angles, returning fire at those out of sight in the bushes. It occurred to me how much they looked like the 'Columbians' I'd seen attack the compound back in Bellano. The thought made me instantly break sweat and if I'd been alone, I would definitely have let out a little gas.

Some of the cameras were infrared so we could see movement even in the darkened house above us. And having watched plenty of movies about nighttime assaults on well-guarded compounds, I assumed them to be wearing some kind of night vision gear as well.

Like, how were they finding their way around otherwise? I mean, fair play, I could've used a set of them a while ago back in Ventnor. It might have saved me a whole ball sack full of trouble.

Now, like I said earlier this whole thing must've been prepared. Because as the Columbians naturally, instinctively came into the house, into the dark, to avoid at all costs the brightly lit grounds, plus, I guessed, to search for us, so the lighting switched. Someone must've been controlling it, not Lizzie but someone, somewhere else, because it was instantaneous, devastating. Just as was the reaction and consequences.

I watched, transfixed as the Columbians, all of them freaked out. Not just because their night vision was completely fucking destroyed along with their coordination, shape and 'plan' but because they knew, before it all actually happened, what it would mean. And then I watched as the *real* guns in the garden opened fire. And I furthermore understood the reason for all the big ass plate glass windows.

I glanced at Dad, I guess expecting to see a little look of triumph on his face. I was disappointed, well not really, I was relieved. He looked sick, as did Lizzie, as did everyone else. Rehearsed or not, planned for or not, this was fucking brutal, disgusting.

I mean obviously, it wasn't a choice thing, not at this stage. It was clearly them or us, I'd seen that, as I say, in Bellano. But that didn't make it pleasant viewing.

But I sensed too that this wasn't the end game. I mean it was clever, clearly unexpected and completely crushing, but no-one was looking at the door, getting ready to open it. I frowned and looked from face to face, slightly concerned that I might be missing something.

And then the house shook. Like fucking for real, like a fucking earthquake. The screen flickered, as did the lights in the basement and I'm pretty sure at least a dozen spiders fell from the ceiling above me into my hair. And looking back to the images from the cameras I saw ALL the external floodlights go out, some kind of projectile flash across at least three of the screens that carried views of the garden and then a huge, almighty flash.

The house shook again, like massively, worse than before, with dust and shit and all sorts falling from the ceiling above us. Then the garden lit up brighter than when the floodlights had been on, briefly but it was blinding. All the screens went white and then immediately after all the power went off. And when I say all of it, I mean all of it.

It was pitch black, not even the glow of standby lights.

I sensed that this is what they'd been waiting for, like the first bits were just the starter and this was the main course.

And whilst I was disoriented and properly scared, personally, I was actually kinda reassured that no one around me seemed to be panicking.

"The UPS should kick in any second" it was Lizzie.

I heard Dad in front of me.

"Is he here?"

I guessed the query was directed at Lizzie; she'd been staring at the screens as closely as him. But Franc answered.

"Let fucking hope not, eh? A few fucking doors aren't gonna to help if he is."

Who were they talking about? Was this the same *he* as Terry mentioned?

What the fuck was this?

And then finally we got some power back on, not like before, like not *all* the lights came on but enough. Plus, some of the computers came back to life along with the screens.

I mean I say *finally* but like, it was only a few seconds really, not even a minute.

I looked around immediately, and noted some of the books had fallen off the shelves and a couple of the lights that normally hung close to the ceiling were now swinging at a wonky angle. Other than that though, it seemed like the basement had survived pretty much unscathed.

"Fuck."

I spun back round to see what Dad was stressing over. He was staring at the screen which had sorted itself out enough for a couple of the camera feeds to be back on. One of them just showed the tiled floor of the kitchen where the shaking had wobbled it enough for it to have drooped down.

The other one though was still rolling just as before and showed a view from inside the hallway just outside the room I'd stayed in. I mean I say 'stayed in' but it was literally just one night wasn't it, and it was only yesterday. Dad was watching the screen, as was Lizzie.

I saw the front door open, and some bodies pass through and then a bit of back and forth. The guys we were watching were moving in a far more relaxed way than when all the shooting was going on a short while ago. It was clear, even on the grainy images, on the small screen that something significant had changed, that the combat they'd initially come in prepared for was all but done.

I think I understood the bangs and flashes now. I thought briefly about Pieter and his buddies but didn't dwell, at least they'd had guns, the Gowon's didn't. And they'd had kids with them. Unless they had got completely clear before the *bird* landed, I couldn't imagine how they might have survived. It had been too busy, too messy out there. Fuck.

Franc had dragged the same guy round to the other side again and now reappeared.

"We need to go," he said bluntly.

I looked at him, more than happy with that, even if I had no idea what or how or when or whatever.

"Hold on," Dad held up his hand.

Lizzie frowned, she clearly agreed with Franc. She turned her back quickly and began closing down more stuff on her computer. In moments she was done and then standing and beginning to move away.

"He's here," Dad said quietly, again holding up his hand.

Everyone, bar Franc and his helper turned back to the screen.

"Are you sure?" Lizzie challenged quickly.

Dad nodded but said nothing. I looked from one to the other and then back at the screen. Who were they talking about?

"Then," she hesitated, "then, Franc's right. We need to go."

Again, Dad nodded, and now Franc reappeared.

"Guys we're going to miss our window if we don't go now...."

Lizzie touched Dad on the shoulder.

"Keith,"

This time he turned, his face was pale, and he looked panicked. Bollocks, this was getting proper scary now. Never mind the big bangs and shit, if Dad, the man who died but was now alive, was worried, then we defo had problems. Also, the girl who shot Shirley in the face was clearly unhappy too, so, like, that was more than enough for me.

"Fuck sake, who's *he*? Who are you talking about? Can someone fucking tell me who we're running from?"

No one looked at me, but Dad answered quietly, with real fear in his voice.

"Someone with a very dark mind, son. Someone we have no choice but to run from."

I nodded, hearing but not really hearing.

"So can we fucking go then please? Like, I've no idea where we might be going to, but, seriously, it's gotta be better than here right?"

Again, nobody looked at me, but I think my sentiment was shared.

Lizzie nodded and took my hand.

"Come on," and over her shoulder; "Keith."

I noticed, even then, that she was trembling. I mean there was a lot going on right? But even so it surprised me, because, like, she was tough. Plus, they'd planned for this, in detail, at least it seemed like they had.

She walked me across the room and into the corner where Franc had been, Dad followed and the last of the big guys at the rear. We passed round and under the staircase that came down into the basement and ducking under a low lintel we passed into a narrow corridor.

Lizzie made me wait while Dad and the other guy - Mani - pulled the door, which was disguised as a shelving unit complete with paint tins and dirty rags, closed behind us. I couldn't see it from the other side, but Lizzie assured me later that it would easily fool the casual observer and buy us some time.

It was properly dark in the corridor, so we went forward with flashlights. I followed Lizzie and I guessed she followed Franc even if he was somewhere far up in front and out of sight. Very soon the corridor turned into a proper rough tunnel. We walked for about ten minutes, straight at first and then with the 'tunnel' angling downward quite steeply for five minutes it levelled off. Then started a slow sweep round to the right.

I got completely disoriented if I'm honest, and quickly too. I had no idea where we were in relation to the house, grounds and access road above. I guessed, rightly, so I was later informed that this tunnel was something to do with the diamond mine. It has been dug during the time Lizzie's Great grandfather had worked the mine himself. Obviously, the house had been torn down and rebuilt at some point, but the tunnel remained pretty much intact.

But beyond that I had no idea which direction we were heading and panicked, for a brief moment, that we'd pop out somewhere in the vertical wall of the huge fucking hole I saw earlier.

Jesus, was that seriously only earlier the same day?

Anyway, the tunnel kept going for a bit before we heard voices and saw the others waiting for us. I was kind of relieved but also still nervous, I mean, where were we going? Who was going to be waiting for us? Assuming we were going to be getting out of this tunnel or whatever.

And if not, where did it lead? Were we stuck in here? Shit, it was so far out of my comfort zone it was ridiculous. Like, the closest I'd ever come to anything like this was when we broke into the grain warehouse on Whaddon Wharf. It had been abandoned for fucking years and was running with rats the size of Shetland ponies. But we'd spent a summer mooching about in there, crawling along the conveyors, in and out of the silos etc. Between tinkering with all the old machinery and shooting at the rats with the same air rifle I shot Skinny Mitches mums' cat with, we played hide and seek. Like, it sounds a bit wet but fuck me it was an amazing place to do it. It was fucking great, apart from the rashes and the sore eyes we all got. But no, it was a great summer. Shame it burned down really. Not that we had anything to do with it.

Honest.

Anyway, it was dark and a bit creepy, like this tunnel. But this tunnel, plus the shooting and the explosions and shit going on upstairs were real, weren't they? I mean hide and seek and shooting pests with pellets is one thing, massive explosions, real guns, dead guys and a tunnel deep under a South African diamond mine were something else entirely.

But I didn't really have time to think about it did I, because we were passing through a heavy metal door, there was talking, decisions and stress and then we were moving again.

It was cold down there, at least colder than it was up top. And that was taking into account that it was nighttime too. But it was ok cause we kept walking, and I was focusing more on not falling over or doing anything that might get us all killed, rather than how hard my nipples were.

I was also counting my steps and casting my mind back to try and work out where we were and where we'd eventually come out. Assuming that was actually the plan, and we weren't intending to stay down here like Gollum. I mean I'm sure it was fine if you liked the dark or were part mole, but I did, and still do prefer the sun.

Eventually we came to the end of the tunnel and another door. It was heavy, like the first one and squeaked when Franc pulled it round. He told us to wait while he squeezed through and went to check things out.

We waited quietly, me fully expecting to hear either footsteps coming up the tunnel behind us, or two or three sharp pops as Franc had his ass capped. Thankfully none of the above happened. Instead, after a couple of minutes he reappeared and beckoned us through, his finger over his lips by way of telling us to keep schtum.

I would tell you what everyone else was looking like, you know, their reactions, expressions etc, but it was dark, as I've already said so, you know, I've got nothing. Sorry.

Suffice to say though that without exception we did as told and followed him through the door.

On the other side it appeared, upon first glance, to be just as dark and fucking miserable as it was in the tunnel, albeit a bit more spacious. I assumed immediately that it was just another chamber but as soon as he had eased the door shut - and locked it - Franc gathered us up and moved us across to a vehicle covered by a tarpaulin or netting or something.

We all helped to pull it off and drag it across the floor to sit in front of the big door. And then we got in. Franc was up front, with his mate, then Dad and Lizzie and then me and the other two at the back. It was like a massive off-road thing, huge fat wheels and heavy metal bars on the front. It was painted dark, but I could see a shit ton of lights mounted on the roof. It also had fuel tanks strapped to the side and rear and shovels and shit hanging off on various locations.

Inside it was nothing like Cubby's Merc. The seats were soft but hard, if you know what I mean and there were more bars and stuff strapped in place. It wasn't built for comfort that's for sure. And as I thought that I considered that if not built for comfort maybe it was built for survival.

It certainly looked like it would ace a zombie apocalypse - if the need arose.

It took a moment to get us all in and settled and for Franc to go round the outside and do his pre-flight checks. And then he was back, and we were ready to go. Now it's worth pointing out that no-one has actually spoken, apart from the old grumpy cunt himself since we'd left the basement. I mean there'd been a bit of mumbling and some urgent whispering and shit but no actual talking. Which was weird, but I guessed probably appropriate under the circumstances.

Anyway, now Franc turned and addressed us all.

"In the event you don't know, what comes next is gonna be rough. It's gonna be rough if we make it out without being seen. It's gonna be fucking shit if they *do* see us."

I looked around but still couldn't really see anyone, so I focused back on Mr Happy.

"The van has mods to deal with small arms but not much more, so if we get cornered it's a bust."

Apart from Franc it was silent in the van. Apart from the blood rushing like mad in my ears that is.

"It's also had mods to give us an advantage if they come after us, on or off road, so hopefully getting cornered won't be a concern. You all need to strap in and brace, at all times, it's gonna be fucking bumpy."

I felt Lizzie lean over from the seat in front and check my seatbelt. She said nothing but I could smell her sweat and feel her heat. It was nice, quite a mumsy or big sister kind of thing to do.

I would've thanked her, but Franc went on.

"We're going out quiet and dark. Me and Alex have NVG, so we won't need lights. Keep your fucking heads down and your mouths shut."

Rude, as standard, but fuck it, I didn't need telling twice. Once more I found myself entirely in the hands of someone operating a scary ass machine which was likely to make the difference, for me at least, between life and a messy death. I just hoped I didn't have to watch any of these guys die like I did last time.

Especially my Dad.

Oh, and Lizzie too, obviously.

Everyone settled, sort of, and checked their belts and stuff and then Franc started the motor. I'm sure it was quiet, like really quiet, under normal circumstances. Here though, having been slinking about in the darkness and quiet of these tunnels like a bunch of stressed-out Dwarfs for god knows how long it seemed shockingly loud. I clenched my teeth, and my arse cheeks and braced for the shooting. I could almost picture the bullets punching through the door panels and windows and ripping into and through Lizzie's face and upper body. I imagined Dad groaning as his lungs filled with blood and he lost the feeling in his hands and legs.

Bit melodramatic I know, sorry, but I was shitting my pants. Again.

But none of that happened. Instead, the vehicle jolted forward and began to move. It was slow at first whilst Franc got the hang of driving with his NVG on. And then he sped up.

Now as I say they'd clearly rehearsed this, planned it down to the smallest detail. I mean, they'd got the tunnels clear, sorted the doors so they opened, closed and locked as required. And they'd got the vehicle in there, big as it was. But that didn't mean it was plain sailing to execute the plan, did it? Like, the truck only just fit the tunnel. And with the bumps and ruts in the floor, the roof rack whacked the tunnel walls and rocks above plenty of times before we crept slowly out into the night. I was starting to feel a bit sick by that time if I'm honest, not sure if that was nerves or hunger, the smell from the braai was still teasing me. So, I was glad to finally to see we were out and to smell the fresh, burnt poo air of the African night.

I confess I was glad not to smell, see or hear anything of the house we'd escaped from. There's that word again; escape. When did that become an acceptable and standard part of my vocab? Fuck sake.

Anyway, we must've travelled a reasonable distance because I couldn't even hear the helicopter. But then I realised that it had probably landed which bolloxed the theory of a safe distance.

Franc stopped, switched off the engine and turned round in his seat:

"Right. We're switching to electric now, there's a bunch of huge batteries under your seats which should, I'm hoping, get us eight or nine clicks away. At that point we switch back to the motor and make like we're on fire, which of course we probably will be."

I'm fucking certain that was supposed to be a joke, but nobody laughed, or even smiled, and yes I could see now, it was dark but not pitch black like before in the cave. But Franc made no effort to communicate humour with his face so I remained quiet, unamused, but hopeful that we might not burn to death.

Because that really would ruin, what had so far been, a nice weekend.

He turned back around and flicked a couple switches and then we moved off again, this time almost completely silent. It was weird, being in a moving vehicle but without the sound of an engine. But it was good because it enabled us to hear the whine of the helicopter motor as it restarted. And that was shit because if it lifted off and scanned around, lights or no lights I was pretty sure they'd spot us. No one reacted, save for Lizzie frowning and turning to look out the rear window.

All the while we kept going, the sound or the rotors both increasing as they sped up, whilst at the same time growing quieter the further we got from them.

After a couple of miles, or 'clicks' as we call them in the trade Franc sped up a little. The helicopter had lifted off but was hanging low and circling the house and grounds about a mile out. They had a huge spotlight fixed to the front nose and as they circled they lit up the ground like daylight. I didn't give it much thought at the time, but Dad pointed out later that they were relying solely on this big ass torch to find survivors / escapees / *us,* rather than night vision or infrared. It was comforting later, you know, the thought that we were kinda safe even though, as Franc said we wouldn't be properly safe until at least twenty clicks away and surrounded by other vehicles or in a built-up area.

Until then we were battery powered shitting ducks.

See what I did there?

Anyway, I had no idea what time it was, how long since we'd first heard the bird and how much of the night we had left to scurry away and hide. But that was ok, it just heightened the excitement, anxiety and the feeling that it was pointless to even try. Like, they had helicopters, guns, bombs and all sorts of tech. We had a battery powered Toyota Land cruiser and some shovels. I'm joking of course, making light of it. Truth was I was terrified, we all were, and that made time go slowly.

But it did go.

One moment followed by another, and with each moment we moved forward. One click, then Franc sped up. Two clicks, then three, then four.

I looked out of the window and couldn't see the helicopter anymore. I mean obviously I could see the hills and evidence of the mine but being unfamiliar with the area I still couldn't really work out how far we'd gone and where we were going.

And here's another thought. I'd assumed, based upon the hours preceding this that I was escaping, again. But fuck it, based upon the *weeks* preceding that, I'd have every right to think instead that I could actually be in the process of being kidnapped, again. I mean that's crazy right? My Dad was there, and Lizzie who, whilst she'd gone to lengths to scare the crap outta me early on, had gone on to prove that, actually, she was cool. A bit psycho for sure but cool too.

Kind of.

But I'm being daft aren't I. Because as I say my Dad was there and the guys that stormed us clearly weren't there for the barbecue, sorry *braai*. They certainly didn't give me the impression that they were interested in my wellbeing, or anyone else's for that matter.

Which reminded me, painfully, how hungry I was. Like, I never even got a fucking sausage, let along any potato salad. Wankers.

So, escape it was, yes definitely (or possibly kidnap). And who better to escape with (or be kidnapped by) than your very own Dad? Right? So, fuck it. I was in it and going with it even if I had no actual choice in it. And, actually, I was pretty ok with that to be fair.

Sort of.

Another click, then another. And then we heard the helicopter again.

22: Italian Jobbie

The sausage, or lack of it, was still playing on my mind. I mean, I never actually got to see the meat cooking so it's possible, in reality, that it was never going to be an option. But based purely on my council estate barbeque experience, which must be said was extensive and varied, sausages were the thing. Like, if the One Stop had them, they were going on, chipolatas, bangers, fancy organic pork and orphan jellyfish wrapped in the skin of virgin badgers, it didn't matter. If they had em, they were going on, never mind the packaging and the dubious expiry date. Never mind the fact that they all got burned to a crisp and always tasted of smoked coal no matter what they started out as.

I mean, of course, there might be burgers and chicken too, but, seriously, who the fuck trusts barbequed chicken? You've gotta be a literal fuckin psycho to trust barbequed chicken.

But I wasn't on the estate anymore now, was I? Nor was I in Kansas, or to my acute frustration, and growing hunger, was I back at the braai, with grease on my chin and tommy sauce all over my cheeks. Like an eleven-year-old boy.

Bastards.

I wondered if there were snacks under the seats. Cubby kept snacks in his car, or at least Karol did, bless him. Come to think of it, I never did find out whether those wafers were for me or if they were his lunch. Never would now either would I. Fucking Shirley.

But maybe that was the answer to my earlier question. Maybe, only people who were abducting you brought snacks, you know, to lessen the impact, to seduce you a bit with sugar. I guess that would depend on how susceptible you were to that kinda thing, I think we know the answer for me.

Shit plan if you prefer cheese or pork pies.

But then again, maybe it was the other way around. Maybe the people who abducted you didn't bring snacks. I didn't see any in the back of the car that scooted off with Danny in, and I defo didn't see any at the house in Wroxall where Shirley had his *first* little accident. That said, if treats were going to be required, I did leave them something nice on the carpet at the top of the stairs.

And when I got to Bellano, at least when I woke up properly, Freya made sure I had a full belly. Come to think of it, that was fucking barbeque food too. WTAF?

Anyway, no, there were no snacks below the seat, I checked. Instead, there was more, useful, survival shit like First Aid kits, maps, plastic sheets, blankets, and the batteries Franc mentioned earlier. So, it looked like I was being kidnapped then, maybe. That, or I was being irrational and childish.

I know right, ridiculous.

I looked out of the window miserably and we clicked on.

But what about the helicopter? I hear you ask, petulantly, (and I'm not even going to bother with the whole 'if you're still reading' shit cause, to be frank, it doesn't really matter)

Yeah, well here's the thing Captain Continuity, it's my fucking story, so I'll get to it when I'm ready. Ok?

Ok I'm ready.

So yes, the helicopter. It was still buzzing around somewhere out there albeit too far, or too low for us to see. Franc had already gone beyond his 8 or 9 clicks but kept us on the batteries whilst he could in case we were spotted. I could hear him and Alex talking about it up front, but my little brain couldn't cope with another problem, so I just concentrated on staring out of the window.

Lizzie was busy looking at maps and talking to Dad and the guys next to me were snoring. Seriously? Fucking snoring whilst we're mid escape from a bunch of highly resourced, highly motivated mercenaries? I could barely sleep through heavy rain let alone a violent and coordinated attempt on my life.

Mental.

I guess it was the training.

Or perhaps the lack of sausages.

Or both.

Eventually, Franc stopped and told us we could get out to stretch our legs. I wasn't bothered to be honest; I'd have been just as happy sitting there for another couple of hours if we were making progress away from the flying bogeymen.

But I got out anyway and pretended to stretch.

Franc did some checks on the bus while Dad and Lizzie spread the map over the bonnet. They were arguing about a choice between two destinations. It sounded like it wasn't the distance, or route that was in question but rather the security of each should we reach it.

"You can't stay together," she said simply, crossly.

He shook his head.

"I disagree, I understand why you're saying that but you're wrong."

"For fucks sake Keith, you're not thinking straight." Now getting pissed.

Franc walked past me and noticed I was watching them.

"Don't stress, they'll work it out."

Still grumpy but different from the 'she'll eat you for breakfast' advice he'd given me not so very long ago. I nodded but said nothing. I was learning quickly just to keep my mouth shut, something that would've made life so much easier had I learned it ten years ago.

"The Clemente house is the right move for Matthew with you and Franc going out to Farside and then on to site two. You know as well as I do that they'll track us, if not now then certainly within the next 36 hours." She huffed a bit and put her hands on her hips. "If you're caught together then it's over, it's a bust."

Second time I'd heard that phrase.

He shook his head again, not stressed but clearly unhappy with her proposal.

"I've just got him back, I can't...."

"You have no choice. Fuck it, if Temcore take you together it's done, we're done. You know this."

"Maybe, maybe not...."

"How *maybe not* Keith?? How *maybe not*?? They've still got Danny. Matthew is the last lever, he's the key. If they got him *and* you...." She was angry now, clearly invested. "We *planned* for this, remember......?"

He stepped back and rubbed his face. Franc finished his vehicle checks and approached them quietly, rubbing imaginary grease from his hands on a dirty little rag.

He put his hand on Dad's shoulder before turning him to face me.

"Look at that boy," he said. They were looking at me, Franc was pointing. "He's there, in front of you, flesh and bone, can you believe it?" Now to me:

"Do you know how much this one has talked about you? Do you know how many hours I've spent listening to him talk about you and your bloody brother?"

Dad's shoulders relaxed a little.

Franc continued, this time to Dad, all of which surprised me if I'm honest, cause up until that point I thought he didn't really know how to talk, you know, like a proper person.

"And look at him Keith. Seriously. He's a man, he's not a kid." And now he turned Dad back further round to look at Lizzie; "Plus look who he'll be with. Think about it, seriously man, you couldn't make him any safer if you tried."

And at that we all thought about the house, the braai, the pool and the big plate glass windows being blown in by gunfire and explosions. I thought about the big spear over the fireplace. Oh, and the last little bits of Shirley that were burned away by the flash bangs.

I wonder if the Colombians #2 took the spear when they came through? I know I would, I liked it. I could've used it to hunt rodents, paedophiles or the kids that smashed Mum's friend Moira's kitchen window last August Bank Holiday.

Anyway, thanks uncle Franc but *safe* was bollocks wasn't it. It didn't exist and we all knew it. We were now on the run, that's right ON THE RUN. Which sounded mental when you said it, to me that is, not you. I mean fuck, on the run, but from who, from what?

And who does that actually ever happen to? Have you ever been on the run? I'll wager not. Sure, you've run for trains, buses and taxis, possibly a rickshaw or two. Bet you've run when you've needed a shit once or twice as well haven't you? But you've never run for your life, like actually run from someone intent on causing you serious harm.

Danny and I ran a few times as kids. And to be truthful, in the moment, it felt like life or death. But the reality was, we were running from a kicking, or the feds, or a stray dog or some shit like that. We also ran from Mr Patel who owned the corner shop in Lay Avenue who chased us with a cricket bat for nicking four cans of Vimto and 20 Benson and Hedges.

Looking back though, it was never run, or die was it, never like it was now.

"Who are we running from?" I asked, not expecting an answer.

Dad shrugged Francs arm off and came over to me. He was beginning to look pissed now, with everyone, even me. Or was he just worried, shit I didn't know, I couldn't tell, which in itself was bollocks because it highlighted the huge gap, you know the *dead* bit of our relationship.

"There's other stuff you don't know," shit. "Stuff that won't make sense to you, at least not now."

"Right," I was trying not to be smart or sarcastic, like I would if Cubby was telling me the same.

Maybe we shouldn't do some things because of more than just what people think. Maybe popular opinion is generally archaic, you know, like so old that it's evolved from something bigger, something more substantial? And now it just sits there, looking awkward and out of place, without this high-level thing, that no one's aware of to give it context. I mean, take some of the things people do that are illegal, like murder and stuff. Why is that illegal? Like obviously I know why it *should* be, it's pretty clear, at least to me. But why is it clear? Why do I know it's wrong?

Is it because I was told it? Taught it? No. It's because it feels wrong, right? But why? If no one told me it was wrong, why do I feel like it is?

See this is what I'm talking about, instinct or something like that. It's in me, the knowledge, the feeling. But if it's not taught, at least not overtly, then it must be a more general, societal thing. A general, widespread understanding or acceptance that that behaviour is bad, that it has negative consequences for my social group, or something like that.

So, follow this thought then to everything. Follow it and see that it, or at least the principal question *behind* it could be applied to every social norm, to every normalised behaviour. Why do we do these things? Why don't we do these things?

For some, I'm betting there is no substance whatsoever other than some out of date courtesy, religious or hierarchical construct that has zero foundation in common sense or the common good.

For example, smoking weed.

I know, shocking right.

But not really. Because the *reality* of it is that habitual use of weed as a relaxant is far less harmful than the same with alcohol. It's been proven. It's science. And I'm sure I'm not the first person you've heard say it.

But ok, if that's legit then why the taboo, why the illegality?

And that's the big motherfucking question right there. Conspiracy guys would tell you it's big alcohol and big pharma, insofar as they perpetuate the use of alcohol as it props up their businesses. Obviously, right?

But historians would differ, because they'd have some context. And they'd see the social complexities that form the foundation upon which we've settled. See the bit above about the evolution of the social norm.

Maybe the truth is in the middle, like Malcolm, or that Baldwin brother that no one remembers; part of something significant but not important enough to warrant attention. Sorry Nigel Baldwin.

Anyway, where am I going?

Oh right, yeah, the things we do, or that others do, or don't do, or think about, things that we feel we shouldn't do, even if there's no tangible reason why not. Or tangible reason but we should.

If you know what I mean?

Right, so *those* things, why are they, like, *there*? In our brains? Is it conscious? Is it behaviour learned? Or instinct? And if instinct then is it right? And how would we know either way?

Fuck this is mental.

I mean take this for instance; so basically, here I am, thousands of miles from home, out in the middle of nowhere, and make no mistake, it was a huge fucking expanse of nowhere, with people I don't know, with no resources of my own, completely dependent on them, and I guess I'm including Dad in that. And I'm getting weird urges, weird thoughts.

Not, like sexual or freaky or anything, nothing that would scare children, just kinda 'out of place', if you know what I mean. And I appreciate this is a pretty elaborate set up for the next bit, but this is how my brain works. Maybe not fully like this back in the day but certainly now, with the benefit of a lot of self-reflecting moments in the shower.

If I'm honest it happens a fair bit, maybe a lot. Always has. As a kid I was known for drifting off into little corners of weird contemplation. I had these dreams or visions, or whatever, normally featuring bee's or honeycombs or some weird coastal location with raging white water and dark rocks on the regular. Mum said I'd go vacant for ages before coming back and asking something she had no idea how to answer.

Went down a storm at school, as you can imagine.

Anyway, I'm here, having thoughts, probably looking a bit spaced, if anyone was watching me, and at the same time I'm conflicted. Cause, despite the discomfort and the fucked-up nature of where I am, why, and who I'm with; I AM with my Dad right? Plus, I'm with people he trusts aren't I. So why the trip? Why the moment?

"Matthew?" Dad was standing in front of me, the rest were staring. "Are you ok son?"

I must've glazed over. I blinked and focused.

Fuck, I'd drifted off.

"You ok? We lost you for a short minute there mate," Dad gestured for Franc to pass him a water bottle. "Here, have some of this."

I looked at the bottle in his hand, brown skin, tattoos, big watch. I looked up into his face. It was a face I knew, like I *knew*. It was safe, it was safety, it was an anchor.

His eyes were brown, his skin was marked in all the places I remember. And I did remember.

I remember him kissing me goodnight. I remember him smiling, laughing, crying once or twice, and I remember him looking at me the way, I guess that Dads should look at their kids. Because he was my Dad, right? I mean this was him, this was the guy, the same guy that was there before, you know, before he wasn't. And fast forward past all the pain and shit in between, here he was again. This was the guy, right?

I took the bottle and looked at the water, my head was spinning. Where was all this coming from? What the fuck was wrong with me?

"Yeah," was all I could manage. I took a few mouthfuls and immediately felt different, like lighter, more *there*.

I looked at his face again, then at the others there with us. They had all turned back to what they were doing and weren't looking at me anymore.

Did I know any of them? Did I know anything *about* any of them? Did I *know* anything? How had I got here? Quite literally, two days ago, minus the mega long flight, I was in the British Consulate in Milan. Two days before that I was taking a shit on a boat I stole from Simon and Garfunkel. And two days before that I was getting my ass kicked by the beautiful Freya on the lawn of a fancy house on the banks of an Italian lake. A lake, by the way, I had no place being on.

I was fucked. Maybe it was a delayed reaction to the flash bang panic of a few hours ago. Maybe it was a piece of Shirley that got lodged in my inner ear, like the tooth my old pal Sausage kidnapped for a bank holiday weekend back in the day.

I didn't know, I couldn't think. Something was off, and I don't just mean that Franc or Alex had dropped half a cheese and ham sandwich down between the seats last weekend and it was starting to stink, I mean something was *off*. Something didn't feel right. For the first time in what seemed like the longest time I wanted a smoke, or a crumpet, fuck I'd settle for an omelette.

"Who are we running from?" I asked again, and then: "Is this really about Danny? Or you? Or is this really about me?"

I don't know why I asked, it didn't really fit with the moment, not *their* moment anyway. Dad, still looking at me, shifted his eyes. It was like a nervous thing, and far more significant, to me anyway, than it sounds. Why would he do that? Why would that question cause *any* kind of reaction? Why did I even ask the question?

He glanced back over his shoulder, and then back to me.

"It's complicated.... you know...." he began.

Lizzie cut in.

"Fuck, Keith, we don't have time......"

Dad looked back over his shoulder at her again, frowning. And then back at me.

"Matty," he hesitated. "Listen, it's about all of us. And right now we just have to keep moving."

It's weird isn't it, how there are those moments when your brain, having been told all it needs to know, just won't sit the fuck down and shut up. Like, it's not like the moment could be described as ideal.

"But there's more though, isn't there? There's something bigger."

He shook his head. Behind him Lizzie huffed and started folding the map.

"Bigger? Yes," another hesitation. "Yes, there is something bigger. But I don't think now is the time...."

"Am I adopted?" I just blurted it, like I did back then. Like I still do now if I'm completely honest. My worst fears, my base terror. I've never been able to hold it in.

Dad looked at me, a strange and not wholly reassuring expression on his face. He shook his head again.

"No Matty, you're not.... it's not.... it's not like that."

Now Lizzie.

"Fuck sake guys. Sorry, I know you've got some catching up to do, but can we do it later? Or in the fucking bus?" she was pointing at the truck.

I looked past Dad at her, and saw genuine anxiety, which was both terrifying, and strangely reassuring. It was enough to bring me back to the moment.

I shook myself, wet dog style, inside anyway, and refocused. I smiled at Dad.

"Ok, good."

The moment passed, clearly, and then we were back on board. Dad and Lizzie came to an agreement, one he was less than happy with so you can guess what it was and then we were off.

Using the big diesel now without too much fear of being heard by the Columbians we made good ground and soon I could see houses, well what appeared to pass for houses in these parts. We went through a few villages, all dusty and fucked up, like parts of east London but without the high rise and rain. And then we started to get into the outskirts of what turned out to be Johannesburg again.

Like, full circle, only without most of the sweaty goons I'd set out with a couple of days ago.

We headed to a centre of sorts where we drove around a bit to check we weren't being followed before diving into lock-up down a dirty little side street, all litter and homeless people. You know the kind of thing.

It was all very familiar if I'm honest. Actually, reminded me strongly of Vic's place under the arches, a place of pretend car mechanics, dodgy bank notes and illegal firearms. Also, a place Danny and I spent many a Saturday afternoon trying very hard to look, well, hard actually.

Vic never took any notice of us, save the odd clip round the noggin for not putting enough sugar in his tea. No, he was always focused on the menacing looking lumps that drifted in with paper bags full of cash, and who left shortly after with something heavy wrapped in an oily rag tucked quite fucking obviously down the front of their trousers.

But I didn't tell you that.

Actually, come to think of it, I wonder if that 1981 Vauxhall Chevette HS *hatchback,* (not the HSR, they were super rare and mostly ended up as stock racers), ever made it off the lift. It was there collecting rust and spiders the whole time Danny and I frequented.

I also wondered if the old bill, who paid him visits on the regular, I know that cause I also made them tea, some with spit in, some without, ever rumbled that he knew fuck all about motors and wouldn't know how to change an oil filter if his life depended on it.

Anyway, this place wasn't under a railway, but it was dark and musty and smelled strongly of petrol and rodent piss. And I use the term rodent loosely, cause I couldn't guarantee it was rats, I mean it could've been a crew of rabid fucking hyenas for all I knew, we were in Africa after all. But regardless, it smelled rank, and kinda nice too, if you get my weird, reminiscent drift.

So we all jumped out and did the whole stretchy thing, arms legs and backs creaking and groaning like a bunch of newly minted zombies. Franc whizzed round doing his checks whilst Lizzie and Dad checked and divided up the kit.

Pretty sure he got more than his fair share of wafers.

Dad was still grumbling but Lizzie was quiet. Seemed like she knew he was miserable but didn't have the energy to talk about it. Like when you're a kid and you've refused to eat your

Findus Crispy Pancake rolls, even though you asked for them, but still want a slice of Vienetta, and your Mums quietly pissed, but too worn down by your bullshit to engage.

And mine was, quite a lot of time, worn down by mine and Danny's bullshit.

And then it hit me.

Which sounds so fucking cliche, and which in itself is a word I've never used before now. But still, it is, cliche I mean. And it's true.

She'd just lost her home, a home and a house that's been in her family for fucking ages. Lizzie, I mean, not Mum. Generations, to double down on the previous. I know that, because she told me.

The big windows, the piano, the braai, even all the techy stuff she had squirrelled away in the basement. I mean shit, you didn't have to be a scientist to know all of that stuff, the stuff that was *in* all the photos she'd shown me, was important.

Anyway, it was all gone now wasn't it, flash bang boom, all gone. I mean I was only there for like 36 hours or something. Maybe 48, I can't remember clearly. I was asleep for a fair bit of that, covered in Shirley's brains for another big chunk, pun fully intended, and in the basement watching the house above me turn to dust and ash on the CCTV for most of the remainder, so if I'm honest I only really missed the sausages I never got to eat. Oh, and the cheese and pickles that I did.

Come to think about it, right now I missed the shower too, because as we know I spent a bit of time in there too but whatever, I was getting used to living like a feral cat so 'one more day' and all that....

So I missed it, a bit, sure. But it must've been fucking killing her. And likely, to some degree the others too. I'm clearly connecting dots I can't properly see but I would think they'd all have been feeling it, because it seemed like a base of some sorts. Like there were a few people there, the vehicles, the computers and stuff. Plus the photo album, the one with my Dad, Lizzie, *her* Dad, and all the events and family stuff. Surely it was, like, *special*?

And even as I thought it, I remembered someone else saying something similar about somewhere else. And then, the way my brain does, I skipped over to making comparisons. The house, the people, the *defences*, and the tech down in a basement etc.

And next I'm wondering if that's where the similarities ended?

Fuck my head was hurting, I needed some chocolate, or a sit down in a dark room, or to stroke a dog. Cause that's calming, isn't it? In fact, I've recently heard of actual *calming dogs* whose sole purpose, aside from being a dog and just living their best life, is to assist in calming people with anxiety. Which is great if big piles of dog shit and having your sofa eaten two or three times a year didn't stress you out too much.

Calming *goats* are also available - but that's in my other book.

Anyway, as standard I'm jumping about from one weird conspiracy theory to the next. I mean, who's house wasn't special right? Who's gonna say welcome, make yourself at home, this place is a fucking shithole, I really hope you like it. Nobody, right? Well nearly nobody, old Manky Mandy, Jerry Coils older sister (and ex missus too so it's been widely rumoured) was quite happy living in her hole. It was actually a council flat, but she treated it like a squat and let all and sundry get up to all sorts in there. Plus she had, frankly, less than ideal personal hygiene habits.

Anyway, aside from one or two of the Nutters delinquent old school friends, why would you not take at least a little bit of pride over where you lived. I always cleaned up my leftover kebab. Unless of course Benny, or more recently Fat Julie got to it first.

But rewind, why wouldn't Lizzie's place have similarities to Terry's? I mean they were kinda in the same business weren't they. And one had to house one's personal effects somewhere, right?

Of course. It was bullshit, I was going mental. Maybe it wasn't sugar I needed, maybe it was sleep.

Because, just when did I last sleep? No, I don't mean cat nap, nor snatching a few zeds whilst the armoured truck bounced along. And not, while I'm at it, a night in what I thought was a cell fearing for my life, convinced that Shirley, or Bob, or whatever his fucking name was, was going to make his breakfast with my liquified remains, and some 'all berry' flavoured proteins shake.

It was all bollocks. The quiet, the small triggers that set my brain fizzing, and the feeling that 'something was off' were just that, nonsense. They could all be put down to the loss, the violent, loud and terrifying loss of something, somewhere they all considered special.

That or I had awakened my supernatural inner self and could now perceive things beyond the physical.

No, me neither.

So, I settled down. I chilled, and I maxed, and I let it wash over me.

And then they blew the fucking doors off.

There was wood splinters and dust, and real fucking bullets whizzing about all over. It went from dark, quiet and smelling of piss, to loud, bright and chaotic in the blink of an eye. And I've no idea what it smelled of, probably still piss, more than likely mine.

Of course, given the choice I'd have stayed together with Dad and the rest, no question. But I didn't have the choice, no one does in these situations do they. I mean ok you probably don't know because you've never been chased by an international team of highly trained assassins.

So it's just me then, which makes this all a little bit awkward.

But whatever, no I didn't have a 'choice' because before I knew what was happening Lizzie, bless her cotton socks, pulled me by the actual fucking hair backwards out of the lockup. Very ladylike.

Me not her.

Note: this wouldn't have been possible at Vic's place, mainly because there was no back door. Which has no bearing whatsoever on the above.

Thank you.

Anyway, I was properly kicking and screaming, or at least moaning a little bit like the big boy I am as we exited stage left, fingers and toes intact, grateful for that, thanks mate.

Our backpacks were half on, half off, and there was dirt and crap and dust all over. My ears were ringing, and I could hear myself shouting words to the effect; 'What the actual fuck' and other likely fruity phrases.

I was looking for Dad, eyes streaming, to see if he was caught, to see if he was shot, to see which way he went but it was all just a big confusion of mess, noise and bright flashes. And no sooner were we in the alley at the back, a big cloud of smoke and shit billowing out after us, then we were back inside again, *inside* the opposite building.

Ok so Lizzie wasn't dragging me anymore, I was moving on my own, all crouched down and ninja style, but I was still looking back and shouting in panic.

We moved through this building and then into another alleyway and then the penny dropped, and I got the hang of it, which was pretty quick for me, and if you've paid even the slightest bit of attention, you'll know what I mean. Oh and if not, which I suspect is the case, because let's face it this book isn't aimed at the laser focused is it, no offence; then wtf? Why are you still here??

Anyway, so I followed her as we ducked through and through and through, sometimes going left, sometimes right, sometimes crouching, even crawling. Not so long before I'd have been completely disoriented, discombobulated even, which is a word I've used before, I know, but it's so good I'm sure you'll agree it warrants a second outing. Anyway, yes, properly fucked to the point of paralysis. In fact, she'd probably have had to shoot me to get me moving.

Which would've made the second book interesting wouldn't it?

Weirdly though, for some reason, she didn't shoot me, and I wasn't bothered, I just went with it. It did seem like Lizzie knew where she was going, so I guess that helped, or I was shocked, and on auto, which is just as likely.

Either way, eventually, a bit later, like ten minutes or something we popped out into a huge car lot. You know, like all on one level, out in the open with the little kiosk, lift up barriers, chain-link all the way round and orphans chasing coppers for a windscreen wash. And when I say coppers I mean coins not the police, because police are only referred to as 'coppers' in the UK. Plus, that would be fucked up, right?

Anyway, sorry, before we go on, is orphan the correct word here? Should it be urchin or something? Or maybe pixie, or gremlin?

Whatever, their prices were quite reasonable and if I'd had a car, I'd have been more than tempted...

But I didn't have a car, did I? So why are we talking about it?

You need to try and focus here.

Right, anyway, Lizzie caught the attention of one of them that she seemed to know. And as we scurried across and around parked cars, looking over our shoulders all the time, he made his way over to us. And then it turned out then, that *he* was actually she.

Obviously I'm assuming again here that *she* had always been she, and that us appearing like we did, when we did had absolutely no bearing whatsoever on it. But as you quite rightly say; 'you never know'.

And I think I've demonstrated, I'm not one to judge.

So anyway, the girl came over and she and Lizzie exchanged a few words in the local lingo which sounded rough, like they were insulting each other rather than agreeing terms.

The girl fished around in her bag and brought out a wire coat hanger which she then used to unlock or *break into* the car that Lizzie had pointed at. She and Lizzie exchanged a few more words before Lizzie gave her some green, or money for you civilians, and the girl disappeared.

Lizzie then gestured for me to climb in the open door, which I did of course, and slid across. But on reflection I only got in because she said to. I was on autopilot, my body was just reacting, like it had been for the last; I don't know how long. I wasn't really in control. But then there I was, in the car with no idea what might come next.

I mean great, so we had a car. But how were we going to get out of the carpark, and where were we gonna to go? Was it one of the places she and Dad had been stressing over, the safe-houses or 'sites'? Was it somewhere else? And if we went to one of those places, or bases or whatever, who's to say these fuckers weren't gonna already be there waiting for us? Or weren't just gonna track and follow us there anyway?

I mean it's not like we hadn't had all the tools and prep previously to make a good stab at getting away. Jesus we'd had a fucking battery powered armoured truck before, and even with all that it had gone to shit. This time, now, it was just me and her, and no shovels, no first aid kits or anything. How the fuck did we think this was gonna work?

I was confused, my head was spinning. And I don't think I really knew it at the time, but I was also bitter. Bitter because I was tired, because I didn't get a sausage off the braai. Bitter because I still had no idea where my little brother was. Because the Nutter was still back home, alone and stewing in a pot of nicotine-flavoured misery, and bitter because I'd just got my Dad back, and now it looked like I'd fucking lost him again. He might even be dead for fucks sake, for real this time.

I mean, that is big right? That there is the really big one, isn't it? Considering how elated I was, how different my life suddenly became, in an instant, just a few hours ago, this, now, was shit.

Proper shit.

But more than that, I was pissed, because things just seemed to be getting fucking worse. Day by day. Getting my Dad back should have been the first step towards something better. It should have been the first step towards getting Danny back, or at the very least finding out where he was, where those fuckers took him. And then getting home to pay mums parking fines and try and get things back to the way they were. It should have been, shouldn't it, but it wasn't. Instead we'd got attached, bombed and chased, and then fucking attacked again.

Bastards.

And now here I was sitting in the passenger seat of a shit, soon-to-be stolen car, nice as it might be, covered in cuts and bruises, alone but for the company of a girl I'd known for less than two days. I was ten thousand miles away from anything I knew, ten thousand miles away from my local kebab shop and I didn't have a clue what I was doing. I looked at my hands, they were shaking, covered in shit, and tingling, with some weird pain or anxiety fuelled panic thing.

Christ, was this ever going to end? Was I ever gonna get home? Was I ever gonna find out if old George was still alive, if the Scab had had her leg off, or if Fat Julie had actually now moved in and was paying rent? Bitch.

Was I ever going to see the Nutter again? Was I ever going to find my little brother?

Was I ever going to find out what the fuck this was actually all about?

I jumped as Lizzie climbed in next to me. She was sweaty and had just as much dust and shit on her face as I knew was on mine plus a few new cuts and scrapes too. She looked hot though, of course she did, like she had the first time I'd met her, after she'd been fighting with the crocodiles. She pushed her bag between the seats into the back before turning and looking at me. I think she tried to smile, I guess to reassure me or something, but it was wonky, and she looked like she'd rather be crying than smiling. I tried to smile back, but, like hers it was shit, really, because, like her I felt like shit.

"Did you see them? Did they make it out?" I asked quietly, not really sure if I wanted to hear the answer. Not really sure if she'd even be willing to answer. I mean yes, clearly she'd have been concerned, *consumed* possibly with how Dad and the others were and whether they escaped. But I suspected the first thing she'd be wanting to actually talk about would be getting the fuck out of here, and what was gonna happen next.

She looked away, out the windscreen in front, and took a deep breath. I'm pretty sure she'd have shrugged then, I mean, not only would it have been a legitimate answer to my question, but I can't imagine a time where it would have been less offensive, less inappropriate.

However, and make no mistake, this, more than any other was an appropriate occasion for the use of *that* word; before I could see how she was reacting, and before she had a chance to say anything I was pinned back into my chair by a massive fucking hand around my neck. And then, just as quick, a big black gun barrel was pressed roughly into the side of my head.

None of which I was expecting, and none of which was ideal. Obviously.

I wanted to look across to Lizzie, to see if she was ok, to see where she was, to see if she was biting, spitting and gouging per her MO. But there was a knee in my chest, and a fair bit of sweaty, angry shouting going on all around, both inside and out of the car. I got the impression that there wasn't just the one or two guys out there, but quite a few more.

I struggled briefly, for a moment, like a baby squirrel trapped under the wheel of a large car, but it was no good, the hand was strong, and the knee heavy and pressing into my ribs.

I concluded then, you'll be surprised to hear, with little or no further persuasion, that at that point, I was fucked.

Sadly, but again.

Properly and completely.
Fucked.

23: Protocols

Lágymányos, Budapest, May 1982

"Ok did we get anything from Colos?"

"No, not as yet, data is still coming through, some indications but nothing solid."

"And what about Akram?"

"Again, the data's new, we're just going through it. But as Juno reported, we're showing 16% wide spectrum coverage with readings lighting up all the way back to stage 12."

Scariades ran his fingers through his hair, momentarily removing his glasses and squeezing the bridge of his nose. He took a breath.

The room was three levels below the street. A relatively new space for them of course, but in reality, just another concrete, soviet era building they all hated. But it was home, at least to their project, their team, for now, and was a vast improvement, for a number of reasons, over their last few locations.

And now they had both funding, enough, for the moment to push through the last of the technical obstacles they had encountered, of which there had been many, and the backing, finally, of enough stakeholders to keep Harket out. But whilst exciting, this new project was also terrifying, and impossible to conceive of without previous successes, specifically Lens and then what followed. Which is why the whole idea of keeping *Harket out* was both necessary and contrary.

“16%. That’s disappointing.”

No one disagreed with him.

"Ok let's move onto the secondary readings."

Vanessa looked back down at her screen. She was tired. The last run had been both thrilling and exhausting, almost like it had been back in the beginning. She knew too, that he was struggling; they all did. It wasn't just work. She suspected that the results of the MRI had come back overnight, and she knew it wouldn't be good, they all did. Hopeless was a strong word of course, but she was close enough to him and Alexia to be aware of the prognosis, even in the best cases. Sadly, the child was nowhere near 'best case'. It made her eyes water just to think about it, she couldn’t imagine how her old friends would be coping.

She swallowed.

"Ok, so as discussed and per protocol we're using platform 3 to analyse the primary. So far, we're up to 40% input with lots more data still to come in and be placed on the track. As you know we lost access to site 1 during field pre-set," she said, wishing immediately that she hadn't, "but sites 2, 3 and 4 are up and contributing." She clicked a few buttons and a new graphic appeared in the centre of the large up-front display. "That said, what we're seeing so far is as expected in the platform 3 simulations. In fact we're seeing an almost perfect match for the AOD and only marginal deviation from the HIERR."

Scariades looked up from his own screen to the main display. He then looked across at Vanessa, wondering again, as he did all too frequently; where Proctor was. He frowned, and not just because her voice wavered as she spoke.

"Quantify the deviation?"

"Less than one percent. It is climbing, but it's still well below the threshold for escalation."

"Under simulation conditions."

"Yes, of course," she looked back at her screen as new data was added to the packet. "But even so, we ran these variables through the platform with no adverse effects."

"At what capture?"

She hesitated as the same thought occurred to her.

"Shit," she said slowly, "68%." Pushing her glasses up her nose, memories of the old lab; faded signage, cracked windows and *fear* rose briefly to mind.

Scariades didn't acknowledge, he was already staring back at the central display watching the lower arc, a lovely pink line, climb gently up and diagonally across the screen.

Jesus Christ.

"A O what? Sorry to interrupt," Gerrard Vorner held his hand up apologetically, again. "So sorry, but what is AO...." he looked down at the notes, and then; "D?"

Scariades looked up, irritated. He would have shaken his head but these people, some of them at least, were funding this operation *and* knew as much about the project origin as him. Time had moved on, of course. They were all older, and much had changed but that didn't mean all the ghosts of the past were gone. Nor did it mean relationships with those that sponsored him were any less awkward.

He shuffled his papers and allowed himself a quiet huff. The air conditioning stopped him from sweating, which was good, a pleasant change from his normal workplace. His complaint, if he had one, beyond the inconvenience of getting here, was that it was always so dark in these rooms during briefings.

The facility was vast and brand new and from what he had seen, still in development. The investment was obvious and considerable, so he could only surmise that the technology and methods by which they operated were the latest and in line with the most cutting-edge standards. He wondered to what degree that was connected with this and earlier projects.

"AOD stands for *Arch of Disturbance* and refers to the speed with which the impact of the occurrence moves through the matter upon which it acts. HIERR stands for *High Impact Energy Replication Rate* and refers to the waves generated by the push down effect and to the accumulated force, measured in terawatts."

"Thank you," Vorner nodded. Understanding more than he let on, he smiled disarmingly.

Scariades ignored the social qué and went back to his papers.

"As you can see the AOD dipped even against the PL3 expectations, which whilst mildly frustrating wasn't entirely unexpected. We had worked on a 70% capture with the model whereas in reality our capture was far less efficient, so in many ways it was a flawed control."

Vorner nodded again, as did civilian observers; Monik at the far end of the table and the man sitting behind and next to her. Scariades suspected neither had actually been listening. There was no *suspicion* when it came to the French contractor however, or Magnus, the two Americans whose names he couldn't remember, and the two lawyers who Scariades had, justifiably, he felt, ignored throughout his presentation. He wasn't sure about the cohort of uniformed military persons assembled along the left-hand side of the room, albeit they did seem to be engaged.

Nevertheless, he appreciated the effort Monik continued to make and so pressed on with the remainder of his summary.

"Having said that if we look now at the HIERR, that's the pink line, we can see a noticeable deviation from the model. Again, the data was a long way short of the model but in this case that works in our favour. Using this path, we can extrapolate that the...."

"Sorry," Vorner interrupted again. He was frowning down at the paper, his finger tracing the lines Scariades had been reading from: "It says you only achieved 16% capture during the test but modelled at 68%?"

Scariades nodded, why was he the only one in the room asking questions?

"Correct."

Vorner smiled again.

"But you just said you modelled at 70% capture?"

Scaraides coughed and rubbed his face, the pressure behind his eyes was almost intolerable. Removing his glasses, he pinched the bridge of his nose again. He needed to sleep, he needed to be at home, he needed to be with Alexia. He replaced his spectacles.

"Mr Vorner..." Baros addressed him formally, for the benefit of the meeting.

"Gerrard, please."

"Mr Gerrard, as you know the capture works on a prime ratio of four point six, eight parts per million. The model allows for deviation. In fact, PL2 had a 12% discrepancy rate, PL1 14%. We are working on tightening up the models but are currently hampered by lack of wide spectrum feedback and engagement by our external partners."

As he knew he would, the Proctor sat forward and coughed.

"Sounds like a subtle request for additional funding to me."

Magnus and the two lawyers nodded but did not laugh. *Most* of the rest of the table ignored him. Which was ironic based upon the complex relationships in the room. Scariades might have grinned had his head not been pounding.

Regardless, whilst happy he'd conceded and this time brought Kruno with him, Scaraides was regretting telling Vanessa she wasn't needed, similarly Elias. It wasn't the data, or the explanation of the findings, it was the impact the deviation was going to have on modelling going forward. And for this project that had been her thing, she had built the models.

Kruno, like Luke, Henry Fielding, Khaled and Arun and the rest of the team, whilst absent through most of project Lens had been there with him through every phase of *this* one. Questionable loyalties in the recent past or not, they had been in his cohort at the Academy, so were there at the beginning. He hoped they would remain with him all the way to whatever the end looked like.

But he was getting the feeling that selling the next phase to these external groups might be difficult, irrespective of this new data. Without it however the work they had done up until now would be wasted, or at the very least diminished and in that case they would be forced to revert once more to the 'asset'. A circumstance that was entirely unacceptable, on all and any level, to him at the very least.

He knew the ongoing investment that was being made. This wasn't the only site, so he hoped that if there *were* doubts, the momentum they clearly had now would be a positive and deciding factor. He hoped they might push through to the next stage.

"Can I make a suggestion?" Monik sat forward quietly; she had the chair, as she had since foundation. They all looked round and waited for her to elaborate; "Why don't we allow Dr Scariades to finish his presentation before we begin our questioning. We all understand the principles of the exercise, it's all very standard, it is far from our first time in this room. And following recent events, and the conversations I know that have taken place as a result, I think it would be good if we allowed him to work through the narrative and tell us what we have asked him to."

Vorner smiled and nodded again.

"Yes of course."

No one else commented so Monik gestured to Scariades.

"Please go on, Baros."

Once again, he was grateful, although he noticed the quiet man behind Monik touch her elbow as he was turning back to his work.

"Thank you," he gestured to the screen, pleased to make Vorner twist round in his seat to see the screen. "As you can see, the pink line, the HIERR climbs steadily, initially in sync with the PL3 expectations, but then, even with the reduced capture we see it deviate," he clicked through to the next image. "Using PL*4* we have modelled a revised HIERR trajectory all the way to threshold and beyond. As you can see it reflects a noticeable increase in yield, not to mention a modelled efficacy of 98% over input." He looked up briefly to see how this data was received.

"It's worth noting that this is the first time we have allowed HIERR to run its course *physically*. It's also worth noting that an older version of PL1, one of the first we ran at the very beginning, back at Site 1 saw this as a probability. In fact it modelled this very line. It even went as far as to suggest a degree of exponential perpetuation..."

The room remained quiet for a short while after he had finished, with just the AC buzzing gently in the background. Scariades was familiar with the data. He had also, with Vanessa et al, had time to process the implications of the findings and to project further forward into PL5 & 6. They'd already shared with Proctor, obviously, and he was confident Monik would see it in a moment. The military contingent too perhaps, but he was less sure of Vorner and the lawyers. That said, the delivery of such *game changing* news to a high profile group like this was a far cry from how it had felt to announce his success with project Lens to the faculty.

He remembered Vanessa saying at the time that it was too much for one person to deliver alone, and that it would need to be re-presented more than once to drive home the subject control protocols. She hadn't been wrong.

But then she'd said it again recently, this time not only talking about the latest yield performance figures, but the larger project too. Maybe she was right, again, but he had come this far. He looked up at the observers and then at the lawyers. Vorner was buried in the paperwork he had in front of him and although it wouldn't have helped, Scariades suspected he was once again wishing for a calculator.

"Sorry," Vorner looked up again, this time frowning. "I'm not sure I understand. Are you saying that the yield on HIERR was *greater* than the upper threshold? Even at 17%?"

"16%" Kruno cut across him.

Scariades frowned at his assistant but Monik, at the other end of the table nodded and added:

"Yes, Mr Vorner, as Dr Scariades explained, and detailed quite succinctly in his presentation, the HIERR exceeded the PL3 model, and the later models used to establish a control."

"But that cannot, sorry but that doesn't..."

"I think you'll find it does," Proctor cut in. "I've seen it."

Monik frowned across at him before she focused back on and spoke to Baros:

"Dr Scaraides, this is very exciting, I think we would all agree," there was nodding around the table, "and in line with what was predicted at project foundation. Is it scalable?"

Scariades had always liked her, they'd always got on, even if they had disagreed occasionally in the past. She had a quick mind, and he liked her absence of diplomacy, her directness. But he had also, always been slightly wary of her impatience and willingness to cut through to actionable responses. He wondered, on this occasion, where that might lead, and what promises she was making in the background.

"In time, yes I believe so."

She nodded.

"And the test material? Bear in mind Dr the extreme uniqueness of its origin," she said, Baros felt sure, entirely for the benefit of the room.

He hesitated now, not for the first time, conflicted. He coughed.

"The subject is...." fidgeting, "the material is resilient."

Few in the room noticed his discomfort, least of all Monik. She nodded before pressing on.

"Degradation?"

He coughed again, conscious suddenly, of his pager vibrating against his chest. The air conditioning seemed loud now, and ineffective. Kruno looked at him and nodded reassuringly.

"Some," Scariades nodded, "But it is manageable, and measures are in place to revert event effects."

"Good, thank you. Develop a timeline for me please. And Mr Vorner," he looked up; "your report on recent local containment failures on my desk by COB tomorrow please. I am being chased by the new European Environmental Health Commission."

Both Vorner and Scariades nodded, the latter certain that Monik had no real concept of what he had described, nor what she was sanctioning. He was also, again slightly shaken by the speed with which things were moving, and how far they had come since J4 first sustained. It was certainly a far cry from begging for access to samples, and assembling their own instruments from whatever they could lay their hands on.

Monik stood and in doing so called the meeting to an end. She addressed the contractors, civilians and lawyers first.

"We have resolved our recent issues and so must move forward. It has been a painful and as you know complex transition but an essential one I think you'll agree." No one commented. "Either way, we are fully settled here. We move to Corpus with immediate effect. You all know the process; we have planned for it. Your input here will be sought as and when Dr Scaraides believes it is necessary," she then turned to Vorner. "Funding for the next stage is approved, Mr Vorner. Ensure Dr Scaraides has all adequate resources to proceed. I cannot stress how important to the administration this project is."

She now turned formally to Baros.

"Baros, thank you, again, for the work you have done up to now, and the work you are continuing to do here, you and the team, all of you" she nodded at his colleagues that had gathered loosely around him, "I think you know how fundamental this is, we all do now. I know it has been difficult and time consuming." Now specifically to Baros, "I hope your son, the child is more comfortable, you have our utmost sympathy, of course. If there is anything we can do to assist you and Alexia at this time, please do not hesitate to ask. Once again, thank you."

And now back to the room.

"Thank you, gentlemen, ladies, we will reconvene here for level three and four in sixty days unless something of significance occurs midterm. Those of you involved in Arcex and the Redaction Protocol project please observe calendar dates issued, there will be heavy penalties for leakage and late delivery. We are, of course, still anticipating and planning for further contact, but regardless things will begin to speed up now."

The room emptied quickly, with only the most cursory pleasantries exchanged. Baros would have found it hard under normal circumstances to say hello and goodbye like most people did, he just wasn't made that way. But now, as things were, he found it impossible. He needed to get back to the DCV as soon as possible. He would carry out another site inspection, then hand off to Kruno, Vanessa and Elias and leave, his pager had been pinging away all morning. He *needed* to be back with Alexia and the child...

Out in the corridor Proctor was chasing Monik down the hall, pushing through and past other meeting attendees as he did.

"Monik, please," he called ahead, determined to catch her before she made it out into the lobby.

She slowed as she heard him call and glanced at her watch. She didn't have time for this. He knew, they ALL knew the terms of their contracts, and there were no extenuating circumstances, not yet anyway. She stopped and waited for him to catch up.

"Miss Leutzinger," he repeated, slightly breathless as he came alongside. "Monik. Thank you. Apologies but I wanted to catch you before you left."

She stared at him briefly before she started walking again, forcing him to do the same. She didn't acknowledge his apology, so he pressed on.

"As you know we're big fans of the work Baros...."

"Mr Baros or *Dr* Scaraides, pick one," without looking at him. Her mind was fizzing. This was her third meeting of the day, and it was barely 9:00am. She had five more stops before a dreaded 3pm debrief with the Minister himself which itself was followed by drinks with the head of fisheries and her counterpart in the UK, a tough meeting to chair, a tougher prospect to go to bed on. She really didn't have time for this.

He chuckled;

"Right. Of course," he nodded. "*Dr* Scaraides, still finding that odd to say, he's always just been Baros to me. Anyway, excellent work, excellent data, really outstanding, and obviously the results from PL3 shared today are, as we thought they would be, are extremely exciting."

Through a set of doors, security either side. Then a right and a left and then another long corridor.

"And challenging. Get to your point."

"Right, yes, of course," he hesitated as they squeezed past a couple going the other way. Monik looked at her watch, praying that her car was ready outside. The last thing she wanted was to be left standing in the cold again. He continued.

"Look, *Miss* Leutzinger, Monik, listen, I know we've been through this before, many times in fact but have you given any further consideration to some of the other uses for this tech, this project?"

Ok, so here it is, again. She was surprised that it had taken this long for him to get to it again, that he hadn't actually asked when still in the room. She remained silent which he took for encouragement.

"And I say that because, as you know, we've both been involved in this project and observing its development, closely in fact, from the beginning. We have both concerns over the longevity of the research model," which, as far as she was concerned meant longevity of the publicly enhanced funding programme, "And in its current form, the sustainability of real world uses," which, in her mind meant he had parties interested in it for commercial or military use.

Through another set of doors, another left, another right and then out into the large glass lobby. It was a huge space, and busy, people coming in, deliveries, visitors etc. A bit like an airport arrivals terminal.

Under different circumstances she might have slid quietly past the coffee stand and picked herself up a toffee latte. Possibly to kill a minute whilst she waited for her car to appear through the huge glass frontage. Possibly to allow a conversation to reach a natural break.

But not today. She'd heard enough, both recently, and before, and knowing her car *was* waiting, she was in no way inclined to give away any more of her time. Particularly to him. She pressed on towards the revolving doors but stopped short. Turning to face him.

"Mr Proctor...,"

"Hey, come on, David, please.... really?....." he spread his hands and smiled.

She looked around and huffed and felt her cheeks flush.

"*Mr* Proctor, the research that we are doing, *have* done, has cost this institute, our earlier iteration directly before and our international partners, of which your organisation is now one, a significant amount of money. And that speaks nothing of the public funding cycles we so exhaustively pursue through and via a myriad of technical finance initiatives. It has been carried out, from the outset with present and future *global* public interest in mind and is of critical importance to the future of both domestic and overseas infrastructure investments." She didn't mention their shared history, the projects that had led to this, or the *other* thing, partly because she didn't trust him anymore, and partly because of their previous personal relationship.

"Of course Monik, but...."

"To answer your question, and to be as clear as I possibly can be. No. We have not, nor will we give any consideration to *other uses* either via our own licensing arrangements or by any other means."

She looked at him, stared at him in fact for a few seconds to drive home the point. The Minister, for what it was worth, would agree, regardless of his widely accepted moral fragility. Proctor nodded. But she hadn't finished.

"In its current form, you and your organisation's position on the panel is one I resisted. And for different reasons, so was your government's. And as previously discussed, I will be maintaining that resistance. I therefore suggest you 'et al' contain your involvement to observing, per your remit, and to providing the resource, services and R&D facilities requested of you *as and when* the PD does so."

Proctor nodded, again. And smiled, although not so widely as before.

"Of course, absolutely no problem, Miss Leutzinger, Monik, all things considered," he nodded. "It's just..." as she was turning away:

"David, please! Don't..." she swung back round, struggling to remain professional. She paused and brushed hair from her face as she composed herself: "This is difficult enough as it is. I have a very full day, and no time for...." she gestured vaguely at him, ".... this."

If he was intimidated, he didn't show it:

"The asset," standing his ground like he had before, like the fool he was: "We are concerned about the asset. And we are concerned about Harket."

Monik stared at him, wanker. He was no more concerned about the asset than anyone else. He was only worried about the security of his investment. He was only concerned about how long the income stream would be, how long his resources would be committed before he started seeing measurable returns.

That plus they'd all agreed never to mention *Harket's* name again.

Eventually:

"*We*?"

"Yes we," he lowered his voice and looked over his shoulder. "As you well know, a number of us, have for a time felt...."

"David, stop. Harket is gone. All that is in the past. You know that."

"Gone?" He raised his eyebrows, trying somehow to bridge the gap between them. "Really? Are you sure? Because we need to *be* sure."

She looked away, her cheeks flushing again. Proctor pressed, and reached out to grip her arm:

"Because, Niki, if he's there, somewhere, somewhere out there, and he finds a way to get back in......, it's not just the asset at risk, it's every...."

"I *am* sure!" She was angry. "He *is* gone and will not be returning, and the *asset* is none of your fucking concern. It never was." She'd cut across him. "David, we've had this discussion before, more than once, *too many times!* The structure has been in place since the beginning and nothing has changed. You know this. You had your turn with," she lowered her voice slightly, "with Lens, Contact, the Extraction exercises and MFFI1 *& 2*. You played your part early on, very well, you always have, thank you. But this is different, the structure is different, it's *so* much bigger, there is *so* much more at stake. And your role within is clear. Don't be tempted to 'overstep'," she stepped back, pulling her arm away, and straightened herself. "Now, Mr Proctor.... David," she made a show of looking at her watch again, noting as she did the indent on the 3rd finger of her left hand where her ring used to be; "I really must go."

She turned back towards her car.

"But...."

This time she spoke sharply over her shoulder.

"The safeguards outlined in the pre-contract are in place Mr Proctor." she was walking away. "If you have any other concerns, please contact my office."

She did not anticipate a reply. Nor did she wait for one.

Proctor watched her go; his face neutral.

"Thank you for your time, *Miss* Leutzinger." he called softly, none of the frustration he felt bleeding through.

But the lovely Monik was already part way through the revolving glass doors and didn't hear him.

About the Author:

David was always creative, but only started writing in his mid-thirties. He now he writes as often as he can, hoping to fit his love for a rich narrative around a busy home and demanding professional life.

Other works by *David Browning-Paine*:

The Spaceman

Printed in Poland
by Amazon Fulfillment
Poland Sp. z o.o., Wrocław

32314381R00222